RANDOM FACTOR

Maxwell chased the wind-driven ball of crumpled paper down the busy sidewalk—then squalled indignantly as a woman tripped over him, dropping her bundles. Murdoch, pursuing his errant kitten, apologized profusely for Maxwell. That was how he met Anne. . . .

Maxwell watched, fascinated, as the vagrant wind held the crumpled paper fluttering against a lamppost. A young woman shopper stopped and directed Murdoch's attention to the crouching kitten and went on her way. Murdoch called his thanks after her . . . then forgot about her.

A moment in time can be re-lived—but never in *quite* the same way. . . .

Also by James P. Hogan
Published by Ballantine Books:

INHERIT THE STARS

THE GENESIS MACHINE

THE TWO FACES OF TOMORROW

THE GENTLE GIANTS OF GANYMEDE

Thrice
Upon
A Time

BY

JAMES P. HOGAN

A Del Rey Book

BALLANTINE BOOKS • NEW YORK

A Del Rey Book
Published by Ballantine Books

Library of Congress Catalog Card Number: 79-55178

ISBN 0-345-30886-7

Manufactured in the United States of America

First Edition: March 1980
Second Printing: June 1982

Diagram by Chris Barbieri based on an original by the author.

Cover art by Rowena Morrill

To all at Del Rey Books—the other half of the team who never get mentioned on the cover

PROLOGUE

The digits, glowing bright red in the upper corner of the computer display screen, changed silently to count off the final seconds.

00:05 . . . 00:04 . . . 00:03 . . . 00:02 . . . 00:01 . . . 00:00.

A symbol appeared below the clock-readout to confirm that the program had begun running. A moment later, the main area of the screen came alive to present the display:

30 December 2009, 2325:00 Hours.
TEMPORAL RETROTRANSMISSION TEST NUMBER 15
Group 4, Sample 3. Transmission advance 60 seconds.
073681
END

The elderly man sitting in front of the console gazed expressionlessly at the display for a second, and then tapped a pad on the touchboard array below the screen. A mild whine came from one of the racks of electronic equipment standing next to him; at the same time a hardcopy of the information on the screen slid smoothly from a slot and into the tray below. The screen went blank. The man took the hardcopy, ran his eye casually over it, then sat back in his chair to wait. In the upper corner of the screen, the clock-readout had reset to sixty seconds and begun counting down again.

The man's body was tall, and his shoulders still broad and straight, but the hair that had once glinted jet-black was now white, and the beard jutting stubbornly from his chin had faded to gray. Remnants of flames that had once blazed bright still smoldered in the eyes looking out over the ruddy crags of his face, but the fire was beginning to give way to a fatigue accumulated over many long years of life.

1

After a while he shifted his gaze to the fluffy black-and-white kitten lying curled up in the half-open, lower-most drawer of the desk that stood alongside his chair.

"Aye, it's a strange pair we are, Maxwell, and that's for sure," he murmured. "Still at work here at an hour when any folks with a dram o' sense would long have been away to their beds. Enough's enough. We'll make this the last for tonight now."

Alerted by the man's voice, the kitten opened a sleepy eye to look at him, and then glimpsed the reflex twitching of his own tail. He awoke, pounced back into the depths of the drawer, and began whirling in futile circles amid sounds of swishing fur and crumpling paper. A yellow plastic pushpin flew out in the con-fusion, bounced on the floor with a hollow clatter, and rolled away in a drunken curve around the base of one of the equipment cubicles. Maxwell's head ap-peared peering from the opening with ears erect and eyes following the rolling button like twin tracking-radars. Then the kitten cleared the side of the drawer in a bound, rounded the corner of the desk in an uncontrolled skid with all four paws flailing ineffec-tively at the shiny floor, reengaged forward drive sud-denly, and scampered away in pursuit.

A faint smile softened the corners of the man's mouth as he watched. Then he looked back at the screen in front of him. The countdown had almost reached zero.

00:01 . . . 00:00.

A display similar to the previous one appeared. The man carefully compared the number contained in it with the one in the hardcopy record that he was still holding. They matched. He nodded slowly to himself. At that very moment, if the phrase retained any mean-ing at all in the strange realm of topsy-turvy logic that he had uncovered, a man was watching those same lines appear on that same screen for the first time—the gray-haired man who was sitting in that same chair, sixty seconds in the past.

He hardcopied the second display, attached the copy to the first, added the sheets to a pile lying on the desk, and entered the details in a notebook lying open be-side him. Then he closed the book and turned back to the console to begin the brief routine for shutting down the system.

"Enough's enough," he repeated as he finished and rose from the chair. As he moved toward the door, the pushpin rattled back into sight from behind a part of the machine. The tip of a black-and-white nose poked round the base of a cubicle. Then, slowly, Maxwell's face slid fully into view closely followed by Maxwell, his body elongated low near the floor like a snake with legs. The kitten gathered himself to spring, then paused and looked up curiously as the man reached for the lightswitch.

"Och, come on now," the man called. "There'll be time enough for that kind o' nonsense tomorrow. It's nearly tomorrow already as it is." Two saucer-eyes turned wistfully toward the pushpin and then up again before the kitten stood up and trotted for the doorway. "Aye, you're no' so bad for all your mischief, ye wee scallywag," the man said gruffly. He turned out the light, waited for Maxwell to leave the lab, and closed the door behind.

The passage outside was bare, with plain, white-washed walls rising up from a gray stone floor. At the end of the passage they came to a narrow wooden staircase leading up to a heavy oak door. The man waited again at the top of the stairs and held the door ajar while the kitten tackled the steps manfully, half leaping, half scrambling up one and then bunching himself for the next.

They emerged from the doorway into a large, paneled hall, gloomy in the feeble light of the single lamp that had been left burning halfway along a corridor opening off the far side. The floor here was covered by deep, rich carpet. Vague shadows of portraits stared down from the walls, and the furnishings, most of which dated from the early twentieth century or before, were solid, well preserved, and dignified in keeping with their surroundings. A full suit of medieval armor stood impassively at the foot of a broad carved staircase that disappeared into deeper darkness above, where glints of reflected light traced ghostly outlines of Scottish claymores and battle axes mounted on the walls.

The man flipped a switch to illuminate the stairs

3

and began climbing slowly. Two circles of mirror-brightness were already staring back at him from the darkness just above the top step. "You'd no' be so nimble on your feet with seventy-two years on the wrong side o' ye, Maxwell," the man said. At the top of the flight he turned to follow the railed gallery that overlooked one side of the stairwell, and stopped outside one of the doors opening off the short passageway beyond. A shaft of light lanced across the floor as he pushed the door open.

"We've done it, Maxwell," he murmured. "There can be no doubt about it now. It works, all right. We'll have to be telling Ted the good news first thing in the morning." He paused for a second. "And Murdoch, of course. . . . It's time we were involving Murdoch in what's been going on." He nodded to himself. "Aye. Murdoch will be very interested indeed if I'm not very much mistaken."

The door swung shut and plunged the household once more into gloom.

CHAPTER ONE

Kennedy International Airport had shrugged off the snow that fell after Christmas, and was again a bustling oasis of business-as-usual amid the white-blanketed suburbs stretching along the southern Long Island shoreline. Steady processions of groundcars and monocabs flowed between the airport complex and Manhattan to the west, while overhead swarms of airmobiles arrived and departed like bees on never-ending foraging missions. From within the perimeter, a succession of Boeings, Lockheeds, and Douglases sailed vertically upward on the first stages of their suborbital trajectories through the ionosphere; higher above, arriving dots from Europe, Japan, Australia, and elsewhere slowly acquired shape as they dropped from the flawless blue that had come with the first day of the new year.

In the Arrivals Concourse of the glass-fronted marble sculpture that constituted Terminal Three, Murdoch Ross stood among a group of waiting people and divided his attention between scanning the faces of the passengers streaming from Flight 235, just in from San Francisco, and taking in a few more lines of an article on graviton wave-mechanics featured in the current issue of *Scientific American*. He was in his late twenties, on the lean side of average for his medium height, and clean-shaven to reveal a fresh and healthy complexion. His eyes were bright and alert as they glanced up every few seconds from the magazine in his hand, and almost as dark as the wavy black hair above the collar of his overcoat.

He saw the head of copper-colored hair protruding above the rest of the new arrivals at the same time as the head saw him. Its owner changed direction to wade obliquely through the river of humanity toward Murdoch. He was dressed in a dark-blue, open-necked shirt, navy windbreaker, and gray cords, and carrying a leather travel bag slung across one shoulder; he moved unhurriedly, but with a powerful, easy-going stride. Murdoch thrust the magazine into the pocket of his overcoat and grinned as they shook hands. It was like grasping a double-thick cut of spare rib that hadn't died yet.

"Lee, great to see you again! It seems like a lot more than five months. I'm sorry about the short notice, but that's all I had myself."

Lee Walker's mouth barely twitched, but his eyes came as near as they ever did to smiling. "Hi, Doc. You're right—it seems a lot longer. I guess that's the way things go." He heaved his bag onto his other shoulder and produced a pack of cigarettes from his windbreaker. "What time is it here? How long have we got before the flight leaves?"

"It's on schedule—just over fifteen minutes."

"Get my ticket fixed okay?"

"You're all set."

"Thanks."

They began walking briskly toward the nearest escalator leading down to the automatic shuttle system that connected the airport terminals.

"So," Murdoch said. "How are things back west? Dynasco going okay?"

"Pretty good," Lee replied. "The checkout's finished, and the documentation's all done. I think they're pretty pleased with the whole deal."

"Good."

"In fact if you hadn't called, I'd have been coming on over to New York in a week or so anyway. How's it been looking?"

"Promising. How about Tracey? Did you get her untangled at last?"

"Yeah. It's all . . . 'untangled.' "

An empty shuttle-car was waiting with doors open. They crossed the platform skirting the track at the bottom of the escalator and stepped inside.

"Okay, so tell me more about it," Lee said. "You reckon your grandfather has actually done it—he can send information *backward* through time?" His face was creased into a frown and his tone skeptical.

Murdoch nodded. "That's what he says."

"But it's crazy. In principle it's crazy. What happens to causality?" Lee drew on his cigarette and blew a cloud of smoke toward the roof of the car. "What's he done exactly? How far has he sent it back?"

"You know just about as much as I do," Murdoch told him. "He wasn't exactly generous with details when he called me either. He just said it worked and told me to get over there right away. He knows I've talked to you about it a lot, and figured it was about time you two met. So I called you. The rest you know."

"But it's crazy," Lee insisted. "I never thought he'd get anywhere with it. If it's true, the whole of physics goes down the tubes. I mean—"

"Save it," Murdoch said. "There's company on the way. Let's talk about it on the plane." A trio of businessmen approached along the platform and stepped into the car talking loudly about some company's market share or something or other. They were followed a few seconds later by a couple shepherding two young, tousle-haired boys. The car doors bleeped a warning and then closed, and the shuttle slid forward to rejoin the through-track, then accelerated smoothly into the tunnel that led to the next terminal on the circuit.

Twenty minutes later they were sixty miles up over the mid-Atlantic at the apex of a shallow parabola that joined Kennedy to an artificial island constructed a few miles off-shore from Edinburgh in the Firth of Forth. The seats on one side of them were occupied by two pleasant but inquisitive middle-aged English ladies who plied them continually with questions about the States; on their other side sat a Bostonian who maintained a steady monologue on football despite their repeated proclamation of total ignorance of, and disinterest in, the subject. At no time during the thirty-five-minute flight did they get a chance to talk further about Murdoch's grandfather.

CHAPTER TWO

"Did you ever hear of Bannockburn?" Murdoch asked over the muted humming of the car's engine.

"Some kind of Scotch baron?" Lee guessed.

"It's a place, not far off down that road on the left

there. They had a battle there in 1314. The Scots had kicked the English out of the whole of Scotland except the castle at Stirling, which is the town we're just coming into. One of the English kings, Edward II, brought an army up to get them out, but he got wiped out by Bruce."

"Scotch?"

"Yes, except that's the stuff you drink. There was another battle here before that too, in 1297. That was when Edward I lost out. I guess the Edwards didn't have much luck around here."

"I didn't know you went in for all this," Lee said.

Murdoch shrugged. "Maybe it's my grandpa coming out in me. You know, I wouldn't mind moving over and living here somewhere one day. Look at the stonework in some of those buildings. I bet they were put up before anybody heard of California."

They had decided not to use the local jet service from Edinburgh to the town of Inverness, just over one hundred miles to the north, since it would have made little difference to their total journey time. Instead they rented a groundcar at the island-airport and drove below the Firth to emerge on land some miles west of Edinburgh, heading toward the Scottish Central Lowlands. Since then, with the groundcar running automatically under remote guidance on the controlled main highway, they had turned northward to pass through Perth, the repeatedly besieged former capital, where they would cross the river Tay.

Lee draped his arm along the lower ledge of the window and surveyed the scenery for a while. "It's a pretty country," he conceded at last, which from Lee was as near a eulogy as one was likely to get.

Murdoch pursed his lips and nodded. "Now you know why I like coming over here whenever I can."

"How come your father never talks all that much about it?" Lee asked. "I'd have thought that with a name like Malcom and being a generation nearer to it, he'd have been full of it. Are you the odd one out or something?"

"More like the other way around," Murdoch replied, shaking his head. "He's the odd one. Grandpa was— still is—a theoretical physicist. His father was a mathe-

8

matician. I guess I'm mathematical. As far as I know, my pa was the only one in the whole line for way back who couldn't balance a checkbook. Didn't stop him making money though."

"That's probably the reason," Lee said. "Buy at sixty, sell at a hundred and make ten percent. Now I know why I can't read balance sheets. Ah well . . . I guess I'll never be rich." He fell silent for a moment, then went on, "Your father is definitely all-American. So if your grandfather's different, what's he like? Does he wear kilts and go around with daggers in his socks, and all that stuff?"

"Dirks," Murdoch said, grinning. "No . . . not often anyway. Only on formal occasions. But you're right— he is pretty traditional. I guess that kind of thing tends to run through the Rosses too. Maybe that's why I like Scottish history."

"And he's still that way after— How many years was your grandfather in the States before he moved back to Scotland?"

"About forty, I think. But people like him don't change very easily. You'll see what I mean when you meet him."

From Perth they followed the Tay valley into the Grampian Highlands, a fifty-mile-deep, storm-tossed giant's sea of granite waves quick-frozen by the winter snow. At the town of Kingussie in the valley of Strath Spey, Murdoch switched to manual drive and turned off the main Perth–Inverness highway and into the mountains of Monadhliath for the last leg of the journey to Glenmoroch. Within minutes the few remaining signs of the space age had disappeared completely. The road became a single track, winding its way carelessly among the feet of regiments of steep, boulder-strewn slopes that had fallen hopelessly out of step, and around frosty streams and rippling lochs, chattering and shivering with the winter cold. Woods of larch and Norwegian pine appeared at intervals, stretching from the roadsides in irregular patches to form ragged skirts along the lower parts of the hills. Higher up, they thinned away or huddled into narrow gorges where they cowered beneath steep slopes of pebble screes and brooding buttresses of naked rock. Only the occasional

9

farmhouse, bridge, or run of dry-stone wall remained as a reminder that the human race existed.

They rounded a bend by one of the farms to find the road blocked by a miniature sea of sheep, which a dour farmer, a helper, and three tireless dogs were herding through a gate into one of the adjacent fields. Murdoch eased the car to a halt a few yards back from the scampering, bleeting tide.

Lee shook his head incredulously. "This can't be true," he said. Murdoch grinned and sat back in his seat to wait. For a while he watched the dogs. On his previous visits to Scotland he had come to admire the uncanny ability of sheepdogs to coordinate their movements and anticipate every gesture and whistle of command. Trained dogs enjoyed working and soon grew restless if deprived of it; like many people, animals could become addicted to the habit. During one of Murdoch's previous visits to Glenmoroch, a sheepdog belonging to Bob Ferguson, who owned a farm on the outskirts of the village, hurt a leg and was prescribed a week's rest by the vet, which meant no going up onto the hills. The dog occupied itself by herding chickens around the farmyard instead.

Murdoch shifted his eyes to study the older of the two men, who was clad in a thick tweed jacket with trousers gathered into knee-length gumboots. He wore a flat peaked cap on top of graying, short-cropped hair. His face was the color of boiled lobster, lined and weathered, and below his bushy eyebrows his eyes burned keenly through slits narrowed by a lifetime's exposure to mountain winds and rain. It was a face, Murdoch thought, that, like the granite crags, had been carved by elements that had ruled the Highlands since long before the ancestors of the Picts and Celts drifted northward from England, or migrated across the sea from the lower valley of the Rhine. It was a face that belonged here, he told himself—just as a part of him, somewhere deep down inside, belonged here.

The last few strays were rounded up and dispatched through the gate. The farmer raised his stick to acknowledge the driver's patience, and Murdoch responded with a wave of his hand as he eased the car into motion again.

"I'd like to see that happen on the Frisco–L.A. freeway," Lee said.

"Time waits for people here," Murdoch told him.

The mention of time sent Lee's mind back to the things they had discussed briefly at Kennedy. They had covered another two miles when at last he spoke. "Suppose your grandfather's right. What happens to free will? If you can send information backward through time, you can tell me what I did even before I get around to doing it. So suppose I choose not to?" He half-turned in his seat and looked defiantly across at Murdoch. "What's there to make me? So I don't, and no information ever gets sent back to say I did. But I've already received it." He shrugged. "The whole thing's crazy."

"Serial universes," Murdoch suggested, keeping his eyes on the tortuous road ahead. Evidently he had been doing some thinking too.

"What about them?"

"Suppose that all the pasts that have ever existed, and all the futures that will ever exist, are all just as real as the present. The present only gives the illusion of being more real because we happen to be perceiving it . . . in the same kind of way that the frame of a movie that happens to be on the screen right now appears real, but that doesn't make all the other frames in the reel less real. Does that make sense?"

"Depends what you mean," Lee answered. "Are you saying that all those pasts exist exactly the way we remember them?"

"No. That's the whole point. They could be different. For instance, the 1939 that exists 'now' back up the timeline might not contain a Hitler at all. When it arrives at its own 1945, World War II won't have happened, and it will have evolved a history that doesn't read like ours at all. From there it will go on into its own future, fully consistent with its own part but different from ours." Murdoch cocked an eye and glanced at Lee.

Lee sat back and frowned into the distance through the windshield. "So that universe will eventually arrive in its own 2010, maybe with a Doc and Lee in it who aren't in Scotland at all . . . or maybe without any

11

Doc and Lee in it. By that time this universe that we're in will have gone forward to its, what would it be? . . . 2065 . . . carrying an internal history that would be consistent with what it remembers. It wouldn't know anything about what's happening way back upstream. Is that what you're saying?"

"More or less. What d'you think?"

"Mmm . . ." Lee turned the suggestion over in his mind. "Could be, I guess. But if it does work that way, I can't see much of a future for it."

"Oh. How come?"

"You could send information back to a past universe, but you could never be affected by anything that anybody in that universe did as a consequence. It might help them, but it can't help you. You could tell them not to do something that you did, but you're stuck with it. So why should you bother? Why should you want to put that effort into helping somebody else solve his problems, even if he does happen to be an earlier version of yourself, when it's not going to do anything to help you solve yours?"

"Curiosity," Murdoch offered with a shrug. "Or philanthropy maybe. There's all kinds of people in the world. Why save souls?"

"Because they count as tax credits on your own return," Lee said. He shook his head. "If it does work that way, I can't see it ever being more than an academic curiosity."

"Pretty sensational for a curiosity though, being able to talk to whole new universes that you didn't know existed. Isn't that exciting enough?"

"That's what bothers me. It's sensational, but you can't use it. Suppose you end up deciding it's pointless talking to past universes because they can't do anything for you, and then you find that future universes aren't taking calls because they've come to the same conclusion. Then what do you do? You're sitting on the biggest breakthrough in physics since electricity, and it's no good to you. It'd be like Robinson Crusoe inventing the telephone."

Murdoch thought about it, grunted, then fell silent. Lee had a habit of suddenly dumping whole new trains of thought by the shovelful for Murdoch's mind to sift

12

through. Sometimes Murdoch wished that he would find a smaller shovel.

At last the road ahead of them unfolded into a two-mile straight leading across bleak, snow-covered grouse-moor textured by scattered rocks and clumps of gorse. Murdoch announced that they had only a few miles left to go. For some time they had been ascending toward a skyline formed by the crest of a vast ridge, and the surroundings had been growing more wind-swept and barren. The final slopes that led up to the ridgeline itself began on the far side of the moor; the road climbed across them in a series of tight hairpins to vanish at a notch of sky pinched in the snow. To the right the ridge rose steeply and swelled to become a bulging shoulder of the three-thousand-foot peak of Ben Moroch, the towering sentinel that kept watch over the pass leading through to the valley-head of the glen beyond.

The sun was soaking into the hills to the west by the time they reached the high point of the pass. To their left the southwest ridge of Ben Moroch marched away in a line of descending spurs before rising again to blend with a more distant peak, while on the right the mountain itself soared upward in glowering ramparts of rock and ice. In front of them and below, the ground fell away into a vast amphitheater formed by the meeting of the west and southwest ridges, which curved away on either side to become the arms that held the ribbon of Glenmoroch in between. For a min-ute or two they were able to look over the crestline of the west ridge at the Highlands stretching away like a sea of rose-tinted icebergs with glimpses of the sun-burnished waters of Loch Ness in between; then the road began meandering downward once more, gently at first and then more steeply, between the frozen peat bogs and shale slopes that formed the upper reaches of the glen.

Soon the whole of Glenmoroch was spread out in miniature beneath them, and Murdoch felt the elation that always came when he saw the familiar landmarks again for the first time after a long absence. The road traced its way down the flanks of the ridge to leave the crest high on the left, and converged on the valley

13

floor with the wandering line of the brook where the streams flowing off Ben Moroch mustered for their long march to Loch Keld and onward en masse to the sea. He could make out the stone bridge where the road crossed the brook before disappearing into a small wood, and beside it the rectangular lines of walled fields that marked the beginning of Ferguson's farm. The road emerged from the far side of the wood into a scattering of houses, copses, and tracks that consolidated themselves lower down into the huddle of Glenmoroch village, already looking sleepy beneath faint plumes of chimney smoke and showing a few lights in the shadow advancing from the foot of the west ridge.

Below the village the road again plunged into trees, which fanned out on either side to form a rough crescent around the near end of Loch Keld. To the right of these trees, the land shelved gently upward for a distance from the shore of the loch, and then swept upward sharply to form the terminal spur of the west ridge. The shelf between the loch and the spur was thickly wooded, and through the trees a compact cluster of roofs and turrets protruded to catch the last rays of the dying sun.

"That's it," Murdoch said, pointing. "The place sticking up through the trees between the mountain and the water behind the village. That's the Storbannon estate."

"I thought it was supposed to be a castle," Lee said after a few seconds.

"Well, that's what people round here call it, but it isn't really. What did you expect—portcullises, guys in armor, and damsels in distress hanging out the windows?"

"I'd have settled for the damsels," Lee replied. After a moment he added, "The dis-dressed ones."

Murdoch groaned.

The village was quiet as they drove through its main street between terraced stone cottages interspersed with an assortment of tiny shops and a few cosy-looking, warmly lit pubs, and past the ancient, iron-railed churchyard. A couple of figures outside the red-fronted Post Office, which also served as grocery and general

14

store, turned to watch the unfamiliar car pass by, but otherwise there were no signs of life. Nothing had changed.

They left the village and entered the crescent-shaped wood that extended to the shore of the loch. A track took them off the main road and brought them out of the wood again, this time pointing toward Storbannon. Minutes later, Murdoch turned off the track between two large and imposing stone gateposts, and into a wide driveway that curved away upslope through the trees. Lee realized after a while that the brief bird's-eye view of the estate that he had seen from high up on the far side of the valley had been deceptive, for they had covered what must have been almost a mile before the lights of the house itself became visible. And then the trees opened up suddenly before a large, oval-shaped area around which the driveway looped, widened, and then rejoined itself to form the fore-court of "Storbannon Castle." The main entrance was in the center of the building, set back on the far side of a small courtyard enclosed on three sides, which was formed by the main body of the house and its two projecting wings. Murdoch steered into the courtyard and stopped at the foot of the broad flight of shallow steps leading up to the doors.

"We're here," he said needlessly, as Lee craned his neck to take in as much of the frontage as he could see in the light reflected by the snow from the two spotlamps above the entrance.

The building could have been an "E" shape without the middle bar, Lee thought, or maybe he was looking at one side of an "H." The doors at the top of the half-dozen or so steps were heavy and solid, with ornate hinges and hanging hand rings of wrought iron; they seemed in good repair, as did everything else that formed his first impressions. The arch framing the doors was formed from columns of round, recessed, stonework ribs, which flowed upward on either side like staggered banks of organ pipes before bowing into flattened curves that met in a point at the top. The walls, extending away into the shadowy corners formed by the wings, were faced in dressed gray stone etched by the battle scars of many long, harsh Scottish winters.

Midway between the entrance arch and the wings, the walls angled outward for a short distance to form two broad piers of double bay windows encased in florid masonry, which extended upward to join the parade of castellations that marked the roof line. At least it's a change from high-rise glass and duroplastic, Lee thought to himself.

"I can see now why they call it a castle," he said. "The tops of the walls up there are built like square-waves."

"Recent additions," Murdoch informed him. "They were part of renovations that were carried out by one of the Rosses in the nineteenth century. That was when the turrets were added too. I guess he put up the castellations to give the place a matching frontage."

"And that's recent?"

"Sure."

"So how far back does this place go?" Lee asked as they climbed out of the car and walked around to begin lifting luggage out of the trunk.

Murdoch paused long enough to take in the South Wing with a gesture of his arm. "That's the oldest part of it. It used to be a nobleman's manor house some-where around the middle of the fifteenth century, but there was something there before that; some of the stonework in the foundations is thought to go back to the twelfth." He shrugged. "But so much alteration and rebuilding has gone on over the years that it's difficult to say exactly which part of what you can see now appeared when. That wing hasn't been lived in for a long time now, though . . . mainly storage and stuff. The front part is the garage, and the part that sticks out back is stables; the whole thing's laid out roughly like an aitch."

Lee closed the trunk and straightened up to survey the front of the central bar, facing them. "So what about this part?" he asked. "Did that come later?"

"In the 1650s," Murdoch answered. "Most of the character is in there. Look at the Tudor arch and the mullions across the windows." He nodded his head in the general direction of the North Wing. "The rest of it appeared in bits and pieces over the last three hundred years or so. A lot of it was the late 1800s.

16

The family had connections with the Clydeside steel industry, which was going through fairly good times, so they had plenty of cash to throw around on things like that." He made a face and added, "That part's typical of a lot of Victorian 'inspirations,' for want of a better word, though—revived Gothic windows, Georgian portico around the other side, mock Doric columns, and baroque ornamentation. Goes together like ice cream and gravy."

Lee stared at the incongruous blend for a moment, and then shrugged. "I'll take your word for it, Doc," he said.

At that moment the doors swung open to release a flood of light onto the steps. A man with thinning hair and wearing a dark jacket and tie walked out, closely followed by a woman dressed in a plain gray dress and white apron, her dark hair tied back in a bun.

"You're here at last," the woman called in a high-pitched, wailing voice. "We were beginning to wonder what had happened to ye."

"Morna, me fine lass!" Murdoch hugged her around the waist and spun her off her feet, ignoring her protesting scream. "We drove up the whole way. I don't trust those French things they fly up to Inverness." He put the woman down and turned to clasp the man's extended hand. "Hello again, Robert. You're looking great. How's it all been going?"

" 'Tis grand to see you back so soon," the man replied warmly. "Sir Charles has been looking forward to today. And this must be the Lee that we've heard so much about."

Murdoch stepped back and clapped Lee on the shoulder. "This is Lee. Lee, this is Morna. She's got secret admirers all over Glenmoroch. And this is Robert. He's been here since before I can remember." Lee shook hands with both of them. "And how are Mrs. Paisley and Hamish?" Murdoch inquired.

"Both fine," Robert told him. "Hamish is all right when he isn't in some pub down in the village. Is this your first visit to Scotland, Lee?"

"First time ever," Lee said. "I think the place is starting to grow on me already, though. Having this

17

guy in the car is like sitting next to a talking history book."

"He's always been one for anything to do wi' the Scots," Morna said. "Even when he was here for the summers as a boy. But enough o' this. Let's get the two o' ye inside and out o' the cold."

"Sir Charles is waiting for you in the library now," Robert told them. "Go on in. I'll take care of the bags and the car." He took Murdoch's keys and went on down the steps. Morna turned and walked back into the entrance hall with the new arrivals.

"Shall I ask Mrs. Paisley to find ye somethin' t'eat?" she asked. Murdoch threw a quick sideways glance at Lee.

Lee shook his head. "Later maybe," he said.

"Just coffee," Murdoch told her. "We only left New York less than an hour and a half ago." He caught the surprised look on her face and stopped to gaze at the splendid paneling of the hall and the majestic main staircase, then added, "It seems like a thousand years already."

CHAPTER THREE

"So what's happening with the consultancy in California?" Charles inquired. "Are you wrapping that up now?" They had been talking for almost half an hour. Charles was speaking from a large, red-leather armchair to one side of the flickering log fire in the library. Lee was sprawled in the chair opposite, and Murdoch was on the settee between them, facing the hearth. Murdoch had given Charles the latest news regarding the family in Chicago, and the conversation had now drifted to the more immediate topic of Murdoch and Lee.

"We've been running it down for some time really," Murdoch replied. "The last contract we had was for an outfit called Dynasco. They wanted a study on self-organizing energy vortices in plasmas. Lee stayed on for a few months to tie up the loose ends on it while I was setting up things in New York."

Charles took a sip from the brandy glass in his hand and smacked his lips approvingly. "Did it not work out then?" he asked. "I could have told you you're not cut out to be a businessman like your father."

"Oh hell, I know that," Murdoch said. "The idea never was to start a multinational. It was just a way of working on things that were interesting without being owned by anybody, and to make enough to get by on for a year or two. That was all we ever meant to do, and that was what we did. It worked out fine."

"So where to next?" Charles asked him. "What happens in New York?"

"It looks as if we're all set for a commission with a consulting group called Wymess Associates. They're looking for outside help on plasma dynamics. I've been talking to them since November and it's looking pretty certain. Sounds interesting too; they're working with General Atomic on nuplex designs for East Africa."

Murdoch was referring to the integrated nuclear-based, agricultural-industrial packaged complexes, capable of supporting a tightly knit, autonomous community at full twenty-first-century living standards and life-styles that was being developed for export to the rapidly developing Third World. The "nuplexes" were part of an international program aimed at once and for all eliminating from the planet the most basic scourges that had plagued mankind as long as mankind had existed. Later on, the technologies perfected in developing the nuplexes would form the basis for designing self-sustaining colonies in space.

Charles nodded slowly. "Aye, that sounds as if it could suit you more. You've always had a wee bit o' the idealist in you, I suspect, Murdoch . . . wanting to contribute something to making the world less of a mess and that kind of thing. You've got academic talent, but you're no academic by nature. After CIT and Fusion Electric, you've probably seen as much of university campuses as you want to." He glanced across at Lee. "And you're from the same mold if I'm not very much mistaken. And I'll warrant you don't see yourself fitting in with the big corporations either."

Lee crossed a foot loosely over his knee, pursed his

lips for a moment, then shook his head. "You've said it. They get things done, but you've got to fit. If you don't fit the image or the image doesn't fit you"—he spread his hands expressively—"what's the point of wasting your time trying to prove something you've already made your mind up you're not all that interested in proving?"

"Aye," Charles conceded simply. He already knew enough not to press questions, and by nature he was not disposed to dispensing conventional wisdoms in the form of grandfatherly advice unless it was asked for.

By the early 2000s, a great deal of basic scientific research and many of the major research projects had come to be managed and funded by the larger multinational corporations. This trend reflected the tendency of private industry to look more after itself and its basic needs as confidence in government initiative was eroded away by the effects of continual policy reversals, irresolution in the face of electoral whims, and stifling bureaucracy. To insure the supply of trained talent that these expanding ventures would demand, the corporations had become heavy investors in the educational system by the closing decades of the twentieth century; some had gone further by opening their own colleges and awarding their own degrees, which in certain sectors of research and industry had already come to be considered more valuable than some of the traditional diplomas.

Murdoch had studied mathematical physics at CIT and then moved on to the university founded by the Fusion Electric Corporation, a California-based company engaged in the commercial generation and distribution of fusion-generated power, to gain further experience in plasma techniques. There he had met Lee, who, it turned out, was a son of the corporation's Vice President of Research. Despite the opportunities implied by virtue of his father's position, Lee's main interests there lay with the computers, an addiction he had been nurturing since an early age. He didn't find the executive image challenging or inspiring and, like Murdoch, was preparing to go his own way; again like Murdoch, he didn't know where to. After completing their courses at the university they had stayed for a while at FEC, and then left to set up the consultancy at Palo Alto, on the bay shore a few miles south of San Francisco.

"So where are you from originally, Lee?" Charles asked. "Have you always lived on the West Coast?"

"I was born in Osaka, Japan," Lee replied. Charles's eyebrows rose in mild surprise. Lee explained, "My father was chief engineer on a joint U.S.–Japanese tokamak project out there for a number of years. He moved back to the States when they made him a V.P."

"You were very young while you were there, I take it," Charles said.

Lee shook his head. "He was there for quite a while. I was nearly fifteen when we moved back. All I got to see of the States before then was what I could squeeze into vacations."

"He was brought up on karate," Murdoch interjected. "I've seen him break concrete blocks with his fist."

"Good heavens!" Charles exclaimed. "You'll no doubt have a lot to talk about with Ted Cartland when he gets back, Lee. Did Murdoch tell you about Ted?"

"Is that the English guy that lives here?" Lee asked. "Used to be in the Air Force . . . been all over."

"Aye, that's him," Charles confirmed. "He was born in Malaya. His father was major in the Army, attached to the Australians. Ted's quite an interesting chappie."

"Where is he?" Murdoch asked.

"He's been away for a few days, working with one of the firms that we use for components." Charles replied. "He should be back tomorrow." The old man sat back in his chair and drained his glass. "Ah well, it sounds as if the two o' ye are still a solution waiting for the right problems to appear. But there's no rush. You know your own minds better than anyone. There's many a man in this world who's rushed headlong into the wrong thing without thinking, and then had to spend the next half of his life getting himself out o' the mess he's made." He leaned forward to refill the glass from a decanter beside him. The other two watched in silence, wondering when he would get around to the topic of their visit and the reason for it.

Charles leaned back and settled himself more comfortably into the chair with his glass. "So, Lee," he said, as if reading their thoughts. "How much do you know about the background to what Ted and I have been up to here?"

"Doc's talked to me quite a bit about it off and on," Lee replied, uncrossing his legs and straightening up in the chair. "I know you spent a lot of time in the States at places like MIT, Princeton, and Stanford . . . and after that at NASA and the Defense Department, before you came back here. I've read the papers you published on the isolation of free quarks. That was at Stanford, wasn't it? I guess it must have started somewhere around there."

"That was in the eighties," Charles said, nodding. "But I suppose you're right in a way: That did lay the foundation. But the really interesting things started happening about ten years ago. I was with NASA by then, but Stanford was still carrying out experiments involving quarks. Some of the experiments were giving anomalous results that nobody could explain, so they asked me to go down and have a look at them because of the work I'd been involved with there previously."

"Something analogous to nuclear resonances, wasn't it?" Lee said.

"Aye. They occurred in connection with nucleons decaying into three quarks. The specific cases were when a nucleon broke down first into two quarks plus an intermediate particle, and then the intermediate particle transformed into the third quark. The 'quason,' which was the name given to the intermediate particle that had been tentatively postulated, had never actually been detected or observed as such. As you say, it was like a nuclear resonance, but its lifetime was so many orders of magnitude shorter even than that of a resonance that some people were doubting it existed at all. It was simply an entity with certain mathematical attributes needed to account for the slight delay between the appearances of the first two quarks and the third one. The problem was that, in the light of the more accurate measurements that had been made by that time, it was impossible to assign a set of properties to the quason that were internally consistent. There was

22

always something that contradicted the experimental data."

"Yes, I remember reading about that in something that Doc showed me," Lee said. "Didn't you offer an interpretation that didn't require quasons at all?"

"That's right," Charles replied. "But the alternative interpretation that I proposed called for a rather unusual assumption: that all three quarks were created simultaneously, but the data defining the first two had propagated *backward in time*. The magnitudes involved were of the order of ten-to-the-minus-thirty second—about the time light would take to cross a quark—but real nevertheless.

"Results of other experiments from other places too involved the same kind of thing," Charles went on. "To cut a long story short, it turned out that they could all be interpreted consistently on the basis of information propagating forward or backward through time, without quasons coming into it at all. So there were two explanations; one was testable but unsatisfactory, the other consistent but apparently nonsensical. As you can imagine, there was a lot of arguing going on around then."

"That's something I was meaning to ask about," Lee said. "This would have been around when, ten years ago?"

"Aye. Around the turn of the century."

"I checked through a lot of the papers and journals from around then, but I couldn't find much mention of it. The only things I saw were the things that Doc showed me, which I guess he got from you. How come? And if you've proved now that the no-quason interpretation is correct, how come the traditional version is still accepted practically everywhere?"

"Ah well . . ." Charles paused to sip his brandy. "There were two reasons. First there was the obvious thing: A lot of scientists opposed the theory on principle. I can't say I blame them really. It conflicted with all the accepted notions of causality, and the overwhelming tendency among most of them was to stick with the choice that at least retained familiar concepts and made sense, even if it was giving ragged results. It wouldn't have been the first time in the history of

23

science that that had happened. So, I suppose, I was part of a very small minority . . . but then maybe I always was an awkward cuss.

"Then on top of that I was just in the process of moving from NASA to the Defense Department. There were all kinds of security regulations, classified information restrictions and all that kind o' drivel to contend with, and some silly ass somewhere got it into his head that this particular topic might have defense implications. I can't for the life of me imagine why, but that was enough to keep most of the story out of the limelight.

"Anyhow, I was convinced I was on the right track, never mind what the rest of them were saying, and through the work I was doing at the Department, I kept in touch with a few people at places like Los Alamos who thought the same way. You see, there were a few unofficial experiments going on here and there even though it was supposed to be restricted work. Eventually everything started coming out of the woodwork and the whole thing turned political. I got fed up with the whole damn business and came back here to be left alone. As Murdoch has told you, I've worked here ever since. It must be, oh . . . three years or thereabouts now."

"And has this guy Ted Cartland been here that long too?" Lee asked.

Charles nodded. "I got to know Ted while I was still at NASA. He was at Cornell, involved with designing orbiting detectors for X-ray astronomy. He'd been mixed up with shuttle and satellite design and testing while he was in the RAF . . . a lot of liaison with other countries and that kind of thing. He'd worked with the people at Cornell in the past, knew them all, and moved there when he left the RAF. They were doing work for NASA, and that was how we got to know each other.

"When I decided to move back to Scotland, I had the feeling that I wasn't far from the point of producing a device to test the theory I'd been working on. Now I'm not much of a practical man when it comes to putting together gadgets and electronics and such, but

24

Ted is. So I invited him to come back as well to take care of that side of things."

With that, Charles emptied his glass for the second time, set it down on the edge of the hearth, and stood up. "Anyhow, enough of all this witterin' on like three old women," he said. "You must be wondering if I'm ever going to show you the machine itself. Let's get along downstairs to the lab."

CHAPTER FOUR

The lab was much as Murdoch remembered it from his last visit, although it seemed to have sprouted a few additional items of equipment. One side of the room was taken up by a large workbench running almost the full length of the wall, littered with tools and unidentifiable electronics assemblies in all stages of confusion. Along the back of the bench stood a line of stacked waveform analyzers, synthesizers, power supplies, and other instruments studded with buttons and covered in screens, and interconnected by unraveled rainbows of tangled wire. A section of ceiling-high storage racks, crammed with books, boxes, and components, occupied the space between the bench and the door; the wall opposite supported a large blackboard, covered with formulas and calculations, above a long metal table sagging beneath a load of charts and papers.

The machine itself stood along the wall facing the door. It consisted of a main display and control console; a DEC PDP-22/30, obtained secondhand through one of Charles's friends who worked for British Admiralty research and complete with its own high-density memory subsystem, plus some options from other sources; an auxiliary terminal connected to the national datagrid; a trio of enclosed, four-foot-high cubicles; and a jumble of electronics strung together in open racks. A cluttered desk beside the operator's chair at the main console and a set of heavy cables running through the wall to the generators in the next room completed the scene.

Saying nothing, Charles walked to the console and brought the system to life with a few rapid taps of his fingers. He glanced at the main screen, issued another command-string, and cut off the display. A few winking lights on the main panel were all that was left to show that the system was active. Then a sheet of glossy, plasticized paper slid from the hardcopy slot and into the tray beneath. Charles picked it up, ran his eye quickly over whatever was printed on it, folded it in two with the printed side inward, and then looked up.

"Now, Murdoch," he said. "Would you be so kind as to sit yourself down there at the console." Murdoch obliged. Lee moved forward to watch over his shoulder. "There's a clock-readout counting down seconds at the top of the screen there," Charles went on. "When it gets to zero, I want you to type in a string of numbers and letters, up to a maximum of six characters."

Murdoch frowned up at him. "What, anything? No particular length?"

"It does not matter. Anything you like."

Murdoch shrugged. "Okay." He waited for the zero to appear, and then rattled in a random sequence. The main screen in front of him displayed:

2H7vi9

"That it?" he inquired.

"That'll do," Charles said. He unfolded the sheet of hardcopy that he had been holding and passed it to Murdoch without saying anything. Murdoch looked at it; Lee gasped audibly behind him. The sheet read:

1 January 2010, 2038.00 Hours.

TEMPORAL RETROTRANSMISSION TEST. No File Reference.

Manual Input Sequence. Transmission advance 60 seconds.

2H7vi9

END

Although they had been more or less prepared for what to expect, Murdoch and Lee were too stunned for the moment to say anything. Talking about this kind of thing in the car from Edinburgh was one thing; seeing it demonstrated was quite another.

"It works with computer-transmitted numbers too," Charles commented matter-of-factly after a few seconds. Murdoch continued to stare with disbelieving eyes at the sheet of paper in his hand.

Lee looked slowly up at Charles, his brows knotted in bemusement. His lips moved soundlessly for a second or two. Then he whispered, "That . . . that was printed before Doc even knew what you were going to ask him to do. This really isn't some kind of conjuring trick? Are you saying those characters were sent backward through time?"

"Aye. Sixty seconds, to be exact." Charles looked back at him impassively.

"They exist!" Murdoch breathed, finding his voice at last. "The tau waves that you've always predicted—they really do exist!"

"So it would appear," Charles agreed.

As Murdoch slumped back in the chair and began turning over in his mind what it all meant, Lee gazed with new respect at the array of equipment surrounding him. It didn't look particularly spectacular; in fact, as far as external appearances were concerned, it could have been any one of a hundred lab lash-ups that he had seen before in all kinds of places. And yet what he had just observed had shaken him more that anything he could remember in his twenty-eight years. Murdoch had told him enough about Charles's work for him to have a general idea of how the machine worked, but inwardly he had never believed that anything would come of it.

The influence that propagated through time originated with the annihilation of matter, that is, the conversion of mass into energy. The mass–energy equivalence relationship became nonlinear at high energy densities; under extreme conditions, less energy appeared for a given amount of mass than traditional theory said ought to. The hadron decay into quarks that Charles had mentioned had been the first instance to be noticed; at the high energy density prevailing inside the infinitesimally small volume of the interaction, less gluon binding energy had been measured than had been predicted. Where did the rest go? According to the theory developed by Charles and his colleagues, it had propagated away as tau waves and rematerialized as mass–energy at another instant in time. Because of the small scale of the events, the resulting time shifts had been of the minute order that Charles had described. But at higher energy densities they promised to be more.

Charles's machine achieved high energy densities by focusing an intense beam of positrons onto a magnetically confined concentration of electrons. It employed a laserlike pumping technique perfected in the USSR about fifteen years before to generate energetic gamma photons, which in turn bred electron–positron pairs. The positrons were channeled by tuned fields and directed at a confined, negative space-charge to produce the sustained annihilations that the process demanded. Unlike the giant particle accelerators, which were designed to produce a few isolated events but at enormous energies, this machine produced many events at moderate energies within a tiny volume of space; it was the energy *density* that mattered. That was why the machine didn't need to be as large as the whole Storbannon estate; it also explained why the discrepancies attributable to the tau waves had remained undetected through the earlier decades of particle physics.

The result of the annihilation process was a burst of conventional energy, which was absorbed by a cooling arrangement, and a pulse of tau radiation that would reappear in detectable form elsewhere along the timeline. The energy of the gamma photons could be varied, enabling the point in the future or in the past at which the tau pulse would materialize to be adjusted with a high degree of precision. The machine therefore functioned more like a telephone than a radio; the sender could "aim" a pulse at a selected instant, in the past for example, but a receiver in the past, or future, had no means of "tuning in." A receiver could do nothing but wait for incoming calls.

Lee was unable to identify which of the cubicles and racks contained which components, but he would have ample time in the days ahead to become familiar with such details. For the time being he just wanted to know more about the basic principles.

"How is the character information modulated onto

28

the positron beam?" he asked Charles. "Do you interrupt it somehow to get a serial code?"

"That would introduce too many complications, as you'll appreciate later on," Charles replied, shaking his head. "It sends one data-frame in parallel code. The beam is split forty-eight ways to give forty-eight simultaneous tau pulses. Thirty-six of them are used to encode six-bit characters, which is why we're restricted to a six-character message at the moment. The other twelve bits are for control and timing signals."

"So the sequence that Doc keyed in was stored first, then transmitted all in one block."

"That is correct," Charles said.

Lee nodded slowly and rubbed his chin while he looked at the equipment again. The shock was wearing off, and he was beginning to think more coherently. "So what's its . . . its range?" he asked. "How far back can it send?"

"That's determined by three factors," Charles answered. "The magnitude of the pulse sent, the sensitivity of the receiving detector, and the absolute velocity of the Earth through space. You see, the tau pulse reappears as detectable energy at the same point in space as it was generated. Theoretically the profile of the reappearing energy wave forms a spherical surface that expands at light-speed about that point with increasing distances back along the timeline. After one second back in time it would occupy a volume one hundred and eighty-six thousand miles in radius, after two seconds one of twice that radius, and so on."

"It can't be," Lee protested. "The machine's not big enough to pack that much power. How could one pulse from it fill a volume that big?"

"Ah, I only said that was theoretically," Charles reminded him. "That's the mathematical limit. Inside that volume, the intensity falls off exponentially from the center-point. The signal exists everywhere inside that expanding volume. However, to receive it, the receiver can only be up to a certain distance from the center of the wave pattern, depending on how sensitive it is."

"So that's where the velocity of the Earth comes into it," Lee said. "The Earth will have moved between

29

the time of sending and the time of receiving. You can only send as far back as corresponds to moving the receiver to its limit of sensitivity."

"Exactly," Charles confirmed. "According to the data from Doppler shifting of big-bang background radiation, the Earth moves about twenty-one million miles in a day. The detectors in the machine will operate reliably up to approximately one hundred and forty-five thousand miles from the center-point of the wave pattern produced by the level of tau pulse that this machine sends. If you work that out, it gives you a range of just about ten minutes."

Lee shook his head in wonder and stared at the characters still preserved on the screen in front of Murdoch. "So how long have you had it working now?" he asked.

"Only since two days ago," Charles told him. "I got it to work for the first time the day before I called Murdoch. Even Ted Cartland hasn't seen it yet. I called him a few minutes before I called you, Murdoch, but he's stuck in Manchester and won't be able to get away until tomorrow morning." Charles cackled wheezily. "The poor fellow was becoming frantic when I talked to him again, earlier today."

Murdoch was only half listening. He was still staring at the console, mentally replaying each step of the demonstration that Charles had given. The question going through his mind was obvious. Finally he looked up at Charles. "When you set this machine up a few minutes ago, you got the hardcopy first. Then you started up a program that would time-out after sixty seconds and send back whatever I typed in. Is that right?"

"Yes," Charles said simply.

Murdoch thought for a moment longer. "Okay. Let's ask the hundred-thousand-dollar question: What would have happened if I'd simply decided not to key in anything at all after the sixty seconds? What would have happened to the characters that were already on this sheet? How could they have gotten there?"

Charles nodded as if he had been waiting for Murdoch or Lee to ask that, and moved forward to reinitiate the system. Then he stepped back. "Try it and see," he invited.

Murdoch looked at the hardcopy slot expectantly and waited. Behind him, Lee moved closer and watched intently.

Nothing happened.

Murdoch's face knitted into a puzzled frown. After a while he looked up at Charles, but there was no surprise in Charles's expression. They waited.

"I don't believe this," Lee murmured at last. "It's no different than last time. Surely an intention inside somebody's head can't make any difference to what the machine does. That's for ESP freaks."

"Wait," Charles told them.

They waited.

Suddenly the slot ejected a sheet of paper. Lee leaped forward and snatched it up.

"It says MURDOC," he announced.

"When was it sent?" Murdoch demanded.

Lee checked the time printed on the sheet and glanced at the time-of-day readout on the console. "It's still set up for sixty seconds," he said. The countdown display had appeared at the top of the screen to confirm his words.

"Right," Murdoch declared. "We'll just see." He sat back in the chair and folded his arms in determination. Clearly he had no intention of doing anything when the zero arrived. Charles watched, but said nothing. The final seconds ticked by; Murdoch and Lee became visibly tense. Then the zero appeared.

And that was that. The paper with its printed record remained in Lee's hand, and time marched on past the deadline regardless. Two faces jerked round toward Charles, demanding an explanation.

"I don't know," Charles said quietly. "I don't know who sent that, or where from, either." The other two gaped at him incredulously. They were too confused for a moment to say anything. Charles stepped forward again and used the touchboard to bring up a color display on the screen. It shows a horizontal line across the bottom, annotated with numbers like the X-axis of a graph with zero at the center; above the line, the main area of the screen was divided vertically into three broad bands: a central white one separating two of gray.

"This is a graphical representation of the machine's window of range," Charles explained. "The horizontal axis is time, with the present instant corresponding to the zero in the middle. The white zone is twenty minutes wide; that's the window of the machine's current range, extending ten minutes forward and back. The gray areas on either side are the edges of the future and the past lying outside the ten-minute range."

To the left of center inside the white area, they could see a short red bar standing up from the scale at the point denoted by —6 —six minutes into the past, and a similar, but dotted, red bar at −5 minutes. There was a second pair of bars, this time blue; the solid one was at −1½ minutes, the dotted one at −½ minute.

"Those two solid lines represent signals that the machine has received and logged," Charles explained. "The red one at minus six minutes is the random sequence of characters that Murdoch sent back a little while ago. Some of the control bits sent with every signal denote the time of transmission, so the computer can plot on the display when the signal was sent, which it does by adding a dotted line of matching color in the appropriate place. You can see that the dotted red line is a minute ahead of the solid one in time. If you watch closely, you should just be able to make out that the whole pattern is creeping slowly to the left as time advances. Thus the zero in the center always corresponds to the current instant." Charles paused and took a long breath, as if he were being forced to say something that he didn't really believe. He raised his arm and pointed at the second, blue pair of bars. "The solid blue line, now at minus two minutes, represents the reception of the signal that Lee read out two minutes ago. And the corresponding dotted line"—he pointed with his finger—"is the machine's reconstruction of where it was sent from—a point in time that is now one minute behind where we are right now." He stopped speaking and waited for the protests that he knew would come.

"That's crazy!" Murdoch exclaimed. "I didn't send

anything one minute ago. You were both watching me. Nobody sent anything one minute ago. There has to be something screwy with the system. How could— What the . . . ?" He sat forward abruptly and stared wide-eyed at the screen. A solid green bar had appeared right on the zero-point of the scale, indicating that another signal had been received at that very instant. At the same time a dotted green bar had appeared sixty seconds ahead of it—sixty seconds in the future. The hardcopy slot disgorged another sheet.

"It says 'CRAZY,'" Lee told them in a bewildered voice. "What in hell's going on?"

A solid yellow bar appeared at zero to the right of the green one, which had already moved a few seconds leftward into the past. Its dotted yellow companion was well over to the right of the white area, denoting that something had come in from about eight minutes in the future. Charles touched a pad to deactivate the hardcopy unit.

"We can look at what the signals actually say later," he said. "I don't think it matters all that much for now." It was almost as if he knew what was going to happen next. The display suddenly went wild. Bars of every shade and color added themselves at the zero-point as fast as the ones already there could shuffle out of the way, producing a solid, rectangular, rainbow spectrum that steadily extended itself relentlessly toward the left. At the same time the right-hand half of the white area, representing the future ten minutes of the machine's range, filled haphazardly with matching dotted bars to complete each pair.

Murdoch slumped back in the chair, shaking his head as his mind abandoned the struggle of trying to find reason in what his eyes told him was happening. The solid bars merged into a block of color that grew until it covered the full ten minutes of the past. By that time the isolated red and blue bars with which the whole thing had begun had been pushed out of the white area completely, and were now standing alone in the left-hand gray zone, beyond the ten minutes of the machine's range; almost twenty minutes had elapsed since Charles's initial demonstration.

And then Murdoch noticed something. He sat forward and peered closely at the block of colors denoting incoming signals. The block was not completely solid; there were a few thin, scattered gaps, indicating points in time during the previous ten minutes at which no transmissions had been received. That much was fact —already recorded and firmly sealed in what was now the past. A thought occurred to him. He pointed toward the screen and looked up at Charles.

"Those small gaps there," he said. "Could we set up the machine to send a signal back into one of them?"

"We could," Charles answered. "Which one?"

"How about that one?" Murdoch pointed. Charles went quickly through the routine of initiating the system to transmit and set the time-shift to select the gap that Murdoch had indicated.

"It's all yours," he announced.

Murdoch studied the display for a moment and paused with his fingers an inch from the touchboard while he thought about exactly what he wanted to do. He licked his lips and mentally composed a message. Anything would do—any nonsense word sufficiently distinct to be identifiable, such as MURDOC or CRAZY or . . .

And then it slowly dawned on him. He was not going to prove anything or uncover anything sensational. What else did all the bars crowded together across the screen tell him but that somebody—somewhere, some time—had already asked the same question as he, and was trying to do the same thing. And that somebody wasn't getting any answers. If he were, why did he keep trying the same thing over and over again? Doing so obviously wasn't getting the somebody anywhere; there was no reason to suppose it would get Murdoch anywhere either. He drew his hands back from the touchboard and sank back with a sigh to find Charles nodding slowly, as if Charles had already read his mind.

"You were thinking of trying to fool it, weren't you?" Charles said. "The screen says there were a few times in the past ten minutes at which nothing came in. Fact. You wondered what would happen if you tried sending something back to one of those times anyway. How could that be reconciled with what's staring you in the face? Am I right?"

Murdoch nodded. "You've thought the same thing, haven't you?"

"Naturally."

"And?" Lee asked.

"I never tried it," Charles answered. Then his voice took on a mysterious note. "Or at least if I did, I don't know anything about it." He looked from one to the other and took in their puzzled frowns, then waved a hand in the direction of the display. "Look there. Who sent all those signals that are plastered all over the place? A lot of them were sent in what has become the past already, but none of us here sent them. Somebody must have." The statement voiced what was already written across Murdoch's and Lee's faces.

Charles activated the hardcopy unit to obtain a single-sheet summary of all the messages that had come in. He scanned quickly down it. "There's no real rhyme or reason to any of it," he told them. "Things like TEST1 and TIME1 . . . Here's an interesting one. It says, GAPFIL. It suggests that perhaps whoever sent it was thinking exactly what you were thinking, Murdoch." He handed the sheet to Murdoch and proceeded to shut down the system.

The mystified look on Murdoch's face deepened as he read. "What are you getting at, Grandpa? Are you trying to say that I *did* send all this? That's ridiculous!"

"I don't know," Charles replied. "You tell me. Are those the kinds of words that would have occurred to you?"

"But it worked," Lee murmured. He was massaging his brow with his fingers, still struggling to find some shred of sanity in what had transpired in the previous half-hour. "That first test you showed us when we came in—it worked."

"Aye," Charles agreed. "When Murdoch had no idea of what I was going to ask him to do, it worked. But as soon as he knew what to expect and began forming ideas in his head about trying to fool it, we got nothing but nonsense from that point on."

"I still say the whole thing's impossible," Lee insisted. "It's what you do that affects what comes out

35

of a machine, not what you might do or what you think of doing."

"Yes, but what you think now might be the cause of what you do later," Charles pointed out. "And that's the kind of thing we're messing around with." He started for the door; Lee turned to follow, and Murdoch stood up and moved away from the console. Charles went on, "I think what it proves is that idle playing around like this isn't going to help us make sense out of it. We need to sit down and work out a systematic approach. I agree with you, Lee. I don't believe in mystical forces or any of that trash either. As I've said, I've only been working on this myself for a matter of days, so I don't pretend to have many answers as yet. This whole thing takes us into a new realm of physics that's stranger than anything you can imagine. But I believe it is part of physics, nevertheless, and there is some kind of sense at the back of it all. That's what we have to see if we can work out."

As Murdoch turned to follow them toward the door, a slight movement from the lowest of the storage shelves by the workbench caught his eye. A tangle of wire and cabling, balanced precariously on the edge of the shelf, was moving as if alive. As he watched in amazement, it rolled off and tumbled to the floor. A sleepy, bewildered, black-and-white, whiskered face poked itself out and gazed about.

"Hey, who's this?" Murdoch said, stooping to disentangle the kitten from the wreckage. "A new member of the household?"

Charles looked back from the door. "Och, the wee rascal must have followed us in. He's been here a few weeks now. Do you remember John Massey who runs the garage down in the village? His wife gave it to Morna. Their cat had a litter o' five."

"He's cute." Murdoch picked up the squirming ball of fluff and held it up in front of his face. "The black chin and white patches make him look mad, kinda like a pug. What's his name?"

Charles told him.

Murdoch's mouth opened in surprise. "What!" he exclaimed. "James Clerk Maxwell? You can't call a cat that!"

"And why not, might I ask?" Charles demanded gruffly. "It's a grand name of science, and a good Scottish one on top o' that." He closed the lab door and began walking along the passageway toward the stairs that led up to the main hall. "I'll no' have any of your 'Kitty' or your 'Tibbles' or such other damn trash for as long as I'm master o' this house," he told them.

CHAPTER FIVE

Despite having been born in Los Angeles, Murdoch Ross did not consider himself to be truly an American at heart. He was by inclination more of a thinker than a proverbial American man of action. The Americans seemed to get things done while the rest of the world found time to think about what it all meant, and therefore to criticize.

One of the things he valued in life was peace and quiet. He appreciated friends who talked when they had something to say and shut up when they hadn't. That was probably one of the reasons why he had always got along well with Lee.

Breakfast next morning in the kitchen, which was where Murdoch preferred to eat when he was late in rising, was marked by a distinct lack of conversation. The meal passed with hardly a word being said, and at the end of it Murdoch found himself gazing at his empty, egg-smeared plate with the riddle of the previous night's events still turning over and over in his mind. On the far side of the table Lee, presumably occupied with similar thoughts, was toying idly with a fork while behind him Mrs. Paisley, Charles's middle-aged, buxom, gray-haired cook, was pouring coffee into two large mugs.

Evidently, Murdoch told himself, future selves did exist who were just as "real" as the selves that existed at a given present moment. That had to be so since somebody had sent the "phantom" signals. Whoever had sent them had clearly not existed in the universe that Murdoch had perceived and formed part of, and for that matter that he still perceived and still did form part of. Therefore whoever had sent the signals had to exist in some other universe. But what universe?

There appeared to be only two possibilities. First, the phantom selves might have existed elsewhere in a system of "serial universes" similar to that which Murdoch had described to Lee during the drive from Edinburgh. On that basis there would be a future universe, one ten minutes ahead of the present one for example, in which certain events were unfolding as shaped by the past circumstances of *that* universe; when the present universe had advanced ten minutes, it could find that the events that *it* came to experience were not the same. In the meantime the former future universe would have moved onward to lie still ten minutes ahead.

This model would be like a procession of boats drifting down a river on the current, with the river being the timeline and each boat being one of an infinity of universes following sequentially along it. Each boat would be accompanied by its own present circumstances, which would be continually evolving and providing memories of pasts; a past as remembered, however, would not necessarily be identical to, or even similar to, the events that some other boat back in the line upstream was experiencing. Thus a patch of floating weed might constitute a permanent feature in the universe of one boat, but not exist at all in the universes seen by the rest.

The alternative was that the future selves who had sent the signals had existed on a different timeline, or timelines, entirely. That would be another possible way of explaining how those future selves had apparently done things that nobody in Murdoch's universe had later done. This picture implied some parallel branching structure of universes in which every point along a timeline became a branch-point into a possibly infinite number of other timelines, with the branches forking unidirectionally like those of a tree.

Neither concept was especially new; people had been speculating on possibilities like that for a century or so at least. The big difference now, of course, was that previously there had never been any means available of testing such notions. Having separated the two alternatives in his mind, Murdoch turned his thoughts back to reexamining the first—that of serial universes —more closely.

Suppose, he thought, that fixed instants in time corresponded to landmarks along the river bank. A particular tree, for example, could be noon on a particular day. Thus each of the boat universes would come to experience its own noon in turn as it passed on its way by. At the instant that a given boat was passing by the tree, some random event could take place in the "now" of that boat's universe, such as a fish jumping out of the water alongside it . . . or somebody onboard typing a particular string of characters into a computer touchboard panel. Given Charles's machine, the crew of that boat could inform another boat following ten minutes behind that a fish had been seen just as they were passing the noon tree. But in general, the crew of the second boat would not expect to observe the same event when they came to pass the tree, for they would be accompanied by a different body of water with different things happening in it. Therefore, in the serial-universe model, different crews would observe different things at similar times. Some changes might evolve slowly, such as a patch of bad weather that many boats might pass through before it cleared, but insignificant random things like the fish jumping out of the water would have no correlation.

But the string of random characters that Murdoch had typed in *had* matched the one that had been received sixty seconds before. Thus the serial model, or at least that interpretation of it, did not appear to fit the facts. An inhabitant of the boat type of serial universe would be able to influence what happened to other boats following his by advising their occupants of things he knew but they had not encountered yet, but nothing he did could ever alter *his* situation, which would have resulted from events in the universe moving along with him. In other words he wouldn't be able to change his own past. But Murdoch had received the same data as he had later sent. If that data had been perhaps the sequence of a roulette wheel or the result of a horse race, he might well have changed his past very significantly indeed.

He sat back and exhaled a long breath as he relaxed to give his mind a break.

Lee returned from his own realms of thought and looked up. "I don't see that it can be serial."

"No." Murdoch agreed.

There was nothing more to be said about that.

Mrs. Paisley took the sudden burst of conversation as a sign that normal civilities were in order again and glanced around from where she was stacking dishes in the dishwasher. "You're way past your normal time today, Murdoch," she remarked. "The two of ye were late getting to your beds, I'll be bound."

"Well, we had a lot to talk about last night," Murdoch answered. "I guess we must have been up until . . . oh, I don't know what time. Anyhow, we're still on U.S. time, don't forget."

"Every bit as bad as Sir Charles," she declared. "I'd give you another six months here, and there'd be no telling the two of you apart."

"With my accent? You've got to be kidding."

"It's what goes on inside o' your head I was meaning, not what comes out of it." She closed the dishwasher and began returning unused food to the refrigerator. "And did you sleep well after all the talking, Mr. Walker?"

"Fine, thanks. I prefer just Lee."

"I should have guessed you'd be every bit as easygoing as Murdoch," Mrs. Paisley said, nodding. She closed the refrigerator door and stood for a moment looking at the two Americans as if trying to make up her mind about something. Then she moved a step nearer the table and allowed her voice to drop to a lower, almost conspiratorial, note. "There is something I've never really felt I could ask Sir Charles about," she said. Murdoch raised his eyebrows inquiringly. "If you don't mind my being inquisitive, what is it that he's doing down there with all those machines and things?"

"He's making a Frankenstein monster," Murdoch whispered. "What else do people do with strange machines in the basements of old castles?"

"There's many a true word spoken in jest," she murmured, looking doubtful.

"Well, actually he's not."

"I'm very glad to hear it."

"Seriously, he's just using the computers to try and prove some of his mathematical theories. All very academic. Nothing spectacular."

"I see." Mrs. Paisley nodded and seemed satisfied. "I'd have thought that maybe he'd have seen enough o' that kind o' thing in his lifetime. Ah well, I suppose it can become an obsession just like most other things in life." She shook her head and sighed. "And yet it's a strange thing—Robert cannot trust him with the household accounts."

Murdoch spread his arms along the edge of the table and looked across at Lee. "Feel like stretching your legs before we get back to work?"

"That sounds like a good idea."

"Aye, why don't the two of you be getting along," Mrs. Paisley said. "Hamish will be in from the grounds any minute for his cup o' tea."

"Sure. We'll get out of the way," Murdoch said, standing up. "Come on, Lee. I'll show you the rest of the house."

The large room that Murdoch led the way into looked out through the French windows over a stone-railed terrace. There was a small bar at one end, and all around chairs were upended on small tables. Most of the other furnishings were covered by white dustsheets. Lee's footsteps echoed emptily on the bare wooden floor as he followed Murdoch in and stopped to gaze around.

"This part's normally closed down at this time of year," Murdoch said. "It'll be opened up again when the visitors start coming back."

"Visitors?"

"Grandpa keeps himself and the staff to the central part of the house, where we've just come from. The North Wing is practically self-contained. It's got bedrooms, its own kitchen, the lounge here, plus a few other rooms. Grandpa rents it to shooting parties later in the year . . . and sometimes for small business

41

conferences and stuff like that. We call it the Guest Wing."

"I'd imagine the company does him good," Lee said.

"It sure does. He often gets a lot of his pals staying out here. They have some good times when the Scotch starts flowing."

"That's the stuff you drink, right?"

"Right." Murdoch smiled and walked across to the French windows, opened one of them, and led the way out onto the terrace. The balustrade overlooked an expanse of gardens, lawns, a tennis court, and a summerhouse, all looking neat and trim despite the covering of snow.

"This area was laid out by Grandpa's father," Murdoch said, gesturing. "Colonel James Ross."

"Soldiers in the family too, huh?" Lee asked.

"That's right. He commanded a British Army regiment in France during World War I—Infantry. In World War II he was a cryptographer for Military Intelligence in London. You see, there's the mathematical streak coming out again." The air outside was cool and fresh with the breeze coming down off Ben Moroch's west ridge. The sky had cleared since the previous day, allowing the sun to take the edge from the season's chill. "We can walk back around the outside," Murdoch said. "The door will close itself." They descended from the terrace by a flight of shallow steps at one end and began crunching their way along a gravel path that followed the wall of the building.

"There've been some alterations to this part," Lee commented, looking up as they walked.

"Mostly in the 1960s and 1980s. The estate was managed by a trust while Grandpa was in the States. They ran it as a private hotel and shooting resort, which is how the Guest Wing came to be the way it is. When he came back to Scotland, he more or less left it the way he found it."

They rounded a corner of the Guest Wing and crossed the rear courtyard to reenter the house through the door by the kitchen. The kitchen was now empty except for Maxwell, who was lapping noisily over a dish on the floor and paid no attention to them. They walked on through to the front of the house and met Morna outside the sitting room, who informed them that Charles was in his study and had given the impression that he wanted to be left alone for an hour or so. That meant that they would not be able to run further tests on the machine for a while, since they were not yet familiar with the detailed operating procedures. Charles had, however, told them to feel free to browse through any of the records and notebooks lying around in the lab, and they decided to go down anyway to see what more they could learn.

Fifteen minutes later Lee was lounging against one corner of the desk and studying a listing of one of the system's computer programs, while Murdoch was seated in the operator's chair at the console, replaying again in his mind the sequence of events that had taken place there the previous night. After a while Murdoch said suddenly, "It's not parallel."

Lee looked up. "Huh?"

"It can't be, when you think about it," Murdoch told him. "Grandpa asked me to key in a random character string, right?"

"Right."

"If the structure was parallel, then that instant in time should have formed the branch-point to as many parallel branches as there were possible sequences that I might have typed, which must have been thousands . . . tens of thousands. According to the idea of parallel universes, all those branches actually exist as different timelines, and we just happen to exist on one of them."

"I think I know what you're going to say," Lee said, straightening up from the desk. "The instruction to send the sequence back would have been carried along every branch from the point they diverged at."

"Exactly!" Murdoch said. "So *every one* of all the me's who existed on *all* the timelines would each have sent his own particular sequence back down his own branch. And all the sequences would have arrived together at the point where the divergence had taken place, that is, the point where we got the hardcopy print. Everything possible would all have come in at the same time."

"You'd have saturated the receiver," Lee said. "It

would have given a binary full-house—all ones with no information content at all."

"Right. All the codes would have been scrambled up together. The decoders could never have made sense out of it. But it didn't happen that way. We got one code out, and it turned out to be the right one. Therefore the explanation of parallel universes doesn't hold up."

Lee tossed the papers he had been reading down on the desk and paced slowly across the lab, rubbing his brow thoughtfully with his knuckle and frowning. Then he about-faced and returned back to where Murdoch was sitting.

"So it isn't serial and it isn't parallel," he said. "There wasn't anything else, so what the hell is it?"

"I don't know." Murdoch propped his elbows on the armrests of the chair and swiveled it absently from side to side, his fingers interlaced across his chest. "Let's go through the whole thing again, step by step," he said after a while. He swung back to face the console and swept his eyes over it, as if the act of seeing it again might aid his memory.

Lee perched himself back on the edge of the desk. "It worked okay until you decided you were going to try to fool it," he said. "You were going to wait for a signal to come in and then not send it when you were supposed to. We waited for a long time, and nothing happened."

"Right. But we did get a signal without any problem the time before that, in the demo we got from Grandpa when we first came in. We didn't think of trying to fool it that time because we didn't know what was going on. So what was the difference?"

"You just said it," Lee replied. " 'We didn't know.' Somehow that in itself was enough to change what happened afterward." Murdoch nodded. Lee thought for a moment, then went on, "Maybe that's not so strange. Present intentions affect future actions all the time. You decided you weren't going to send anything, and sure enough nothing got sent. So we never received anything. The future you was simply not doing what the earlier you had decided not to do. So far it makes sense."

"So far," Murdoch agreed. "But then something did come in, so evidently the future me changed his mind. The message said MURDOC, so I assume it was from a 'me' somewhere, and from the look of it a me who was a few minutes ahead of that point in time. What would have changed my mind and made me decide to send something after I'd made my mind up not to?"

A brief silence descended. Lee straightened up, walked slowly across to the storage rack by the door, and stood toying idly with a section of waveguide that was lying in a cardboard box. Then he turned to face back across the room.

"You hadn't made your mind up not to send *anything*," he pointed out. "You'd only made your mind up not to send whatever came in. So let's assume that the future you who sent MURDOC had also decided the same thing. And since there's no reason not to, let's also assume that he stuck to it. That means he couldn't have received any signal that said MURDOC in his past, because if he had he wouldn't have sent it. But obviously he did send it. So the question is: What made him send that signal back on the spur of the moment, at a time when he hadn't received anything at all?"

"I shouldn't have to ask that question because I ought to know the answer," Murdoch replied. "A few minutes after I received that signal, I should have become him. But I never was him because I never sent it." He sighed with exasperation and pivoted the chair through a full circle.

Lee waited until they were facing one another again. "Well, let's imagine first for the sake of argument that you did become him," he suggested. "What were you thinking of a few minutes before that signal came in?"

Murdoch sat back and covered his eyes with his hand as he tried to cast his mind back to the previous night. "Let me see now . . . I'd been waiting for a signal to come in. When it came, I wasn't going to send it. We waited . . . Nothing happened. We've been through that. What then? . . ." His face screwed itself into a frown as he thought. Lee watched and waited in silence. Then Murdoch went on, "After a while I was starting to get fed up with waiting. I was looking

45

at the screen here and seeing the time-axis empty with nothing on it. I started wondering . . ." Murdoch's voice trailed away for a second. Then he looked up sharply. "Hey! I wondered what would happen if I decided to send a signal back to a point that was already recorded as having had no signal coming in. I thought maybe I'd try fooling it that way instead, since the other way didn't seem to be getting us anywhere."

"And the you that sent the MURDOC signal would have existed at just about the time that you were thinking that," Lee said, an undertone of excitement creeping into his voice. "So perhaps he was thinking the same thing. Only maybe he did send something. And maybe that was what we received a few minutes earlier."

"So what happened to him?" Murdoch objected. "Where is he right now?"

"You could ask the same question about all the other you's who sent all the other garbage you never sent."

"Okay, I'll ask it. What happened to all the other me's who sent all the other garbage I never sent, and where are they right now?"

"Well, if you don't know, what am I supposed to say?" Lee said. He spread his arms wide, then folded them across his chest and rocked back on his heels until he was propped against the door.

"Okay then, let's go back to the me that was me," Murdoch said. "I was getting fed up waiting, and I was thinking of sending a signal back anyway, but I hadn't got to the point of actually doing it. Then suddenly the signal that said MURDOC came in, which changed everything. At that point I forgot all about what I'd been thinking, and went back to what I'd made up my mind up about in the first place: not to send any signal that came in, when the time came to send it. A signal had come in; I wasn't going to send it."

"And sure enough, you didn't."

"And we couldn't understand it."

"And a little while later, others started coming in. What were you thinking then?"

"I'm not sure," Murdoch confessed. "I think I was too confused to think of anything. Then the garbage started coming out of the sky. The next thing I remember is noticing the gaps, and wondering what would happen if I sent a signal back into one of them." An intrigued look appeared on his face. He pulled himself upright in the chair suddenly. "Say . . . that's the same situation that we've just been through. In another minute or less I'd have been at the point of trying it."

"Which is precisely where all the garbage was coming from," Lee pointed out.

Murdoch became visibly excited. "And it did look as if whoever sent all that stuff had thought exactly that. Think of some of the signals that came in— GAPFIL, FILGAP—things like that. See, they're just the sort of mnemonics you'd pick if you were trying to do what I'd started thinking of doing. Whoever sent those signals must have seen gaps just like I did, and had the same idea."

"And they succeeded," Lee said, nodding. "But they couldn't have known they were succeeding. If they'd known, they wouldn't have kept on doing it over and over."

"And that means none of them could ever have been me," Murdoch said. "Otherwise they'd have remembered seeing what I saw." He slumped back in the chair again and threw out his empty palms. "Which gets us back to the original question: Who were they and where are they right now?"

Another silence ensued.

"I don't know," Lee said at last. "But it has to have something to do with trying to set up paradox situations, which is what you were doing. When you played it straight, everything worked okay; when you, or somebody somewhere, started trying to fool the system, that was when weird things started happening. That was the only thing that could have made a difference."

"We got results though," Murdoch said. "The problem is they don't make sense."

Lee unfolded his arms and walked back to the console. He stared at the empty screen for a while. "Then perhaps it's our ideas of what makes sense that need revising. After all, what we call common sense is based on the obvious fact that causes always come first and effects later. But this machine says that things no longer have to be that way. Therefore they can violate what we call common sense. We've always called anything that did that crazy." He clamped his hand around the top corner of the console panel and wheeled to face Murdoch. "Which seems, Doc, to lead us to the conclusion that, whatever the explanation turns out to be when we get to the bottom of it, it's gonna have to seem pretty crazy."

CHAPTER SIX

Edward Cartland returned shortly after lunch. Murdoch, Lee, and Charles were discussing further thoughts on the previous night's developments when a squeal of brakes sounded from the forecourt outside the window, and was followed by a clattering of running footsteps, first on gravel then on stone stairs, which terminated in the booming of the front doors being thrown open. Blurred snatches of a man's excited voice came from inside the house and were answered by a few high-pitched syllables that could only have been uttered by Morna. The hurried footsteps sounded again, became suddenly hollow as they moved from carpet to wooden floor, and grew louder. A second later the library door burst open, and Cartland hurtled through.

"What's happened?" he demanded at once, apparently speaking to nobody in particular. "What's it done?" He jerked his head around to take in the room and singled out Charles. "You said it works, Charles. What? What works? Is it still working now?"

Charles stood up and made vague slapping motions in the air with his hand until the stream of words stopped. "Och, calm down, Ted, for God's sake," he said. "Aye, it works. We'll show it to you right away. Now say hello to Murdoch and Lee."

Cartland's manner changed abruptly. He turned toward where Murdoch was rising to his feet, seized his hand, and began pumping it vigorously. "Murdoch! How are you, old boy? Delighted to see you again. Sorry about my appalling manners and all that.

We don't get to see time machines working every day, you know."

"Hi, Ted," Murdoch said, grinning. "You haven't changed. This is Lee, my partner from California."

Lee stuck out a hand, and Cartland repeated the performance.

"Lee Walker, isn't it? I've heard all about you. Delighted. I've worked with all kinds of Americans in my time. Great bunch! Where are you from originally?"

"Japan."

"Good Lord!" Cartland blinked in surprise, then shifted his gaze back to Charles. "Charles, what's happened then? I've driven all the way from bloody Manchester on manual. Nearly broke my neck a dozen times. What's it done?"

Charles sighed. "Oh dear, it's obvious that we're not going to get any sense out o' you until you've seen for yourself," he said. "Come on then. Let's go down to the lab and get on with the demonstration." With that he led the way out of the library with Cartland tagging immediately behind. Lee caught Murdoch's eye for an instant as they turned to follow and frowned quizzically. Murdoch shrugged and returned a faint grin.

Cartland was in his early forties, athletically built, and had dark, slightly wavy hair that was just beginning to recede at the temples. He wore open-necked shirts around the house, usually with a sweater or a sports jacket, but never went out without a necktie. With his distinctive upper-crust English accent, neatly clipped moustache, and unfailing—at times almost schoolboy-ish—exuberance the man could never, Murdoch thought, have been anything but a former British military officer. He was the kind of person that Murdoch sometimes imagined Colonel James having been when at a comparable age in the 1920s. That had been almost a century before; however some traditions still changed only slowly.

In the lab, Charles began with a repeat-performance of the previous night's demonstration and obtained a similar result, this time with Cartland as the operator. Cartland was almost as amazed as Murdoch had been, despite his having virtually built the machine, and soon

49

followed the same line of thought as Murdoch had by trying to fool the system with paradoxes. After about half an hour, a pattern essentially the same as that of the previous evening had established itself. At that point Cartland declared himself to be completely baffled. A discussion followed in which Murdoch and Lee expounded again the thoughts they had been developing since breakfast. Charles said little, evidently reserving an opinion until more hard data had been gathered. Eventually they ended up with Cartland shaking his head at the screen and looking nonplussed, Charles sitting at the desk beside him, and the other two standing behind.

"Well, this won't do," Cartland said. "We could talk about it all day, but it won't tell us any more. We're still no nearer getting to the bottom of it."

"What do you suggest?" Murdoch asked.

"I'm not sure really." Cartland frowned and rubbed his moustache pensively. "It's the human element that's causing all the trouble, isn't it? If we could eliminate that. . . ." He lapsed into silence, then sat up. "I know. Let's do the same thing as we started with, but this time let's automate the process. Then there won't be any possibility of anybody getting clever ideas halfway through and upsetting everything. We'll have the computer handle the whole thing, without any intervention from any of us at all."

"What are you trying to prove?" Murdoch asked.

Cartland had already keyed the system into program-development mode and begun tapping in a header reference. "I don't really know," he replied candidly. "But it's different, isn't it?" The others watched in silence while he set up a simple program that would activate the time transceiver system and run after a delay of two minutes to transmit a random number back thirty seconds.

"Now," Cartland said airily as he added in the final commands. "It's simply not possible for us not to receive anything. The program is running. In two-minutes' time, it *will* generate a random number and it *will* send that number back thirty seconds. Does everybody agree? That much is programmed in, running, and unchangeable." Charles grunted affirmatively from the chair by the desk. Cartland turned in his seat and glanced up at Murdoch and Lee, standing behind him. They nodded. "Good. Therefore we *will* receive it. And now I'll tell you what I intend to do. After we have received the number, I will enter a command to abort the program. The program will then be unable to generate any number, or transmit it, when the time comes for it to do so." He clapped his hands together and sat back in his chair to wait.

"What's the point?" Lee drawled. "I can tell you right here and now what'll happen: You'll wind up with a number coming in anyhow, despite the fact that you don't send it later. We've already seen it."

"I know," Cartland agreed. "And we keep asking who sent it. Well, we know jolly well we never did, so it's no good asking each other, is it? So what I'm going to do is ask the people who did, or at least who look as if they did."

"Who do you mean?" Murdoch asked.

"Ourselves two minutes ahead in time, of course," Cartland answered. "I shall use the machine to ask them whether or not they sent it. Depending on the answer we get, assuming we get one, we may or may not learn something."

Charles sat back heavily in his chair with a sigh and tugged at his beard. Murdoch and Lee looked at each other despairingly. They had been talking about nothing else all morning and neither of them had seen the solution staring them in the face. Why did it always take somebody else to point out the obvious? Before either of them could say anything, something happened on the screen in front of Cartland, who leaned forward to peer at it for a moment, and then announced briskly, "Here's our number, 419725. Jolly good. As things stand right now, this number will be transmitted in just under thirty-seconds' time. Everyone agreed? Right." He rubbed his hands together like a concert pianist about to begin playing and then leaned back over the touchboard. "Now let's tell this fellow to abort its program." He hammered in a rapid sequence of symbols, glanced up at the screen, and sat back with a satisfied nod. "There," he announced. "The program's on its back with all four legs

51

sticking in the air, dead as a dodo. How long have we got to go? About twenty seconds. Okay, we'll see if you were right, Lee."

They waited in silence while the twenty seconds passed. At the end of that period nothing had changed; no signal had been sent.

"There," Cartland said. "Just as we expected. Now when that number came in two minutes ago, it was tagged as having been sent from two minutes ahead of where we were then, which is right now. But clearly we're not sending anything. So what I want to do now is send a signal to two minutes *ahead* of where we are right now, and ask whoever picks up the phone if they know anything about it." He turned back to the console and rubbed his hands together again. "At least it might give us some idea of how all these bloody universes of yours are connected together, Murdoch," he added as an afterthought.

"Maybe we shouldn't have to ask the question at all," Murdoch mused half to himself.

"What?" Cartland looked up, puzzled. "Why not?"

"If they were us two minutes before, they'd remember it. They'd already know what question they wanted to ask."

"That's a thought," Cartland agreed. "I wonder—" He broke off suddenly as something happened on the screen. "Just a sec, something else is coming in. It's *two* frames, one behind the other. They say . . ." His voice faltered as he stared hard, seemingly having trouble believing his eyes. He blinked and shook his head. "They say, 419725 and, NOT US." Cartland slumped back in his chair and finished weakly, "My God, how extraordinary!"

Charles was already on his feet and bending forward to peer at the screen. Murdoch and Lee stared incredulously over Cartland's shoulder.

"You were right, Murdoch," Charles breathed. "They remember thinking exactly what we are thinking at this very moment. They must exist on the timeline that extends forward from where we are now."

"Or one of them," Lee commented.

"They received the same number," Murdoch said in an awed voice. "That was why they sent it as the

52

first frame: to identify themselves as existing in this universe and not in some other one where some other number might have got sent. But they didn't send it either. They knew the question we were asking, and they've answered it."

Cartland sat hunched at the console, drumming his fingers on the edge of the panel in vexation and exasperation. "So who did send the f . . . f . . . faffing thing?" he demanded. "This is getting ridiculous. It's insane. It . . . What? . . ." More frames appeared in rapid succession on the screen below the two that were already being displayed. They read:

WEJUST
BROKE
JAR
CAREFL

"What the blazes?" Cartland said, and then threw up his hands in helplessness. Charles shook his head slowly from side to side and sank back into his chair, while Murdoch's mind took a short vacation from the effort of trying to think.

Lee froze.

The words on the screen had triggered something. They meant something to some deep-down part of his mind, a part of his mind that knew something that hadn't yet filtered through to conscious awareness. Without moving a muscle, he scanned methodically through the information being registered by his senses.

He was half-leaning over Cartland's shoulder with his left hand gripping the backrest of the chair. His right arm was draped loosely across the top of the metal cubicle beside him, resting on a couple of plastic binders and some assorted papers. His hand was open with the fingers loose and relaxed.

Fingers . . . Fingers . . . *Fingertips!*

He started to tense involuntarily, but at the same instant summoned up an effort of will to force his hand to remain motionless. Then he became aware for the first time that his fingertips were just touching something smooth and cold. He turned his eyes and, very slowly, inched his head round.

His fingers were resting against a glass jar half filled with cleaning fluid. Unknowingly he had been pushing the jar away from him, and already its base was partly off the top of the cubicle and protruding into thin air. It was so delicately balanced that a settling fly would have been enough to send it to the floor. Lee didn't dare even to pull his hand back for fear of the vibration such a movement might cause.

"Doc," he whispered, "turn around, slo-owly." Murdoch frowned and moved his head; Lee moved his eyes to indicate his predicament. Murdoch nodded, reached out carefully with his arm, and lifted the jar out of harm's way. Lee emitted a long sigh of relief and pulled his hand back. Charles, who had seen the whole thing, was staring wide-eyed with astonishment.

"What's going on?" Cartland was looking from side to side and behind with rapid, inquisitive movements of his head. "What are you lot doing back there?"

"Where did those frames come from?" Charles asked him, ignoring the question.

"Four minutes ahead," Cartland replied. "They seem to be saying something about somebody breaking a jar or something. Why? What's going on?"

"It almost happened," Charles whispered. "Lee was on the verge of knocking a jar off the cabinet, which I shouldn't have left up there in the first place." He swallowed hard as the meaning of what had happened began to sink in, and then went on in a halting voice, "There was a universe, four minutes ahead of ours, in which it *did* get broken. Whoever sent that message back was trying to find out if he could alter his past. And he did!"

Cartland blinked and thought for a few seconds. "Good grief," he conceded. Only an Englishman could have uttered the remark with that preciseness of tone that qualified it as a suitable response to any event from the whole spectrum of the unexpected; said in just that way, it could equally have attended the discovery of a fly in one's soup or have greeted the news that the Moon had just fallen into the Atlantic.

"Not necessarily," Lee said in reply to Charles. "He might have altered *our* present and *our* future. That doesn't prove anything about *his* past. He might still

54

be standing there looking at a heap of broken glass."

"You're right," Charles admitted. "It could still be serial. I don't think we've done enough to be able to dismiss that possibility entirely."

"There's one easy way to find out," Murdoch suggested. "Call up four minutes ahead of now and ask him."

Cartland looked up sharply, seemed about to say something, then shrugged and turned back to the console. There was nothing more to say. While the others watched, he composed the signal, DIDJAR, followed by a second, BREAK. Then he set the transmission routine to aim the first four minutes ahead and the second to come in an instant later, and pressed a key to execute it. He had barely finished when three new frames came in: NO, followed by, CANTBE, and SERIAL.

"It's from four minutes ahead," Cartland told them. His voice was almost matter-of-fact; he was by now beyond being able to express surprise at anything.

"He knew what we were thinking again," Murdoch said. "Our signal didn't say anything about serial. And the first frame says, NO. The jar in the universe four minutes ahead of us isn't broken. So whose jar did get broken?"

"This is absurd," Cartland declared. "It could only have been in whatever universe is four minutes ahead of us, yet somebody in that universe has just told us that it wasn't."

"Not quite," Lee said, glancing at the clock-readout on the console panel. "A universe that's now one minute behind us asked one that's now three minutes ahead. We're partway between changing from one into the other . . . if you see what I mean. Maybe that affects it somehow."

"Oh, Christ," Cartland moaned miserably.

"In that case, three minutes from now we'll be at the point where the broken jar is supposed to have existed," Charles said. "I'm going to assume that it will still be intact, because it looks fairly safe to me up there where Murdoch put it. Anyhow, we'll know for sure if I'm right in a few minutes' time. So what will that tell us?" He looked from one to the other to invite a reply. Nobody offered anything. "It will mean that the event has not taken place in our universe at the time it was said to have taken place, and we already know that it never took place in the only other universe it could have occurred in—the one that is four minutes ahead of us. That seems to me to say that it never took place *anywhere!*"

"But it did," Murdoch protested. "Look, it's right there on the screen. It happened . . . unless that message is false, but why should it be? Why would we want to mislead ourselves? Where are the pieces, right now, of that jar that got broken?"

"I don't know," Charles said slowly. "But the only conclusion I can draw from what I've seen is that they no longer exist anywhere." He paused. A complete silence enveloped the room as three stunned faces stared back at him. "The event," he went on, "appears to have been completely eradicated in some way. Have you considered the possibility that whoever sent that message succeeded in changing his own past, and in doing so, he somehow *erased* the universe in which he existed?" He paused again to allow what he was saying time to sink in, and then nodded soberly at the others. "Aye. There's a thought to keep you all sleepless for a few nights. Perhaps he does not exist anywhere at all, and that's why you're not having much luck in trying to talk to him."

Nobody spoke for a while. Then Murdoch turned his head toward Lee. "You did say it would sound crazy once we started getting into it."

Lee took a long breath. "Yeah, but I never meant as crazy as this. In fact it's so crazy, it just might be true."

At that instant two signal-frames appeared on the screen. They were Cartland's own questions from four minutes ago. "Somebody back there has just received a warning about a jar," Cartland announced shakily. "He wants to know if ours broke."

"Tell him," Charles advised. "Play it straight. Let's have no more fooling around with this until we've a far better idea of what we're doing." Cartland typed in NO as a reply, and followed it with CANTBE, and SERIAL. Then he entered the appropriate timing commands and sent the three signals.

"You're right," Cartland said. "Let's leave the mucking around with paradoxes until later."

"Then switch the machine off now," Charles said. "Before we get too clever and manage to erase ourselves. And let's have no more meddling with it at all until we've given ourselves plenty of time to think about what we've seen today, and where we go from here."

The others agreed that Charles was right. They also decided to force adherence to his ruling by taking the machine out of service for a while. Cartland had been to Manchester to supervise final testing of components he had ordered some months previously, designed to enhance the machine's performance. First, they would enable larger blocks of information to be transmitted than the current limit of six characters at a time; second, they would increase the range from ten minutes to something on the order of a day. Cartland estimated that he would need seven to ten days to install them and test the modifications. The best time to do all this would be at once, which everybody accepted somewhat reluctantly. Then there would be no opportunity for yielding to flashes of inspiration or trying out premature ideas for probably over a week. By that time, they hoped, they would have recovered sufficiently from their initial intoxication to think rationally.

As they were leaving the lab at the end of the afternoon, Murdoch turned to Charles and said jokingly, "What we ought to do is take the range up to a day right now. Then we'd be able to ask ourselves tomorrow what we'd decided to do. It'd save us all the hassle of having to figure it out from scratch."

"That's precisely the kind of monkeying around I want to make damn certain we steer clear of until we know what the hell we're doing," Charles told him darkly.

CHAPTER SEVEN

"Do you remember Lizzie Muir, Murdoch?" Charles asked. "We said hello to her in Edinburgh last time you were over . . . at that conference on plasma dynamics or whatever it was. Quite an attractive woman for her age . . . getting on for around fifty or so."

"The physicist?" Murdoch said. "Something to do with the big fusion plant up on the coast. Burg-something . . . Burghead, wasn't it?"

"Aye, Burghead. That's her. I think I'd like to bring her in on what we're doing here. She's done a lot of work on the kinds of things we were talking about this afternoon. I've known her for years. She's not the type who'd go blabbing her mouth off about it if we asked her to keep it under her hat for a while. Besides, she could be a big help."

They were sitting with Lee and Cartland in a re-laxed semicircle around the fire in the drawing room. It was late evening, a few days after the incident of the almost-broken jar. Since then Cartland had been fitting and testing the new components that he had brought back from Manchester, while Lee had worked with him on modifying the computer programs; Murdoch had been spending most of his time with Charles, re-examining the mathematical side of things.

"What's Burghead?" Lee asked. He was sprawled full-length in the chair next to Murdoch, watching Maxwell turning somersaults over his feet in frenzied attempts to untie his shoelace. "Wasn't there something in the news a few months ago in the States about it?"

"It's on the Moray Firth about forty miles north of here," Murdoch replied. "Big industrial complex, mainly petrochemicals, hydrogen electrolysis, and power generation. The news items were about the fusion plant they've been building there for the last few years—it's the world's biggest heavy-ion inertial system."

"Working yet?" Lee asked, evidently interested.

"Not yet," Charles supplied. "I think they're still testing parts of it. The last I heard was that it should go on-line sometime in the summer."

"Seems a way-out place to build a fusion plant," Lee remarked.

Cartland looked up from knocking the bowl of his pipe into an ashtray resting on the arm of his chair. "Don't judge the whole of Scotland by this part of it," he said. "The northeast was a boom area in the eighties with the off-shore oil. That was when all the refineries and petrochemicals sprang up, along with a few new generating plants to power it all—oil-fired, naturally. Then they found out that oil wasn't going to last as long as they'd thought it would."

"Hence the fusion plant," Murdoch said.

"Makes sense, I guess," Lee agreed.

"The fusion plant itself is the result of a collaborative European effort," Charles told him. "It was funded and built by the European Fusion Consortium. You probably know about it. It includes the British, French, Germans, Italians . . . aw, and a few more. Lizzie Muir was in on all that when it was being planned and set up. She worked on fusion in Europe before the Consortium was formed."

"So how did you get to know her?" Murdoch asked. "Bump into her at a conference somewhere?"

"Och, no. I've known her from way back when I was in America. I was her tutor for a while at Stanford."

"You're kidding."

"I am not. It was in the eighties, just after your father moved from New York to California . . . around the time you were born, in fact. She'd got her doctorate at Edinburgh and come over to Stanford on a research fellowship." Charles stared into the fire and stroked his beard absently as he thought back. "Aye . . . That was where she met her husband, Herman . . . German chappie. They're still together . . . Live in a nice place just outside Elgin, up on the river Lossie." His eyes twinkled faintly about something, but he said nothing more.

"I must get Herman out on a golf course when this wretched weather clears up," Cartland murmured. "We've been saying we'll have a round some day ever since I came here, and we still haven't done anything about it."

Charles nodded abruptly to himself as if he had just made up his mind about something. "That's what we'll do," he declared. "We'll ask Lizzie to come down here for a day or two; there'll be lots to talk about." He looked across at Cartland. "She'll not believe any of it until she sees it for herself. When do you think we'll have the machine running again?"

"It's going slowly, but we're getting there," Cartland said. "Lee's a big help. He must have learned to talk in binary before English."

"What do you say then?" Charles asked. "Next Thursday perhaps?"

"Make it Friday," Cartland suggested. "Then she can stay on for the weekend if she wants to. It'll give us an extra day too."

"I'll call her right away then," Charles said. He leaned across the arm of his chair and lifted an ancient sound-only telephone from the lowermost of the bookshelves by the fireplace.

Lee raised his eyebrows in surprise. "No pictures? I didn't think anybody still used those."

Charles glanced up at him as he tapped the word MUIR into the array of miniature touchpads on the instrument and held the handset to his ear. "Have you ever had to answer one of those damn vi-sets when you were in your bathtub?" he asked.

"No problem," Lee said, shrugging. "You just cut the video. It's—"

Charles held up a hand for quiet as somebody came on the line. "Hello," Charles called into the phone. "Is that you, Lizzie? . . . Charlie Ross. . . . Fine, of course. And how are Herman and the family? . . . Good. . . . Really? . . . That's wonderful. Look, I— . . . Yes. . . . Yes. . . . Good. . . ." He clapped his hand over the mouthpiece and muttered something while he raised his eyes momentarily toward the ceiling. The sound of indistinct chattering continued to come from the earpiece. Suddenly he said in a stronger voice, "Och, will ye stop witterin', woman. I've something important to tell ye." Murdoch grinned. Lee shifted his feet and winced audibly as Maxwell clung on through his sock. "Liz, how would you like to come down to Storbannon and spend a day or two with us? Ted and I have made some progress on the work we've been doing here. I'd like you to see it. I think you'd find it rather interesting. . . . Oh, not now. It'd take far too long. That's why I'd like you to come down. . . . I thought maybe next Friday. . . . No, *next* Friday. You could stay over until the Saturday perhaps. . . . Yes. . . . I told you. I think you'll find it interesting. . . . Very. . . . Aye, I do. . . . Well, go and see what he says then." Charles looked up at the faces listening around him. "Gone to ask Herman," he explained.

"What does Herman do?" Lee asked Murdoch.

"I don't know," Murdoch said. "I've never met him."

"He used to develop computer algorithms," Cartland said. "Now he writes books about it. You'd get along fine with him, Lee."

"Will he be coming here too?" Lee asked.

Cartland shook his head. "Shouldn't think so. He was in the middle of another book last time I spoke to him. He gets a bit antisocial at times like that. Elizabeth told me once she thinks he's going to write a book one day called *How to Lose Friends and Not Be Influenced by People*." Then Charles began talking into the phone again.

"It's all right, is it? Good . . . glad to get rid of you, is he? I see. . . ." He chuckled at something. "You tell him from me that I'm way past being interested in any o' that nonsense. . . . Disappointed be damned! Oh, and there's something else. We've got a couple of visitors here with us. Do you remember my grandson who I introduced you to in Edinburgh once? . . . Aye, Murdoch. He's over again. He's got a friend with him this time, the one I told you about. . . . Yes." Charles looked up at Lee unconsciously as he listened to something. "Oh, a big chappie with red hair. . . ." He frowned suddenly and raised his voice. "He's just another American. God damn it woman, what else do you want me to say? He's sitting right here. . . . I know you're only teasing. . . . I am *not* getting huffy. . . . Nonsense. . . . Very good. So we'll see you next Friday. Around noon it is then, for lunch."

"Regards," Cartland sang out.

61

"Ted sends his regards," Charles repeated. "Aye, to Herman too. Tell him he's welcome if he changes his mind and feels like a break. . . . Well, you never know. . . . You too, Lizzie. Bye now." He replaced the telephone on the bookshelf with a sigh.

"Some woman," Lee commented.

"Oh, that's just her way," Charles said. "She likes to tease a little now and then, but she's not so bad at all really. She has a good head on her shoulders, and that's what matters."

Suddenly the stand, coal tongs, shovel, brush, and poker that formed the hearth set collapsed with a loud metallic crash. Maxwell streaked out from underneath the heap of wreckage, dashed under the nearest armchair, and about-faced to survey his latest accomplishment. Charles looked on dourly as Murdoch leaned forward to pick up the pieces. After a few seconds he stroked his beard thoughtfully and said, "Do you think, Ted, that when you've got the machine up and running, we could find a way of erasing that animal into some other poor, unsuspecting universe?"

CHAPTER EIGHT

By the time they sat down to dinner, early in the evening of the Friday just over a week later, Elizabeth Muir appeared to have recovered from the shock of having a lifetime's unquestioned beliefs demolished before her eyes. The notion of being able to send information or any type of causal influence backward through time was something that she, as a physicist, had always dismissed out of hand. The whole of physics was based on the observation that causes never worked backward. If causality reversal was allowed, physics couldn't work. That physics did work said causality reversal was a myth. Therefore it could never be demonstrated. In the course of the afternoon, she had been obliged to rethink a lot of her convictions. She was still a long way from having answers to the things she had seen, but at least it no longer showed so much.

The meal was served in what had once been part

of the banquet hall of the original manor house, which had since been partitioned off to form the less spacious but more serviceable formal dining room. It was a high-ceilinged, stately room with walls paneled in dark oak that extended to its hammer-beam roof, affording a suitably dignified setting for the cut glass and gleaming silver that had been laid out for the occasion. Forty-odd years of living in America had made not one scrap of difference to the habits that Charles had formed in his youth, and he appeared in a dinner jacket with black tie; the others conceded as far as dark, conventional ties with white shirts. Elizabeth, knowing Charles's whims, wore a long, satiny, purple dress that she had brought for evening wear.

Murdoch had met her only briefly during his last visit to Scotland, and his recollection of her had been vague, but in the course of the afternoon he had come to appreciate what Charles had meant when he described her as attractive for her age. Her hair was neatly styled in waves that held just a hint of orange, and her figure, though thickening slightly at the hips and bust, would not have dismayed a girl twenty years her junior, but what made her attractive had nothing to do with things physical; it was more her composure, and the elegant way in which she managed to speak and carry herself. Many women try vainly to cling to youth and glamor until long past the years when the effort becomes self-defeating; others, like Elizabeth, draw more from life than life can drew from them and learn how to work with nature, allowing girlish good looks to give way to something more subtle and far more enduring. Such women mature gracefully, but they never grow old. If he ever did get married, Murdoch couldn't help thinking as he watched Elizabeth across the dinner table, he hoped it would be to a wife about whom he would be able to think the same things when she was about to enter her second half-century.

For propriety's sake the conversation made token reference to such things as where Lee was from and what he had done, the progress of the trials at Burghead, and Charles's experiences in America; but the events of the afternoon were bubbling too near the surface to be contained for long. Soon Elizabeth was describing the aspect of her own work that had led Charles to suppose that she might have something of value to contribute to the task ahead.

"When I was working in France, I was part of a group looking into theories of entropy states and the general thermodynamics of plasmas. The natural rate of entropy increase in a closed system defines the flow of what is perceived as time. We were trying to develop a better insight to the synchronization between apparently uncoupled systems, in other words to explain how time manages to flow at the same rate in different parts of the universe; for example, how does a nuclear reaction inside a star 'know' how fast the same reaction is taking place inside another star or perhaps in a laboratory? Why do they all keep in step? It seemed to us that there was something that had simply been accepted as fact and taken for granted for too long." She paused to pick up her knife and fork to resume eating.

Cartland nodded from the other side of the table. "I met a couple of chaps when I was in Hamburg a few years ago who said they were mixed up in something very similar," he said. "They were from the big physics research institute there. Otto . . . Gauerlick, or something like that, one of them was. Can't remember the other. Ever hear of him?"

"Otto Gauerlicht!" Elizabeth exclaimed delightedly. "Yes, from the Wien Institute. He worked with us for a while before the Consortium was formed. How on earth did you come to meet him?"

"It was just before I left the RAF," Cartland replied. "I did quite a bit of touring around Europe . . . liaison on spacecraft designs and so on. I got to know Otto through somebody at Farben who worked on propellants. Amazing, isn't it."

"The world gets tinier," Elizabeth agreed. "Anyway, where was I? To cut a long story short, we ended up by deriving a set of mathematical expressions that interrelated entropy functions, quantum energy-states, and spacetime coordinates of quantum events. In particular, certain variables that could be interpreted as time and energy turned out to be covariant."

"You mean there was some kind of equivalence relationship?" Lee asked, sounding surprised.

"Not quite," Elizabeth answered. "But you could almost think of it that way. It meant that the universe could be represented by an ensemble of 'events,' each characterized by a set of energy states and spacetime numbers; nothing more. And in such a representation of the universe, conservation of mass-energy did not hold; it was replaced by a conservation of the product of that quantity with spacetime. By means of mathematical transforms, it was possible to transform one universe into another in which either quantity varied inversely with the other. If you made all the spatial variables constant, the spacetime functions reduced to pure time; so you could transform energy to time or vice versa. We had no idea what that meant, but it was fun playing games with the equations."

"You're kidding," Lee said. "I've never heard of anything like that. They don't seem similar in any respect at all. There just isn't anything in common."

"That was why I said it wasn't really correct to call it an equivalence relationship," Elizabeth said. "What it seemed to say was that energy could be extracted from the universe, which is where conventional conservation breaks down, and injected into another version of that universe in which the time coordinates of all the 'events' were shifted by some amount. The more energy you transformed, the greater the time-shift would be." She looked around the table and shook her head in wonder. "If that was interpreted as taking place within the same universe, it seemed to say that energy could be transferred through time. We couldn't see any physical significance in it at all, and dismissed the whole thing as a theoretical curiosity like tachyons and negative mass. And that's what I've always believed—until I saw the machine downstairs."

"Elizabeth showed me some of the mathematics a while ago," Charles commented. "I realized then that some of the expressions could be identified with parts of my own work. That was why I thought she'd be rather interested in what we're doing."

"*Rather interested?*" Elizabeth echoed. "Charles, that must be the biggest understatement to date in this century. I'm overwhelmed, fascinated . . . completely hooked, to use our guests' parlance. In fact I'm even presumptuous enough to assume that I'm part of the team now. I am, aren't I, Charles? You wouldn't keep me in the dark about what happens next now that you've shown me this much. You wouldn't dare."

"Och, you don't have to tell me that at all," Charles replied, raising his eyebrows. "It would be more than my life's worth and I know it." He stopped eating and placed his knife and fork down. His expression at once became more serious. "Of course you're part of the team now, Liz. I'm certain you could be a big help in making sense out of this whole thing. I'm assuming we'll be seeing a lot more of you down here now, whenever you can find some free time."

"Well, I'm glad we can see eye to eye on that, Charlie Ross. You'd have been in trouble if you'd said anything else." Elizabeth paused to give her mood a second or two to adjust to Charles's tone, then went on, "Very well, where do we go from here? What are your thoughts, Charles? Don't tell me you haven't been turning a few speculations over in your head in the last week."

Charles took a sip from his wine glass and nodded at once as if he had been waiting for the question. The others watched him and waited expectantly.

"We must conclude that past and present versions of the universe in which we live exist and are equally real," Charles told them. "We thus have a continuum of some kind. I think we're all agreed that it can't be of the popular infinitely branching, parallel variety; that would introduce too many impossible complications. In any case, it isn't supported by the data we've seen." He looked around to invite comment, but the others just nodded silently. "Neither can it be of the simple serial variety that we considered initially; in such a model it would be impossible to affect the present by manipulating a past, and again our results seem to indicate that this is not the case. The only model I can think of that could be consistent with what we've seen is a more complex serial one in which altering the events in a past universe does affect not only the future of that particular universe as it evolves in time, but also the presents of all the other universes that lie ahead of it. In other words there is some mechanism of causal connection through the continuum that the simple serial model doesn't take account of."

"You mean like with the jar," Lee said. "That one message changed what happened in all the universes involved, not just in the one universe where the message was received."

"Precisely that," Charles confirmed. "To be anywhere near the reality at all, the model will have to possess a mechanism that explains such evident facts." Those at the table became quiet.

After a while Cartland asked, "Any ideas?"

"I think maybe I have," Charles replied. The others looked at him with suddenly renewed interest. "Everything we have discovered so far," he continued, "seems to add up to two things: First, the universe that we see around us and form part of is simply one of many, equally real universes that appear to be strung sequentially along a single timeline; second, events that happen in this universe affect not only its future, but the situations in all the other universes that lie ahead of it. That, of course, suggests a continuity throughout the system; the future universes ahead of us form a progression of states that are evolving from the present state. We need to ask ourselves what the mechanism is that provides that continuity. That same mechanism will turn out to be, unless I'm very much mistaken, the same mechanism that enables events in one universe to alter what happens in another. Obviously we're talking about a causal influence that must be propagated by some means."

"Agreed, but I don't think you'll find you have to look very far," Cartland said with a shrug. "The continuity follows from the fact that objects don't suddenly just appear and vanish; they endure in time. So a universe an hour, say, ahead of this one will contain the same objects. They provide the continuity."

"Objects?" Charles repeated in a mildly challenging tone. "A candle, such as the one on the table there? A mayfly? A cigarette? They'll endure in time?"

"Oh, all right," Cartland conceded. "I used the wrong word. Molecules then. Atoms, if you like."

"The candle, the mayfly, and the cigarette are breaking down molecules all the time," Charles pointed out. "And they all contain carbon fourteen; atoms come apart too."

"Oh, you know what I mean, Charles," Cartland said, sounding a little surprised. "Protons, neutrons, and electrons if you like. Or quarks and photons—whatever you'll accept as the basic mass–energy quanta. They don't change."

"They don't," Charles agreed at last. "But they do *rearrange.* Bundles of them may come together and remain attached for a while to form a tree, and then fall apart again and disperse when the tree dies and decays. But as you say, Ted, the basic entities endure. They rearrange into different patterns to produce the changes that we call time, and they provide the continuity that enables one universe to evolve from another."

"But you said all the universes were equally real," Elizabeth said, looking slightly puzzled. "How can the same quarks and things be in all of them at once?" She thought for a moment, and her expression changed suddenly. "Oh, wait a minute. I think I can see what you're getting at. You're saying that the continuity *between* universes in the time dimension is just as physically real as the spatial continuity inside a universe. Every particle has a real extension in time, just as tangible as its extension in space. Right?"

"Exactly!" Charles declared. "So if you alter the arrangement of particles in one universe, you alter the arrangement of them in all subsequent universes as well by virtue of that continuity." He sat back, sipping his wine, to allow time for the others to reflect on what had been said. Eventually Cartland shook his head and frowned.

"Sorry, old boy, not quite with you," he confessed. "Are you saying that the whole universe is just a part of some bigger continuum, and that things like particles somehow extend right through the whole thing? The objects we see are only really parts of what they are completely?"

"Yes," Charles replied. He pointed toward the center of the table. "That candle there has burned about a quarter of the way down, but in the universe that's an hour or so behind us, it's still intact; in a universe that's a few hours ahead, it probably doesn't exist as such at all. The whole candle is the sum of all those, and all the points between. But all we see is the part of it that exists in the particular universe that we happen to be part of. The 'real' candle is all of them put together."

"I hear what you're saying," Cartland murmured slowly. "It's a bit difficult to visualize though."

"Try thinking of a two-dimensional analogy," Murdoch suggested. "Imagine that the universe is flat, and that everything it contains is flat. It's a plane, okay? Now form a solid continuum by stacking an infinite number of zero-thickness planes like that together, like the pages of an infinitely thick book. Every page is a universe. The basic particles are ink particles, and they form character shapes, that is, objects. But unlike in an ordinary book, where all the pages are different, the ink particles continue through like 'threads,' so the patterns they form can only change gradually, not abruptly. Also all the pages move together in one direction along the threads as they slide down the entropy slope that Elizabeth talked about earlier. So anybody inside one of those universes, us for example, will see the patterns changing sequentially. That's what he calls time."

"Ah . . ." Cartland nodded and pulled his moustache. "Yes . . . I think I can see what you're driving at."

Murdoch thought for a moment, then fished inside the pocket of his jacket and retrieved a piece of paper, which he unfolded. "Here's a sketch I drew when Grandpa and I were talking about it yesterday," he said, smoothing the paper out and placing it in the center of the table. The others leaned forward to look at it more closely except Charles, who continued to drink from his glass.

"That's supposed to be a solid continuum of stacked, two-dimensional universes," Murdoch informed them. "Each universe consists of a space containing objects and inhabitants that are all made up of particles, at least that's what it looks like to you if you happen to live inside one of them. But we, in our privileged

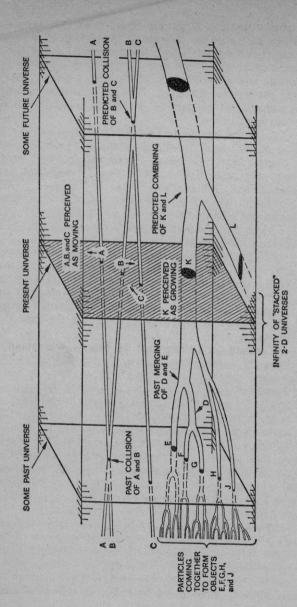

SOME FUTURE UNIVERSE

A

B
C

PREDICTED COLLISION OF B and C

PREDICTED COMBINING OF K and L

A,B,and C PERCEIVED AS MOVING

PRESENT UNIVERSE

A

B

C

K PERCEIVED AS GROWING

K

L

INFINITY OF "STACKED" 2-D UNIVERSES

PAST MERGING OF D and E

SOME PAST UNIVERSE

PAST COLLISION OF A and B

D

E
F
G
H
J

A
B

C

PARTICLES COMING TOGETHER TO FORM OBJECTS E,F,G,H, and J

70

position as superobservers looking in from the outside, can see that every particle is really an infinitesimally thin slice of a thread that passes through all the universes. As the universe moves along the threads in some kind of supertime, the particles, or slices, appear to move through space. That gives a visible rate of change that is observed as normal time within the universe."

"You can see there how, to Murdoch's superobserver, all of the universes are equally real," Charles commented. "Only the one that you happen to be part of and moving with gives the illusion of appearing more real to you than the rest."

"So in theory it ought to be possible to send signals from one to another," Lee observed.

"Aye," Charles agreed. "And I maintain that that is exactly what we've managed to do."

Morna and Robert entered at that point to clear the dishes and prepare the table for the next course. The conversation reverted to small-talk for a while, mainly among Murdoch, Charles, and Lee. Cartland picked up Murdoch's sketch and examined it silently while Elizabeth stared thoughtfully at the center of the table.

Cartland looked up just as Morna was about to leave the room behind Robert. "Compliments to Mrs. Paisley," he called out. "Tell her the duck was splendid. Absolutely first-class." A murmur of endorsement rose around him. Morna nodded, smiled, and closed the door. A few seconds elapsed while the former mood around the table reestablished itself.

"Okay," Lee said. "We've explained how they're all real and how they're connected. So what about events in one universe affecting other universes ahead of it? I can see how causal influences can move forward in time and affect the future. That much is everyday experience. But the universe that a cause happens in is moving forward too, so the effects would be observed inside the same universe, which makes sense intuitively. But you sound as if you're saying the causes can run on ahead and get into other universes that lie in front. Am I right?"

Murdoch glanced at Charles, who motioned for

him to continue. "That's the way it looks," Murdoch said. "If they only propagated at the same rate as the universes themselves move, then it would be the way you said: The effects of a cause would be permanently trapped inside the same universe that the cause occurred in. But that would give you a simple serial model, and we've already rejected that possibility."

Lee stared at him dubiously for a few seconds, then said, "You mean that the patterns that exist in all the future universes could be rearranged into something different?"

"Yes," Murdoch replied simply.

"Wait a minute, wait a minute," Cartland broke in, raising a hand. "What are we saying now? Is this how the universe in which the jar was broken managed to get itself 'erased,' as Charles put it? Is that what we're into?"

"Yes," Murdoch said again. "A universe existed in which the objects and inhabitants formed by the thread pattern included a broken jar. It broke because of causes that lay behind it, in the past. Then a signal was sent back that eliminated those causes. The pattern from that point onward was re-formed into a new one that represented a different sequence of events."

"What, *all* of it?" Cartland sounded distinctly skeptical. "The *whole* universe? Surely not."

"Not necessarily all of it," Murdoch agreed. "Probably only a small part of the total pattern was altered —the part that corresponded to the fraction of the universe that the lab downstairs represents. I wouldn't think the signal caused any alteration of the threads that made up a fisherman off the coast of Thailand or somewhere and changed anything in his life, or an event that took place in the Andromeda galaxy. But it certainly did alter what happened to us."

"But what about the people in the lab who *did* break the jar?" Cartland demanded, still looking unhappy. "What happened to them? Where are they now? Do you mean that these threads simply . . . 'jumped' somehow into a completely new arrangement when the signal was received? The people who broke the jar were simply . . . 'reset' into us, who didn't?"

72

"That is just what I mean," Murdoch said, nodding emphatically.

"And we know nothing about it?" Cartland asked disbelievingly. "Surely that's preposterous. Why don't we remember anything connected with the incident?"

"Because our memories consist of circulating electrical currents and certain DNA structures," Murdoch answered. "Electrons and quarks—basic quanta. They are all threads too! So are data bits in computer memories and characters sprayed as ink-jets onto printout paper. *Everything* that formed any record of the original pattern was reset. Hence our memories are consistent with the new pattern that now exists. On the timeline as it now is no jar was ever broken. Yes, it's preposterous, but it accounts for the facts."

Cartland slumped back in his chair and transferred his gaze to the tablecloth. He had evidently followed what Murdoch had said, but was still having difficulty accepting it. Elizabeth remained very thoughtful and said nothing.

"It accounts for a lot of the other things we've seen too," Charles added after a while, speaking slowly and seriously. "It would explain, for example, how we could receive a signal and then fail to send it later on. A universe existed that contained in a tiny part of itself a couple of inhabitants who had no record of any signal having been received at some point in the past. They sent a signal to that point. In doing so, they rearranged the threads that constituted themselves, their memories, and their instruments into new patterns that did include memories and records of the event. The fact that they failed to send the signal later wouldn't matter at all, since the people who did send the signal would already have ceased to exist as such anyhow."

"And here's a sobering thought," Murdoch added. "Exactly the same mechanism explains why we always see records of other 'selves' in the future who tried aiming signals back at points where they'd never received any, but we never get around to trying the same thing ourselves: If we did, we'd simply join the list of the ones who had been reset."

"Good God!" Cartland exclaimed. "That means

73

we've already been through it—every one of us here at this table."

"Seems that way," Murdoch agreed. He made an effort to keep his voice nonchalant as he spoke, just to enjoy the expression on Cartland's face.

Cartland's eyes widened, and his moustache seemed suddenly to bristle of its own accord. His throat convulsed soundlessly for a moment while he struggled to regain his voice. "Good grief," he managed eventually.

"Obviously this is all very hypothetical at this stage," Charles told them. "The first thing on the priority list is to see if we can devise some way of trying to test the theory more thoroughly."

Lee had been finishing his dessert and listening without interrupting. When a short silence descended, he placed his spoon in his empty dish, looked up, and said, "You're saying it's like an old newspaper picture that's made up out of dots. Let's say they form a picture of Ted. The dots are really the ends of a bundle of wires that has been cut across. The plane of the cut is a universe; Ted exists as part of that universe. Okay?"

"That's a good enough analogy," Murdoch agreed.

Lee nodded. "Fine. Now the threads are suddenly rearranged. We're in the same universe because we're still looking at the same cut, but the ends of the wires now make a picture of Charles, say. Everything in that universe that formed part of Ted is still there, but Ted isn't. And nobody else in it will ever know anything about any Ted ever being there. That it?"

"That's it," Murdoch said. "The mythical superobserver would remember it because he's on the outside and perceives supertime, but nobody inside the continuum would know about it."

"It's the 'suddenly' that bothers me," Lee told them, taking his eyes from Murdoch to look around the whole table. "The cross sections of the wires are material particles. To rearrange their pattern, they have to move perpendicular to the time axis. That means they have to move through space in all of the plane universes they pass through. How could they do that instantaneously? They should still be subject to relativity constraints."

"A good point," Charles agreed, nodding. "We asked the same question. But don't forget that we've never said anything about the process being instantaneous; there could be a finite propagation delay along the continuum that we haven't any data on yet that would enable us to measure it. And there is a theoretical consideration that could turn out to be a way round the problem. You see, the basic entities that constitute the threads may be more fundamental than quarks or photons. If a quark comes apart into something simpler, the attributes that define mass may disappear in the process. Hence you could find that it's possible to decompose mass at one point into components that themselves do not possess mass individually but only when they're combined together, transport those components to some other point without a relativistic restriction, and reconstitute the property of mass there. But that takes us right out on the fringe of the whole business, and there's a lot of work to be done there yet. In fact this is something I'd like to talk to Elizabeth about while she's here." He turned toward her as he spoke. "You haven't been saying very much for a while, Lizzie. What's your opinion?"

Elizabeth had been listening intently throughout with her fingers pointed together in front of her mouth and her dessert standing untouched before her. "Opinion on what, Charles?" she asked. "Your last point or the whole business?"

"The whole 'reset model' that we've been discussing," Charles replied.

Elizabeth brought her arms down to her sides and paused for a moment to collect her words. "I think you're on the right track," she said at last. "As you say, that explanation does account for the observed facts, as extraordinary as it sounds, and for the time being at least I'd be completely at a loss to suggest even the beginnings of any alternative. However, there are two things that bother me about it as it stands.

"The first is that the model is *static,* at least if we forget for the moment about being able to send signals up and down the continuum. By that I mean that future events are predefined by the patterns that exist in the threads. The future is already determined but unknown,

75

and is just waiting to be consciously experienced. There's no scope for human decision, free will, and chance. I don't like that. I believe that those things are real and important."

"I agree," Lee tossed in. "I can't buy that they're just illusions either."

"But I never said that," Charles protested. "Take the incident with the jar. That was something that had every appearance of chance about it, and the event was changed. That says to me very clearly that such things are not permanently and unalterably predetermined."

"I know," Elizabeth said. "But the model doesn't explain it. According to the model you described, that event was always written into the timeline until the signal was sent back to change it, which means that only a machine like yours can alter the thread pattern. So was the whole of human history and evolution before that simply a playing out of a fixed script? I can't believe that, Charles. The model has to show how such things as chance could operate before you built your machine, and at present it doesn't."

"I agree with you," Charles said at once. "And I've no answer to give. What's your second problem?"

"Maybe another way of saying the same thing," Elizabeth said. "The experiment with the jar, for example, seemed to indicate that the people in a particular universe did manage to alter their own past. But the model still doesn't explain that fully; it only half explains it."

"How's that?" Murdoch asked, looking surprised. "I thought we covered it okay."

Elizabeth shook her head. "Let's imagine somebody decides to change something in his past, in other words something he remembers," she said. "So he sends a signal back that resets the timeline and remains imprinted upon the fabric of the new timeline that it creates instead. Because of information contained in the signal, the something that was to be changed is changed, and the new somebody who is formed on that timeline perceives nothing that requires changing. Hence our original premise—that he began by deciding to change something—becomes untenable. So how and *when* did the signal ever come to be sent to begin with. Or to be a little more specific, how did the people who sent the signal about the jar manage not to receive the signal when they were at the time you were at when you received it? Either a signal was or was not received at that time. If it was, why didn't they receive it; if it wasn't, how did you?"

Murdoch swung his head round to look at Charles. Charles thought for a while and nodded slowly. "She's right," he murmured.

"In the model, causes and effects remain as we would normally define them," Elizabeth went on. "But instead of being simply related in sequence along a unidirectional timeline, they exist on a complicated loop that takes place in time. The loop makes the whole thing an impossible situation, at least it does if the loop is postulated as a permanent feature of the model like the threads. It can't be always there, but the model doesn't explain how it can come and go."

"You mean the model needs to be dynamic," Cartland said.

Elizabeth nodded decisively. "Yes, dynamic. That was what I meant when I said I was bothered about it being static as it is." She picked up her spoon at last and looked at Charles before returning her attention to her meal. "As I said, I think you're on the right track. But we need to add something that will give free will and random influences a chance to operate—something that injects an *element of uncertainty* into the whole process. The loops must be allowed to appear and disappear dynamically."

"Something like a quantum dynamics of spacetime," Murdoch remarked.

"Yes, something very much like that," Elizabeth agreed. "We need to extend quantum uncertainty, or something very like it, throughout the whole continuum of universes. When the model includes that, I think it will be getting extremely close indeed."

CHAPTER NINE

On Saturday morning they ran tests to try out a few ideas that had occurred to Charles. In the course of the experiments they communicated several more times with future versions of themselves who they did not subsequently evolve into. Although these tests were simple in nature and far removed from the rigorous experiments that Charles was planning, they seemed to support the general form of the model discussed over dinner the night before. The experience of witnessing evidence of a small part of the universe being wiped out and re-formed into something else was still strange to say the least, but by lunchtime, such being the adaptability of human nature, it was no longer disconcerting.

The range of the machine had by then been extended to twenty-four hours as Charles and Cartland had predicted, and some of the signals coming in were from well beyond the ten-minute limit that had previously been the maximum. To avoid the possibility of missing anything that might be important, they decided to leave the machine switched on and running permanently, thus establishing an always-open "line" to receive and record automatically anything that the inhabitants of the universes ahead of them in time might have to say. Since the message capacity had also been extended well beyond the previous six-character limit as part of the modifications, there was now room to accommodate significant amounts of information from the mysterious future universes.

Elizabeth decided, without much coercion, to extend her stay until Sunday night. This gave Murdoch and Lee an opportunity to make a trip into Kingussie, the town about fifteen miles away where they had turned off the Perth-Inverness road on their way from Edinburgh, something they had been wanting to do for over a week but had put off. Murdoch had made up a list of things he needed that were not available in the village, and Lee wanted to buy some warmer clothing;

he had not taken full account of the Scottish winter before leaving California. After lunch, therefore, they bade farewell for the afternoon and left Charles, Cartland, and Elizabeth to continue yet another seemingly interminable discussion in the library. They stopped in the vestibule just inside the main doors to put on their coats. Fascinating though the work was, the thought of taking a break was nice, and they were in high spirits.

"I can't say I'll be sorry to get out into some fresh air," Murdoch said. "It looks like a nice day for a drive."

"Suits me," Lee agreed.

Murdoch moved ahead and swung open one of the heavy wooden doors. He paused and drew in a deep lungful of air. "Mmm, smells nice and fresh. Blue sky again at last."

"Watch it doesn't give you oxygen poisoning," Lee said, pausing just behind him to light a cigarette. Murdoch grinned and went on down the steps while Lee stood there for a second to draw the cigarette into life in his cupped hand, at the same time holding the door partly open with his elbow. Down near the floor behind him, an inquisitive black-and-white face poked itself from between Charles's overshoes and the umbrella stand. Lee pocketed his lighter and let the door go to close as he began following a few paces behind Murdoch. Maxwell squeezed through the gap just before the door closed and tumbled unsteadily down the steps a few feet behind Lee's heels. The cat reached the car just as the door slammed above its face, and stood in the snow peering up with wide, bewildered eyes.

"All set?" Murdoch asked as Lee settled down in the seat beside him.

"Sure. How will we be for time? I figure maybe I could use a pint of that Scottish beer."

"No problem," Murdoch said as he started the engine. "I've only got a few——" He frowned suddenly. "Hell!"

"What's up?"

"We should have told Mrs. Paisley we might be a bit late. I'd better go back inside and fix it."

"I'll do it." Lee swung himself out of the car and headed back toward the steps, leaving the car door half open. Murdoch sat back to wait, and after a few seconds switched on the radio. The music was enough to mask the scratching noises of Maxwell scrambling in at the bottom of the passenger's door and worming his way under the seat toward the back of the car. A minute later Lee reappeared, climbed in, and closed the door.

"Okay," he said. "She'll leave us some sandwiches."

"Great. Let's go," Murdoch answered.

The car turned out of the forecourt and disappeared into the curve of the driveway, between the snow-crusted trees.

Kingussie was a quaint little town straddling what had been the main Perth-to-Inverness road before the opening of the bypass fifteen years before had rescued it from the automobile invasion of the twentieth century. Since then Kingussie had reverted to a picturesque jumble of narrow streets, haphazard buildings, and a few church spires that made a convenient stopping-off place for travelers on the nearby throughway to have a meal, shop for souvenirs, or simply browse along the main street's parade of shopfronts displaying everything from tartan plaids and Scottish woolens to skiing and mountain-climbing equipment.

The main street was busy with Saturday-afternoon shoppers making the best of the fine weather when Murdoch and Lee slowed to a halt just ahead of an empty space in the line of vehicles parked by the sidewalk. Murdoch backed the car into the space and cut the engine.

"They don't exactly have a surplus of parking lots in this town," Lee observed, looking around.

"What would you pull down to make some more?" Murdoch asked him.

"Mmm, okay, point taken. Where to first?"

"Well, if you still want a beer, why don't we do that now. Then we won't have to carry lots of junk all over town. There's a place you'd like just around the

80

corner, all oak beams and stuff. Must be three hundred years old."

"Sounds fine."

Murdoch climbed out into the road and closed the car door. Lee opened the door on the other side, then paused for a moment to check his pockets for the list of things he needed to buy. In a flash, Maxwell slipped out and vanished between the underside of the car and the curb. A few seconds later his nose poked out from behind the rear wheel as he surveyed the strange world of people and movement flowing by in front of him.

There was a lamppost near the edge of the sidewalk just a few feet from where the car was parked. Its base was hexagonal, and a crumpled ball of paper had lodged against one of the corners, carried there by the breeze. The ball of paper fluttered nervously in delicate equilibrium while a trillion molecules of air played thermodynamic roulette to decide the issue. Maxwell watched, his eyes widening slowly. The ball teetered precariously for an instant longer, then broke free from the lamppost and tumbled across the sidewalk.

Maxwell's first pounce missed by an inch. A split-second later he had gathered himself again and was streaking in pursuit after the erratically rolling ball as it veered into the doorway of one of the shops.

Murdoch was halfway around the car when a startled shriek, coinciding with an ear-rending S-Q-U-A-W-K, stopped him dead in his tracks. At the same time Lee, who was just straightening up from closing the door on the other side of the car, spun around. They were just in time to see a girl who was coming out of one of the shops with an armful of packages stumble over something and drop most of the bags. The bundle of fur that disentangled itself from her feet and fled into the crowd was unmistakable.

"Oh, shit!" Murdoch said miserably.

"Jesus, it's Maxwell!" Lee yelled. "He's taken off! Check the damage, Doc. I'll go get him." With that he plunged away into the throng, plowing a swath through the ranks of startled onlookers.

"What is it, Maggie?" a woman wailed in a high-pitched voice to her companion.

"They're Americans, I think" was the reply.

"Och, aye." A man nodded dourly to his wife, as if that adequately explained all.

It had all happened so quickly that the girl was still staring at the wreckage around her feet, and had made no move to recover the bags. Murdoch walked over and squatted down to begin collecting the spilled contents. He groaned inwardly at the sounds of tinkling glass that came from several of the boxes and paper bags, and braced himself for a tirade of abuse from above. But none came. Instead the girl squatted down opposite him and began gathering the rest of the items with calm, unhurried composure.

"Gee, I—I don't know what to say," Murdoch stammered. "We didn't even know he was there. Here, I'll take that. Oh hell, this one sounds like bad news."

"It can't be helped," the girl said simply. "Obviously it was nobody's fault. Was that your kitten?"

"Yes, I'm afraid so. He must have hitched a ride. We didn't know he was in the car."

"I do hope I didn't hurt him."

Her voice was as calm and controlled as her manner. It was a rich, melodious voice, carefully cultivated, and her accent was more English than Scottish, Murdoch thought. They straightened up, she holding the rest of the bags and he with his hands full of boxes and burst wrappings. He found himself looking at a face that was a classically oval composition of finely molded features built from lines that were clean and sharp but without any hint of harshness; it was framed by hair that fell in loose, dark waves to her shoulders. Her nose was straight, her mouth full, and her chin just pointed enough to be dainty without losing its softness. And the eyes—looking out from beneath long, dark lashes, which had to be real to suit the rest of the image—were dark, clear, and unwavering. They were infinitely deep, intelligent eyes—the kind that could take on expressions of their own to mirror the thoughts within or, with equal ease, remain aloof and inscrutable. She was dressed in a brown sheepskin coat whose hood was thrown back to reveal fleece inner lining, with matching knee-length boots of suede.

Murdoch realized that he had been staring for what

was about to become an impertinently long time. "Oh, he'll be okay," he said. "He's young. . . . Hasn't gotten around to using any of his nine lives yet." He motioned with his head at the items he was holding. "Look, ah . . . about this mess. Naturally I'll take care of the damage for you. Why don't we get off the street and find someplace where we can take stock."

"You don't have to," she replied. "If I had been looking where I was putting my feet, it would probably never have happened. I think the damage sounds worse than it is. There wasn't really a lot in there that could break."

"It sounded like you had a collection of chandeliers in there to me," Murdoch said dubiously. "Let's check it out anyhow. It'd sure make me feel a lot better."

Her mouth softened into a smile that seemed to come easily and naturally. "Very well. Thank you, that's very considerate." She turned her eyes away to gaze along the street. "What's happened to your friend? I hope he hasn't lost the kitten." As she said this, Lee came back into sight through the crowd, holding a squirming, protesting Maxwell clamped firmly inside the front of his jacket. At the same moment the door of the store opened, and a man came out bearing a worried expression. He was bald except for two patches of thin, gray hair smoothed down above his ears, and was carrying a pair of thick-rimmed spectacles in his hand. His dark suit worn without a topcoat said that he was not a customer; from his age, Murdoch guessed he was probably the store manager.

"That was a terrible piece of bad luck," the man said to them. "I saw the whole thing. Bring everything back inside now, and we'll have a look at what's broken. You weren't even off the premises, so there will be no problem in replacing it. We can always send the stuff back as damaged in transit."

"There's no reason why you should have to do that," Murdoch said. "Just replace whatever needs replacing and let me take care of it." The manager took some of the girl's packages and held the door open with his back as she turned to reenter the store. Lee bundled Maxwell onto the back seat of the car, slammed the door, and joined Murdoch a few steps behind her.

"I guess we're in trouble," Lee said.

"I don't think so," Murdoch told him as they walked over to the counter inside the door. "We seem to have picked a very understanding victim." He dumped the packages he had been holding down on the counter and turned toward the girl. "This is Lee, by the way. I'm Murdoch."

"Anne," she informed them. "I'm pleased to meet you both, even if the circumstances are a little unusual. I gather you're Americans."

"Both from California," Murdoch said.

"It's a strange time of year to visit your family," Anne remarked casually. "Most people would have done it the other way round—winter there and spend the summer in Scotland."

Murdoch's mouth fell open in surprise. "I didn't say anything about any family. How the hell . . . ?"

Anne gave a quick laugh, uncovering a row of perfect teeth. "Oh, just a lucky guess. With a name like Murdoch, you had to have some Scottish blood in you. And Lee is still wearing summery clothes, which says you haven't been here very long."

"Good grief!" Murdoch exclaimed, realizing as he said it that he had been adopting some of Cartland's expressions in the last few days. "What are you? Do you work for Scotland Yard or something?"

"Oh, nothing as exciting as that. I just notice things, I suppose."

Behind them the manager was examining the contents of the parcels, and every now and again pushing one of them aside with a sad shake of his head while he called out the design numbers to an assistant who began wrapping up the replacements.

"Are you from around here?" Murdoch inquired.

Anne shook her head. "I live at Nairn, north of here near Inverness. I'm just driving home from Edinburgh. Kingussie seemed a good place to stop for a snack and do some shopping."

"Have you had your snack yet?"

"Not yet."

"We were just about to go for a drink. How about joining us? I think we owe you one."

Anne's brow furrowed slightly. "I couldn't face a

drink at this time of day," she said. Murdoch decided it just wasn't his day. Then she added, "But a cup of tea and a sandwich would be very welcome. Could you stand that?"

"We'll take the risk," Murdoch said and grinned.

The manager finished adding up prices on a scrap of paper and cleared his throat to attract their attention. "Ah, are you sure you still want to pay for this, sir? Really, I'd be quite happy to write it all off as I said."

"We'll pick up the tab," Murdoch insisted. "What's the damage?"

"As you wish. It comes to thirty-four pounds and seventy pence. Will it be cash, credit, or on account?"

"AmEx okay?"

"Certainly."

"Here." Murdoch produced his card. The manager inspected it briefly then inserted it into a slot in the front of a small, desktop terminal on one end of the counter. A few seconds went by while a communications satellite high over the Atlantic redirected downward and westward a stream of binary code prefixed with the number of Murdoch's New York bank account.

"Are you enjoying your visit to Scotland, Mr. Ross?" the manager asked as the terminal's miniature screen came to life to validate the transaction.

"A lot, thanks."

"A grand Scottish name, I see. Would you be related to any of the Rosses in these parts?"

"My family's from near here—a place called Glenmoroch, over toward Loch Ness," Murdoch said.

The manager snatched his spectacles from his ear and looked up abruptly. "Not Sir Charles Ross of Storbannon?"

"Yes. He's my grandfather. You know him?"

"I most certainly do." The manager's voice warmed suddenly in surprise and evident delight. "There aren't many around here who don't know Sir Charles. Then you must be his grandson from America. It's not your first visit here either; I've heard about you from time to time." He extended a hand and shook Murdoch's firmly. "It's a pleasure to meet you at last. How long will you be staying?"

"We don't really know for sure. We're helping Grandpa with some of his work for a while. Oh, this is Lee, who's over with me from the States. And this is Anne, who we've just bumped into . . . or rather our cat did."

"My pleasure," the manager said as they nodded in turn. "I've only known Sir Charles since he came back to Scotland, you understand. A grand man he is . . . a grand man. Remember me to him when you get back —Andrew McKenzie from Kingussie, tell him. He'll know who you mean."

"We sure will," Murdoch promised. He inclined his head in the direction of his AmEx card, still protruding from the slot in the terminal. "Are you finished with that?" McKenzie extracted the card, thrust it back into Murdoch's hand, and stabbed his finger at a button on the panel beside the screen. The word VOID appeared superposed in red across the details being displayed.

Murdoch started to protest, but McKenzie brushed the words aside with a brisk wave of his hand. "I'll not listen, and that's the end of it," he declared. His voice left no room for argument. "I'm Pamela McKenzie's uncle, you see. It's the least I can do for the Rosses of Glenmoroch."

Murdoch and Lee exchanged puzzled looks. "Sorry, I'm not with you," Murdoch said. "Who's Pamela McKenzie, apart from being your niece?"

"Oh, I see. They didn't tell you about that, eh." McKenzie nodded to himself. "Ask somebody to tell you about it when you get back to Storbannon. Ask them to tell you about Pamela McKenzie."

They all left the store together and stopped to deposit Anne's packages in her car, a fairly new-looking Audi lowline, silver-blue metallic with black trim, which turned out to be parked just a few spaces ahead of Murdoch's. Then they found a quaint olde-worlde tea house tucked away in one of the side-streets off the main thoroughfare, and were soon settled at a secluded corner table with a heaped plate of sandwiches and currant buns, while a subdued background of Strauss polkas played cheerfully from somewhere among plant pots and timber beams up near the ceiling.

Her name was Anne Patterson. She was originally from Dundee but had spent many of her earlier years at school in England, which accounted for her almost complete lack of a Scottish accent. As Murdoch listened to her speaking at greater length, however, he began to detect a slight lilt that added an undertone of texture to her voice that made her even more fascinating. She was single and lived alone. Nairn was a pleasant little town, she found, with plenty of variety to offer without being so large as to become overpowering. Furthermore it was conveniently close to where she worked—the fusion plant at a place called Burghead, about forty miles farther north, as a junior doctor and assistant to the Head of the Medical Department.

"Burghead!" Murdoch exclaimed when she told them this. "Can you beat that? The world gets smaller every day."

"Do you know it, then?" Anne asked, sounding slightly surprised.

"We know of it," Lee said.

Murdoch passed on. "Do you know somebody there called Muir—Dr. Elizabeth Muir?"

"Of course. She's very well known there. She's the Principal Physicist. I take it she's an acquaintance of yours."

"She's an old friend of my grandfather's. In fact she's staying with us for the weekend right now. Incredible, isn't it."

Lee shook his head disbelieving. "It seems like nobody can move in this country without bumping into somebody they know. That oughta keep a guy on the straight and narrow."

"They all seem to know Murdoch's grandfather anyway," Anne remarked. "Sir Charles, wasn't it?" She said it matter-of-factly, without any trace of deference or awe. This at once made Murdoch feel more at ease, and he was certain she had done it intentionally; he wanted to be just Murdoch Ross, not the grandson of somebody famous.

"Yes," Murdoch replied, in a way that he hoped was

87

off-hand but not enough so to sound careless. Anne continued looking at him over the rim of her cup, her eyebrows half raised. In one expression she was able to convey that she was naturally interested but didn't want to appear inquisitive. "He's a scientist," Murdoch went on. "A theoretical physicist. He spent most of his life in the U.S.A. which is how I come to be an American. He retired about three years ago and moved back to Scotland."

"He sounds very interesting. What kind of work does he do now?"

"Oh . . . private research. Particle phenomena . . . connected with communications mainly."

"You must be physicists too then," Anne said, shifting her eyes from Murdoch to Lee then back again. "You told Mr. McKenzie that you were over here helping him with his work."

"I guess we are . . . sort of," Lee said with a shrug.

"Sort of?"

"By inclination anyhow," Murdoch said. "But the world only seems to have room for graybeards, bomb-freaks, and aspiring executives. So what can you do?"

"I see," Anne said simply. Murdoch had the feeling that she did see—exactly; there was no need to explain further. "So what do you do?" she asked. "Apart from kidnap kittens."

"For the last couple of years we've been on our own," Murdoch told her. "I suppose a theoretical consultancy would be the best way to describe it. We think about other people's problems for a price, and maybe solve them for a bigger price."

"That's one way of getting paid without being owned by anybody, I suppose," Anne remarked. Her radar was uncanny. Again there was no need to elaborate; she already understood all there was to be said. "Who's looking after the business while you two are over here?" she asked.

"Actually we pretty well wrapped it up about six months ago," Murdoch said. "We were looking at some other possibilities in New York when my grandpa asked us to come over." He shrugged and showed his empty palms. "So here we are."

"No plans for what happens next?"

"Guess not. It all depends on the winds and the tide." Murdoch refilled his cup from the pot of tea that had come with the sandwiches.

"How about you?" Lee asked her. "Where do you plan on going after Burghead? Anything in particular in mind?"

Anne emitted an almost inaudible sigh and shrugged, more with her eyebrows than her body. "I'm hoping to qualify as a specialist in nuclear medicine while I'm there. After that? I don't know. I might go abroad somewhere . . . America possibly."

"No ties here at all, huh?" Lee said.

"Not really."

"What about your folks in Dundee?" Murdoch asked.

"Oh, I left there a long time ago. We get along well enough, but"—she paused just long enough to avoid sounding indelicate—"we really don't have all that much in common. They're content enough in their own kind of world, if you know what I mean." She made it a plain statement of fact with no attempt at any implied apology; at the same time, her eyes asked why there should be any.

She was another odd-one-out of the family, Murdoch realized. They were all three of them the same: Three young people adrift on life with supplies for a voyage of eighty-odd years, but with no port singling itself out on the charts as an obvious destination. The major trade routes were well marked, but exactly what the trade was that took place at their ends was obscure. Eighty years of battling storms could be a long time to spend discovering that a cargo was valueless.

They talked for a while longer about nothing in particular. Anne's manner throughout was pleasant and not unfriendly, but there was a mild, vaguely defined reserve beneath her conversational exterior—a studied aloofness that seemed to define an invisible boundary of familiarity beyond which strangers were not invited. Murdoch was too intrigued by her to allow her to walk out of his life as suddenly as she had walked in, but at the same time he sensed a need for caution. So, when at last the time came for them to leave, he forced his voice to remain casual and said simply, "We'll all have to get together again sometime. Would you like us to give you a call if we wind up near Nairn?"

"You could," Anne replied. It was simply a statement of the fact. "My number's in the directory. It's the only Patterson with Anne spelled in full." As she spoke, Murdoch watched for any hint of eagerness in her response, but her expression and her eyes gave away nothing. It made her all the more fascinating, and he wondered for a moment if it was deliberate. And then he remembered that he had already decided she was the kind of person who never uttered a word or made a gesture that wasn't deliberate.

The sun had dipped behind banks of sullen, wet-looking clouds that were moving in from the west by the time they topped the pass on the shoulder of Ben Moroch and began the descent into the glen. Lee was idly watching the road ahead while Maxwell perched unsteadily on his shoulder, hypnotized by the views sliding past the window. Every now and again Lee turned his head to study Murdoch, who had been unusually quiet all the way from Kingussie.

"Quite a gal," Lee remarked at last after an exceptionally long silence.

"Uh huh."

"Classy. Don't see a lot of that around these days."

"Uh uh."

Lee studied his fingernails for a second, then said, "Just imagine, the world's biggest heavy-ion fusion plant. You don't get a chance to see that every day."

"Lee, what are you talking about?"

"Oh, just a thought . . . It occurred to me that if you happen to know the Principal Physicist of a place like that, it shouldn't be too much of a problem to get yourself a tour." He paused as Murdoch's head swung round sharply, then went on in a matter-of-fact voice, "Especially for people who are physicists themselves, and even more especially if they happen to have worked on fusion."

"You're right," Murdoch said. "We've got a lot of

90

work to do, but, aw hell . . . everybody has to have a break once in a while. We ought to talk to Elizabeth."

"Yeah. Just what I was thinking," Lee agreed, nodding his head slowly.

CHAPTER TEN

Virtually any scientifically conducted experiment can, at least ideally, be reduced to two broad steps: first, determining the variables that affect the outcome of the experiment; second, setting up conditions such that one of the variables at a time may be altered while the rest are kept constant. From the data obtained in this way the experimenter can, with luck, begin constructing a picture of which variables matter, in what way and to what degree they matter, and which don't.

In the case of the proposed time-communication experiments there were essentially three variables to be considered: the data content of the signal sent, the instant in time that the signal was sent from, and the instant it was sent to. An additional complication was that all three of these factors were themselves consequences of decisions made at some point or other in somebody's mind; exactly when, and in what manner, the results of such decisions became accessible to observation was something that was still far from clear.

To simplify as far as possible the task of differentiating the effects of all these influences, the team agreed upon a schedule of tests that fell into two broad phases. Each phase would consist of transmitting a series of signals containing data of a particular type: phase one, determinate data; phase two, randomly generated data. For the first series of tests, the signals sent would comprise the results of complex algorithms run on the computer. These results would thus be effectively determined from the moment the schedule was fixed and long before the tests actually came to be performed; because of the complexity of the algorithms selected, however, nobody would have any way of knowing in advance what the results would be. The second series of tests would use signals that advised the outcomes

91

of events decided randomly, such as random-number generating programs run on the computer, tossings of coins, or arbitrary choices and decisions made on the spur of the moment by the people involved. By combining the results of these tests, the team hoped to make at least a start in finding out more about the role played by the elusive elements of chance and free will.

That covered the data content of the signals, but still left the two other variables that had been singled out for investigation: the times of transmission and reception. To isolate the effects of these, the team decided to divide each of the phases into two groups of tests, with one of the quantities being varied and the other held constant in each group. The first group in each of the phases would comprise tests to study the effect of varying the transmission time of a signal. The computer would wait for an incoming signal from the future, determine the moment in time from which it had been sent, add one second to that time, and then transmit a different signal after the one-second-extended period had elapsed. This process should, the team reasoned, generate a whole series of loops back, all "aimed at" the same instant in the past but transmitted from a series of points advancing progressively at one-second increments into the future. Then they would repeat the whole procedure, but this time with the loops shortening by one second with each repetition instead of lengthening. After that, for the second group of each phase, they would go through the whole thing again, this time keeping the time of transmission constant and varying the time of reception.

To eliminate, or at least minimize, the human element, the team agreed to adhere rigidly to the schedule once it had been worked out in detail, regardless of what took place thereafter. Also, to avoid the risk of unnecessary complications, they made a rule forbidding any further dialogues with past or future selves, or the transmitting of anything at all that was not specified in the schedule. The matter was already complicated enough.

The computer would be programmed to record every measurable quantity relating to every test. Then analysis would begin of the data left imprinted on the final timeline preserved at the end of it all. From this analysis the team hoped to gather more clues to assist them untangle which events were erased by what and under what conditions, and thus gain more of an insight to the workings of the strange mechanics that governed the feedback loops through time.

Murdoch was on his way through the dining room to rejoin the others in the library when he stopped for a moment to gaze out through the window over-looking the rear courtyard. It was around midafternoon on Sunday. The steady drizzle that had arrived during the night had continued unabated through the day to turn the snow covering the ground into a sea of dreary, watery slush. Behind him, Robert and Morna were preparing the table for dinner later that evening.

"Looks lousy out," Murdoch threw back over his shoulder. "I think I've figured out why the Scots are crazy."

"And why would that be?" Robert's voice asked from somewhere behind him.

"They're descended from crazy ancestors. Who in their right minds would have settled in a mess like this?"

"Well, if it's crazy we are, then you're no better yourself," Morna declared. "You're as much a Scot at heart as Sir Charles, American mother or not."

A few seconds passed. "Are the others still talking in the library?" Robert asked. "Ye've all been at it since first thing this morning, and through most of yesterday too. There must be something very important happening. Mr. Cartland seemed very excited about something at breakfast, I noticed."

"Nothing that'll change the world," Murdoch replied. He turned his back to the window and moved nearer the center of the room. "It's starting to look as if some things might work the way Grandpa's theories have been predicting for a while. Ted's just excitable by nature. I don't expect any revolutions." As he said it, Murdoch had the fleeting thought that, if things worked out the way he was beginning to suspect they might, one day that last sentence could well qualify as the biggest lie told in history.

"There was something I meant to ask you," Murdoch went on, more to change the subject than anything else. "Who is Pamela McKenzie?"

"Have you not heard about her?" Morna asked, sounding surprised. "I'd have thought Sir Charles would have told you. There, isn't that just like him to go not mentioning a word of it." Murdoch looked inquiringly at Robert.

"She's a young lass from just outside of Kingussie who was working here at Storbannon for a while last winter," Robert said. He shook his head grimly. "Oh, last winter was a bad one, and that's for sure. A lot of snow we had. . . . Some of the passes up in the hills were closed for weeks."

"Yes?" Murdoch said.

"Pamela was taken sick all of a sudden . . . something quite serious inside, it was. They got her to the hospital just outside of Kingussie, but then a storm broke out so they decided to operate there instead of taking her up to Inverness. She started hemorrhaging, I'm told, and they needed to get some kind of special blood sent down in a hurry. The ambulances were grounded so they sent it down in a police car, but the road from Inverness was so bad that it was touch-and-go whether or not it would get through. But anyhow it did, and everything turned out well." Robert paused from laying out the silver and looked up. "It was only afterward we found out that Mr. Cartland had talked to his RAF friends in the base up at Lossiemouth and arranged for them to have an all-weather rescue team standing by ready to pick up an extra supply from Inverness and bring it down to Kingussie if the police didn't make it. He tried to make out as if it was nothing at all, but there are a lot of folk around here who'll not forget in a hurry what he did."

"I see . . ." Murdoch said slowly. "That explains a lot."

"Where did you hear about Pamela?" Morna asked. "She's been gone from Storbannon a while now."

94

"We were talking to a guy in Kingussie who said he was her uncle."

"Oh, that'll be Andy McKenzie, I'll be bound," Robert said. "Runs the glassware shop on the high street."

"That's him. Bald head. Wears glasses."

"Was that where you had the accident with that wee devil of a kitten then?" Morna asked.

"That's right. When McKenzie found out where we were from, he wouldn't—" Murdoch's voice broke off as he heard the library door open and a sudden flood of voices pour into the hallway outside. "Excuse me," he said. "I'd better go see what's happening."

The others were just coming out to stretch their legs and break for coffee.

Elizabeth caught sight of Murdoch and detached herself from the group to walk over to him. "Change of plan," she announced. "Your wicked grandfather has persuaded me to stay for dinner. I'll be leaving afterwards instead."

"Unless he's managed to talk you into making it a week by then," Murdoch said with a grin.

"I'd love to, believe me. But neglected husbands can be so objectionable. And I simply must be back at Burghead tomorrow. We'll be testing the reactors at full power for the first time very soon now. You wouldn't believe how much there is to be done."

"Say, that reminds me, I was meaning to ask you something about Burghead." Murdoch screwed up his face and scratched his ear for a moment. "You know, with the world's biggest heavy-ion plant just forty miles away, and with Lee and me having worked on that kind of thing, I was wondering—"

"If I might be able to arrange a visit for you. Yes, Lee has already mentioned it. Of course I'd be happy to. In fact that was what I came over to tell you. I'll call you later in the week when I've had a chance to organize something. It will be a busy week, but I'm sure we'll be able to sort something out for you both."

CHAPTER ELEVEN

Murdoch and Lee drove north to visit Burghead on the following Thursday, which turned out to be a convenient time to take a day off. Charles and Cartland wanted to go to Edinburgh to spend the day with some former colleagues of theirs who were visiting Britain from the States; the team therefore declared Thursday a holiday, left the machine to run automatically, and went their separate ways.

The lure of taming fusion, with its promise of practically unlimited amounts of energy from easily processed and abundant fuel in the form of seawater, had captured men's imaginations since around the middle of the twentieth century. The principle was straightforward: Two nuclei of the heavy isotopes of hydrogen, one of deuterium and one of tritium, could be fused together to produce a nucleus of helium and a surplus neutron. A small amount of mass would be lost in the process, appearing in an Einsteinian way as a lot of energy to be carried away mainly by the neutron and partly by the helium nucleus.

In practice the main problem to be overcome was that of finding a way to induce the nuclei to come close enough to each other for fusion to take place since they both carried positive electrical charges. In other words, how could they be confined in close enough proximity for the strong nuclear force to solemnize the marriage when the long-range electromagnetic force drove them apart before they were even on speaking terms? The answer was to cause the nuclei to rush at each other so fast that their momenta would carry them through the repulsive barrier regardless of how the laws of electrodynamics felt about it. That meant that the plasma formed by the nuclei would have to be hot. Very hot. It worked out at around fifty million degrees Celsius. This was fine for anybody who happened to live at the center of a star, where gravitational pressure sustained the necessary temperatures and densities, or in the core of a detonating hydrogen bomb, where an A-bomb trigger heated hydrogen to such temperatures before it could disperse. But human beings had long ago adapted to a more genial type of habitat and had developed a distinct preference for keeping things that way.

Through the latter half of the twentieth century, despite alarmist accusations that research was being sabotaged by political and commercial vested interests in oil, two broad approaches emerged to solving the confinement problem. The first to be investigated was magnetic confinement, in which the hydrogen plasma was trapped inside magnetic "bottles" of various shapes and then heated by the injection of electromagnetic radiation or of high-velocity particle beams. The second approach was inertial confinement, which came later. It consisted of crushing to superhigh densities small pellets of hydrogen fuel at very high speed using the inertia of the nuclei to drive them together and fuse before repulsion could stop them. This was achieved by dumping an enormous amount of energy on the surface of a pellet in a very short space of time —typically measured in thousandths of a microsecond; under such conditions the outer skin of the pellet exploded away and created an opposite, inward reaction-force that imploded the core, rather like a spherical rocket. To convey the required energy to the pellet, three technologies were developed: laser beams, electron beams, and ion beams.

The first generation of working fusion reactors went into operation in the United States and the U.S.S.R. in the late 1980s and early 1990s. Both nations had developed magnetic methods as their primary form of approach, but eventually supplemented them with one of the inertial alternatives, the Americans opting for lasers, the Russians for e-beams. Although they both pursued research on ion beams, neither nation gave priority to perfecting techniques involving them.

The European Fusion Consortium finally got its act together in 1990 after a spate of delays and bickerings resulting from jealousies and petty-politics that should have been forgotten generations before. The choice open to the Europeans by this time was either to buy into the technologies that had been pioneered elsewhere, which would have cost them considerably in money, prestige, and national pride, or to go for ion beams. They chose the latter. Besides the obvious reasons, the approach promised several distinct technical advantages. For one thing, ions were more massive than electrons and could carry far more energy at a given velocity; also, because of their high inertia, they could be focused onto their targets from relatively long distances, thus reducing substantially the problems of designing final-focusing equipment that would withstand the bombardment from a sustained barrage of fusion microexplosions. And on top of this the techniques for generating and controlling particle beams were well understood after decades of high-energy accelerator physics, which meant that a lot of lost time could be made up by exploiting an already mature technology. In fact the attractions of ion beams were so evident that the Europeans wondered why neither of the superpowers had concentrated on them in the first place. But that wasn't the Europeans' problem.

In a rare revival of the enterprising spirit that had inundated the world with bibles and gunboats in years gone by, the nations of the European Fusion Consortium elected to go whole hog with a project that would surpass in concept and scale any of the first-generation reactors that had been conceived by the end of the twentieth century. It would be a gigantic, heavy-ion facility designed to perform a triple role: It would produce power and deliver thousands of megawatts into the European supply grid; it would use a portion of the fast neutrons produced in the fusion process to convert abundant deuterium into tritium, thus manufacturing its own fuel; and it would breed heavy isotopes to help satisfy Europe's fission-reactor needs.

The haggling, of course, began when they tried to agree on where to build it. In the end, ironically, the issue was decided by oil. Although the long-term picture was at last beginning to look quite cheerful, oil would still be needed for many years to come to keep the wheels of Europe turning. The British had acquired the lion's share of the oilfields developed in the North

Sea; they could therefore sell oil to the other Consortium nations far more cheaply than the traditional overseas suppliers could, or at least were disposed to. And in the 1990s the prospect of cheap oil for a while was not something to treat lightly. Furthermore, if British oil was going to be channeled into Europe, it was only fair exchange, surely, that European fusion power should be sited where it could sustain the industries that the availability of that same oil had engendered. And besides, the British pointed out, they would be much nicer people to do business with than those insufferable Arab chaps with their never-ending squabbles and price hikes. Breeding would tell, and all that. . . .

It all added up to an as-near-as-made-no-difference unassailable position at the bargaining table. And so, finally, Burghead it turned out to be.

Sunday's rain had turned to snow by Monday, and then the weather had cleared once more. Murdoch and Lee's first view of Burghead was from the top of a range of low hills that lay between Elgin and the sea, from where they found themselves looking down over a narrow strip of coastal plain, standing crisp and white against the blue waters of the Moray Firth in the distant background.

The complex stretched away out of sight along the shoreline and extended for perhaps two miles inland. It was a dense sprawl of refineries, storage tanks, chemical plants, and generating stations interconnected by tangles of roadways, pipelines, and power cables. The whole resembled a sculpture of frosted concrete and steel. The reactor facility itself was located at the end of the complex nearest them, occupying a site that had obviously been developed more recently than the rest. They were able to pick it out easily.

Very easily.

It was square, and must have measured three miles along a side.

At least the area enclosed by the line of the perimeter fence looked square; the far side of the site was distorted by the perspective and its details obscured by distance, but it seemed to extend all the way to the shore. The road was high enough, however, to present a good idea of the general layout.

There were four identical clusters of buildings, one inside each corner of the perimeter square, and a compact group of larger buildings at the geometric center. In fact, as far as surface constructions went, the whole site had a distinctly barren look about it; the reason for its size was the symmetrical pattern of straight-line segments and circles that it framed, which revealed the arrangement of underground accelerator tracks and storage rings that generated, merged, and concentrated the beams before hurling them inward at the target chambers located beneath the largest of the central group of buildings. The largest and most conspicuous of the rings was centrally situated in the perimeter square. It was two miles in diameter, and marked the outer edge of a wide, circular belt made up of many identical structures of some kind; they didn't project far above the snow and could have been just the upper parts of something that went deeper. Four smaller rings, each about a fifth of a mile across, occupied the corners and encircled the four outer clusters of buildings. A web of straight-line segments, intersecting the rings at tangents and connecting the large one to the four smaller ones, completed the design.

Lee pursed his lips in a silent whistle as he took in the sight. "Ma-an!" he breathed after a few seconds. "Take a look at that."

"That's what I call engineering," Murdoch murmured in an awed voice. "Real engineering. . . ." Burghead had received coverage from time to time by the U.S. news media, but the pictures had never been able to convey anything that approached the impact of the real thing. Murdoch sat forward in his seat to study the facility in detail while the car hummed along contentedly under the control of its own guidance system, aided by routing data transmitted from computers in Inverness or wherever. "That must be the main storage ring in the middle," he said after a while. "It's gotta be two miles across at least. The ones at the corners must be secondaries. The primary probably pumps them up in sequence."

"I guess so," Lee agreed. "With a wraparound factor

of about ten, I'd guess. They look about a tenth the size. They must fire inward underneath the primary."

"They do, but not directly," Murdoch said. "I talked to Elizabeth about it. The secondaries pump up a battery of tertiary rings, and they unload onto the target. That wide belt of stuff just inside the big ring must be where the tertiaries are buried." He paused for a moment, then added, "That means the final pulses are aimed from something like a mile out."

"Jeez!" was Lee's only reply.

The road descended from the crestline of the hills in a series of shallow, sweeping curves that eventually straightened out on the flat below to run alongside the perimeter fence for its full length. The fence was a monotony of wire, twenty or so feet high, strung between concrete posts and standing a few hundred feet back from the edge of the highway. The fence marched by endlessly on their left for a while, and then at last gave way to a huddle of low, flat buildings flanking two wide, steel-framed gates. At this point a road formed a junction with the main highway and ran along one side of a fenced-in parking area before passing through the gates and disappearing into the site. A sign by the highway at the turnoff read:

EUROPEAN FUSION CONSORTIUM
BURGHEAD HEAVY-ION FACILITY
SOUTH GATE

Murdoch flipped the car into manual drive to leave the controlled highway, turned into the parking lot, and found an empty space not far from the gatehouse door. They entered through double glass doors and announced themselves to a security officer, wearing a navy-blue police-style uniform complete to the black-and-white checkered cap-band also worn by the Scottish constabulary, who was sitting behind a long counter that partitioned off the rear part of the reception area. The officer checked a computer screen to confirm that they were expected, examined their ID's, and issued them lapel name-tags; then he called to somewhere to announce their arrival and asked them

101

to wait in the gatehouse lobby, which was through another door to one side.

They passed the next ten minutes or so examining a five-foot-square model of the facility that, together with some pictures and other exhibits, formed a display in the lobby, and chatting with a couple of service engineers from Honeywell who were also awaiting a plant escort. The engineers had come to make some final adjustments to equipment before the first full-power tests of the reactors, scheduled to commence on the following Monday. Elizabeth had mentioned that the tests were imminent, but she hadn't been specific about when.

At last the door opened and a tall, lean, youngish-looking man ambled in. He looked the kind of person who had never quite got past being a student, with un-tidy, sandy-colored hair, a mottled brown, rolled-collar sweater, and tan corduroy trousers. He stopped and looked inquiringly from one pair of faces to the other.

"Mr. Ross and Mr. Walker?"

"Us," Murdoch informed him.

"Ah." The newcomer came across and shook hands with both of them. "Michael Stavely. I work with Elizabeth Muir. She's got herself tied up with some-thing that won't wait, I'm afraid. I've been volunteered to look after you between now and lunch. She'll be joining us then."

"Fine," Murdoch said. "I know you've got a busy week coming up. It's nice of you to find time for tourists."

"No trouble at all. Anyhow, I gather you two belong to a rather special category of tourist." Mike led them back through into the reception area and opened an-other door that led to the outside, but on the inner side of the perimeter. "This way. I've got one of the firm's buggies outside. You can leave your car out front. You haven't left anything in it that you might need, have you?" They descended a few steps to a smaller parking area at the rear of the gatehouse, and Mike led them over to a heavy-duty pickup truck, painted sky blue and bearing the golden lightning-bolt insignia of the European Fusion Consortium on its doors, which was parked at the end of a short line of assorted vehicles. "Is there anything in particular you'd like to see first?" he inquired as they climbed in.

"We'll leave the tour to you," Lee said.

"Right-ho. We'll start at the beginning and end at the end then. I'll take you to have a look at one of the injectors. They're where the beams are formed and start out from. Then we can follow the whole gubbins through from there."

They followed the main road from the gate for a short distance, and then turned off into a perimeter track that brought them to one of the corner-groups of buildings. Outwardly there was nothing especially distinguishing about them. They made up a lonely huddle of fairly standard three-storey office blocks and a few bungalow huts, interspersed with open parking spaces. A somewhat larger construction stood in the middle; it was windowless, and looked squat and impregnable, vaguely blockhouselike, as if it belonged more in a space-launch facility. They parked beside the large building and entered through the single door that formed the only break in its otherwise blank and featureless walls. A few minutes later they emerged from an elevator several levels belowground and walked into a different world.

It was a world fashioned and shaped by the uncompromising dictates of high-voltage engineering. Banks of transformers larger than any that Murdoch had ever seen reared upward amid an intricate, three-dimensional tapestry of superconducting busbars and coolant pipes. Between them were batteries of insulator stacks ten feet high and more, carrying lines to immense torroidal windings built around sections of partly visible cylindrical constructions that stretched away through labyrinths of steel structural frameworks.

Mike led them down a series of metal staircases through several levels of railed catwalks and maintenance platforms, and onto a walkway surrounding the base of what looked like a huge, round, steel tank, bristling with insulators and wrapped in cables; a long cylindrical structure emerged from one side of the tank and disappeared through concrete casemates in the approximate direction of the primary, two-mile-diameter storage ring.

"This is one of the injectors," Mike told them, gesturing upward at the tank. "Inside that are high-voltage arcs for peeling off electrons to give us our ion supply. That tube is the first of a series of initial accelerating stages. Initial acceleration is up to a million volts. The accelerators are charged from a capacitor bank located on the next level down."

"What ions do you use?" Lee inquired.

"Mercury."

"How many injectors are there altogether?" Murdoch asked.

"Sixteen," Mike replied. "There are four like this at each corner. This whole arrangement is duplicated by a second system running parallel to it on the other side of that wall." He pointed behind them, and then started to lead the way along a catwalk that followed the wall of the tube, which was at least ten feet high, through the concrete supporting structure and out onto a fairly wide observation platform. They found themselves looking along a vast, brightly lit tunnel in which relays of steel supports carried the tube away into rapidly shrinking perspective. A few hundred feet farther on, they could see the point where the other tube, running almost parallel, emerged from one side to join the first at a fine angle.

"This stretch is the first booster stage," Mike informed them. "From here to the junction along there, the beam is pushed up to ten million volts. Exactly the same thing happens to the beam from next door. The two are then merged to give one double-current beam."

Murdoch leaned his elbows on the parapet surrounding the platform and gazed for a while at the intricate webs of piping and windings that encased the gleaming surface of the tube wall for as far as he could see. "What kind of current are we talking about?" he asked.

"Oh, not much at this stage," Mike said cheerfully. "Even after the two beams merge, it's still only on the order of tens of milliamps—but that's at ten megavolts already, don't forget."

"I thought you said there were four beams at each corner," Lee remarked.

"There are. Come on, let's take a walk. I'll show you where the other two come into the act."

They descended to the floor of the tunnel and followed it to the junction, where they were able to stand and look up at the two massive tubes coming together over their heads. Beyond that point the tunnel became higher, and soon opened out into a huge vault, encircled by more catwalks and platforms, where the tube merged with one angling downward from somewhere above. The combined tube was even thicker than before, and marched away relentlessly into a wider tunnel that continued on in the same direction.

"The whole double-beam setup you've seen is only half of it," Mike explained. "There are two more injectors on a higher level, and their beams are merged in the same way to produce another double-density beam. The two double-density beams come together here."

"So you've got a quad at this point—combining the outputs from all four injectors," Lee observed.

"Quite."

"Still at ten million volts?" Murdoch queried.

"At this point, yes." Mike pointed across to the other side of the wide bay in front of them, which went down several levels deeper and separated them from the mouth of the larger tunnel that continued from there. "That's the beginning of the second booster chain. The first stage of it is another garden-variety linear accelerator that shoves things up to twenty-five megavolts. The other end of the chain is a fair distance away. In fact it's at that primary storage ring, which you must have noticed as you came over the hill."

"We did," Murdoch said. "So what's the beam up to when it reaches the ring?"

"One hundred billion volts," Mike replied.

Murdoch whistled.

They skirted the bay by way of a railed walkway running around its edge, and came to a concrete apron from which rose the massive steel supports that carried the accelerator tube into the next section of tunnel.

From this vantage-point the tube looked like a gigantic gun-barrel converging away into the far distance. The tunnel was wide enough to accommodate an underground roadway that ran along below and to one side of the tube itself. One side of the roadway was flanked by the steel structural work supporting the tube and its coil assemblies, the other by white, tiled wall lined with layers of cable; looking along it, Murdoch felt like a mouse that found its way into a wiring conduit.

A local control center looked out over the bay from a point above the apron and next to the tube. Mike took them up there to meet some of the engineers who were responsible for that section of the plant and able to answer Murdoch's and Lee's more detailed questions. After that the three of them returned to the apron and boarded a small, electrically powered car to continue their tour toward the central zone of the site.

On the way, Mike explained that the same thing happened at all four corners of the plant, yielding four identical beams that entered the primary storage ring at four equispaced points around its circumference. Each corner-battery of four injectors was designed to produce two hundred and forty quad-current-density ion pulses every second, which were then boosted up to virtually the speed of light. Each pulse lasted for just under a half a thousandth of a second, which meant that a pulse would be some sixty-three miles long; obviously, therefore, its leading edge would arrive at the primary ring long before its tail end had emerged from the injectors. The ring drew the pulse in and wrapped it around on itself ten times, rather like a length of string being coiled onto a reel, and in the process multiplied the ion current by a factor of ten. At the same time it merged the compressed pulse with the ten-times-wrapped-around pulses from the three other injector batteries, achieving a final combined current of the order of amperes circulating in the primary ring.

The tunnel opened into a long, wedge-shaped space, again going down to deeper levels, one side of which was formed by the curving wall of the primary ring itself. Above it, the final, one-hundred-billion-volt booster section of the tube continued, suspended amid

106

girders and latticework, to merge into the structure of the ring, thus forming the pointed end of the wedge. From the ends of the chamber, a brightly lit gallery curved away out of sight in both directions to carry the roadway along the ring's periphery, no doubt connecting with other, similar tunnels coming in from the other corners of the site.

"There are four places like this around the whole ring," Mike said as he halted the car to allow them a few minutes to take in the scene. "Every one is an entry port where a combined beam from four injectors is sucked in. There are four exit ports as well, situated between the entry ports. Every time the ring is pumped up, it unloads a full charge through each of the exit ports in turn."

"Like dealing out four hands of cards," Murdoch said. "Yes, we've come across it before."

"You've got it," Mike said, nodding. "Would you like to see one of the exit ports?"

"Sure. Why not?"

"Let's drive round the ring a little way and have a look at one."

They made a U-turn around the blunt end of the wedge to enter one end of the curving gallery, and followed it around until it opened out into another wedge-shaped chamber similar to the one they had just left. The difference here was that the tube disappearing into the tunnel that terminated in this chamber carried the ion pulses away from the ring instead of into it.

They turned off the ring-road and followed this tunnel for a long distance back out toward one of the corners of the plant; exactly which corner, Murdoch was by now no longer sure. It brought them to yet another similar, but smaller, chamber where the same story was repeated on a smaller scale. The tube from the primary ring fed a secondary storage ring, which was one tenth as large; obviously the secondary was one of the four one-fifth-mile-diameter structures located at the corners of the site that Murdoch and Lee had spotted earlier from the road. Each secondary ring achieved a further wraparound current-multiplication of ten, ending up with a trapped, circulating

107

load of sixty amperes. The primary discharged two hundred and forty times every second, feeding each of the secondaries in turn; thus every secondary was pumped up to full load sixty times per second.

They drove around the secondary ring until they came to its single exit port, which pointed back to the central part of the plant. A diverter enabled the concentrated pulse coming from the ring to be channeled away through any one of four tubes, which diverged from each other across a long, fan-shaped vault before disappearing into the mouths of four separate tunnels. Mike drove them to the far end and into one of the tunnels to reveal yet another seemingly endless procession of lamps and struts marching away to a distant vanishing point. Murdoch was beginning to wonder just how much there was of this incredible subterranean network.

This tunnel led back to the center, all the time following a gentle incline that took it beneath the structure of the primary ring, passing en route through a lower level of one of the wedge-shaped chambers that housed the entry and exit ports; for all Murdoch knew, it could have been one of the two that they had already passed through higher up when they were going in the opposite direction.

The tunnel ended in a low, circular space a hundred feet or so across, which contained one of the tertiary storage rings. The tube they had been following entered the ring at a tangent in a way that was by now familiar, and the exit tube led away at another tangent from the same side. There were sixteen such tertiary rings in all, Mike informed them, lying edge to edge in a belt around the heart of the plant like a circle of coins. Each of the secondary rings at the corners fed four tertiaries in sequence via a diverter arrangement like the one they had seen in the fan-shaped vault. Since a secondary ring discharged sixty times every second, every tertiary was pumped up fifteen times per second. Further wraparound in the tertiaries gave another current-multiplication factor of ten, producing six hundred amperes in each.

Thus, fifteen times every second, a point was reached where there were six hundred amperes of multiply ionized mercury atoms moving at relativistic speed inside every one of the sixteen tertiary rings. When the plant eventually went to full power, all sixteen rings would be discharged simultaneously, and a total of ten thousand amperes would converge in the final rush along the three-quarter-mile-long guides that climbed gently upward to the target chamber. The compression achieved at that stage would be such that the pulse delivered from sixteen directions at once would last only for nanoseconds.

The power that smashed into the target pellet in those nanoseconds would be in excess of a thousand trillion watts.

Murdoch and Lee gazed out through a long, glass wall at the place where the beams ended their brief lives in a flash of fusion plasma. They had arrived at last in the Main Control Room below the Reactor Building, which was the large building dominating the cluster at the center of the site. Beyond the glass lay a vast, circular cavern in which the thirty-foot-diameter, steel-clad bulk of the reactor vessel reared up through tiers of access levels and maintenance platforms. Around its base and below the level of the control room, a circle of massive steel yokes carried the beam tubes from the tertiary rings into the reactor wall.

Mike waited a while for them to digest the view, then moved forward to stand beside them and gestured with his arm.

"That's where it all happens. The target chambers are in there, of course. Actually they're not as big as you might think. Most of what you can see from the outside is due to shielding for neutrons and radiation."

"How come 'chambers'?" Murdoch asked. "How many are there?"

"Three. The first phase of full-power testing will be to run one of them flat-out. If it all goes okay, we'll go the whole hog and double the firing rate of the injectors. Then the accelerator system will deliver thirty full packets a second. That will drive two reactors in parallel. The third is a standby, so the plant will always be capable of chucking out two reactors' worth."

Murdoch looked out at the forest of girders and

pipes encasing the reactor vessel, scattered among which a dozen or so technicians were making final adjustments and measurements in preparation for the coming Monday's tests. "How long before you try running two chambers in parallel?" he asked.

"Practically straight away," Mike replied. "Every section of the system has already been tested through individually, and the whole thing has been run up to moderate power lots of times without any major snags. On Monday we'll run two chambers at full-blast individually. Then, if all goes well, we'll double up on Tuesday morning. After that it will be solid testing for at least a few months."

"On-line by summer then, huh?" Murdoch said.

"With luck. Tentatively we're saying by the middle of July."

Lee looked down at the sample target that he was holding in his hand, one of two that Mike had presented as souvenirs. It was a thin-walled, hollow glass lens over half an inch across, filled with a mixture of deuterium and tritium. Inside one of the reactor chambers, a stream of pellets at a precise spacing of fifteen per second would be directed through the beam focal point like machine-gun bullets to be hit on the fly by the titanic bolts of energy from the accelerators. The inner surfaces of the target chambers comprised "waterfall" screens of liquid lithium metal, thus affording no solid area to be eroded by the particles and debris generated in the fusion process. The fast neutrons produced were slowed down in the lithium blanket, where their kinetic energy was transformed into heat to be carried away by the liquid and used to generate power in another part of the plant. As an alternative, the fusion plasma could be directed out of the chamber and its energy tapped directly via magnetohydrodynamics, but that capability would be added later.

"I think Elizabeth said the blanket was a breeder as well," Lee said. "Don't you seed it with deuterium and breed your own H^3?"

Mike nodded. "Yes. It's got fertile fissiles in it too . . . U^{238} and thorium 233. After neutron activation and beta decay, they end up as plutonium 239 and U^{233}. We run a sideline flogging it to fission plants up and down the country—and abroad, come to that. It brings in a bit of extra beer money and helps pay the rent."

The two Americans gazed for a while longer at the scene beyond the glass wall, and then turned back to face Mike. "Any more questions?" he asked them, glancing from one to the other.

"I don't think so for the moment," Murdoch said, shaking his head. "I guess you've covered just about everything."

"Quite a show," Lee conceded.

"We try and give value for money," Mike said cheerfully. "Anyhow, if you've seen all you want to for now, we ought to be thinking about making a move. It's almost twelve-fifteen, and we're supposed to be meeting Elizabeth in the cafeteria over in the Domestic Block at half past. We'll need just about all the time we've got."

"In that case let's go," Murdoch said.

As they began moving between the panels and consoles toward the main door of the control room, Murdoch turned for a last look out at the reactor. He had seen fusion plants before and had come not really expecting any big surprises. But he had to admit that he was impressed.

CHAPTER TWELVE

"That was good," Lee said approvingly, pushing his empty plate away. He nodded his head to indicate the whole of the self-service cafeteria, which the senior executives at Burghead shared with everybody else. "They sure look after you people here."

"We do our best," Elizabeth acknowledged from across the table. She looked feminine as usual, but at the same time businesslike, in a pale-blue, two-piece suit with a white blouse. "You seemed to find the salmon to your liking, I noticed."

"Beats burgers and French fries."

Elizabeth moved her gaze toward Murdoch, who was deep in thought while he finished his coffee.

"You're unusually quiet today, Murdoch," she said.

"Oh . . . I guess I've seen too many new things this morning. It takes a while to filter in."

"Savoring the pride of being a member of the human race, eh?" She made her voice sound flippant, but Murdoch knew by now of her habitual British tendency to use flippancy as a softener when she was being her most serious. "Thirty years ago they thought they had an energy crisis; today we make our own suns to order."

"Not really anything like that. I'm just . . ." Murdoch checked himself and thought for a moment. "I don't know though . . . Maybe you're right."

"I think maybe he's a bit mad because this place isn't in Arizona," Lee said.

"I wouldn't worry about it, old chap," Mike commented. "It wouldn't be here either if the Germans and the Froggies hadn't paid for everything except the doorknobs. How much do you think jolly old England was worth after forty years of being run by plumbers' mates? Do you know that in 19——" He stopped speaking and looked up as a figure approached and stopped by the table. It was a middle-aged man with a ruddy complexion, wearing a heavy tweed jacket. Elizabeth greeted him with a look of obvious recognition.

"Jack, hello. I was keeping an eye open for you. We'll need those figures this afternoon, early if possible. How are they coming along?"

"That's what I came over to mention," Jack said. He looked at Mike. "Jan's finished the flux-count matrix. She's stuck until she gets the G2. Morris says you were doing it." He glanced briefly at Murdoch and Lee. "Sorry to butt in, but it's a bit urgent."

"Don't mind us," Murdoch said, shrugging. "The work has to come first."

"Jack, this is Murdoch, and that's Lee," Elizabeth said. "They're over from the States. Murdoch's grandfather is Charles Ross down at Glenmoroch. This is Jack Belford. His group looks after target-chamber instrumentation."

"Hi."

"Hello."

"Charlie Ross, eh." Jack raised his eyebrows. "I've

seen some good crowds down there in that castle of his. Give him my regards when you get back. Maybe we'll see you later on this afternoon in Maths and Physics."

"Yes, they'll be paying us a visit," Elizabeth said. "They had the tour this morning. That was what tied Mike up. My fault, I'm afraid."

Jack looked appealingly at Mike. Mike rose to his feet and spread his hands in a gesture of apology. "Well . . . it looks as if duty calls. You'll have to excuse me. I enjoyed talking to you both. We'll probably see each other again later in the afternoon." He turned and began talking to Jack as they walked away.

Elizabeth moved closer to the table to talk in a lowered voice. "How are things at Storbannon? I've been meaning to call Charles but never seem to get a chance. Is there anything new to report?"

"Not really," Murdoch answered. "We've just been running strictly according to the schedule. The machine's running and piling up results, and none of us even knows what any of them are yet. It's all exactly the way we agreed."

"Oh, I see." Elizabeth sounded slightly disappointed. She sat back in her seat and turned her hands upward briefly to signal an end to that topic. After a short pause she went on, "So . . . you've seen our main attraction here. Is there anything else you'd particularly like to add to the list? If not we can go on over to Math and Phys, and you can meet some more of the people."

"Sounds good," Lee said.

Elizabeth glanced inquiringly at Murdoch. Murdoch thought for a moment. "As a matter of fact there is something else we could do," he said. "There's a friend of ours who works here. I was thinking maybe we could look in and say hi while we're around."

"I see no reason why not," Elizabeth replied. "Who is he?"

"It's a she. Do you remember that girl we told you about . . . the one we bumped into in Kingussie last Saturday? She asked us to drop in if we ever found ourselves up this way. She works in the Medical Center here, or whatever it's called."

"The Medical Department," Elizabeth said. "Yes, we could go by that way; it's practically next door. What did you say her name was?"

"Anne . . . something." Murdoch shot a questioning glance at Lee.

"Patterson," Lee supplied, in a tone that said Murdoch already knew damn well what it was. Elizabeth studied Murdoch's face for a second, and her eyes began twinkling in a knowing kind of way.

"Ah yes," she said. "I think I know the girl you mean—longish dark hair; dresses well; carries herself nicely? . . ."

"Yeah. That sounds about right," Murdoch agreed, nodding his head casually. Too casually.

"She's very pretty," Elizabeth said. After a short pause she added, "And it would be terribly impolite to come all this way and not even take the trouble to say hello, wouldn't it."

"Terribly," Murdoch agreed solemnly. Lee raised his eyes toward the ceiling and looked away with a sigh.

"Nothing personal, of course," Elizabeth said. She kept her face straight, but there was just enough mockery in her voice to be detectable.

"Of course not," Murdoch told her.

He was beginning, he realized, to get into the English habit of voicing the opposite of what he meant. It could be subtly more emphatic than making direct statements, which would have sounded coarse by comparison, and it had the advantage that a person could never be taken to task on the record of what he had actually said. Perhaps, he thought, that was why the British had never needed a Fifth Amendment.

Murdoch and Lee entered a large room full of X-ray machines, a gamma camera, a body scanner, and an assortment of electronics consoles, and saw Anne working at a computer terminal through the half-open door of a small office off the far side. They had left Elizabeth in another office next door, talking with a Dr. Waring, who was the head of the facility's Medical Department. Waring had told them where they would find Anne, and to go on through for a few minutes.

He had given Murdoch the impression of being the kind of person who didn't really approve of social calls during business hours, and Murdoch had taken ". . . a few minutes . . ." to mean just that. They walked across to the office door and stopped, but Anne was facing away and too intent on what she was doing to notice them.

"Excuse me," Murdoch said. "We're looking for a black-and-white kitten. You haven't seen one around here by any chance, have you?" Anne turned in her chair and looked up. The surprise on her face lasted for no more than a fraction of a second. Then she smiled, swiveled the chair around to face them, and stood up.

"Well! If it isn't the two cowboys from California. I wondered how long it would be before you showed up here."

"You . . . what?" Murdoch looked at her uncertainly. She was doing it again already.

"You said you worked on fusion in America, and that Dr. Muir was a friend of your grandfather. It didn't need an Einstein to work out the rest." Anne thought for a moment. "In fact it must have been Dr. Muir who got you in here. Where is she—in Dr. Waring's office?"

That took care of most of the obvious continuations that the conversation might have followed.

"So . . . what do you do here?" Murdoch moved forward to look at the screen she had been working at. It was packed with lines of computer instruction code. Although Murdoch was primarily a mathematician, machine-language programming was not one of his strengths; he was experienced in using high-level, almost English, languages to formulate problems to be run on computers, but the figures on the screen were used for manipulating processes down at the fundamental level of the machine's registers.

Lee studied the screen with casual interest for a moment. "Real-time I/O coding," he commented. "I didn't know doctors worried about what goes on inside computers. I thought you only needed to know how to talk to them from the outside."

"Oh, that was something I got hooked on when I was at university in London," Anne told them. "We were

115

doing a lot of image processing at one point. I became fascinated at the way in which the computers created pictures you could interact with, so I got myself into a special course to learn how to program them myself." She shrugged. "After that it grew to a kind of hobby. It's come in useful many times though."

"So what's that?" Murdoch asked, gesturing toward the screen.

"It's an image-encoding communications handler I'm working on for linking our system here to the Health Authority's big computers in Edinburgh," she replied. "Part of an idea that Dr. Waring had and wanted to try out." She turned away from the terminal. "Anyhow, what about you two? Have you seen much of the facility yet?"

"Most of it, I reckon," Murdoch said. "We got a bit lost in the subway a few times."

"And what did you think of our modest attempt?"

"Jeez . . ." Murdoch threw out his hands. "I'd thought I'd seen fusion plants before. What do you want me to say? It's tomorrow today, already."

Lee leaned against the doorpost and inclined his head to indicate the large room behind him, through which he and Murdoch had entered. "Where are all the patients?" he asked. "I know this is a pretty big plant, but why a place this big, equipped with everything? You look all set up for World War III."

"It is a quiet day today," Anne said. "Actually, the fusion facility is only the first phase of what it will be like eventually. Once that's up and running, all kinds of other things will be built over it on the surface . . . a steel plant, for example. I'm not much of an expert on those things though. But the Medical Department was designed with that kind of growth in mind."

They talked for a while about Murdoch's and Lee's first impressions of Burghead and about its future growth. Murdoch was unable to prevent himself searching her face continually for some sign that she was being more than just polite to a couple of casual acquaintances who had dropped in to say hello, but the eyes that were supposed to mirror the soul worked one way. Eventually it was time to go.

"Maybe we could all get together later since we're

up here for the day anyway," Murdoch suggested. "Maybe a bite to eat somewhere. Did you have any special plans?"

"Nothing definite," Anne replied. "I had a large lunch though, so I don't think I could manage a meal. But I could take you up on that offer of a drink that you made last time."

"Sure. Where?"

"There's a pub in a village about half a mile off the main road not far from the plant," she told them. "A lot of Burghead people stop off there for a drink after work. I could meet you there. Maybe you could get to know some more of the people from here too."

Murdoch wasn't particularly interested in meeting any more of the Burghead people, but he tried to sound enthusiastic. "What's it called?" he asked.

"The Aberdeen Angus. Take the main road west for about three miles, and turn off at a sign that says *Achnabackie*. It's right in the middle of the first village you come to. You can't miss it."

"About when, six?"

"That would be fine. We usually go in the Lounge Bar. It's straight on through the bar that's inside the front door. Until about six, then?"

"Sure. See you there."

"Take care," Lee said.

Ten minutes later they were walking with Elizabeth toward the Engineering Block, which contained the Mathematics and Physics Department, along a path below the looming bulk of the Reactor Building.

"So, how was your lady-friend?" Elizabeth inquired. "Pleased to see you, I trust."

"Of course," Murdoch replied. "Two handsome, husky, unattached American males—what more could a girl want? We're meeting her later for a drink."

"My word! You don't waste much time. Now I know how you people got to the Moon so quickly. Anyway, I'm glad I was able to help."

"You always did strike me as a romantic at heart," Murdoch said.

"Perhaps I felt I owed you a favor." Elizabeth was smiling mischievously.

"What are you talking about?" Murdoch asked her, puzzled.

"Maybe I should say I owed the Rosses one. Charles was a professor at Stanford when Herman and I met, you know. He fiddled the timetables around just so that we could work on the same projects together. So, you see, there are romantics at heart in your family too."

CHAPTER THIRTEEN

"Anne, come on back over and join the party. We don't have splinter groups in this pub. It isn't sociable." The voice was Trevor's, calling above the background of voices from a circle of Burghead people seated around a table filled with bottles and glasses in one corner of the spacious, oak-beamed lounge. Trevor was a square-built six-footer, with a pink-hued face and wearing a dark blazer with striped tie, who was sitting with three of his pals, Nick, Sam, and Steve, at one end of the group. Anne had been talking to them when Murdoch and Lee arrived at The Bull some two hours earlier. Since then she gravitated toward the two Americans to introduce them to the rest of the crowd, and for the last twenty minutes or so had been talking to Murdoch by the bar, off to one side. Trevor appeared to have grown visibly more irritated by this as the empty glasses in front of him accumulated. At the other end of the table, the rest of the group were talking with Lee about Stateside plans to supplement the U.S. fusion program with orbiting solar-to-microwave converters and other proposed developments.

"Who is he?" Murdoch asked in a lowered voice. "I thought you didn't have any regular guy. I mean, I don't want to make some kind of ass out of myself here."

"Oh, don't take any notice," Anne said, keeping her eyes on Murdoch. "He can get a bit bombastic when he's had a drink or two. He belongs to a rugby club, and I've been there with him a couple of times because they're a good crowd to have a laugh with. That's all there is to it."

"He sounds like I'm trespassing or something." Murdoch looked past Anne's shoulder, but Trevor had turned his head away and was talking to somebody next to him.

"Nonsense," Anne said. "That's for me to decide. I told you, don't take any notice. He's forgotten already that he said it. Now, what were we talking about?"

"You were telling me about Jenny and her disappearing tricks."

"That's right. How about you? Do you have any brothers or sisters?"

"One of each. They're both a bit younger than me. They live with my folks."

"In Chicago?"

"Yes. Iain's twenty-five. He's a born businessman like my pa. My sister wants to be a dancer in the movies. She's mother all over."

"What's her name?"

"Tanya. She's eighteen."

"That's nice. I like that name."

"Hey, Doc," Lee called suddenly from one end of the table. "These guys won't believe we're gonna dig a tunnel under the Atlantic. Come over here and tell 'em I'm serious." It was a chance to rejoin the party without looking submissive.

"Let's go talk to the people," Murdoch murmured. He picked up their glasses from the bar and moved over to where Lee was sitting. Anne followed, pretending not to notice Trevor's glare from the other end.

"He's serious," Murdoch said. "We're gonna dig 'em all over—New York City to the West Coast . . . Toronto to Texas. Airplanes will be strictly for backwoods routes and museums."

"It makes sense," Lee declared, turning back to the faces listening around him. "Why have to shove all that air out of the way when you can go through tubes where there isn't any air? Why lift motors up and then bring them down again when all you really want to move is the passengers?"

"Just like that," Jerry said flatly. Jerry was a cryogenics specialist who worked at one of the injector nodes. "Like a well in the garden."

"Why not?" Lee asked simply.

Sheila, an artist of some sort from the plant, looked up incredulously at Murdoch and then back at Lee. "But what are you going to dig them with? You simply can't get coolies these days, and even if you could, there aren't enough shovels."

"You melt your way through," Lee said. "Heavy currents are pretty good at melting rock under high pressure. They're doing it in Utah for deep mining. The shield even makes its own glass to line the tunnel behind it as it goes. It works great."

Tom, who worked with Jerry, gave Murdoch an appealing look. "Okay, but . . . fourteen thousand miles an hour? . . . Lee's saying the bloody trains will be able to do fourteen thousand miles an hour. Surely not."

"That's what the studies predict," Murdoch said with a shrug. "Coast to coast in just over twenty minutes, city center to city center. Why not? There's no air drag, and if you levitate the cars magnetically, there's no friction worth talking about either."

Anne moved through between two of the chairs and sat down in one of two vacant seats between Sheila and Tom. Murdoch took the other.

"That's fantastic," Tom said. "I'd read a few things about something like that, but I didn't know it'd got a definite go-ahead."

"I've had a thought," Jerry said suddenly. "If they got it up a little bit more, to eighteen thousand, they wouldn't have to bother levitating it at all. It'd be in orbit!"

"Hey, an underground satellite!" Lee exclaimed. "How about that?" They all laughed.

"So when will all this happen?" Sheila asked, leaning forward to look at Lee. "What dates are we talking about?"

Lee finished a long swig from his pint glass and wiped his mouth with the side of his hand. "They should start the transcontinental ones inside a couple of years. You'll have to wait a while longer for the Atlantic one though. They've still got to figure out exactly what they're gonna do about crossing tectonic plate margins."

"These people make me bloody sick." The voice came suddenly from the far end of the table. The conversation died abruptly. It was Trevor, sounding slightly slurred. "I'm sick of these b-bloody Yanks, coming over here and telling us how bloody clever they are all the time," he pronounced. As he spoke, he looked from one to another of his own henchmen at the far end, but his voice was loud enough to carry to everybody, obviously deliberately. His eyes had taken on a detectable glaze, and his face was a shade redder than it had been earlier. From the corner of his eye, Murdoch saw Lee stiffen.

"Aw, shut up, Trev," Jerry threw back, trying to make his tone sound bored. "Now you're spoiling the party. We don't want to talk about that."

"That's a point," Tom said, turning to Murdoch and getting back to the previous topic. "How are they going to get around that?" Murdoch started to describe a recent proposal that involved telescopic sections of tunnel that would pivot inside twenty-mile-long excavated caverns to compensate for the drift of the plates. As he spoke, he stole a glance over Anne's shoulder at Trevor, who was glowering at them while draining the last of yet another Scotch.

"It's true though," Trevor came in again from the far end. "We all know they've done some clever things. Why can't they leave it at that? Why do they always have to come over here and act so bloody superior about it? *We* beat them hollow with heavy-ion fusion, but we don't keep on about it all the time, do we?"

"Nobody's acting superior," Anne said curtly. "But *some* people seem to be doing their best to appear inferior."

"Well said, Anne," Jerry approved. "Shut up, Trev."

"You can't tell Trev to shut up," Sam said from the far end, feigning a note of surprise in his voice. "That won't do. Whose side are you supposed to be on?"

Sheila sighed and looked imploringly from one end to the other. "There aren't any sides over anything. For

121

Christ's sake don't start getting silly, Trevor, why don't you go onto Cokes or something?"

"I prefer to stay with the Scotch, thank you. Why? What are you trying to say?"

"She's trying to tell you you're over the mark," Tom said. "It's time you laid off."

"I'm all right. All I said was some of these foreigners make me sick. . . ." Trevor leaned back heavily in his chair and seemed to lose the thread of what he had been about to say. He scowled and raised his eyes to look in Murdoch's direction. "Coming over here and carrying on as if it was *them* who educated the world . . . all talk." He brought his eyes to focus on Murdoch directly, squinting as if he were trying to peer through a haze. "You see . . . there is this thing called *cul-ture*, old boy." He pronounced the word slowly, as if expecting them not to have heard it before. "There is more to life, you may be surprised to learn, than just making more and shoddier machines. But the colonies probably haven't got round to finding out about that yet."

"I was over there last year," Sam said casually. "Do you know, they put ice in sherry?"

Nick, who was sitting on Trevor's other side, gave an exaggerated gasp of disbelief. "You're joking! That's as bad as serving unchilled white."

"Oh, they do that too," Sam told him. "In fact they—"

"Stop it!" Anne cut in sharply. "If you can't hold a few drinks, then don't make a spectacle of the fact. Aren't manners supposed to count somewhere as well?"

"It's a sham society," Steve joined in, ignoring her. "Know what I mean—all plastic and tinsel on the outside, but nothing inside. Anything that glitters fascinates them."

"Did you ever come across that sissie thing they call football?" Nick asked.

"They wear spacesuits for it," Sam said. "Air-conditioned and spray-sanitized, I think." He shook his head wonderingly. "They make a big fuss about it though."

Trevor leaned forward and held his jacket out to display the badge on the breast pocket. "See that?

English League rugby badge, that is. What you call a *man's* game. . . . I wonder why it never caught on in the States. I mean, they're always *talking* about their he-man footballers and their bloody Marines, aren't they?"

"Maybe we grew out of needing to prove things," Murdoch suggested, deciding that things had gone far enough. He held Trevor's eye steadily and forced himself to remain calm.

"What's that supposed to mean?" Trevor demanded.

"Burghead's quite a place. I'm impressed. I didn't expect to find it being run by schoolkids. I thought you'd have left such nonsense behind a long time ago."

"Are you saying we're incompetent?"

"No. I'm just saying that right now you're acting pretty dumb."

"Dumb?" Trevor shot a puzzled glance at Nick and Sam. "What does he mean, dumb? I'm speaking, aren't I? Is the poor chap deaf or something?"

"They get their words mixed up," Sam said. "I think he means stupid."

"Oh, I see. . . ." Trevor set his glass down on the table and nodded slowly. "We're getting personal, are we? I wasn't being personal. I was just talking about things in general. Wouldn't you say he was being personal?"

"Very personal," Nick agreed. "Quite uncalled for, I'd say."

"Listen, Yank," Trevor said, looking back round abruptly and speaking in a harsher, and now openly derisive, voice. "*I* happen to be at Burghead because I qualified to work at Burghead. *I'm* here because I'm a bloody good engineer, and I've got a degree from European Energy Community's university to say so. Why are *you* here?"

"You know why he's here," Sam said, making little effort to disguise the sneer. "He's traveling tourist-class. His grandad knows Lizzie Muir."

"You mean they're not qualified?" Nick asked in mock surprise.

"I think they dropped out," Sam replied.

"God knows what business it is of yours," Sheila

123

said, sounding exasperated. "But if you must know, Murdoch's grandfather happens to be a Nobel Prize winner . . . for physics."

"So?" Trevor demanded, gesturing toward Murdoch. "What's that supposed to make him? My father was a surgeon. That doesn't make me a member of the BMA."

"It means I don't need pieces of paper and boy-scout badges on my coat to remind me who I am," Murdoch said, allowing his tone to become sarcastic. "What's left in there when you peel it all off?"

"Wrong. They stand for something that matters," Trevor shot back.

"That's what people who wrap boxes in plastic and tinsel say."

Trevor's face darkened. "Are you trying to make a fool of me, Yank?"

"There's no need. You manage okay on your own."

Trevor stood up from his chair, lurching against the table in the process and slopping some of the drinks. His jowls had inflated, and his expression was ugly. Lee was on his feet in the same instant, facing him from a few feet away. His movement had been smooth and catlike; his face was expressionless, but his muscular frame stood poised on a hairspring. Murdoch gripped the arms of his chair and forced himself to stay put. Lee could probably have taken all four of them even without Murdoch's help, but that wasn't the way.

"Lee, cool it," he said. "It's not worth breaking up a nice pub over."

Lee kept his eyes fixed unwaveringly on Trevor. "I've had enough of all this double-talk," he grated. "If you're trying to say something, let me hear it to my face straight-out. We don't have to mess up the pub. The parking lot outside'll do fine."

"Sit down, you silly sod," Nick hissed at Trevor from the corner of his mouth. "He'll take you apart after the amount you've had." Trevor obviously wasn't going to be able to count on any backup from that quarter. Suddenly he looked less certain of himself.

Murdoch relaxed, moving back in his chair, in an attempt to defuse the situation. "Okay, Trevor, we agree with you," he said. "Rugby's a tough sport. So why don't we leave it out on the field where it belongs, huh? This is getting crazy. The way we're going on, a guy's gonna need a spacesuit soon to have a drink."

"Oh, thank God," Jerry said, sounding relieved. "Come on, Trev. Knock it off. The man's talking sense."

"Now let's see a bit more," Sheila suggested.

Trevor hesitated for a moment longer. Lee remained motionless, watching him. Then Trevor lowered himself slowly and heavily back into his seat, and made an awkward pushing motion with his hand. "If that's what you want . . . What's the point anyhow?" He sounded surly, but underneath grateful to let the matter go at that. Lee said nothing as he uncoiled back into his chair, shedding tension like a spring being unwound. An uncomfortable silence followed.

At last Tom turned to look across at Murdoch. "I didn't know about your grandfather. When did he get a Nobel?"

"Back in the eighties," Murdoch said, keeping his eyes on Trevor for a moment longer before shifting them toward Tom. "It was for some work he was involved in at Stanford."

"What kind of work?" Sheila asked.

"The first isolation of free quarks. He moved there from Princeton to work on the big Stanford accelerator."

The conversation gradually picked up again. Trevor and his three pals talked among themselves about other things until a respectable time had passed, then got up and left together with a few perfunctory goodnights to the rest of the company. At once a more relaxed atmosphere descended.

"Whew, that feels better," Jerry said. "For a moment I thought we were going to have a real barney. What on earth's got into Trev tonight?"

"I think he thought he had territorial rights," Tom murmured, nodding toward Anne.

"Gee, I didn't mean to start anything like that," Murdoch said. "As far as I was concerned, we were just talking."

"Shut up!" Anne exclaimed indignantly. "You're sounding as if you're apologizing for something. If

125

Trevor had any thoughts like that, he should have asked me first. If anybody needs to apologize, it ought to be me . . . for calling you cowboys earlier on today. You handled the whole thing very well."

"Cowboys are from Texas," Murdoch told her, grinning. "Californians are different."

"You mean Californians don't wear their hats and smoke cigars in the bathtub?"

"Certainly not," Murdoch replied. "We take showers."

"With hats and cigars," Jerry threw in.

"Of course."

Sheila laughed and sipped her drink, then looked at Lee. "Were you bluffing?" she asked. "For a moment you really looked as if you'd have had a go at all four of them, never mind Trevor."

"He would have," Murdoch said. "Don't worry about it. Lee can handle himself if he needs to."

"Ah, what the hell," Lee grunted. "It's over. Forget it."

"He's right," Jerry declared. "Look, we've got a nice-sized crowd for a party now. How about going on somewhere? We could go into town and try one of the clubs. I could use a bite to eat too. What's the vote?"

"Sounds good," Tom said. The others nodded.

"Right then," Jerry declared. "Unanimous it is. One more round before we go. This one's mine. Same again for everybody?"

Midnight had come and gone and been forgotten. Murdoch and Anne were sitting with their heads close together, talking across a corner of the table in a dimly lit alcove of the nightclub. Tom and Sheila were together on the dance floor, while Lee and Jerry were at the bar talking with a couple of girls who had come in about an hour before. The band had burned off its surplus energy and was slowing down in preparation for calling it a night.

"Know something?" Murdoch said. "You smell nice. What is it?"

Anne smiled and shrugged without looking up. "Nothing special. I've been at work all day. Maybe it's

126

just something that exists in the nose of the . . . oh, I don't know. What's a word like 'beholder' that means smell?"

"Hell, how should I know? I don't write dictionaries." He thought for a second. "How about 'philodorer'? That ought to mean 'liker of nice scents.' "

Anne giggled and placed her hand on his arm. "You really are crazy. What would a Texan have said?"

"I can't imagine."

"Where did you get black hair like that? I like men with thick, black hair."

"Grandpa's used to be the same. You'll have to meet him sometime."

"I'd like to. He sounds fascinating."

"You know," Murdoch said, leaning closer, "a guy could get really fond of somebody like you, given enough time." He traced his fingertip lightly along her arm. "Why don't we do something like this again soon . . . just the two of us?"

Anne appeared to think about it for a second or two, then answered, "Yes, I think I'd like that. Is it a promise? I'll hold you to it, you know."

"You'd better believe it."

Anne slid her fingers over the back of his hand and entwined them loosely with his. They felt cool, smooth, and exhilarating. "Are you going to be over here for very long?" she asked.

"Who knows?" Murdoch replied. "I guess it depends on how things go. We're not really sure yet how much work there is to do at Storbannon."

"Then I hope you run into all kinds of problems that you didn't bargain for," Anne told him. She smiled, and Murdoch could see that the one-way mirrors had been switched off.

CHAPTER FOURTEEN

The time-communication model that had been tentatively proposed held that a signal transmitted back from the future would remain imprinted on the new timeline established in the process. The whole of the timeline that lay after the event of the signal being received, however, which included the event of its being sent, would be altered according to the new circumstances. One of the purposes of the tests that had been run throughout that week was to test this hypothesis more thoroughly.

In one set of tests, the machine had been programmed to send a signal back to a point in time advanced one second from the point at which the machine had last received a signal in the past. On the new timeline thus established, the receipt of the time-advanced signal would itself become the most recently received one; therefore the process would repeat to give a series of loops back into the past. Every loop would be one second shorter than the previous one. Hence the previously received signal would remain imprinted upon the part of the timeline that lay ahead of, and therefore outside, a loop executed later. This would happen with every loop, and every signal transmitted in the series would remain on the final timeline left at the end of it all.

According to the model this would not be observed when the converse procedure was applied, that is, when the loop was lengthened by one second with each iteration instead of shortened. In this case a later loop would fully enclose an earlier one. The whole of the earlier loop, including the events of both its being sent and received, would lie on the section of timeline that the later signal would reconfigure. Therefore no trace of any loop except the final one should remain at the conclusion of tests of this type.

By Friday morning the first phase of tests, which involved signals derived from determinate computer algorithms, was complete. The team eagerly inspected the results and found to their elation that they were as the model predicted. Accordingly, in a great flurry of excitement they began to prepare the system for the first part of the second phase of test, which would use random data, intending to allow the system to run automatically once more while they got down to the task of analyzing the phase-one results in more detail.

But when they went down to the lab to set up the second phase, they ran into an unexpected difficulty: The receiver was registering continuous activity, but the computer was unable to extract anything intelligible from whatever it was receiving. In the early afternoon the problem suddenly disappeared for about two hours, then reappeared, continuing until late evening. At ten o'clock that night all was well again, but shortly after midnight the trouble began once more. By Saturday morning the situation was still the same. Cartland concluded that there had to be a fault somewhere in the system. He announced to the impatient team that there was no choice but to strip the machine down and put off the intended tests until the trouble could be located and cured.

Cartland rested his elbows on the edge of the bench and peered intently at the waveforms being displayed on the screen of the signal analyzer connected to the exposed electronics inside one of the system cabinets. He consulted a chart draped over the bench beside him, frowned, clicked his tongue several times, and shook his head.

"There isn't a bloody thing wrong with the phase decoder or the array generator," he pronounced. "This is preposterous. Run the output diagnostic for the Bragg coupler and see what that says."

"I just did," Lee told him from the main console. "It checks out okay. No faults."

"Preposterous," Cartland muttered again. "That's twice through the whole ruddy system from end to end, and not a thing. There has to be something in here that's doing it. What about that vector address dump, Murdoch? Found anything?"

Murdoch shook his head without looking up from

the desk behind Lee, where he was poring over a sheet of densely printed hardcopy. "I haven't got through all of it yet, but it looks clean so far."

"Well, get a move on then, there's a good chap," Cartland said. "We can't make a start on the discriminators until you've finished that."

"Sorry. I guess I'm not thinking too fast today."

"He's in love," Lee remarked casually as he keyed another block of code onto the screen in front of him.

"Oh, God help us," Cartland muttered.

At the desk, Murdoch smiled to himself but said nothing. Yesterday he had called her twice, once in her office at Burghead to ask if she had a hangover too, and once at home in the evening for no reason in particular. That morning she had called him, ostensibly to ask if he had found out who Pamela McKenzie was. They had arranged a dinner date in Inverness for Sunday evening. Sunday was only tomorrow, but Sunday evening seemed a long way away.

Early on Saturday evening the problem suddenly disappeared again. By ten o'clock that night it hadn't returned, and Cartland began to suspect that it wouldn't.

"That's a strange thing you seem to be telling us, Ted," Charles said from his chair in the library late that night as they sat talking about it. "You mean the machine has been working perfectly all evening? What did you do to it?"

"Nothing." Cartland shrugged and showed his palms for emphasis. "All I've done is take bits out, test them, and put them back. But I tell you there's nothing wrong with it."

"How about some kind of intermittent fault?" Charles suggested.

"Possible, I suppose. But if so, there isn't a trace of it now. I've tried all kinds of things to reproduce it, but the whole machine is as clean as a whistle."

"So we can carry on from where we left off?"

"I don't see why not."

Lee turned around to face the room from where he had been standing deep in thought for the last few minutes. "How do we know it was any kind of fault?" he asked. "The problem didn't show any signs of being intermittent while it was there. And if it wasn't intermittent, why isn't it there now?"

"What else could it have been?" Murdoch asked.

"I'm not sure," Lee replied slowly. "But I've been thinking about those raw detector waveforms we looked at while it was going on. I'd have said it looked more like some kind of interference."

"Interference?" Charles looked puzzled. "From where? How could it be? It would have to be something propagating through tau space to affect pair production. What else is there that produces tau waves?"

"I don't know," Lee replied. "But we could go back over everything and have a look. We've got portions of the waveforms stored. Maybe if we played them back through the analyzers, they'd show up something."

"We could," Cartland agreed. His tone was dubious, as if he saw little point to such an exercise.

Charles said the rest for him. "Och, why should we be bothering with stuff like that? We've lost enough time as it is. If the machine's working now, let's just be thankful for that and stop messing around with it. If we get any more trouble, we can worry some more about what's causing it then."

"I agree," Cartland said.

"Me too," Murdoch declared. "Sorry, Lee, but you just lost the vote. We're a strictly democratic institution."

Lee shrugged and left the matter at that.

A few minutes later Charles bade the others good night and went to bed. Cartland suggested to the other two that it wouldn't take the three of them long to tidy the machine up in readiness to commence the phase-two tests first thing in the morning. Murdoch and Lee agreed, and they all proceeded on down to the lab.

Cartland reassembled the subunits strewn across the top of the bench, rapidly ran through a series of checks, nodded his head in satisfaction, and slid the assembly back into the equipment rack from which he had taken it. Then he began reattaching wires and connectors, his hands moving swiftly and deftly with practiced ease. Lee leaned with his elbows resting on one of the low cubicles and watched with the unspoken respect of one professional for another.

"Doc says that you spent a lot of time in the British Air Force," Lee said after a while. "Was that where you studied electronics?"

"*Royal* Air Force, old boy," Cartland said without looking up. "Yes, I suppose I did pick most of it up there. I was mixed up with military types and gadgets long before I joined the jolly old RAF though . . . ever since I was a boy, in fact."

"Charles once said that you were born in Malaya. Is that right?"

"Yes . . . born into an Army family. My father was an instructor in a school of jungle warfare that the Australians ran in Malaya in the 1960s . . . mainly for U.S. Rangers and Special Forces, actually. He was with the British Army, of course, but attached to the Aussies. When the war in Vietnam fell apart in 1970 whenever-it-was, he moved to Australia, so that was where I grew up." Cartland shrugged as he tightened the restraining clips of a bus microconnector. "You know how it is—the town wasn't much more than a glorified Army camp and air base. I got interested in electronics and flying and that kind of thing, and when we moved back to England I went to Cambridge for a while, then joined up."

"The RAF?" Lee said.

"That's right. After a while they sent me to the U.S.A. for shuttle training in Nevada. Spent a year there. Then went to Germany to work with the people who were designing the E.S.A. shuttle, then to the Sahara to fly it."

"You sure got around."

"That's not all of it either," Murdoch threw in from where he was tidying up the cables at the rear of one of the racks. "Tell him the rest, Ted."

"Well," Cartland said, "to cut a long story short, I suppose I became a sort of Air Force consultant on designing orbital vehicles. I did that in the U.K. for a while, then went back to Australia to do testing at the missile range at Woomera. Then when the Americans and the Europeans merged their space programs, I went to Washington to do technical liaison."

"So how did you wind up at Cornell?" Lee asked. "That was where you met Charles, wasn't it?"

"That's right. I got to know him fairly well while working in Washington. They were doing some interesting things for NASA on orbiting observatories. Charles was with NASA at the time, and that was how we bumped into each other."

"I can see why you never got married, Ted," Lee remarked.

"Good heavens! No time for anything like that." Cartland looked positively shaken by the idea, as if the possibility had occurred to him for the first time in his life. "Mind you, there's no shortage of popsy on that kind of circuit, so there's no reason to miss out on anything. I mean . . . just because a chap likes a drink now and then, it doesn't mean he has to go mad and buy himself a whole bloody pub, does it?" He straightened up and placed the tools that he had been using back on the bench, where Maxwell was pawing frantically at a CRT screen in a futile attempt to trap the flickering trace. Then he moved over to the console and ran quickly through a sequence of system checks. "There," he announced. "That seems to be it. I'll leave it running in monitor mode in case anything comes in. Talking about drinks, I wouldn't say no to a quick noggin before turning in. How about you chaps?"

"Sounds like a good idea," Lee said.

"I might as well put these covers back while I'm at it," Murdoch called from behind the rack. "You go on upstairs and set 'em up. I'll be there in a couple of minutes." Cartland and Lee left the lab, and Murdoch heard their voices fading away along the corridor outside.

He finished replacing the covers, came around from behind the rack, and stood for a while staring at the console of the machine. It was strange, he thought, that everybody could appear outwardly so nonchalant and matter-of-fact about it—a discovery that seemed on the verge of rocking the whole of established science back on its heels. And yet, inside, surely the others were all as excited as he was. He tried to picture the possibilities that would be opened up when they could relax the rules and communicate freely with pasts that had been and with futures that still lay ahead. Staggering possibilities, which in all probability none of them had even glimpsed yet.

His eyes strayed to a sheet of hardcopy printout that was lying on the desk by the console. It was a memory map that he had used earlier in the day, showing which parts of the system's memory were reserved for programs and other purposes and which were left free. For no particular reason he mentally selected a portion of the unallocated space and decided that, when the time came, there would be his own personal mailbox from the future. Crazy!

And then an intriguing realization dawned on him: By virtue of his having made that simple decision, every version of himself who existed along the timeline ahead as it then stood would possess that same knowledge, by remembering having been him now. For the same reason, they would remember having thought exactly what he was thinking at that very moment. Therefore, if any of them had anything to say that was sufficiently important to warrant breaking the rules for any reason, this would be the obvious moment in the past to send it to.

With a shrug and not really expecting to find anything, he moved a step forward and tapped a code into the touchboard to interrogate the mailbox. As he had expected, nothing was there. He laughed inwardly at himself for being silly, scooped Maxwell out of the trash bin below the desk, and closed down the lab for the night.

But the thought still intrigued him as he walked back along the white-walled passage that led to the foot of the stairs. He would continue to check his mailbox regularly from then on . . . just in case. Something might come in one day. And there was no harm in simply interrogating an area of memory. That wouldn't involve the breaking of any rules.

CHAPTER FIFTEEN

As Murdoch came down the main staircase after getting up and showering the next morning, the first thing he heard was Morna's high-pitched voice coming from somewhere immediately below him.

"I cannot see him, Robert. He's gone right down inside. I can hear him scrabblin' around somewhere down here near the leg."

Murdoch came down the lower flight to find Robert dismantling the suit of early sixteenth-century English armor that stood by the foot of the stairs, while Morna watched anxiously from behind his shoulder. The helmet, gorget, and pauldrons were on the floor surrounded by a heap of ironmongery that had once been an arm. Robert was muttering profanities to himself while he fiddled with the straps securing the breastplate.

"What's the idea?" Murdoch asked cheerfully. "Thinking of selling it on the side as scrap?"

"Och, it's Maxwell," Morna told him. "He stepped off o' the stairs and into the helmet. The visor fell shut behind him, and now he's gone down inside."

"He's fallen into the leg and cannot get back up," Robert grumbled blackly. "I'll have to be takin' the whole damn thing to pieces now to get him out."

"Grilled cat for dinner today, huh?" Murdoch said with a laugh, and walked away in the direction of the kitchen.

After breakfast he went down to the lab just for the hell of it and checked his mailbox. There were no deliveries. Then he went back upstairs and joined Charles in his study. Charles had some calculations that he was particularly anxious to complete in time for a clean start on Monday morning, and Murdoch had agreed to spend the whole day helping out until the time came for him to leave for Inverness to meet Anne. The work divided itself conveniently into two parts that could be tackled separately and merged together later on, and they worked largely in silence throughout the morning. They broke off to have lunch with Cartland and Lee, who had been in the lab setting the system up for phase two, and resumed immediately afterward. It was a necessary but not especially exciting part of the research, and Murdoch found the hours dragging. But he consoled himself with pleasant anticipations for the evening that lay ahead.

It was approaching five in the afternoon when Murdoch suddenly screwed his face into a puzzled frown. A check-function that he had just finished evaluating had failed to give the expected result. He sighed and began the procedure again, using a terminal connected into the datagrid. Ten minutes later the same, wrong, answer was staring him in the face. He gritted his teeth against rising impatience and recalled to the screen a summary file of the results he had stored before lunch. It was five-thirty when he groaned aloud and slumped back in his chair.

"What is it?" Charles asked, looking up from his littered desk on the far side of the study.

Murdoch gestured wearily toward the screen. "I got the third integral of the theta field wrong. It's carried on right through all the envelope profiles. Everything I've done since lunchtime has been garbage." Charles got up, came across the room, and stood looking from the papers lying at Murdoch's elbow to the screen and back again while Murdoch explained briefly what had happened.

"Ah well," Charles said with a heavy sigh. "I suppose it's better you found out about it now than in a week's time. Why don't you pack it in now and give your brain a rest. You can straighten it out tomorrow. Anyhow, it's almost time you were thinking of getting away to your fooling around in Inverness, is it not?"

"Ah hell, that'd mess up all your plans for tomorrow," Murdoch said. He heaved a long sigh and cursed himself inwardly. "Look, I'll give her a call and put tonight off. Now I know where the problem is here, I'll still be able to get it done tonight. It'll be a straight substitution when I've figured the right integral."

"You can't do that," Charles protested. "That's no way to be treating your lassie."

"No, really, I'd feel better about it if I fixed it and got it out of the way."

"There's no need. Dammit, a day sooner or later won't make any difference to me," Charles said dubiously.

"It will to me," Murdoch insisted.

He called Anne fifteen minutes later from the vi-set in the sitting room. The way her face lit up when she saw him made him feel worse. She was obviously disappointed when he explained the situation, but understanding, and insisted that he couldn't think of letting Charles down under the circumstances. She was due to work late-shift on Monday and Tuesday, but could make-it for Wednesday. It seemed a hundred years away.

All through dinner Murdoch was far from happy. By then, his imagination was starting to play tricks and blow the whole thing out of proportion in his mind. He could see how it must have looked to her, even though she hadn't actually said anything to suggest it—a precedent that said computers and theories would always take first place. That wasn't true, of course, but how could Anne possibly be expected to know it wasn't when she had no inkling of what was happening at Storbannon and what it all meant? And *his* knowing that it wasn't true made matters all the worse. The rational part of him conceded that he was probably exaggerating everything in his mind, but still there was an emotional part that wouldn't stop worrying about it. He knew it was adolescent, but that didn't help much.

After dinner, still moody, he left the others and started walking through the main hallway on his way back to the study to begin work again. As he passed the door that led down to the lab, an insane thought hit him from nowhere. He stopped dead in his tracks.

The mailbox! It could remove the whole problem—literally. At this very moment he, or at least a "him," could be halfway to Inverness.

A sinking feeling came with the realization that something inside him was yielding to the idea. The rational part of his mind clutched wildly for straws, reciting over and over in his head all the reasons why such an action would be utterly and completely out of the question. But even as he contemplated it, the emotions that were in control were guiding his feet to the top of the stairs.

His reason came spluttering back to the surface when the message was composed and staring back at him from the screen, awaiting only the press of a single key to send it back to the destination that he had specified. He shook his head and blinked at the words in front of him, as if he had just awakened from a dream and was seeing them for the first time. What the hell did he think he was doing? Nobody fully understood the complexities of meddling with things like this yet. And besides, doing so was against all the rules that he had agreed to. No, it was unthinkable.

He had never sent back a signal that would alter a past event. None of the team had. They couldn't, because of the way the process worked. Anybody who sent back such a signal would alter the past that had molded his recollections, and in doing so would establish a new timeline that included a new self whose recollections would be consistent with the signal being received and whatever else followed as a consequence of it. The "self" who sent the signal would no longer exist on the new timeline; he would have been erased, and therefore could never exist to remember that the event had ever taken place.

Erased? Murdoch had been about to erase himself? Something cold and slithery was turning somersaults along his spine at the thought of it. He sat back slowly in the chair and shook his head.

And then suddenly, he heard the door leading down to the lab being opened. Footsteps began descending the stairs, and the voices of Charles and Cartland came floating in from the passage outside. Murdoch was seized by an irrational panic; his finger shot out instinctively to delete the words that were glowing on the screen. But for a long time while he had been sitting there thinking, his mind had been subconsciously fixating on the *Send* key with a morbid fascination.

He hit the wrong button.

His eyes widened with disbelief as they stared

stupefied at his hand. But nothing had happened. He didn't know what should have, but something was surely wrong . . . like the feeling he always had in the dentist's chair when he wanted to tell them that the anesthetic they had just given him wasn't going to work. . . .

"He's fallen into the leg and cannot get back up," Robert grumbled blackly. "I'll have to be takin' the whole damn thing to pieces now to get him back out."

"Grilled cat for dinner today, huh?" Murdoch said with a laugh, and walked away in the direction of the kitchen.

After breakfast he went down to the lab just for the hell of it and checked his mailbox. A second later he had sunk into the operator's chair in front of the console and was staring in astonishment at the screen.

It was saying something about the theta-field integral connected with the work he had promised to do that day with Charles. He swallowed hard and shook his head in disbelief as he leaned forward to study the message more closely. It seemed to be nothing more than a detail of a trivial error. The whole thing was ridiculous. What could possibly have been so important about something like that that it justified breaking all the team's rules? He had no way of telling; the message didn't go into any detail. He shrugged to himself, noted the information on a scrap of paper, deleted the record from the system and, still mystified, sauntered back upstairs to join Charles.

The dinner had been superb and the wine pleasantly mellowing. The music was soft and slow, and Anne's body swayed like warm, liquid velvet as she danced close to him.

And she smelled nice.

"I don't want to go home," she murmured into his shoulder.

"You shouldn't even be thinking about that," he told her. "There's lots of time left yet."

"Not enough. It's been a nice evening."

"Mmm . . ."

"You wouldn't believe how much I've been looking

139

forward to tonight. I had an awful premonition you were going to call at the last minute and put it off." She giggled softly. "There, doesn't that sound terribly schoolgirlish?"

"Nope. It sounds crazy. Why would I go and do something like that?"

"Oh, I don't know. . . . You might have got too wrapped up in that work you're doing to tear yourself away. Something like that."

"Now that's really crazy. You don't think I'd have called it off just over a few lousy sums."

"You never know with scientists."

"No way in the world."

A week later Murdoch was still puzzling from time to time over what could have been so important about a trivial third integral that it was worth breaking the rules and jeopardizing the whole experiment.

CHAPTER SIXTEEN

Dr. Ahmul Shajawnpur stood frowning thoughtfully out of the window of his office in the Casualty Department of the Jawaharlal Nehru Hospital in Calcutta, absently fingering the tie cord of the surgical mask dangling below his chin. In over twenty years of medicine he had never come across anything like this. He turned away from the window after a while and looked again at the computer-generated body-scan still being displayed on the large wall-screen opposite his desk.

The body from which the scan had been generated belonged to an insurance broker who had been admitted a few hours earlier that day, and who was still recovering under sedation. The man had collapsed suddenly on the deck of a boat on the river, in the course of a day's sailing with some friends. Heart attack, everybody had said.

The thin line, enhanced by computer to stand out clearly on the image, entered the lumbar region above the waist and to the right of the spine; from there it traced a smooth, shallow curve through muscle, arteries, lung, and bones to exit through the left shoulder an inch behind the clavicle. Analysis had shown it to comprise a microscopically thin hairline of devastated cells, seemingly torn apart by some agency and, from the lab tests performed on tiny samples of the cell debris, subjected to considerable heat. The line reminded Shajawnpur of a track from a bubble-chamber picture, as if something had passed right through the broker's body from lower-right back to upper-left front. Something such as what? What was small enough to pass through a man's body without killing him, dense enough to drill through bone, and hot enough to ionize sodium, potassium, and carbon?

He leaned forward and touched a pad on the panel by his desk to switch to another view. The new image showed the broker's body positioned on the scanning table bent at the waist with the left arm extended forward and the right arm flexed and drawn back. According to the friends who had seen the incident, the broker had been hauling in a rope just before he collapsed, and to the best of their recollection had been stooped in that kind of posture. It was interesting. Allowing for the approximations involved, with the body in that position, the mysterious track became a straight line. What moved more or less horizontally over water and passed through a man's body as if it wasn't there? Shajawnpur shook his head. He would have to bring a specialist in on this, he decided.

A specialist in what?

He sighed, sat down at the desk, and entered a note into the terminal to bring the case to the attention of the staff surgeon when he made his rounds the next morning. His patient seemed to be in no immediate danger. He closed the file.

Professor Ferdinand Chaurrez, from the Geophysics Department of the University of Bogota, Colombia, stared suspiciously at the data-plot pinned to the wall before him in the cramped laboratory trailer. The trailer was one of two parked amid a small jumble of portable cabins, tents, oil drums, crates, and a few miscellaneous vehicles at the upper end of an arid valley in the rocky foothills of the Cordillera Orvental, a northern extension of the Andes. The plot showed the computer's interpretation of the latest data relayed from equipment that was measuring cosmic-ray intensities at the bottom of an unused mine about twenty miles to the west. Behind the professor, José Calliano, one of his graduate students, perched on the edge of an analysis bench and watched curiously.

"That one doesn't make sense," Chaurrez said at last. "According to the readings, a single particle occurred there"—he pointed with a pen—"that sent everything off-scale. That would mean an energy at least four orders of magnitude greater than anything that has ever been recorded. And it could even have been much greater than that; from this there's no way of telling."

"I thought the same thing," José told him. "I've never heard of anything like it either, but I thought you ought to see it. Another strange thing is the associated trajectory coordinates. Look at them. According to those figures, the particle would have been moving practically horizontally. I've never heard of a cosmic-ray particle that traveled through a mineshaft sideways, have you?"

"Was this the only one?" Chaurrez asked.

"Just that one."

"That's not a cosmic-ray particle at all," the professor declared. "You've got a fault in the equipment somewhere. I'd forget this batch of data if I were you; it's probably all corrupt. Make sure the computer's okay. If anything like it happens again, take a jeep up to the mine and check the equipment there. Otherwise forget about it."

"You don't think it could be something else?"

"Yes, it could. If you can think of something that flies through solid rock horizontally with at least a hundred thousand times more energy than the most energetic cosmic-ray particle ever detected and probably a lot more, then yes, I suppose it could be that. Alternatively it could be the result of an intermittent equipment fault. Now, which of those two hypotheses do you think best accounts for the facts and requires the minimum of assumptions?"

"Okay," José said, grinning. "Point taken. I'll go and check over the computer."

In a structural analysis laboratory of the Instrumentation Commissioning section of the Skycom Corporation's space-launch facility on the edge of the Western Australian desert, John Skelly, Director of Quality Control, gazed grimly at the 3-D color hologram being presented at medium-to-high magnification.

"Somebody's head will roll for this," he growled in a bass-baritone rumble that was barely above a whisper. A few of the other men standing around the display table shuffled their feet uncomfortably.

The hologram, generated from the output of a scanning electron microscope, reproduced a small part of the surface of the mirror for an astronomical telescope being assembled in orbit; the mirror had been scheduled to be lifted into orbit for mounting in the telescope in two months' time. For over a year the mirror surface had been ground, polished, measured with laser interferometers, and then polished some more until it was accurate to within a small fraction of a wavelength of light. And now, after all that painstaking care, this. . . .

Whatever it was had gouged a microscopic furrow for a short distance along what had yesterday been a flawless surface. The furrow was shallow at one end, but deepened rapidly toward the other, where it terminated in a hole that continued on into the glass. X-ray images had shown that the hole continued on in a straight line right through the body of the mirror, making a slight descending angle with the surface. The far end of the hole had been located a small distance down the mirror's edge on the opposite side. The furrow was undetectable by the naked eye, but it was enough to make the mirror useless for the delicate measurements for which it had been designed.

"Do we know yet what did it?" Skelly demanded, looking up at the circle of faces. The heads shook wordlessly from side to side. Somebody shrugged and showed his hands. "But bloody hell, don't we even have a clue?" Skelly raged. "There was nothing wrong with it yesterday. We must know what's been going on around it since then, for Christ's sake!"

"We've checked all the records and logs," one of the technicians told him, not for the first time. "Everything has been kept well inside spec. There hasn't been anything unusual in any way. No accidents reported, no faults on anything, no—"

"Something bloody unusual has happened all right!" Skelly exploded. "Look at that, man. Are you telling me something just came out of nowhere and drilled its way through five feet of solid glass?" He straightened up from the image, and his face darkened even further. "By the end of today I want an answer," he told them. "I want to know what did it, and who was responsible. The salary of whoever it was can go toward paying the penalty clause in the contract." With that he turned on his heel and stamped out of the lab.

An uneasy silence descended.

"So, what next?" somebody asked at last. "Where do we go from here? I'm not even sure what we're supposed to be looking for."

"Whatever did that," somebody else replied, waving toward the hologram.

The first speaker pulled a face and stared glumly at the image.

"The only thing that could have done that would be an armor-plated bacterium with a rocket motor up its ass," he said. "Now you tell me, where do you start looking for something like that?"

CHAPTER SEVENTEEN

January turned to February, and the Scottish Highlands remained frozen in the grip of winter. At Storbannon the results of the second phase of tests, which used randomly generated data as the content of the signals sent back through time, were analyzed and revealed a strange phenomenon: On a few occasions the number received was different from the number that was later sent.

Many of the tests involved programming the system

144

to record an incoming number from the future, waiting until the time came to send it, then, at that point, generating a random number and sending it back to the point at which it had been received. In tests of this type where the whole process ran automatically, the pair of numbers always matched; there were no anomalies in the thousands of numbers recorded.

In some later tests, however, the team tried experimenting with the effects of arbitrary human decision. They set the program exactly as before, allowed it to run through to the point where the signal was about to be sent, and at that point made an arbitrary decision, sometimes based on flips of a coin and sometimes by other means, whether or not to switch off the transmitter. In the cases where they did switch it off, the computer produced a number anyway but couldn't send it. The number that had been received, therefore, the team reasoned, must have been sent from a timeline that had been altered only to the degree of containing a transmitter that had been switched on, but which was switched off on the new timeline. This should not have affected the value of the random number produced; the number received should still have matched the number later observed, whether it was sent or not. And indeed, in most of the cases the two did match. But in a tiny fraction of the large number of results, they didn't. Murdoch and Lee discussed the anomaly one day in mid-February while they were tramping from Storbannon down to Glenmoroch village for some fresh air and a spot of exercise, which was as good an excuse as any for a drink.

"Let's go through it, very simply, one more time," Murdoch said. They were following a footpath that led from a side gate in the grounds down toward the crescent-shaped wood. "Here is the machine waiting, and at some time a number comes in—let's say, 123."

"Okay," Lee agreed.

"So 123 gets stored. Now nothing happens until the time comes for it to be sent back. The random-number routine runs and generates a number."

"Check."

"Now we know, from the data we've collected from lots of tests, that if the number that's just been generated is sent, it always matches what has already been received. If it isn't sent, then most of the times it still matches, which is what we'd expect. But sometimes, just sometimes . . . we end up with 123 recorded as having been received, but the program outputs something else, let's say 456. Now try and make sense out of that for me." By now they had entered the wood. The silence was broken only by the steady crunching of their boots in the snow and the occasional swishing sound of snow sliding off the branches in the trees all around.

"There had to be a timeline with a computer on it that generated 123," Lee said after a while. "There had to be because there's no other way that 123 could get received in the first place. Agreed?"

"Okay, I'll buy that."

"But by the time our computer has become that computer, it doesn't produce 123; it produces 456. Therefore the computer that did produce 123 doesn't exist any more."

"Which says it got reset onto a new timeline."

"Which says it got reset onto a new timeline. So what reset it?"

"That's where it gets crazy," Murdoch said. "The whole sequence was preprogrammed so the events of both sending the signal and receiving it had to be on the original timeline that involved 123. Nothing changed from that situation until we took the decision to switch off the transmitter. But that couldn't have had any effect on what was happening inside the computer. So what made the number come out wrong?"

"And why doesn't it ever come out wrong when you leave the transmitter on?" Lee completed.

"Exactly," Murdoch said.

The path brought them to a flight of iron-railed stone steps that led up to the road running from the wood to the village. As they came out onto the road, Bob Ferguson from the farm on the far side of the village drove by in a rickety van with one of his sheepdogs hanging out from the passenger-side window. He tooted the horn and waved cheerfully as he passed, then disappeared around a bend in the road heading in the direction of Loch Keld.

"There's only one answer," Lee said after they had covered a few hundred more yards. "Something else must have reset the timeline . . . something that's got nothing to do with signals being sent back or not being sent back."

"What are you getting at?"

"Well, look at it this way. Here I am with 123 stored as having come in. Now suppose that *something* affects the timeline I'm on, after that moment but before the time comes to send the signal . . . something that leaves my record of 123 intact, but causes the computer to generate 456. Now if I switch off the transmitter, 456 never gets sent. So I'm left with a mismatch, which is what we got."

Murdoch thought about it for a few seconds, then said, "But if you leave the transmitter on, 456 does get sent. That would reset the whole timeline from the moment the signal was received on, so that it would show 456 coming in. In that situation it would overwrite 123 and you'd end up never knowing that 123 ever got sent at all. Yes . . . and that was what we got too: Whenever the number was sent, we never had a mismatch."

"It's sneaky," Lee declared. "The something else alters the timeline and sets up a mismatch situation. But when you send the signal, it changes things in such a way as to cancel out the effect of it. It's only when you don't transmit that you can hope to catch it."

"So what's the something else that affects timelines?" Murdoch summarized.

"Yes. And why doesn't it do it consistently? Why does it only happen every now and then instead of every time?" Lee added.

They reached the outskirts of the village without speaking further. The few people who were out and about acknowledged them with nods or a few words of greeting as they passed.

"Something unpredictable," Murdoch mused, half to himself. "It has to be something that operates randomly and can affect random numbers generated by a computer. What kinds of things work like that?"

"Noise fluctuations," Lee said. "Thermal effects. Relaxation sequences of excited atoms. All kinds of

147

quantum . . ." His voice trailed away, and his pace slowed abruptly as he realized what he had said. He halted and turned to stare back at Murdoch, who had already come to a halt a pace farther back. In the same instant they had both realized the same thing.

"It's exactly what Elizabeth said," Murdoch breathed. "She said that an adequate model would have to include some kind of quantum uncertainty. Now we've found exactly the same thing, but from actual experimental data." They stood silently for what seemed a long time as the full implications sank in. A woman who was clearing snow from a path leading to the side door of a house across the road stopped to look at them curiously, but they took no notice. Then they started walking again, this time more slowly.

"The particle threads can't be precisely defined," Lee said after a while. "They're only defined within uncertainty limits. At the quantum level, the pattern is dynamic. It can change spontaneously, independent of whether any signals are sent or not. That says it must happen all the time, machine or no machine."

"So at the quantum level events are not frozen into the thread pattern and predetermined," Murdoch said excitedly. "And all kinds of macroscopic phenomena can be decided by random quantum-level fluctuations. That could be where chance and free will come into it. That's exactly what Elizabeth wanted to see!"

They reached the main street of the village and came at least within sight of the Argyll, Glenmoroch's hotel and principal pub. "We'll have to get Elizabeth involved again as soon as we can," Lee said. "Any idea when she's due back?"

"Next week, according to Grandpa. They're still having problems up at the plant."

Elizabeth had visited Storbannon a few times since mid-January. She had hoped to have even more time to spare after the full-power tests of the reactors were completed, but an unexpected snag had developed. The tests had begun on the Monday as planned and continued through to Tuesday morning. Then the control computers at Burghead had announced an emergency condition and shut down the reactors. Subsequent in-

148

vestigation had revealed severe erosion on the under-sides of the reactor chambers, resulting in a vacuum loss that the sensors had detected. None of the engineers at Burghead had been able to explain what had caused the erosion. The proposed schedule for taking the plant on-line by summer was threatened, and Elizabeth had been tied up day and night with her staff, trying to track down the cause of the problem.

They reached the door of the Argyll, and Lee ducked to follow Murdoch through the low threshold. The bar inside was cheerily lit by a roaring, open fire, and pleasantly warm after the ear-nipping cold outside. A few heads turned among the knot of farmers and other locals gathered at the bar. In the middle of them was Hamish, the gardener from Storbannon, a wild-looking man with eyes that always seemed wide and staring like a maniac's, a bald head fringed by two dense tufts of unruly, red hair, and a full, rust-colored beard.

"Well, if it isn't our two Americans come to join us," one of the farmers said. He had a weathered face, laced with a network of fine purple veins, and was wearing a flat cloth cap. "Hello, Murdoch Ross, and hello, Lee. Will you be joining us for a drink?"

"Hi, Willie," Murdoch replied. "Pint, thanks."

"Same," Lee said. "Hi . . . and thanks."

"T'is good to see you're cultivating a taste for *real* beer at last," Hamish told them, wiping a trace of froth from his beard with his sleeve. "All that American synthetic rubbish does nothing for a man at all."

"What's wrong with our beer, Hamish?" Murdoch asked, feigning surprise. "It's not synthetic, it's natural. It's made from natural ingredients, under natural conditions, grown with natural organic fertilizers. The ads on the TV say so."

"Aye," Hamish growled, screwing his face into a scowl of distaste. "And it tastes like a certain natural organic fertilizer that I could mention too."

CHAPTER EIGHTEEN

Murdoch collected the few remaining dishes together into a stack and dropped the two crumpled napkins on top, leaving the glasses and the still quarter-full bottle of burgundy on the table. Then he picked up the stack, balancing it carefully, and turned to the door that led through to the kitchen.

He enjoyed the evenings and all-too-infrequent week-ends that he found time to spend in Anne's Nairn apartment. Storbannon was all very grand and imposing, and quite cheerful in its own lofty way, but this was what he called homey. He was never quite sure what it was that Anne did that made the apartment seem that way, but every time he walked in, he was instantly aware of something subtly different about it from the places belonging to girls he had known in California, New York, and elsewhere.

There was no one thing that stood out on its own, but rather lots of little things that contributed some-how to an overall effect merely by being there—such as the collection of small, hollow glass sculptures on the bookshelves, always containing a few flowers that were fresh, or the frilly covers on the armchair backs and side tables that always matched. And then there were the things that were slightly more elaborate and slightly more ornate than they needed to be, but in a particular kind of way such that each of them served the dual role of fulfilling the purpose it was ostensibly designed for while at the same time con-tributing something to the mood of the whole setting. The writing paper on the bureau in one corner, for example, could have been just writing paper; it was, but in addition it was pale brown and richly textured, with a simple floral design in green and yellow at the lower left-hand corner of every sheet. The envelopes could have been just envelopes, but they matched the paper. The cabinet opposite the window could have contained just bottles and glasses; it contained an *arrangement* of bottles and glasses, along with a cut-crystal decanter and set of goblets. The vi-set screen, standing on its flexible supporting arm on top of the cabinet, could have been the standard black-and-gray model that came at the standard rental, but it was coffee-brown two-tone, which cost slightly more; the room needed coffee-brown two-tone. It was the same with the funny fluffy animal figures in the corners and over the door, the china figurines on the ledge above the heater vent, and the embroidered, tasseled mats underneath the table lamps. They achieved nothing individually, but had any of them not been there, something would have been missing.

Or maybe Murdoch was imagining it all; maybe the only thing different was that Anne lived there.

He carried the stack through to the kitchen and set it down beside where Anne was loading the dishwasher with the rest of the dishes from dinner. She was wearing a figure-hugging, navy-blue dress that seemed to continue the curves of her legs in a flowing wave all the way through to her shoulders. Murdoch slipped his arms under hers and around her waist, nibbled her ear, and squeezed her breasts lightly. She giggled and wriggled, but not too much.

"You know you shouldn't do that in front of the children," she said, meaning the picture that was taped to the refrigerator door, showing a pair of scampish-looking puppies staring out of a garbage can.

"They have to learn sometime," Murdoch replied as he let go of her and drifted back to the door. "There's still about two glasses of wine left. Want me to fill yours up?"

"Mmm, please. I'll be through in a second."

"Ice?"

"Heathen!"

"Just kidding."

He strolled back into the lounge, refilled the glasses, and settled down with his in the armchair by the window to look out over the lights of the town center. Anne had known exactly what she was looking for when she chose this place, he thought to himself . . . just like everything else. A minute or so later, Anne came into the room, picked up the other glass from the table, and curled herself up on one end of the sofa, facing him.

"Don't you get claustrophobic in this humble abode after your castle?" she asked, smiling.

"I told you before, I like it," Murdoch replied. "It's Texans who have to have everything big. You're forgetting."

"But .Storbannon isn't just big," Anne said. "It's magnificent. There aren't many people who can go home to somewhere like that these days, especially with the taxes and things. How does your grandfather do it . . . if it's not a rude question?"

"Oh, he has a few sources of income—and a good lawyer in Kingussie, who's worked for the family for years. On top of that, my father in Chicago channels some of the profits from his business into keeping the estate intact." Murdoch could have added that it was a problem that he would almost certainly inherit one day, but he never broached that issue in his conversations with Anne. It was something that she had never touched upon or hinted at either. Murdoch was glad of that.

"He told me you'll be opening up the Guest Wing again next month," Anne said. "Won't that make things impossible? I mean, you've got more than enough to do without worrying about looking after visitors, and conferences going on and things, surely."

"He's got an agent in Edinburgh who takes care of all that," Murdoch informed her. "They supply their own people, who live in and handle contractors for decorating, catering, and all that stuff, so the whole thing runs itself . . . kind of self-contained." He paused and sipped his drink. "Say, I was meaning to tell you, Grandpa's been thinking about that suggestion of yours for extending the visitors' parking area behind the summerhouse and putting some shrubs there. He likes it. Robert's getting the agent in Edinburgh to look into it."

"I'm glad," Anne said. "It looked too cramped and bare by the wall there."

"Grandpa also wanted to know when you're coming down again," Murdoch said. "We thought maybe we could fix something for Saturday . . . dinner maybe."

"I thought Dr. Muir was going down there on Saturday. Won't it be all business talk?"

Murdoch shook his head. "She had to cancel out. She's still tied up with the reactor problem they're having at your place. Have you heard anything about how it's going?"

"I'm afraid I haven't. I don't get to hear very much about that side of things. I do know it's causing a lot of concern though. We've had all kinds of people coming up from London, and over from Brussels and places."

"I see." Murdoch shrugged. "So, how about Saturday?" he asked again. "Is it okay?"

"Fine. I'll probably turn up around midafternoon because I've got to go into Inverness for something in the morning," Anne replied. She smiled suddenly. "I can say hello to Maxwell again. How is Maxwell?"

"In disgrace. He's discovered that swinging on drapes is great fun. Unfortunately it breaks vases."

Anne laughed and stretched herself out more comfortably along the sofa. After a few moments of silence she nodded her head in the direction of the vi-set screen, standing on the cabinet. "Do you want to watch the news?" she asked. "It'll be on in about three minutes."

"Not especially. It'll just be the usual garbage."

"I thought you might be curious to see if any more bugophants had turned up anywhere," Anne said. "You're always talking about them with Lee."

"Bugophant" was the name that the media had given to the still unidentified objects that had been drilling holes through people and things in various widely scattered parts of the world ever since late January. The term had been coined after an American scientist had described the properties of whatever was responsible as being comparable to "something like a bug with the weight of an elephant." Eleven incidents involving these strange objects had been reported in the three months that had elapsed since January. The most recent had occurred in Scotland itself, and involved a housewife in Glasgow who had fallen down some stairs when a sudden stabbing and burning pain caused a

153

convulsion of her leg. Subsequent examination had revealed a "bugophant burrow" through her knee.

"Oh, I'm not interested in hearing any more inarticulate eyewitnesses and their inane accounts," Murdoch said. "When somebody finds out what's doing it, I guess we'll know anyhow. How about some music instead?"

Anne reached out and picked up the carry-around communicator pad that controlled the apartment's electronics. She used its miniature screen to pick out a prespecified medley, and the strain of a popular orchestral piece began issuing from the built-in sound system.

"What are your latest ideas on them?" Anne asked as she replaced the pad. "Have you had any brain waves? They seem to be baffling all the experts."

"Not really," Murdoch confessed. "The only thing I can think of is that they have to be extraterrestrial, like some astronomers are saying."

"A shower of high-density particles from some other part of the galaxy?"

"Or even some other galaxy," Murdoch said. "That's where the highest-energy cosmic rays come from. Who knows? It makes about as much sense as anything else."

"But if that's true, why do they move horizontally?" Anne queried.

Murdoch shrugged. "Maybe it's just a probability effect. It could be that there's more chance of something or somebody getting hit by one that just grazes the surface of the Earth. Maybe most of them do come straight down, but we don't hear about those because they don't hit anything."

"It could be, I suppose," Anne mused. She thought for a second, and an impish smile formed on her face. "I take it that you don't exactly subscribe to the explanation in the *Herald* last week, then," she said.

"What explanation?"

"They're parts of debris from an orbiting UFO that was powered by some revolutionary kind of drive based on neutronium. The Americans or the Russians mistook it for a MIRV-satellite that the other one had put up despite the treaty, fired a nuke at it, and now they're hushing it up."

154

Murdoch snorted. "Garbage! That's even crazier than some of Ted's satellite stories."

"Oh, how is Ted?" Anne inquired. "I was meaning to ask."

"He's as well as ever. Did you know, he spent some time once at one of the places that had a bugophant? It was the place in Australia . . . Skycom Corporation's launch site. That was where the telescope mirror was wrecked just before it was supposed to be put up into orbit for assembly."

"They fired a couple of people, didn't they?" Anne said. "Then they had to reinstate them with lots of apologies and compensation when more bugophants began turning up in other places."

"That's right. In fact Ted once knew the guy who fired them. He used to handle the contracts that Skycom had for the RAF when Ted was out there. He sounded like a real mean bastard, from what Ted said."

"Maybe he won't be so mean in such a hurry in future," Anne said. "People should keep their words soft and sweet; they may have to eat them later." She relaxed against the end of the sofa and lapsed into silence while she listened to the music and tasted her wine. Then she went on absently, "We had a doctor at university in London who was perpetually mean. He was a neurophysiologist who taught programming. Later on they found out that he had an incipient brain tumor, which was what was making him behave like that. Rather funny in a way . . . like having a dentist with bad teeth."

"Did he get fixed okay?"

"Oh, yes. He's fine now, as far as I know."

Murdoch thought for a moment. "Was that where you learned to program real-time . . . the image-processing and things you talked about once?"

"Yes. That was where I started getting interested in it anyway."

"What kinds of other things did you program?" Murdoch asked.

"Oh . . ." Anne sighed. "I tried to program computers to compose music once, but it never really worked. The programs did what they were supposed to, all right, but . . . oh, I don't know . . . the result never sounded what I would have called right."

Murdoch smirked to himself. He couldn't resist it. "Maybe it was because your Bach was worse than your byte," he suggested.

Anne squealed and threw a cushion. Murdoch laughed and caught it a foot in front of his head. "Ooh . . . That was simply awful," she moaned. She leaned back and watched despairingly while Murdoch tossed the cushion back onto the sofa, then said, "Try being serious instead. What's the latest news with your grandfather's machine? I've been hoping you'd have something exciting to tell me."

"There is," Murdoch told her. "I was saving it until after dinner." Anne pulled herself up into a more attentive position and raised her eyebrows expectantly. Murdoch hunched forward in the chair to prop his elbows on his knees, and paused for a moment to collect his thoughts.

Although the machine was not, strictly speaking, secret, there was an unvoiced agreement among the members of the team that the time was not yet ripe for outsiders to be aware of the nature of the experiments. But Anne, being Anne, had been naturally curious about the work Murdoch was involved with, and as time went by he had found himself letting slip odd hints that he hoped might suffice as answers to her questions without giving too much away. In no time, however, she had fitted the pieces together for herself, and bit by bit led him to fill in the rest of the story. At first she had thought the whole thing to be an elaborate joke on Murdoch's part. However, as it became clear that he was being absolutely serious, her incredulity had given way to a rational, though astounded, acceptance of the whole thing.

Although Charles had taken well to Anne, Murdoch had not as yet mentioned anything to him about how much she knew of what was happening at Storbannon. Although Murdoch himself had no qualms about Anne's discretion, he did have mild apprehensions regarding Charles's possible reaction. Later, Murdoch was sure, when Charles had had a chance to get to know her even better, would be a more suitable time.

156

It was one of those things that would always sound better tomorrow.

"We think we've more or less got the model figured out," Murdoch said. "Qualitatively, at least. . . . A rigorous, quantitative theory will probably take years to come together. The model is dynamic in the way that we figured it had to be, but the latest indications are that it's far more stable than we'd expected."

"How do you mean, stable?" Anne asked.

"The particle threads that are woven together to form the timeline are not static," Murdoch replied. "They vibrate within limits defined by quantum uncertainty. In fact we're beginning to suspect that the Uncertainty Principle of classical physics might be nothing more than a manifestation of the fluctuations in threads passing through a particular universe."

"Yes, I remember that," Anne said. "What we call chance events have their roots down at that level. That was how it was possible for the timeloops not to be permanent fixtures."

"Right. Sometimes a quantum-level event can have effects at the macroscopic level. When that happens, the timeline can reconfigure itself spontaneously such that the part of the total pattern affected by the event can alter itself macroscopically all the way through from that point on."

"Let's just get this straight," Anne said, raising a hand. "While you were talking, I just happened, for no reason at all, to brush my hair out of my eyes with my right hand."

"Okay."

"And from what you've said before, there's another 'me', who exists ten seconds back along the timeline we're on, who hasn't done that yet."

"Right."

"Now you're saying that in her universe, random quantum events could be taking place differently to the way they did in ours. For instance, something at the atomic level could perhaps decide the difference between a finely balanced neuron firing or not firing, and that neuron could be enough to trigger a different behavior pattern. So she might do the same thing as I did, only with her left hand." Anne paused and looked inquiringly at Murdoch. He nodded. She continued, "That action would reconfigure the part of the timeline that contains me so that a new me would exist, right at this instant, whose memory and everything would be consistent with the new thread pattern: I'd have used my left hand, remembered that I'd used my left hand, and I wouldn't know anything about it ever having been any other way."

"That's right," Murdoch confirmed. "And for all we could ever know, it might have happened in exactly that way, except you'd have switched from left to right."

"And that kind of thing could be going on spontaneously all the time?"

"Yes."

"Sounds spooky."

"Don't worry about it. You've been living with it all your life."

Anne pulled a face. "Very well, I won't. So where does the stability part come in?"

"That's where it gets interesting," Murdoch told her. "You see, at first we had this vision of the whole pattern being in a state of tremendous agitation all the time . . . with the threads coming together and bouncing apart, and reconfiguring all kinds of events at the macroscopic level from instant to instant. But in fact it doesn't happen like that; the timeline doesn't change macroscopically at anything like the rate at which quantum events take place. At the large-scale level, the system is amazingly stable."

"So there aren't millions of me's spaced microseconds apart over the last couple of minutes, all deciding to brush their hair with different hands."

"Exactly. The overwhelming probability is that the situation will stay stable . . . in other words, the way you remember it. It's as if there were some kind of noise-filtering process that operates as you go up from the smaller, unpredictable level up through to the larger, more stable level. Only very, very rarely does a quantum event avalanche upward in scale and produce significant changes that are tangible. So at the everyday level things become more determinate, but chance still gets its innings."

"I see." Anne leaned back and drummed her

fingertips lightly on the back of the sofa while she digested what Murdoch had said. After a while, a puzzled frown formed on her brow. She looked back at him. "How could you possibly test something like that experimentally?"

"By realizing that we'd never thought of something obvious."

"What's that supposed to mean?"

"Here's a paradox," Murdoch said. "We program the computer to do a very simple thing. We program it to examine its record for some point in the past and decide whether or not a signal was received at that point. If one wasn't, the computer sends one there; if one was, the computer doesn't send anything. Now let that program run continually. What happens?" He sat back and waited while Anne frowned with concentration as she stepped mentally through the tortuous logic of visualizing timeloops.

"It's absurd," she said slowly at last. Murdoch nodded in satisfaction. She went on, "You'd keep going round the same loop forever. There wouldn't be any way out of it." Her eyes narrowed thoughtfully as she remembered what Murdoch had said a few moments previously. "It's obvious, isn't it . . . the first thing that you'd imagine anyone would think of. So what are you saying—that you never thought of trying it?" She paused as a new light of understanding flowed into her eyes. "Or should I say that if you did try it, you've no recollection that you did?"

"You've hit it right on the head," Murdoch told her. "We're nearly at the end of April now, and we've been running the machine since January. And in all that time something that should have been first on the list of things to try never occurred to us. But if we had tried it, the machine would have gone into an infinite loop. What does that say to you?"

"There must have been timelines on which you did try it."

"Yes," Murdoch agreed, nodding. "That loop would have sustained itself permanently, *unless* some quantum fluctuation got us out of it. For example, somebody who existed on the timeline inside the loop might have made a decision for no particular reason to discontinue the experiment, or maybe somebody ahead of the loop decided not to commence it in the first place . . . or, maybe . . . *never thought of it in the first place!* It would have to be something with billions-to-one odds against, but it would happen sooner or later if the loop iterated indefinitely. When it did happen, the loop would disappear, and on the final timeline we'd end up right where we are now in April, with no record preserved that any experiment like that was ever performed."

"And having acted very much out of character," Anne remarked.

"Which is just what you'd expect from those odds," Murdoch said.

"So how did you test it?" Anne asked again. "Or did you have to infer that indirectly?"

"No, we found a way," Murdoch replied. "We set up a program just like I said, but in such a way that it incremented a count every time it went around the loop. When the count reached a preset number, the program discontinued the test. So there was a mechanism to break out of the loop built in. The loop couldn't become infinite. Tests like that gave us enough data to figure out how the loops are structured. Later on we included random factors, which was how we managed to measure the stability. That was the part that was really unexpected. You have to run tens of millions of numbers to get a handful that don't match."

Anne subsided into silence for a while, and then picked up the communicator pad again. "Would you like a coffee?" she asked.

"Good idea."

She tapped a brief code into the pad, and in the kitchen the percolator began filling itself. "So where do you go next?" she asked. "Has your grandfather lifted the ban on ad hoc dialogues with the future yet? I'm dying to find out what happens then. Just think how we could clean up at the races."

Murdoch shook his head. "Not yet. There are still a few more things that he wants to find out about first. The model seems to imply some dimension of 'super-time' that the patterns can reconfigure in. He wants to know what the relationship is between time and super-time. There are reasons for believing that causal influences can only propagate along the threads at a finite rate in supertime. What's the rate? What's the rate at which tau waves propagate? He wants to know a lot more about things like that."

"It certainly sounds as if there's still a lot more to do," Anne said. She sighed. "Oh, I do wish you'd clear up this business about my knowing what you're doing down there. I'm sure your grandfather wouldn't mind as much as you think. I'd love to be able to help in some way, even if it was only by debugging a few programs or something. Are you going to talk to him about it?"

"Okay," Murdoch said. "I'll talk to him tomorrow. Maybe you're right."

"Do . . . please."

"I will. I already said I would."

"Oh, dear, aren't I getting to be an old nag. Okay." Anne smiled, got up from the sofa, and disappeared into the kitchen. She came back a minute or so later, carrying two steaming mugs and some mints on a tray.

"There was something else I remembered while you were gone," Murdoch said as she set the tray down. "Grandpa has figured out another interesting thing: The quantum-level vibrations of basic particles can absorb energy from tau waves."

Anne's brow knitted as she handed him one of the mugs. "I'm so glad you told me that. It was just what I was wondering. Now tell me what it means."

"It means that normally, without anybody sending any tau waves through time, the timeline is highly stable; alterations at the macroscopic level due to avalanching quantum effects are rare. But an incoming tau wave raises the energy-level of some quantum processes, and makes them far more likely to alter large-scale events on the timeline. So every time we use the machine, we destabilize the system to a degree at the moment in time that receives the signal."

"You mean that it interferes with the outcome of chance events in the universe that the signal arrives in . . . and therefore all the universes after that as well?"

161

"Yes," Murdoch replied simply.

Anne looked slightly uncertain. "Chance events where . . . at Storbannon? In the lab? . . ."

"No, everywhere," Murdoch said. "You're forgetting that the wave rematerializes in a volume that expands at light-speed as it gets farther away in time from the instant of transmission. The range of the machine is one day. In that time the Earth moves about twenty-one million miles. So everywhere inside a sphere of that radius, the signal is at least as strong as it needs to be for the machine to detect it. In other words if it can affect chance events in the lab when it rematerializes, it sure-as-hell can do the same thing here in Nairn, or come to that anyplace else on Earth too."

Anne remained very quiet for a moment. "I hadn't realized that," she said, for the first time sounding genuinely awed. "You mean that whenever you use the machine to send a signal, you could be changing the outcome of chance events all over the world in the universe that you inject the signal into?"

"Exactly that," Murdoch said slowly. His tone had become very serious. "Imagine a guy somewhere in New York who made a million last night on the spin of a roulette wheel. The overwhelming probability is that the part of the timeline that includes him in it has remained stable since then, and tonight he's out somewhere whooping it up. But now suppose we decide to run a test on the machine at Storbannon right now. Suppose that in the course of that test we happen to send a signal back to the exact moment in time at which the ball on the wheel was balanced between falling into red or black last night. The tau-pulse field materializing at that instant, here, in New York, and everywhere else inside twenty-one million miles of where the Earth is right now could be enough to make the ball go the other way, and reconfigure that part of the timeline from that moment on. So tonight, instead, the guy's on a bridge, about to jump into the East River.

"It makes you think, doesn't it."

CHAPTER NINETEEN

When Murdoch returned to Storbannon in the early hours of the following morning, he was surprised to see Elizabeth Muir's car parked outside the main entrance. He hurried inside and found the team and Elizabeth gathered in Charles's study. Charles was at his desk with his tie loosened and his waistcoat unbuttoned, and Cartland was propped wearily against the blackboard to one side, his arms folded across his chest. Elizabeth was sitting in another chair, and Lee was standing by the window. The room was littered with papers and empty cups, and evidently the scene of much hard work for many hours. There was an atmosphere of tension about the place.

"What's happened?" Murdoch asked.

Charles looked up and passed a hand across his brow. "If it's what we think it is, it's bad, Murdoch," he said. "Elizabeth called earlier today about some thoughts she'd been having on the wee wormholes that are appearing all over the place. She came down later to go through some of our formulas. We think we know what they are."

"The bugophants?" Murdoch stared at Elizabeth. A smile flickered briefly on her mouth to acknowledge his arrival, but she was evidently too tired to volunteer a lengthy explanation. Murdoch shifted his gaze to Lee. He couldn't imagine what the mysterious objects could have to do either with anybody at Storbannon or with Elizabeth.

"When is a fusion pellet like a supernova?" Lee asked simply. There was no humor in his voice.

Murdoch blinked back his bewilderment at the question. "What the hell is that supposed to mean?" he asked them.

"Think about it, old boy," Cartland said quietly. Murdoch stared helplessly around the circle of somber faces. Nobody was offering any clues. So he thought about it.

A supernova: a catastrophic explosion of an abnormally large star. Throughout its stable life, the star maintained an equilibrium between the gravitation of its mass, which tried to make it collapse, and the radiation-pressure resulting from the fusion reactions going on inside it, which tried to blow it apart. The radiation was conveyed to the surface by photons, which moved extremely slowly because of their repeated absorption and reemission by matter along the way. The inside of the star generated energy faster than the surface could radiate it away, so the core got hotter . . . and hotter. Eventually it reached a temperature of sixty billion degrees—at that number, who cared on what scale?

At that critical temperature, the rate of production of neutrinos suddenly increased abruptly to an enormous figure. Neutrinos hardly reacted with matter at all; they went straight out through the body of the star, carrying away with them lots of the energy that up until then had gone into producing photons. So, all of a sudden, there were far fewer photons being produced, and consequently far less radiation-pressure to hold the force of self-gravitation in check.

At that point the star started to collapse, suddenly and violently.

In the process it released gravitational energy at a phenomenal rate—far faster than the material of the star's outer layers could absorb it. So they exploded away into space, producing a supernova. The opposite reaction of that explosion drove the already collapsing core harder and faster inward toward the star's center.

A fusion pellet was imploded in the same way . . . almost. The difference was that, because the pellet possessed negligible self-gravitation, the energy to implode it had to be supplied externally, such as by lasers or particle beams. But apart from that, the mechanics were similar. An inertial-confinement fusion reactor was, in effect, a supernova in a test tube. And a supernova produced . . .

Murdoch gasped in disbelief as the answer to the riddle at last became clear. "Oh, Jesus Christ!" he murmured, sinking weakly down onto the nearest chair, the color draining from his cheeks.

A supernova compressed its core all the way down to a black hole!

CHAPTER TWENTY

Ralph Courtney, Chairman and Managing Director of the local Board at the Burghead Heavy-Ion Fusion Facility, and Associate Director of the European Fusion Consortium, studied the faces of the dozen or so people sitting around the polished oak table that formed the centerpiece of the main conference room. Some of the faces were wearing worried frowns, some were still looking bemused, and others were just deep in thought.

Elizabeth Muir was still standing where she had finished speaking a minute or so before, in front of a large map of the world pinned to a board halfway along one side of the room, opposite the middle of the table. The meeting had been specially convened at her request. In the half hour that it had been in session, she had already said all there was to say. In fact she had said that in the first ten minutes; it had taken the rest of the time for the turmoil that followed to die down, and more than a few of those present were still only beginning to recover their capacity for coherent thinking.

She had begun by announcing her conviction that a serious flaw existed in the body of theory upon which the design of the Burghead reactor system had been based. Despite the decades of research that had gone before, and despite the carefully verified formulas and figures, she claimed, something completely unexpected, and at that stage inexplicable, had occurred during the full-power tests that had been conducted in January: The target pellets had been crushed down into miniature, probably nuclear-sized, black holes. The black holes had fallen through the floors of the reactor vessels toward the Earth's center, and that was what had caused the erosion that nobody had yet been able to explain.

The dynamics of what would happen after that were unclear. However, she told them, she had evaluated some approximate models, and the possibilities were alarming. The swarm of tiny black holes could form a mutually orbiting system within the Earth's core, exchanging energy among themselves and undergoing further excitation and agitation as new arrivals from the surface supplied gravitational energy and components of surface rotational momentum. Some of them could be thrown into violently eccentric orbits in this process—sufficiently eccentric to penetrate back up and reemerge on surface-grazing trajectories. Hence the "bugophants" that had been making appearances in recent months, Elizabeth suggested.

What was the evidence?

First there was the erosion through the lower casings of the two reactors used in the January tests. Analysis had shown that the erosion comprised a dense concentration of tiny tunnels that were identical to the ones being reported from various parts of the world. Second, the tests had been performed in mid-January; the first bugophant had been reported less than two weeks later. Third, all the incidents reported to date were scattered along a band that extended from the northern British Isles southward across the Atlantic to Panama and the top of South America, down over the southeast Pacific to miss Antarctica, and then northward from there to rejoin itself via Western Australia, northern India, central Russia, and Scandinavia. When this band was drawn on a globe, it formed a great circle around the Earth; if Elizabeth's account was correct, this marked the line of intersection between the Earth's surface and the orbital plane of the black-hole system. It was as simple as that.

There was one other thing. The two reactors had been run first independently for a day at fifteen pellets per second, and for about half of the second day in parallel at a combined rate of thirty per second. That meant there would be something like two million black holes down there.

"Surely . . . God, I don't know . . . This whole thing is preposterous, Elizabeth," Courtney said at last. "Black holes . . . milling around in the core like a swarm of bees? It's too far-fetched. I can't accept anything like that purely on the basis of what you've said. That isn't evidence; it's just a collection of coincidences . . . wild hypotheses, if you don't mind my saying so." Some of the heads around the table began nodding in mute agreement.

"I know that, Ralph," Elizabeth said wearily. "I know there isn't anything quantitative to support it. But it *is* a consistent explanation of what these things are and where they've come from. *And* it explains the erosion. It's the only one that fits both sets of facts. How many experts have been racking their brains and haven't even been able to offer a clue?"

There was one other item of evidence, an item that was conclusive, but she was obliged not to mention it. At Storbannon on the previous day, she and Charles had analyzed the data collected by the machine at the time in January when the system had been malfunctioning, which covered from Friday to Saturday before the Monday on which the Burghead test had commenced. As Lee had maintained at the time, the cause of the problem had been interference from tau waves coming from some source other than the machine itself. Cartland had analyzed the groupings and timings of the interference pulses, and found that it matched exactly with records brought by Elizabeth of the pellet-firing sequence followed in the tests at Burghead. The two had matched exactly, which could never have been explained away by coincidence. Therefore the interference picked up by the machine could only have come from the reactors being tested at Burghead. But the interference had been picked up at Storbannon *two full days before the tests at Burghead took place*.

Therefore the Burghead reactors must have generated tau waves that had propagated back two days in time. But tau waves were generated by the annihilation of matter. The Burghead reactors were not designed to annihilate matter; they were designed to convert matter to energy via fusion. Nevertheless, they had generated tau waves; therefore they must have annihilated matter. According to the established theory upon which the designs had been based, such an eventuality was impossible. The facts said it had happened. Therefore there was something greatly amiss with established theory.

Elizabeth and Charles had spent most of the previous day reviewing the physics of fusion plasmas in the light of Charles's newer theory, and had discovered some significant discrepancies. The compression of a target pellet to black-hole density was clearly predicted from Charles's equations, though for reasons that could never have been taken into account using conventional concepts. They had agreed that Elizabeth would have to inform the Burghead directors of the conclusions, and accordingly she had called the meeting for the afternoon of the following day. Charles had been reluctant to publicize details of his research if it could be avoided, and Elizabeth had therefore elected to try in the first instance to convince the directors of the facts without mentioning the Storbannon machine or its function. She knew that this would be a tough assignment, but she had to give it a try. The first indications at the meeting were that she was unlikely to enjoy much success.

Max Wehrbaum, from the EFC's Munich laboratories, was shaking his head and looking openly contemptuous. "What is all this talk about a fundamental flaw in the theory?" he demanded. "The theoretical foundations for fusion and plasma physics have been well understood for half a century. Where is there room for any kind of flaw?"

"I agree," Simon Vickers, Technical Director at Burghead and Elizabeth's immediate boss, said from Courtney's right. "Accepted theory appears to be more than amply validated. Experimental results have always been consistent with prediction, and there are machines working all over the world without problems." He shrugged. "We've got holes through the reactor casings that we can't explain yet, and some other people in other places have found a few holes here and there that they can't explain either. I don't see any compelling reason to assume that the two are

168

connected at all. It's certainly no reason to go tearing up physics all the way back to Galileo."

"There just isn't enough energy delivered to a pellet to get it anywhere near to black-hole density," somebody else threw in from the far side. "We all know that. It's elementary. Surely you're not suggesting that every scientist who's worked in the field over the last fifty years couldn't get a few sums right."

"Nobody has ever worked at the same combination of high energy and energy *density*," Elizabeth replied. "Plasma phase changes are notoriously nonlinear at high-density regimes. I'm saying that I suspect we have invalidly extrapolated lower energy-density results into a realm where they don't apply. The tests entered a completely new phenomenological region dominated by processes that we failed to anticipate."

"What kinds of processes?" Courtney asked dubiously. "Substantiated by what data? What reason is there for postulating processes that nobody's had any inkling of before? . . . As far as I'm aware, anyway." He glanced from side to side and was rewarded by a few solemn shakings of heads. "Nor anybody else by the look of it," he added.

"Oh, I can't describe them in precise detail at this stage," Elizabeth said. "But I contend we must assume they exist, and we should investigate them. Look at the map here. The plot passes right through Scotland . . . and the first incidents were reported within days of the tests here. Surely that tells us something."

She couldn't tell them that Charles had already determined where the flaw in conventional theory lay and explained how it was possible for the beams to crush the pellets to far higher densities than had been predicted. In the energy-dense core of the pellet, pair-production of electrons and positrons would be induced, followed by mutual annihilations sufficiently concentrated to generate minute tau waves; these tau waves would amplify rapidly as a consequence of a complicated, positive-feedback mechanism. The amplified tau waves would propagate out of the universe entirely, carrying away energy that should have been available to oppose the implosion. This process would invalidate the predictions of conventional theory completely by effectively increasing the beam-power in the core region by a factor of millions. Conventional theory took no account of tau waves.

"That track on the map is a pure fabrication." The speaker this time was Maria Galdarini from Turin, another member of the European delegation that was at Burghead that week to investigate the erosion problem. "There is only a handful of points on it. The trend is illusory. There's nothing but a scattering without any statistical significance at all."

"Anyway, besides all that, there's another thing," Simon Vickers added. "Even if we suppose for the moment that you are correct and these things are black holes, Elizabeth, they'd be microscopic. You said that yourself a few minutes ago. They'd be very short-lived because of Hawking radiation. They could never have continued to exist since January. But the latest bugophant was reported only a few days ago. So how could it have been a black hole that was produced here when we ran the tests? It's impossible."

Elizabeth had discussed this issue at great length with Charles as well. According to accepted quantum mechanics, a particle trapped inside a black hole had a certain probability of being able to "tunnel" its way out. The probability grew larger with particles that were more energetic, and with holes that were smaller. A small hole would therefore lose particles at a higher rate, and continue to do so in an accelerating fashion until the hole "evaporated." But accepted quantum mechanics failed to allow for the energy lost to the tau waves produced whenever a new particle fell in. Therefore the trapped particles would be left with less energy than accepted theory said. Therefore they would not be able to tunnel out as easily as accepted theory said. And that meant that the hole would last longer than accepted theory said.

"I do know about Hawking radiation," Elizabeth said. "All I can say is that if we did drive the plasma into a new region of nonlinearity, then we might be mistaken in assuming that we can apply the same concepts that work for other regions." None of the listeners appeared very convinced. What Elizabeth had said sounded too much like bending the facts to suit the answer, and she knew it.

"If such things ever existed, which to say the least is very unlikely in my opinion, then most of them will already have extinguished themselves," Max Wehrbaum declared. "After all, weren't there supposed to have been two million of them? Perhaps a few statistically extreme cases have survived for this long. If so, then in a few more days they will have disappeared too."

"So there's really no problem," Vickers said. "If we did manufacture them here, which I very much doubt, all we have to do is turn the wick down a bit when we get the reactors fixed." He paused and reconsidered his words for a moment, then looked up at Elizabeth. "I'm sorry. I didn't mean to sound flippant. Obviously if it did turn out that you were right, we'd all have some very serious problems to think about. It's just that . . . well, I can't see it . . . never in a million years." He shrugged, spread his hands, and left it at that. Elizabeth looked appealingly at Courtney.

"I'm sorry, Elizabeth," Courtney said in a regretful voice. "But I think we all agree with Simon. I must say, I wish you'd given me a better idea of what this was going to be about before we called this meeting. If you could show us something tangible to suggest even that what you've said is possible, let alone fact, then of course that would put an entirely different light on things. We'd have to reappraise the whole world fusion program from basics." He sighed and waved toward the map. "But we need something more convincing than that, I'm afraid. Until I've seen something that's more specific, I'm certainly not going to lose any sleep over it."

"Och, don't worry yourself about it," Charles said from the screen in Elizabeth's office a half hour later. "You did your best, and I appreciate it."

"So where do we go from here?" Elizabeth asked with a heavy sigh. "Are we going to have to tell them the whole story?"

"It looks like it, I'm afraid," Charles said. "I'll talk

to Ralph Courtney myself and see if I can come up and talk to him at Burghead. I'll probably bring Ted along with me as well."

Elizabeth bit her lip and looked unhappy at the idea. "Is it absolutely necessary?" she asked. "You know, I'm beginning to wonder if perhaps we're over-reacting a little bit. If the holes are going to disappear before much longer, what's the point in you coming up to Burghead to tell Ralph and the rest something that they'll find out eventually in their own time anyway? Why can't you simply stay out of it and leave them to it?"

Charles shook his head gravely.

"If I were certain that the holes will just go away, I'd do exactly that," he replied. "But I'm far from certain. I've been running the accretion functions all morning here with Murdoch. We're not sure yet whether or not some of the expressions are convergent so we can't be absolutely sure, but I'm beginning to suspect that the holes *won't* just go away. If the tau losses extend the lifetimes sufficiently for the accretion rate to overtake the Hawking depletion rate, the holes will become permanent. After that, they'll only be able to get bigger."

CHAPTER TWENTY-ONE

The results of Charles and Murdoch's attempt to calculate what would ultimately become of the miniature black holes were inconclusive. The two of them spent the rest of the day examining an alternative method, working through the evening and into the night with Lee to set up the equations in a form that could be submitted to the datagrid for analysis on the network computers. The task was long and arduous. At three o'clock in the morning, by which time the job was still a long way from being completed, they called a halt for the night. There was, after all, a limit.

Murdoch was just finishing a late breakfast in the kitchen the next morning, when Cartland ambled in holding a single sheet of glossy paper. Murdoch recognized it as hardcopy from one of the datagrid terminals, either the one in the lab or the one in Charles's study. Cartland looked around in mild surprise. "Where's Lee this morning?" he inquired.

"Still in bed," Murdoch answered. "I guess he overdid things a bit last night. He'll show up later. What's that you've got there?"

"Something I copied from the *News* about an hour ago. Thought you might know something about it. Even if you didn't, I presumed you'd be interested." Cartland slid the sheet across the table and watched while Murdoch took in the headline over a slice of toast and marmalade: MINISTER DENIES COVER-UP OF HEALTH HAZARD AT SCOTTISH FUSION PLANT. Murdoch moved his coffee cup to one side and drew the sheet nearer to him to scan the text. It read:

In answer to a question raised in the House yesterday, the Minister of Energy Utilisation and Power, Mr Stanley Newell, emphatically denied recent allegations that a hitherto unsuspected and hazardous form of radiation has been discovered, which originates in the process of nuclear fusion. The questioner, Mr Francis Booth, Conservative Member for Tyneside South, where a new fusion reactor is planned for completion in 2015, was referring to the claim made earlier this week by a spokesman for the anti-nuclear action-group 'Pandora' concerning the sudden outbreak of an as yet unidentified sickness among technical personnel at the Burghead plant, on the Solway Firth.

The EFC's Heavy-Ion Fusion Facility at Burghead, the world's largest project to date of its type, was completed last year. Since completion of the construction phase, trials have been continuing in preparation for the plant's scheduled commencement of full commercial operation in July. Within the last seven days, eight employees of the plant, all of them technical personnel who normally work in close proximity to the reactor vessels at the center of the facility, have been admitted to hospital suffering from the sudden onset of symptoms that have so far defied diagnosis. They appear to be associated with a malfunctioning of the central nervous system, the precise nature of which remains obscure. According to Pandora, a new type of hazardous radiation, originating in the fusion process, is responsible for the outbreak, details of which are being deliberately withheld following Government intervention.

In part of his statement in reply to these claims, Mr Newell said, "It is true that eight members of the Burghead technical staff have, within approximately the last week, become victims of an affliction which has not yet been positively identified. The suggestion, however, of this being a result of a form of radiation attributable to the fusion process and hitherto unknown to science, is utterly without foundation of any kind. This being so, the further suggestion, that information pertaining to such mythical radiation is being withheld from the public domain as part of a conspiracy of silence between certain unnamed departments of His Majesty's Government and the governments of other Consortium nations, is ludicrous in the extreme."

Dr M. J. Waring, Head of the Burghead facility's Medical Department, told our reporter during a videocall interview, "Nothing that we have observed is even remotely suggestive of the effects of radiation-induced phenomena. Thank you. That is all I have to say."

Dr Elizabeth Muir, Principal Physicist at Burghead, was stated as being in conference yesterday afternoon and unavailable for comment.

The report went on to give a canned history of the Burghead plant and a few details of its planned schedule for the coming months. Interestingly, Murdoch noted, there was no mention of the erosion problem, which had already made nonsense of the planned schedule.

"No, I hadn't heard about this," Murdoch said when he had finished reading. "That place must have a jinx on it. As if they didn't have enough problems already."

"I'm surprised Anne never mentioned anything about it," Cartland remarked. "What's the matter with you two? Don't you talk to each other these days?"

"Oh, sure we do," Murdoch told him, missing the

tone of voice. "I guess it's just doctors' professional ethics: They don't like talking about things like that." He rubbed his chin thoughtfully. "Unless of course there *is* something funny going on that she's been told not to talk about."

"That's what I was wondering," Cartland said. "Do you think it could have anything to do with these bugger-whatsits? You know—possible focusing of the orbits at the point of origin or something like that."

Murdoch thought for a moment while he finished the last of his toast. "I can't see it," he said. "The doctors would have known if they were bugophants, but from what it says here, it sounds like something completely different. More likely somebody shipped Burghead a case of lousy salmon."

"Unless somebody somewhere didn't want people connecting bugophants with Burghead," Cartland suggested. "Maybe they took Elizabeth more seriously than she thought."

"That's a thought." Murdoch frowned and drummed his fingers on the table. "I wonder . . ." He glanced across at the newssheet again and then looked up. "Do you think Anne might say something about it if I called her? She's bound to know more about what's going on than whoever wrote this. Now it's in the news, she might be in more of a mind to talk about it."

"You tell me, old boy," Cartland answered.

Murdoch downed the last of his coffee and got up from the table. "I'll call her right away," he said as he headed for the door.

"Oh, don't tell me!" Anne exclaimed from the vi-set in the sitting room a few minutes later. "We've had every neurotic and freak in the country calling us. Just now I had a little old lady from somewhere saying it was caused by breathing in neutrons. She'd read all about them. She was sure that if we all wore surgical masks soaked in lemon juice, it wouldn't happen again. Just trying to help, I suppose, but we really could do without it. Dr. Waring has refused to talk to any more of them, so guess who's getting it all."

"But what is it?" Murdoch asked. "All I've seen is

what Ted just showed me. Has it got anything to do with the reactors?"

Anne glanced off-screen and lowered her voice instinctively. "I can't really say very much right now. I'll talk to you about it when I see you at Storbannon tomorrow. We don't know what it is, but it's almost certainly viral so you can forget all this nonsense that's being talked about it having anything to do with fusion. In some ways it resembles a highly virulent and extraordinarily accelerated form of multiple sclerosis. None of the experts we've talked to have heard of anything like it before."

"So how come all the people who've got it just happen to work in the central reactor complex?" Murdoch asked. "That sounds like too much of a coincidence. . . . Or isn't it true?"

Anne sighed. "Yes, it's true. But there must be some other factor they all have in common that's less obvious. The records are being processed to see what else there is that correlates with what; also we're doing a check through London to find out if anything similar has been identified anywhere else. But at the moment, it's still a mystery. There's—" She glanced away again. Her expression changed, and she turned back apologetically. "Oh dear, something's just cropped up. Murdoch, I'll have to go. Sorry. I'll call you back later when it's not so busy." At that moment a flashing red caption appeared across the screen, superposed on Anne's face, to announce: URGENT CALL HOLDING.

"Something's waiting to come in here too," Murdoch said. "Talk to you later, okay?"

"As soon as I can." Anne's face vanished in a blaze of colors that promptly reassembled themselves into the features of a well-groomed woman, neatly dressed, and somewhere in her mid-forties.

"Hello," she said. "This is Mr. Courtney's assistant calling from EFC, Burghead. Could I speak to Sir Charles Ross, please?"

"Sure," Murdoch replied. "Hold on a moment. I'll have to transfer you." He tapped in a code to route the call to Charles's study, waited for the *Accepted* indicator to light up at the bottom of the screen, and cleared down. If the call meant what he thought it meant, Charles would probably be going up to Burghead to see Courtney later that day. That meant there would no doubt be a panic to get the analysis up and running on the datagrid before Charles went. Murdoch sighed. It was going to be another one of those days. He walked out of the sitting room and went upstairs to pull Lee out of bed.

It was approaching lunchtime when Murdoch entered the lab with the latest set of numbers that Charles had produced upstairs in the study. He found Lee slumped back in the chair at the desk, screwing his face into knots and rubbing his eyelids with his thumb and fingers. Lee stopped and blinked uncertainly over his hands at the piles of hardcopy and flowcharts strewn around him.

"Seeing code on the walls?" Murdoch said with a grin. "I'm not surprised."

"Huh?" Lee looked up, aware of Murdoch's presence for the first time. "Oh, hi, Doc. Yeah . . . I guess I've been hitting it a bit hard. Maybe I need lenses. It all went hazy for a while."

"Are you okay?" The grin vanished abruptly from Murdoch's face.

"Oh, sure. . . . Seems to have cleared itself up now."

"How are we doing?"

"Just about there. All I need now are some boundary parameters that Charles was working on upstairs, and it should be all set to run."

"I've got 'em here," Murdoch said. "Grandpa and Ted are taking off for Burghead now. They're leaving us to get the analysis running. How long do you figure from now?"

"Aw . . . say an hour or two to check through the program . . . allow a little bit for bugs . . . I think we should have it into the network and running by midafternoon."

"And how long to run?"

"Oh . . ." Lee thought for a second. "If the network loading is about what it usually is on Friday afternoons, I'd say six, maybe seven hours."

"We should know by tonight then, huh?"

"Guess so."

A short silence followed. Murdoch put the sheet of figures down on the desk and sat back on the edge of the main console. "And what if the *eta* derivative comes out positive?" he asked at last.

"Then there won't be a darn thing anybody can do about it," Lee said slowly.

There were more errors in the program than they had expected, which was unusual for Lee, but by five o'clock the job was at last loaded into the datagrid via the terminal in the lab. Lee was feeling fatigued by this time and went upstairs to lie down for a few hours to catch up on the sleep he had lost the previous night.

Shortly afterward, Murdoch was walking past the door of Charles's room when Robert came out, evidently in a hurry, carrying some of Charles's shirts in one hand and a brown leather traveling bag in the other.

"What gives?" Murdoch inquired.

"Och, I wish I knew," Robert replied. "There's an awful fuss suddenly broken out about something. Your grandfather called about ten minutes ago from Burghead. Himself and Mr. Cartland are going to Brussels tonight with some of the directors on the seven-fifteen flight from Edinburgh. I don't know what's going on, I'm sure."

"They'll never make it," Murdoch said flatly. "It's almost six now."

"Burghead are flying them to the airport in one of their airbuses. They're on their way here now to pick up some things."

"Want a hand with that stuff?"

"Ah, it's good of you to offer, but you've work enough of your own to be worrying about today," Robert said.

"We're through," Murdoch told him. "I'm on free time now. Here, I'll take those things. How long have we got?"

Twenty minutes later, Murdoch and Robert were standing in one corner of the tennis court with a small pile of bags, watching a black dot grow in the sky above the crestline of Ben Moroch's southwest ridge. The dot gradually took on the shape of a short-haul VTOL transporter, slowed to a halt two hundred feet over their heads, and then descended smoothly to land in the center of the court. Before the last whines of its engines had died away, a door opened and Cartland jumped out. He ran over to help with the luggage as Murdoch and Robert approached, and at the same time Charles appeared in the frame of the doorway.

"They're convinced," Charles yelled down before Murdoch could ask anything. "We're meeting some of the EFC people in Brussels tomorrow morning. It should be quite a party. They're flying in from all over Europe tonight."

"On Saturday morning?" Murdoch said, surprised.

"That's the only time you'll get them all together at this kind of short notice," Charles told him. "How did it go this afternoon?"

"Okay. It's running now. There were a couple of bugs though, so it won't complete until sometime late tonight."

"Call us in the morning with the results," Charles said. "We'll be at EFC Headquarters from ten o'clock onward. Ask for Claude Montassier. Got that?"

"Where will you be staying tonight?" Murdoch asked. "I could call you there."

"I don't know. Somebody will be meeting us off the plane. They're arranging all that."

The pilot appeared from somewhere at the nose end and took the last of the bags from Robert to hoist it aboard. "That the lot?" Cartland said, getting ready to climb back inside. "Good show. Thanks for the effort, chaps. Well, I suppose we'd better be toddling along. No time for tea and all that."

Elizabeth squeezed into the doorway from behind Charles. "Hello, Murdoch," she said. "Hello, Robert. It looks as if the cat's really among the pigeons now."

"Glad it worked out," Murdoch said. "I guess they're not so mad now about having their time wasted yesterday, huh?"

"No. They see things a bit differently now. Well, we'll see you when we see you."

"Sure. Have a good trip. I'll call you tomorrow."

"Aye, thanks a lot, Murdoch," Charles called out as he moved back inside to make room for Cartland. "I don't know when we'll be back. It all depends on how it goes." Cartland climbed in. The pilot closed the door and disappeared in the direction of the nose. A minute later the engine started, its sound swelled to a loud note, and the VTOL lifted off. Murdoch and Robert watched as it climbed and turned southward across the glen, and then they turned and began walking back to the house.

As soon as they got inside, Morna informed Murdoch that Anne was holding on the vi-set in the sitting room. Murdoch went on through and saw that Anne was wearing a white coat and was framed by the familiar background of her office at Burghead.

"Still working?" he asked in surprise.

"It's been absolutely hectic all day. That's why I didn't call back earlier," she told him. "I'm just about to leave. Is everything still okay for tomorrow?"

"It's all changed. Things have been hectic here too. Grandpa and Ted have had to make a rush trip to Belgium. In fact they just left here a few minutes ago in an EFC jet. I guess dinner tomorrow's off. There's no reason why you shouldn't still come down though."

"Yes, I'd like to," Anne said. "In fact, if your grandfather and Ted are away, maybe we could go out somewhere tonight. You've had a hard day, and I've had a hard day. Why don't we both relax and have a break?"

"Great idea. I could use one. Where? Any suggestions?"

"How about that place in Tomatin we tried the other week? It's about halfway in between. And why not bring Lee as well? It would be better than leaving him stuck on his own down there."

"Okay. I'll have to wake him up later. He's been burning it at both ends lately and has gone to sleep it off. We'll see you at about what . . . eight, say?"

180

"Just what I was going to say." Anne smiled suddenly and looked pleased. "I'll have to go home and change first. See you at eight." She blew him a kiss, and the screen went blank.

CHAPTER TWENTY-TWO

"It seems to be some kind of sudden deterioration of the myelin insulating sheaths around the nerve fibers of the brain and spinal cord," Anne said, keeping her voice low. "The same kind of thing happens with multiple sclerosis, but that usually takes years to develop. Whatever this is takes hold in a week or two." Murdoch listened from across the booth while he finished his soup. Beside him Lee, who had declined a starter, was staring morosely at the wall and saying very little.

"And nobody's got any clues what's causing it?" Murdoch asked.

Anne hesitated for an instant longer than was natural before shaking her head. "Not as far as I'm aware anyway," she said.

Murdoch caught the curious inflexion of her voice. "How do you mean?" he asked.

"There's something very strange about the whole business," Anne replied, speaking in a low, confidential tone. She paused. Murdoch said nothing. She went on, "I don't know . . . I just get the feeling that there's more to it behind the scenes than is being talked about."

"How come?"

"Strange things happening lately . . . such as lots of scrambled calls coming in for Dr. Waring from various government departments that shouldn't be interested in anything like this."

"Like who?"

"Oh . . ." Anne thought for a second. "Eurospace Medicine at Farnborough, NASA at Washington . . . the Soviet Aerospace Ministry. Why would people like that be interested in a small-scale outbreak of an unidentified sickness in Scotland?"

"Search me." Murdoch shook his head and spread his hands helplessly.

"See the kind of thing I mean," Anne said. "And then we've got a mysterious visitor who keeps turning up to talk to Dr. Waring. And he spends a lot of time at the Infirmary in Glasgow, which is where the cases were sent."

"What kind of visitor?" Murdoch asked, becoming more baffled by the whole thing.

"His name is Sir Giles Fennimore. He's quite famous—a specialist in viral DNA manipulation and an advisor to the Government on genetic engineering legislation. Why would somebody like that be involved with this?"

Again Murdoch could only shake his head. "And that's all you know? No other clues at all, huh?"

"There was one thing I was going to ask you," Anne replied. "What's the *Centurion Satellite?* Have you heard of it?"

"Centurion?"

"That was what it sounded like."

"I've no idea," Murdoch confessed. "Why? Where does that come into it?"

"It was something I accidentally heard them talking about yesterday," Anne said. "They mentioned something that sounded like *Centurion Satellite.* I was curious about what it was."

"What did they say about it? Anything more?"

"I didn't hear any more. It was just a split-second before they closed the door."

"It's a pity Ted isn't here," Murdoch remarked. "He'd know for sure."

They lapsed into silence for a while. Anne looked quizzically at Lee, but he seemed lost in a world of his own and made no response. She looked back at Murdoch.

"Anyhow, I'm tired of being cross-examined," she said. "Now it's your turn. You haven't told me what's going on in Belgium yet. What's this sudden panic all about?"

Murdoch frowned to himself and bought time by breaking a roll and buttering one of the pieces. He didn't want to say anything about the black holes yet, at least not until he had some firm answers from the analysis running in the datagrid. "It was something to do with the erosion in the reactors," he said at last. At least, that wasn't really a lie. "The fusion products at the high energy-densities attained in the tests weren't exactly what they were supposed to be." That certainly wasn't a lie either. "They've gone to the EFC HQ in Brussels to tell the Consortium scientists about the latest findings."

Anne looked at him suspiciously. "Is that all? I wouldn't have thought that your grandfather would have anything to do with something like that." She went quiet for a few seconds. Murdoch chewed a piece of roll and said nothing. "The only work that your grandfather is involved with these days is the machine," Anne went on, talking half to herself. "How could that have any connection with the reactors at Burghead? . . ." Her voice trailed away for a few seconds. She fingered a button on the front of her dress, and her eyes narrowed slowly. "Unless, maybe, the machine somehow picked up something that the reactors radiated. . . . But how could that be? The machine picks up time waves."

Murdoch looked away in despair; she was ninety percent of the way there already. His eye fell upon a group of four men talking around the table in one of the corner booths. Two of the faces were familiar; the other two were not.

"Don't look around," he murmured.

"What is it?"

"There are some mutual friends in the corner . . . pal Trevor and one of his buddies. They're with a couple of other guys I don't know."

"There's no reason why they should bother us," Anne said.

"I know," Murdoch replied. "But why risk making it look like an invitation?"

"I can see them in the mirror on the end wall," Anne remarked after a few seconds. "The other one is Nick. I don't know who the other two are. I'm sure they're not Burghead people though."

"Trust them to pick this place."

"They know we're here," Anne said, still watching

the mirror. "Trevor just pointed in this direction while he was talking." Murdoch moved his head so that he could watch from the corner of his eye without staring directly. One of the strangers turned his head to look back over his shoulder for a moment, then faced back toward Trevor and nodded. Murdoch kept his eyes averted.

"Raincoats," Anne mused absently.

"Huh?"

"There are raincoats on the seat next to them."

"So?"

"On a day in May like this? I'd say they're traveling quite a long way from home . . . probably for the whole day, wouldn't you?"

"Who cares?" Murdoch said with a shrug.

"And we're right on the main road going south," Anne went on, taking no notice. "I bet those two have been at the plant today. They could be on their way back to Edinburgh, maybe to the airport. Trevor and Nick both live near here. They probably arranged to meet them here for some reason. One of them has been using a pocket recorder too. I can see it under his elbow."

"Aw, lay off," Murdoch told her. "Who cares what the hell somebody in—"

"Ah hah!" Anne said suddenly. "I bet I know what it is. Do you remember Sam, that other friend of Trevor's, who was in the Bull that night Lee was getting mad? He was one of the eight who were hospitalized in Glasgow. I bet those two are reporters from somewhere, looking for the inside story."

"Save it," Murdoch said. "They're coming over."

The first of the pair was overweight, and strode toward the booth with a ponderous, self-assertive gait. He sat down and squeezed in next to Anne without waiting to be asked, smiling broadly and flashing a press card. His partner was smaller, thin-faced, and had a curt, no-nonsense air about him; he moved a nearby chair across and sat down at the end of the table.

"You don't mind if we join you for a minute, do you," the first opened. His voice was firm and presumptuous. "Joe Gowling, United News Services, London. This is Harry Squires. We're covering the story of what's gone wrong at Burghead . . . the *real* story from the inside," he added with a knowing wink. "I understand from your friends back there that this lady is a doctor at Burghead." He turned to Anne, still smiling. "Is that right? Miss Patterson, isn't it? Or can we all be friends and make it Anne?" Gowling saw Anne catch her breath and raised a hand to stifle her protest. "Don't worry. It'll only take a minute or two. That's not much to ask out of anyone's life, is it?"

Anne shook her head and looked imploringly at Murdoch. "Oh, not now," she said. "I've had more than enough of this whole thing all week."

"Sorry," Murdoch said shortly. "This is a private party. We're done with work now."

Gowling's smile only broadened further. "I understand, lads. We don't want to take up your whole evening. Just five minutes, okay?" He turned to face Anne again. "Now, Anne, you must have been one of the first to see every new case. What kind of symptoms did these people have when they were first brought in? Were they dizzy, sick, anything like that . . . or what? Were there any external signs of the kind you'd expect from radiation—rashes, burns, or anything similar?" At the end of the table, Squires switched on the recorder he was holding and set it down on the corner between himself and Murdoch.

"The official spokesman on medical matters at the facility is Dr. Waring," Anne said wearily. "You should speak to him on Monday. I'm not in any position to give you any official quotes."

"But you must know," Gowling insisted. "All we want—"

"Look, I've already said this is private," Murdoch cut in. "We haven't got anything for you. Why not just do as she says and let us enjoy our meal."

"You can't get near Waring," Gowling replied. "We tried today. He won't even take calls about it."

"That's tough," Murdoch said. "Maybe when he's got something to say, he'll say it. You can quote us on that. Now would you leave us alone, please." He sounded impatient.

Gowling's smile faded. "Aw, come on, pal," he said.

"Be reasonable. We've got a job to do too. The public has a right to know the facts. If it's all been a bit exaggerated, this is a chance for you to help straighten things out. If it hasn't been exaggerated, the people should know. If you don't say anything, that makes it all sound as if there *is* something to cover up. Know what I mean?"

"BURGHEAD DOCTOR FAILS TO DENY FUSION RADIATION HAZARD," Squires shot at them, looking up suddenly. "See, it doesn't sound good. You're better off telling us about what you do know, even if your account does have some gaps in. We'll worry about filling those in. That's our job."

Gowling had stretched out an arm and was about to take a cracker from the dish in the center of the table. Murdoch moved the dish away pointedly and set it down out of reach. "I don't seem to be getting through to you two," he said. "I've already told you twice that this is private, and we're not answering questions. I'll say it plainer: Beat it. You're annoying us."

Gowling's expression darkened. He didn't reply, but turned his head away to talk directly to Anne, making it plain that he considered the conversation to be none of Murdoch's business.

"You're a doctor," Gowling said. "You understand all about obligations, right? Well, you've got an obligation to the public who pay your salary. You owe it to them to— What the . . . ?" He swung his head around sharply as Murdoch picked up the recorder from the corner of the table, ejected its magnetic cartridge into his hand, and held it over the candle flame, destroying whatever was stored on it.

Squires snatched frantically to retrieve the tape but was too slow. "You had no right to do that!" Squires snapped angrily.

"That information was public property," Gowling seethed. "Can't you see how bad this will read now? Use your head. You've still got a chance to put it straight."

Behind them the restaurant manager appeared, attracted by the rising voices and the flare of the plastic coating on the outside of the cartridge. Heads began turning to look in their direction from the surrounding booths and tables. The manager hovered uncertainly, as if hoping that his presence might be sufficient to calm things down.

Murdoch turned his head to look up over the back of the booth. "Could you get these two bums away from our table? We don't know who they are, they're bothering us, and all we want to do is have a meal. Otherwise call the police."

The manager moved nearer reluctantly and looked from Gowling to Squires. "I'm sorry, but if you two gentlemen wouldn't mind returning to—" he began, but a sudden gasp from Anne interrupted him.

"Murdoch! Look. . . ."

Murdoch jerked his head around to find Anne staring with horrified eyes at where Lee was sitting. He turned fully to follow her gaze. At the same instant the vague thought flitted through his mind that Lee, in a way that was completely out of character, had not been reacting to the hostile exchange at all.

Lee seemed to be unaware of anything around him. He was clutching a glass of water with his arm half raised above the table. His arm was convulsing in short, irregular spasms from the elbow, causing water to spill onto the tablecloth; Lee was staring at it with a stupefied expression, as if it had suddenly acquired a will of its own and was defying his attempts to bring it under control. His jaw tightened visibly as he made a concentrated effort. The glass shattered on the table, and his fingers went limp among the pieces. A trickle of blood ran out from under his hand and began soaking into the white cloth.

"Lee, what is it?" Murdoch said, alarmed. Lee remained staring blankly in front of him. Anne waved her hand to and fro in front of his eyes. They didn't blink.

"I don't think he can see anything," she whispered, and then more loudly, "Lee . . . Lee, can you hear me?" No response. Murdoch stared aghast, not knowing quite what to do.

"He's sick," Anne said in a worried voice. "Very sick. We have to get him to hospital." She looked up at the manager, who was about to say something.

"I'm a doctor. Can we get him out of the restaurant and have an ambulance here as quickly as possible, please? Also I need to use a phone."

"There's an armchair in my office," the manager replied. He turned to one of the waitresses who had appeared behind him. "Peggy, ask Mrs. Graham to call for an ambulance right away, would you. When she gets through, she's to put the call through to my office. Ask her to tell them that we have a doctor on the premises who will be able to give them whatever information they need. Hurry along now."

Anne got up to leave the booth. Gowling, now suddenly subdued, heaved himself out and stood back to make room while Squires got up to get out of Murdoch's way.

Anne lifted Lee's hand gently from the broken glass and swathed it in a napkin. As she did so, his arm began twitching uncontrollably again, and he mumbled fragments of words that made no sense. "You'll have to give me a hand," she said, glancing at Murdoch and the manager. "He'll probably need supporting. I think his balance will be affected too."

Between them they half led and half carried Lee from the restaurant while the shocked silence that had descended slowly gave way to a normal level of noise as people resumed eating and talking. In the office they sat Lee back in the armchair, and Anne loosened his shirt collar and belt. Then she produced a small, black leather wallet from somewhere inside her pocketbook.

She took a plastic packet from the wallet and unsealed it to expose a thin adhesive disk with a blob of what looked like yellow gelatin at its center, protected by a translucent film. She peeled the film away and placed the disk firmly over an artery on the side of Lee's neck. As the drug penetrated his skin and entered the bloodstream, the convulsions in his limbs died away, and his body fell limp. Anne felt inside his jacket and passed his wallet to Murdoch.

"See if you can find his social security number," she said. "They'll need it to access his records in the U.S. Health Department databank."

"Is there anything I can do?" the manager asked.

"If you could get somebody to bring in some clean water for that hand, it would help," Anne said, moving an upright chair underneath Lee's feet. "Also we'll need an area cleared in the car park for the ambulance to land."

"I'll see to it right away," the manager said, and left the office.

Anne produced a penlamp from her pocketbook and lifted each of Lee's eyelids in turn to examine the pupils. She tested his pulse at the temple, and then lifted one of his arms to feel for stiffness in the elbow, hand, and fingers. Just as she was finishing this, the call-tone sounded from the vi-set on the desk behind her. It was a gray-haired woman, presumably the one the manager had referred to as Mrs. Graham.

"I have the Emergency Unit at Inverness Hospital on the line," the woman said.

"Thank you," Anne acknowledged. "And would you try another call for me? I'd like you to call the Royal Infirmary at Glasgow, if you would. Ask to be put through to a Dr. Fisher in Intensive Care Special Isolation. If he's not available tonight, then I'll talk to whoever is on duty there."

"I'll put the call through as soon as I get them," Mrs. Graham said, and vanished. A second later she had been replaced by a young woman wearing a white coat, who announced that she was speaking from the Emergency Unit.

"Hello," Anne said to her. "My name is Patterson, Dr. Patterson. I'm at the Clansman Restaurant at Tomatin on the Kingussie road south from Inverness. We need an ambulance here right away."

"Very good," the woman replied. "Can you give me some information?"

"A man has collapsed here and needs hospital treatment immediately. I've administered a diffusive tranquilizer. This is important: He must be taken to the Special Isolation section of the Intensive Care Unit at Glasgow Royal. They are familiar with this kind of case there." Murdoch stared at Anne in horror as he listened. She went on, "The patient is a United States citizen by the name of . . ." She took the papers that Murdoch was proffering numbly and scanned them.

"Lee Francis Walker; last residing at 236 Bayview Towers, San Francisco; social security number 101-58-1453."

"His records to be beamed through to Glasgow?" the woman inquired.

"Yes, please. And could you arrange for the ambulance to bring a supply of Sotisone 5 and Formactinin. We're clearing a landing area here, and we'll have a car transmitting on Emergency Band for the ambulance to home on."

"Very good, Dr. Patterson. They'll be leaving immediately."

"Thank you." Anne cut the call and turned to Murdoch, who was still watching speechlessly. Her face was grave. "Has he been drowsy for the last day or two?" she asked. "Lack of energy, sleeping a lot . . . temporary blurrings of vision?"

"Yes . . . he has," Murdoch mumbled. "I thought he'd been working too hard."

"Fits of giddiness? Difficulty in coordinating movements?"

"He never mentioned anything like that, but then he isn't the kind of guy who would." He swallowed hard. "You've seen this before, haven't you? It's the same thing you've been getting at the plant."

Before Anne could reply, the call-tone sounded again. This time the call was put straight through, and showed a swarthy, gray-bearded man dressed in what looked like a surgical smock. "Dr. Patterson," he said at once. "Surely you're not still working at this time on a Friday."

"Hello, Dr. Ellis. No, I'm not, but we have an emergency that I'm arranging to be sent straight to you. His name is Lee Walker. You'll be getting all the details soon via computer from Inverness. An ambulance is on its way here to collect him."

Ellis's expression became more serious. "How positive is it?" he asked. "Has voluntary motor deterioration set in yet?"

"Possibly incipient. The diagnosis is tentative at this stage, but I don't want to take any chances. Listlessness and lethargy for the last two days, temporary visual disturbances, and suspected giddiness. Right now we have complete loss of vision, extreme dilation of pupils, and no stimulus responses; involuntary contractions of right arm and partial loss of control of lower limbs; pulse fifty-four; skin cold and moist; stiffening of hands and arms under sedation."

Ellis listened and nodded his head slowly.

"It could be another one, right enough," he said. "Very well. I'll have them prepare for reception right away."

CHAPTER TWENTY-THREE

It was one-thirty in the morning when Murdoch and Anne came out of a side door of the Glasgow Royal Infirmary and trudged across the almost empty parking lot to his car. A wind was beginning to blow from the west, and it was just starting to rain. Anne had flown to Glasgow with Lee in the ambulance; Murdoch had driven, leaving Anne's car at the restaurant in Tomatin to be collected later.

In the Intensive Care Unit of the Infirmary, Ellis had confirmed Anne's suspicions and admitted Lee to the Special Isolation section, where the other cases from Burghead were interned. Ellis had also mentioned to them in confidence that the most recent reports from London had revealed a flood of identical cases appearing in many parts of the world, but especially in the West Coast region of the United States. The victims were from all walks of life, and it seemed safe to conclude that whatever the cause of the sickness was, it had nothing to do with working around fusion reactors. If anything, the common link seemed to be that all of the victims had been in the western United States around eight months previously; Lee, for example, had been living there, and the eight from Burghead had all been members of a party that had spent some time in California in early September as part of an exchange program of European and American fusion scientists. From what had been learned so far from the earlier cases, Lee's condition could be expected to deteriorate rapidly toward total disruption of the central nervous system. To date there had been no fatalities, but all the signs pointed inevitably in that direction, probably within several weeks. As far as Ellis knew, the cause had still not been identified, and no cure was even remotely in sight. There was nothing more that anybody could do.

Murdoch was still shaky from the shock when he climbed into the car next to Anne and closed the door. He sat for a long time, staring out at the streetlamps through the streaky patterns of rain and dust on the windshield. The occasional lights from traffic passing by outside the Infirmary grounds added to the bleakness and emptiness of the scene. And the emptiness of Storbannon would be even worse to return to. Tonight of all nights, he didn't want to be alone. Even as he thought it, he felt Anne's hand close around his in the darkness of the car. He turned his head and saw that she was watching him.

"We can pick my car up tomorrow," she whispered simply. Murdoch barely nodded by way of reply. There was no need to say anything.

They arrived at Storbannon, tired and exhausted, in the early hours of the morning. Despite the events that had taken place that night, one thing couldn't be allowed to wait. When they walked in, Murdoch told Anne that there was something of crucial importance that he would have to check in the lab.

"You look as if you could do with a strong coffee," Anne said as they hung their coats on the pegs inside the main entrance. "Would you like me to make some?"

"Good idea," Murdoch told her. "Black with plenty of sugar."

"You go on down to the lab. I'll bring it when it's ready." Anne disappeared in the direction of the kitchen, and Murdoch hurried downstairs.

As he switched on the lights in the lab, a sleepy-eyed Maxwell detached himself from the shadows in the doorway and followed him in. "Getting lonely, huh, little fella?" Murdoch grunted as he sat down at the datagrid terminal to access the results file of the analysis. Maxwell rubbed himself against Murdoch's ankle and began purring. Murdoch smiled faintly and turned his eyes away as the screen in front of him filled with mathematical expressions. He scanned down them, and then pulled over a pile of hardcopy that Charles and he had used earlier to set up the equations. He began following through the sheets to interpret the results being presented on the screen.

How does a man feel when he finds the end of the world staring him in the face?

Murdoch just stared numbly at the screen, unable to think, unable to move, unable to feel anything. But for him the shock was not total; he had been half prepared for it all along.

The black holes were not going to evaporate.

The loss of energy through tau radiation would sustain them until they became permanent. Then they would grow. As they lost orbital momentum, they would spiral toward the Earth's core, eventually coalescing into larger black holes . . . which would continue to draw in matter and grow even faster. There was insufficient information to determine exactly how quickly the process would accelerate or how long it would go on—maybe months, years, tens of years, or perhaps even longer—but the final result at the end of it would be inevitable:

Eventually they would consume the whole planet.

It was unstoppable, and irreversible. There was no other way it could end.

"Murdoch, what's the matter?" Anne's voice came suddenly from the doorway. She sounded worried. Murdoch looked up slowly and turned his head toward her, but his eyes seemed to be staring straight through.

"Sit down, Anne," he said in a dull, heavy voice. "I guess it's time I told you about what else has been happening at Burghead."

CHAPTER TWENTY-FOUR

"There isn't any way they can be stopped," Murdoch said wearily. "At least, assuming these calculations are correct. We didn't spend time double-checking everything, and we had to make a few assumptions that might be suspect, but right now that's the way it looks."

"You can't be absolutely certain, then," Anne said. She had recovered somewhat from the impact of Murdoch's revelation, although her face was still pale and her voice shaky.

"No," Murdoch admitted. "Not absolutely." His tone said that he was convinced in his own mind nevertheless. A silence descended. Murdoch returned his attention to the curves and numbers that he had been manipulating on the main screen of the machine's console throughout the hour or so that he and Anne had been talking. At intervals he had lapsed into long periods of staring silently and thoughtfully at the displays, but so far he had not told Anne anything of the idea that was beginning to form in his mind.

Anne sat back in her chair with a long, despairing sigh, and tried again to grasp the enormity of what Murdoch had told her. The whole history of the human species was nothing but the tail-end of the saga of the birth and shaping of the Earth itself. Even the story of life was but the final page to be added to the book that had been written so far. It was as if the whole, intricate, billions-of-years-long process had been simply preparation for the story that would begin when mankind at last appeared upon the stage. And now, with the first few lines of the opening act barely completed, the story would never be told. All that would be left to mark that it had ever begun would be a knot of deformed spacetime orbiting the sun.

She looked at Murdoch, still working silently and intently at the console, not knowing what to make of the strange change that she had sensed coming over him in the course of the last hour. An hour ago he had been resigned to the hopelessness of everything; now his mood seemed determined and purposeful. Anne sensed that it was not a time to press him with questions. She waited.

At last Murdoch sat back in the chair and stared for a long time at the data being displayed on the main screen. Then, without turning his head to look at her, he asked, "Anne, can you program one of these computers?"

Anne's forehead creased in bewilderment. "I've worked with DEC 22/40s and 43s," she replied. "Software-wise they're the same as a 30. Why?" Murdoch did not answer directly. Instead he swiveled his chair around to face where she was sitting. There was a strange, distant look in his eyes, one that Anne had never seen before.

"There's no way that a black hole can be destroyed once it's grown large enough to be stable," he said. "From that point on, nothing you do can get rid of it."

Anne shrugged. "I know. So there's nothing anybody can do to change things now."

"There is," Murdoch said. "The phrase I used was: '. . . *from that point on.* . . .'" For a few seconds Anne was completely mystified. Then her expression changed slowly to one of disbelief. She gasped, and moved her eyes involuntarily from Murdoch to the machine beside him.

Murdoch nodded. "Exactly!" he told her. "There is something we can do. We can change what happened *before those damn holes were ever created in the first place!*"

Anne shook her head as she tried to understand what Murdoch was saying. After everything he had said in the last hour, this was too much.

"It's the *only* way," Murdoch said. "Nothing else could make any difference now."

"The machine?" she whispered. "You think we could use the machine to change what's happened?"

"Why not?"

"But . . . but to do that, you'd have to have the reactor tests stopped right at the beginning."

"Yes."

Anne rested her face in her hands while she reached through her mind for something she might have missed. At last she looked up. "But how?" she asked. "The machine only has a range of one day."

"I know."

"The tests were run in January. How can we possibly do anything that will change that?" Anne protested.

"By using the machine as a *relay*," Murdoch said.

Anne sank back and waved her hand in front of her face. "I don't know what you're talking about, Murdoch. What are you talking about?"

"The machine that's here today can send a message back to itself yesterday," Murdoch said. "That one could relay the same message back to the machine that existed the day before that. It could chain back like that for as far as we wanted it to go." Anne's mind began spinning. She stared from Murdoch to the machine and back again, but could find nothing wrong with what he had said. In fact it now seemed obvious.

Murdoch started speaking again, this time more rapidly and with a note of urgency in his voice. "To get in all the information needed about the black holes, we'd have to send a succession of screens full of data that would all arrive in sequence and remain imprinted on the restructured timeline. That means they'd have to be sent simultaneously in supertime from a series of points along the timeline we're on now. Fortunately we know from the shortening-loop tests how to set up a transmission-control program that will accomplish that.

"Another snag is that the machines that exist on the present timeline yesterday and the days before all the way back to January don't have a program in them that will read in an incoming message and retransmit it back down the line. So what we need to do is set up a bootstrap: a set of machine instructions that can be sent on ahead as the first signal to read in the main program. Then the whole package will copy itself all the way through in one-day jumps to January. All we can do after that is hope to God that somebody back there takes notice of it."

Anne's expression had been changing while Murdoch was talking. His scheme was feasible, she realized. In terms of technique, it was identical to the method of down-line-loading used for sending a program out to another part of a computer network and starting it running in a remote machine; the only difference was that, in the case that Murdoch had described, the program would be bootstrapped through a time-link rather than over a conventional optical cable or a laser beam.

"I think you've got something, Murdoch," she whispered, nodding slowly at last. "It could just work, couldn't it. . . ." Her voice rose to a normal level. "It might work. We'll have to put it to Charles and Ted when they get back. I'm sure that—" She broke off as she saw the look on Murdoch's face. Her face became puzzled. "Why not? Surely we've got to tell them about it."

Murdoch half turned and gestured toward the screen on the console. "We can't wait for them to get back," he said. "We don't have any time."

Anne was nonplussed. "What do you mean? I thought you said there was no immediate hazard."

"There isn't," Murdoch said. "But it's got nothing to do with that. We've only got something like twelve hours left in which we can use the machine. If we don't do it in that time, we'll never be able to do it at all." Anne threw out her hands and shook her head in noncomprehension.

"I've been monitoring the noise background here," Murdoch explained. "There are something like two million black holes down there, consuming mass and radiating tau waves all the time. The machine is picking up the radiation from a few days ahead of now as background noise." He took a deep breath. His voice was sounding hoarse. "The holes are getting bigger, and the noise is getting stronger. If my estimates are right, somewhere around twelve hours from now it'll be strong enough to swamp the signal. The machine will be unusable . . . permanently. After that it will only be able to get worse."

"You're not suggesting that *we* do this right now . . . without any reference to anybody," Anne said in a shocked voice. "That's unthinkable, surely."

"We don't have any choice," Murdoch pointed out. "We *have* to do it now, or do it never. If the machine is going to get us all out of this mess, it has to be inside the next twelve hours. We don't have time to convene any committees."

"But, Murdoch, you're talking about changing the whole timeline back to January," Anne protested. "All kinds of people's lives could be affected in ways you can't even imagine. How can we go tinkering with something like that? We've no way of telling what the consequences might be."

"You're right," Murdoch agreed. "But we know what the consequences of the alternative will be."

"We *don't* know . . . not for certain. You said yourself that the results of the analysis might be wrong."

"They might, but it could take years to verify every detail of the theory rigorously," Murdoch said. "We haven't got years, Anne; we've got twelve hours."

"How sure can you be about that?"

Murdoch shrugged. "It's an estimate. I could be wrong about that too, but that's the way it looks right now. You want to just wait around, do nothing, and find out that way?"

Anne fell silent and thought about the things Murdoch had said. Murdoch watched and read from the changing look in her eyes that she was coming around to accept the irrefutable logic of the situation confronting them. It was as he had said: They had no choice.

"Very well," Anne said eventually in a resigned voice. "What do you want me to do?"

At once Murdoch's manner became more brisk. "I'll need you to write the retransmit program and the bootstrap," he said. "The references you'll need are all over there. I'll use Grandpa's latest calculations and the information that Elizabeth brought on the reactor design to put together a message. I'll keep it short and to the point."

"How long have we got?" Anne asked.

"It's four-fifteen now. The background interference could build up faster than I estimated. I think that to play safe, we ought to aim at being ready to go by noon. What do you think?"

"We should make it okay. That kind of programming is really quite straightforward."

"Just remember that it will have to run right first time," Murdoch said. "If that means you have to take longer, take longer."

Murdoch got up and began rummaging through the notebooks and papers lying on the desk. Anne sat down at the console and activated the machine's program-development system. "I'll have to get some things from the study," Murdoch said, and turned for the door. "I'll be back down in a minute."

"Are we still going out for dinner tonight?" Anne called after him. He stopped for a moment and frowned, unable to decide whether or not she realized what she had said, or if she was being serious. Finally he shook his head, ignored the question, and walked out into the corridor.

By five-thirty Murdoch had explained in detail what he wanted the program to do, and Anne had flow-charted an interpretation that he had agreed should work. She began coding the routine, and he commenced selecting the items of information to go into the message. They worked mainly in silence, each fighting off the fatigue of the hours immediately preceding dawn. Maxwell burrowed into a pile of discarded printout and went to sleep.

At seven-thirty-five Anne ran a test of the program by using a separate area of the computer's memory to simulate the machine that would be functioning as the receiver. She found an error and began tracing it back through the coding that she had generated. Murdoch completed the message and loaded it into the computer ready to be accessed and transmitted by Anne's program. He went to make some coffee while she worked on.

Eight-fifteen. Anne had fixed the error but then had found another one. Murdoch ran an analysis of the background interference and found that it was building up faster than he had estimated. He revised the deadline to ten A.M. instead of noon.

While Anne was tracing the second error, Murdoch

checked back through the machine's log to find a good point in the past at which to aim the message. Obviously the recipients should have as much time as possible to grasp the significance of the message and take appropriate action, which meant that the message ought to be sent back as far as possible. The farthest back it could be sent was to the time at which Cartland had increased the message capacity of the machine and extended its range to twenty-four hours; Anne's program would not work correctly with the ten-minute range and the six-character limit that the machine had possessed prior to then.

To get that far back, the message would have to be "hopped" through the two-day period in which the machine had been temporarily disabled by interference coming back from the Burghead tests in January. Luckily the tests had not involved continuous operation of the reactors for the thirty-six hours they had run, but had included several gaps of an hour or two at a time, which were caused by the engineers shutting down the reactors to assess intermediate results and alter the test parameters. The interference pattern obtained at Storbannon had corresponding gaps, during which the machine had been operable. Anne's program would cause the message to materialize in, and be retransmitted from, one of those gaps.

These considerations eventually led Murdoch to select a point midway through a Saturday afternoon shortly after he and Lee had arrived in Scotland. He tried to remember what had taken place on that day so many months before, but too much had happened since, and he was too tired to think about it.

At nine-twenty Anne announced that the program appeared clean. "We can check out the whole system now," she said. "Is your file ready?"

"All set," Murdoch told her. "Vector in at thirty-six thousand. Access levels are zero-five and zero-four. Use mode three."

"Are you using a trap symbolic?"

"Default."

Anne nodded and ran her fingers deftly over the touchboard. Her screen went blank for an instant, and then the first few lines of Murdoch's message appeared at the top, accompanied by a duplicate of itself halfway down; each copy was tagged with a set of numbers and symbols.

From where he was standing behind her chair, Murdoch grinned feebly through eyes that had become red-rimmed. The screen told him that the program, along with the message, had bootstrapped itself into an area of memory that simulated a second machine, and from there repeated the process into a third area. It had stopped there because Anne had inserted a single test-instruction into the program telling it to. For the real thing, she would simply have to delete that test instruction and substitute the target-date data that Murdoch had selected. The program would then relay itself back up the timeline in one-day hops. After each hop it would compare the date that it carried with it against the actual date supplied by the machine that it materialized in. When the two dates matched, the program would stop retransmitting itself, activate the printer, and output Murdoch's message.

"It's all right," Anne said, scanning down the screen. "We're ready to go. It just needs a couple of simple changes now. You'd better bring the transmitter on-line." Murdoch was already flipping the switches beside her to make the system fully operational. He ran through a few switch checks and noted the readings on an auxiliary readout: The interference level was high, but not yet critical.

Murdoch looked down at the long, dark hair falling over Anne's shoulders as she leaned forward toward the console, at her slender arm stretching out over the touchboard, and thought that she had never seemed more beautiful than at this moment. He bit his lip silently and gripped the back of the chair with whitening knuckles.

She had forgotten.

She was so intent on her task that she had forgotten what it would mean to restructure a whole timeline. Events would shape themselves into completely new universes along the new timeline that would result. Everything connected with Storbannon and Burghead, and eventually places far removed from these, would be changed. Everything that he and Anne remembered doing together would be changed—for better or worse. There was no way of telling.

There was no way of being sure even that they would still be together.

Or even know that such a universe had ever been, or could have been.

That was what frightened him.

"The linkages are complete," Anne said quietly, turning her head to look up at him. "It's ready." Something vast and hollow opened up somewhere in the pit of Murdoch's stomach. He felt his body shiver but was unable to control it. There was nothing to decide, he told himself. Everything was already decided. If he didn't do it now, he'd never be able to do it. He leaned forward and stretched out an arm for the *Transmit* key; at the same time his other hand slid onto Anne's shoulder and brushed against the softness of her hair and her cheek. He froze as his finger touched the cold surface of the key; conflicting emotions tore at each other inside him. Anne's hand came up to her shoulder, found his, and squeezed it reassuringly. He swallowed hard and pressed the key firmly.

Somewhere back in time, binary digits were already materializing out of an intangible realm of existence and assembling themselves together before consolidating, and hurling themselves back yet further again a hundred times over. At the end of the chain, causes had already come into being whose effects were rushing back down the timeline toward the present moment, demolishing the universes that lay in between and reforming new ones from the same elements like the patterns in a kaleidoscope.

How long . . . ?

Anne got up from the chair and turned to slip inside Murdoch's arm. He could feel the warm curves of her body flattening against him as she pressed herself close. His arm tightened, and she looked up into his face. His mouth fell open as he saw that her eyes were brimming with tears that she had been holding back for a long time, and he read what was written in them. He shook his head in mute protest.

"I hadn't forgotten," she said.

CHAPTER TWENTY-FIVE

"It looks pretty busy," Lee observed as he looked out of the car at the crowds of shoppers threading their way along the snow-cleared sidewalk of the town's main street. He looked along the line of parked vehicles beside them. "You're gonna have problems finding a space here."

"It just needs patience," Murdoch said, slowing the car to a crawl. "Ah, what did I tell you—there's one." He brought the vehicle to a halt just ahead of an empty space, checked behind them, and reversed into it.

"They don't exactly have a surplus of parking lots in this town," Lee observed, looking around.

"What would you pull down to make some more?" Murdoch asked him.

"Mmm, okay, point taken. Where to first?"

"Well, if you still want a beer, why don't we do that now. Then we won't have to carry lots of junk all over town. There's a place you'd like just around the corner, all oak beams and stuff. Must be three hundred years old."

"Sounds fine."

Murdoch climbed out into the road and closed the car door, Lee opened the door on the other side, then paused for a moment to check his pockets for the list of things he needed to buy, and got out.

Inside a volume of space that extended for millions of miles around, a whispering disturbance materialized out of another realm, perturbing quantum states of energy and juggling with the interactions of a billion submicroscopic uncertainties.

As Murdoch came around the car and climbed over a pile of snow onto the sidewalk, he caught the eye of a girl who was coming out of one of the stores, carrying an armful of packages. She had long, dark hair, and was wearing an expensive-looking sheepskin coat with knee-length suede boots. For an instant he found himself staring. Then he realized that she had stopped, and was looking at him curiously with a faint half-smile playing on her lips. She nodded her head toward the rear end of his car.

"Is that your kitten down there?" she asked. Her voice was precisely cultivated and melodious, sending a strange tingle of excitement down his spine. He and Lee both turned together and looked back. A familiar black-and-white, whiskered nose was peering out from behind the rear wheel of the car, transfixed by a crumpled ball of paper that was fluttering against the base of a lamppost, pinned there by the breeze.

"Christ, it's Maxwell!" Lee exclaimed. "How in hell did he get here?"

"Must have hitched a ride," Murdoch said. He moved back to the car and stooped to reach behind the wheel. Maxwell's head promptly withdrew itself and proceeded to glare balefully out at him from the shadows beneath the car. "Get around the other side," Murdoch called. "Make sure he doesn't run out across the street." Cursing beneath his breath, Lee stamped through the snow piled in the gutter and squatted down to block the line of escape. Murdoch made a few futile attempts to reach the kitten, but succeeded only in getting his sleeve plastered with slush from the wheel arch. Finally he scooped up a handful of snow, crushed it into a hard ball, and threw it hard at the road inches in front of Maxwell's nose. Maxwell recoiled from the exploding snowball, straight into Lee's waiting hand. Murdoch opened the car door again while Lee carried the kitten around and dumped him inside.

"In you go, fella," Lee said. "I never saw him. He must have been under the seat or somewhere all the time. How'd he get out of the house in the first place anyway?"

"I don't know," Murdoch said as he slammed the door. "If it hadn't been for—" He turned toward where the girl had been standing, but she was gone. He looked along the sidewalk and saw her closing the trunk of a silver-blue car parked a few spaces ahead of theirs. She walked around to the driver's side, opened the door, and started to get in.

"Hey . . ." Murdoch called. She stopped and looked up. "Thanks." The girl smiled, gave him a cheerful wave, and climbed into her car. A few seconds later the car pulled smoothly out into the traffic lane and headed away along the street.

Murdoch watched it for a moment with silently admiring eyes. "Say . . ." he murmured. "Wasn't she something. What's the matter with us today, Lee? Why didn't we give her a hand with the parcels?"

"Because we've got things to do," Lee said. "Anyhow, the good-looking ones are always married before you find 'em. How about that beer? I could sure use it."

"Yeah . . . I guess you're right. Come on. The pub's this way."

They turned and walked away along the sidewalk. Behind them, the ball of paper broke free and tumbled along into one of the doorways.

They arrived back at Storbannon early in the evening to find the team in Charles's study, wild with excitement over something. Charles handed them some hardcopy sheets from the lab computer, then stood back to await their reactions. Elizabeth and Cartland watched expectantly. Murdoch ran his eyes quickly over the heading of the first sheet while Lee read over his shoulder. After a few seconds, Murdoch looked up, his face creased in bewilderment.

"Is this some kind of joke?" he demanded.

"It most certainly is not," Charles told him gruffly.

"The machine just started spewing it out," Cartland said. "It was about halfway through the afternoon . . . less than an hour after you left."

"But . . . I don't understand," Murdoch protested. "What the hell is this?"

"You should know," Elizabeth said. "It appears that you sent it."

Murdoch sat down and began studying the sheets more carefully. Exactly how the physics of time communication worked was still unclear, but it seemed reasonable to suppose that a team that existed somewhere in the future would have discovered more about it; presumably that future team had discovered a method of sending multiscreen messages in sequence, which was something they hadn't looked into as yet. From the model of the process that was just beginning to emerge, the team that had sent this message would no longer exist, since they would have existed on a timeline that no longer existed as it had been. Provided that the model was correct in this respect, the team that had sent the message would have known at least as much too. And still they had sent it. That was a sobering thought.

From odd pieces of text here and there Murdoch could see that the message had something to do with miniature black holes and the plant at Burghead where Elizabeth worked, although most of the data and mathematical expressions included with the text meant nothing at all to him. But the thing that staggered him was that the message purported to have come from a date in May. How could that be possible when the machine had a range of only one day? Perhaps they would be able to analyze what had come into the computer and obtain a few clues about that later, but for the moment Murdoch was more intrigued by the contents of the message itself. He passed the first sheet to Lee and proceeded to examine the next.

"We've been going through it all afternoon," Charles told them. "Some of the formulas in there are obviously from my work because they use my own symbology, but I must confess that I've never seen most of those expressions before. Elizabeth says that other parts of it are to do with the physics of the reactors at Burghead. It seems there's a connection between the two that we never dreamed of."

"Have you made any sense out of it yet?" Murdoch asked. "I don't understand a tenth of this stuff, whether I'm supposed to have sent it or not."

"We can follow the gist of it," Elizabeth replied. Her face was grave and her voice unusually serious. "It appears that at high energy-densities and full power, a positive-feedback mechanism can generate a miniature black hole at the core of a fusion target pellet. At this moment I can't explain why conventional design procedures give different answers. That's

206

something that Charles and I are going to have to spend some time looking into."

"Black holes?" Murdoch stared at her incredulously. "But inertial systems don't go anywhere near that kind of density."

"That's what current theory says," Elizabeth sighed. "But current theory doesn't take any account of Charles's tau phenomena. There seems to be an implication that we don't know about, but which whoever sent that did."

"You haven't got to the end yet," Cartland came in. "It's telling us to have next week's full-power tests at Burghead stopped . . . and in no uncertain terms. Apparently they managed to make two million of the bloody things."

"Two million black holes?" Murdoch gasped.

"Aye," Charles said grimly.

"What happened?"

"We don't know," Charles replied. "It doesn't go into details. We've been discussing it here for hours and can think of all kinds of possibilities. But we'd need to run a full computer simulation before we could be sure of anything."

"Whatever the result was, it was serious enough for whoever sent this to do something extremely drastic to change it," Elizabeth said.

"Surely not," Lee objected, looking up from his reading. "Holes that small wouldn't last long enough to do any harm."

"If there's a connection with tau phenomena that we don't understand, anything might be possible," Charles said. "From some of the math in there, it's clear that they had a far better understanding of the whole thing than I could offer now. We're going to have to do a lot of work on the physical basis of plasma theory and see where tau physics comes into it."

"That could take some time," Murdoch pointed out. "The tests at Burghead are due to start a week from Monday. What do we do about that?"

"I'll call the senior directors over the weekend and see if we can go and talk to them first thing Monday morning," Elizabeth said. "If they won't accept this

207

message at face value, then I suppose we'll have to bring them here and show them the machine. If that doesn't convince them, nothing will." She looked inquiringly at Charles.

"I suppose so," Charles agreed reluctantly. "It'll be a pity to have to bring outsiders into it so soon, but from the look of things those tests have to be stopped whatever the cost."

"This is neat." Lee pushed himself back from the main console in the lab and nodded approvingly at the list of code being displayed on the screen. It was late on Sunday morning. Elizabeth and Charles were talking physics in the study; Cartland was upstairs showering and shaving. Murdoch looked up from the datagrid terminal, at which he was running a calculation to verify one of the expressions contained in the message received the previous day.

"What?" he asked.

"The program that read in the message," Lee replied. "It used the machine as a relay and bootstrapped itself back in one-day jumps. There's a test built in to terminate it at yesterday's date."

"I had a feeling it might be something like that," Murdoch said.

Lee turned away from the console and looked at him. "Did you ever learn real-time programming anyplace, Doc? You never said anything about it to me if you did."

"No, never. Why?"

Lee waved a hand at the screen. "Whoever did that knew some neat tricks. I was just curious as to who it might have been."

"Aren't there any clues in there?" Murdoch asked.

"Nope," Lee said. "But I know it wasn't me."

"I guess we'll never know then." Murdoch thought for a moment about the strangeness of the whole situation, and then returned his attention to the terminal.

Charles returned with Elizabeth to meet the Burghead directors on Monday morning. The reactions to what they had to say ranged from open-minded skepticism to downright disbelief. It was all too extraordinary to be assimilated in so short a time and on the say-so of just two people, whoever they might be. Charles had not had sufficient time, nor was he yet sufficiently familiar with the way the machine worked, to be able to substantiate all his claims, so he invited the directors to come to Storbannon to see for themselves. The matter was clearly too serious to be dismissed, however improbable the whole business sounded, and the Board agreed to send a delegation to make the visit on Wednesday morning. The Board agreed also to meet again on the Thursday to debate the outcome.

CHAPTER TWENTY-SIX

"We are agreed then," Courtney summarized for the Board on Thursday morning. "For the time being at least, we are obliged to accept this message as genuine. In view of the extreme gravity of its content, there can be no question of the proposed tests going ahead until the situation has been fully investigated." Heads nodded in assent from around the conference table. He continued, "I propose therefore that the schedule for the tests be suspended until further notice, and that the reasons for the decision be conveyed to the EFC Presidential Committee immediately. The question of where we go next must obviously wait until we obtain a response from there. Are there any dissenters?" There were none. "Very good. Passed unanimously." He paused for a second.

"Obviously the things we have heard this morning are not for publication or for discussion outside this room for the time being, to insure Sir Charles's peace and privacy if for nothing else." He glanced at Charles, who was sitting next to him, as he spoke. Charles acknowledged his words with a slight nod of his head. Courtney concluded, "We will have to leave that side of things with Brussels as a policy issue. Yes, Simon?" He looked at Vickers, who was moving to speak.

"I agree with you that we should keep the whole thing quiet for the time being," Vickers said. "But we'll need an official story to explain the postponement. I mean, with all the publicity that this place has had, we can hardly just refuse to say anything at all. And the people who work here will want an answer as much as anybody else."

"Any suggestions?" Courtney invited, casting his eyes around the table.

"I'll talk to a couple of people in my department who can be relied upon to cooperate without asking questions," Elizabeth said from the far end. "We should be able to put together a story about some piece of equipment needing to be redesigned and modified, or something like that. I'll see if I can get a statement circulated by this afternoon."

"Very well. We'll leave that one with you, Elizabeth. Thanks." Courtney raised his voice slightly to address the whole meeting again. "There is another item that I would like to propose. As you have heard, the physical theory that underlies our work here appears to have converged with the remarkable line of research that Sir Charles Ross has described to us. As soon as the appropriate people within EFC have been made aware of these developments, the next step will almost certainly be a call for a detailed reexamination of the theoretical foundations of high-energy plasmas by our senior physicists. After that, I don't know who might get involved.

"From the purely practical point of view, the first goal must be to determine if, and if so how, the heavy-ion system can be modified to avoid the kind of hazard that appears to have afflicted some"—he frowned for a moment as he sought for words appropriate to a formal meeting of the Board, to express what he still couldn't help feeling was something out of fairyland—"some future universe. Clearly it would be of great help to our scientists if they had access to the knowledge which at present only Sir Charles and his colleagues possess. My proposal is, therefore, that we instigate at once a program of collaboration between a selected group of our research people at Burghead whose discretion can be trusted and Sir Charles's team, acting, for want of a better word, as consultants. There's no reason why we shouldn't begin that straight away on our own initiative without waiting to hear from Brussels. I have already discussed such an arrangement with Sir Charles, and he has stated that he is more than willing to help us in any way he can. Could I have your views on that, please."

"Good idea. Do it," Vickers murmured.

"Have we any idea how long this could go on?" somebody asked. "It could become rather embarrassing. I mean, here we are with this whole ruddy shooting-match ready to go after damn near fifteen years of designing it and building it, and now we don't even know when it's going to work."

"Or *if* it will *ever* work," somebody else tossed in. A murmur of endorsement rippled round the table.

Elizabeth leaned forward to answer. "I don't want to play down the seriousness of the situation," she told them. "But let's be thankful that we've only an embarrassing delay to worry about, and not the catastrophe we would have had if we'd gone ahead in complete ignorance. From what Sir Charles and I have been able to work out so far, the problem seems to lie in the energy-balance equations that describe the plasma phase at the implosion core. To put it simply, the equations as they stand fail to take account of an additional energy-transfer mode, which Sir Charles's theory describes, but conventional theory does not.

"Putting it all in perspective, my opinion at this point is that it should be possible to guarantee hazard-free operation of the reactors as they exist now simply by altering the intensity profiles of the beams, and perhaps by using a redesigned pellet. There's no question of our having to tear the whole plant down and rebuild it from scratch, or anything like that."

"That sounds very reassuring, Elizabeth," one of the former questioners said. "But how can you be so sure of that so soon?"

"I said it was simply my opinion at this stage," she reminded him. "We won't be in a position to make definitive statements until we've done a lot more work."

"And that's exactly why I'm saying we should get Sir Charles and his people involved as soon as possible," Courtney said. "The sooner we make a start, the sooner we'll have some answers."

Colin Harding, Director of Engineering, had been looking thoughtful throughout the exchange. When a lull occurred, he sat forward, cleared his throat, and frowned uncertainly for a moment.

"Look," he said, turning his head from one side to the other to address everybody present. "This may sound a bit ridiculous because I don't pretend to understand very much about this . . . this 'time machine' yet, but it seems to me it could save us a lot of trouble. If somebody in May could use it to send a message back, why couldn't we use it to send questions *forward?* After all, it must be reasonable to assume that months from now we'll know a hell of a lot more about this business than we do at the moment." He shrugged. "So why can't we simply ask 'us' months from now what the answers are, instead of spending lots of time finding out the hard way?"

"That's got to be preposterous," Vickers said, but the confused expression on his face added that he wasn't exactly sure why.

Charles answered the suggestion. "That may not be as daft as it sounds," he said. "There are probably all kinds of strange possibilities that we can't even imagine yet. There's a whole new realm of physical phenomena to be investigated, and at this stage we're not even in a position to describe their effects, let alone explain them. I would prefer us not to go meddling with things that we are still a long way from understanding fully. At the moment we are in the process of preparing a schedule of rigid tests for the machine at Storbannon, designed to provide more data on what these effects are. For now and for the foreseeable future, I would like to use the machine for that purpose and for nothing else."

"A very wise precaution," Courtney declared. He looked up and around the table. "So we've got a lot of work to do, and we'll do it in the way we already know how. The proposal is for Sir Charles and his team to begin working with us as soon as is mutually convenient. Those for?" One by one the hands around the table went up. "Those against?" Courtney asked. There were no hands. "Passed," he announced.

CHAPTER TWENTY-SEVEN

During the weeks that followed, Charles spent a lot of time at Burghead and made several visits to the EFC Headquarters in Brussels, sometimes with Cartland, to discuss the new physics with a selected circle of EFC executives and senior scientists. The media carried an official version of why the much-publicized Burghead tests were being postponed; a brief flurry of cynicism and criticism from some sectors of the public greeted the news, but soon died away.

Murdoch and Lee were left to take charge of the extensive schedule of tests that had been drawn up for the machine at Storbannon. This turned out to be a tedious job involving days spent running variations of the same routines of complex computer algorithms and random-number-generator routines, most of which could be programmed to execute automatically. The two Americans thus found themselves with a lot of spare time. They used the opportunity to visit Burghead in order to look over the plant and meet some of the people with whom they would be working when Elizabeth and Charles had finished the groundwork. One of these was Mike Stavely, a physicist who worked with Elizabeth in the Mathematics and Physics Department of the facility, and one of the few who was aware of the real reasons for abandoning the plans to go full-power with the reactors. On a day in early February, they found themselves with Mike and Elizabeth in the Burghead cafeteria, finishing lunch after their first comprehensive tour of the plant.

"So," Elizabeth asked them. "What do you think of it?"

Lee turned his hands palms-up and shrugged. "Impressed. What else do I say? Anything would be an understatement."

"Grandpa and Ted were pretty excited after they'd been taken around it the other week," Murdoch said. "Now I can see why."

"Where are they today?" Mike asked as he stirred cream into his coffee. "Back at the castle or traveling again?"

"Traveling," Murdoch told him.

"Where to this time? Another Brussels trip?"

Murdoch shook his head. "No, London. They'll be back sometime tonight."

"What are they doing there?" Mike asked, surprised.

"They've gone to talk to a Government advisory committee on technology and science. It looks as if everybody's getting in on the act."

"Government committee?" Mike looked puzzled. "Burghead's got nothing to do with them, surely. Why are they getting their oar in?"

"You're right, Mike," Elizabeth said. "The reactor problem is an EFC matter. But the chaps in Brussels are becoming concerned about the greater significance of the whole thing as a separate issue. They've more or less insisted that the Government get involved with the pure physics aspects."

"They may be a competitive corporation, but the idea of being the only outfit around that knows about messing with timelines is making them nervous," Lee explained. "This one's too hot to be holding."

"Mmm . . . I think I see what you mean," Mike agreed. Elizabeth leaned back to cast a wary eye around the tables in their vicinity.

"We shouldn't really be talking about this here," she said, lowering her voice. "Save it until later."

"Sure," Lee said. He sat back and fished a pack of cigarettes from his pocket.

Murdoch propped his chin on his knuckles and gazed absently around. Suddenly his eyes came to rest on a girl who was setting a tray down and just about to join a group of people at a table on the far side of the cafeteria. There was something about the way she walked and about the long sweep of dark hair over her shoulders that seemed familiar. Then he remembered.

"Say," he said to Lee after a second. "Guess who I've just seen here."

Lee turned in his seat to follow Murdoch's gaze. "Where?"

"Over there by the window . . . just sitting down."

Lee spotted her and frowned as he tried to recall where he had seen her before.

"Kingussie," Murdoch supplied. "The day Maxwell took a walk. Remember?"

"Ah, yeah . . ." Lee said, nodding slowly.

"You know her?" Elizabeth asked, sounding surprised.

"Not really," Murdoch said. "We bumped into her briefly in Kingussie a few weeks ago. It's just that I didn't know she worked here. Any idea what she does?"

"She's from the Medical Department, isn't she?" Mike said to Elizabeth.

Elizabeth nodded. "She's Dr. Waring's assistant, I think." She glanced at Murdoch and Lee, and explained, "Dr. Waring is in charge of the medical facilities here. I'm not sure what her name is, though. Do you know, Mike?"

"No, I'm afraid not. Wouldn't mind finding out."

"We could no doubt find out for you if you wanted to say hello sometime," Elizabeth offered. "I wouldn't make it during office hours though. Waring can be a bit touchy."

"Oh, hell no," Murdoch said. "It's nothing important. I was just surprised to see her here, that's all."

While the others carried on talking, Murdoch's eyes strayed back to where the girl was sitting. Something about the way she sat with her body erect, about the way she laughed, and about the way she used her hands so expressively while she spoke mesmerized him. Never in his life had he found anybody so instantly fascinating. And he didn't even know her name.

Murdoch and Lee spent the rest of the day in the Mathematics and Physics Department with Mike. It was well after six o'clock when Mike suggested a drink for the three of them to finish off the afternoon. The other two agreed without much argument, and Mike suggested a place called the Aberdeen Angus, which, he said, was a popular place among Burghead people, just off the main road about three miles west of the plant and practically on their way home.

Fifteen minutes later, Murdoch was following Mike's somewhat battered VW wagon westward in manual-drive mode at one hundred and ten miles per hour despite the posted limit. Eventually they slowed down to something approaching sanity and turned off at a sign that said *Achnabackie* onto a narrow road that wound its way between stone walls in among wooded hillsides. After about half a mile, they came to a small village nestled in a fold in the hills and found the Aberdeen Angus right in the center. They parked next to Mike's wagon and joined him a few moments later outside the front door of the pub.

"What's up?" Mike asked cheerfully. "Leave your brakes on?"

"Does everybody drive like a maniac around here?" Murdoch asked. "That was a controlled highway. Why not relax a little and let the system take care of it?"

"Too old a model," Mike said, waving toward the wagon as they reached the door. "It hasn't got full auto. Anyhow, it saves on drinking time." They drew up at the Public Bar just inside the front door. "My round," Mike told them. "What's it to be, pints?" Murdoch and Lee accepted the offer. Mike called out the order, and the barman began drawing off three foaming mugs of dark ale.

"So, what were you saying just before we left the office, Mike?" Murdoch asked. "The next phase at Burghead will be to build a steel plant over the reactor site or something."

"That's right," Mike said. "And other things after that. It'll have a separate reactor system of its own that'll use the same beams. Steelmaking's already going nuclear in Japan and the U.S.S.R. It's about time we caught up."

They talked for a while about the attractions of using the high temperatures of nuclear plasmas as the basis for metal extraction and processing in the

216

industries of the coming decades. Such a trend would render the whole cumbersome and relatively costly technology of traditional ore reduction and smelting methods obsolete, since the intense heat of a plasma torch would reduce everything—low-grade ores, desert sand and rock, scrap materials, construction debris—down to the atoms of its constituent elements, which would be ionized and could be separated, and concentrated magnetically. Cost-effective metal extraction would no longer depend on the availability of concentrated geographical deposits.

"And moonrock as well," Lee said. "Didn't they reckon once it'd never be any good for anything?"

"Absolutely," Mike agreed. "Once we've got the technology developed down here, we ship it up there. Then we'll really be able to start building things. I bet they'll start the space colonies inside twenty years. You wait and see."

While they were talking, a group of people had come through from the Lounge Bar and were trickling by in ones and twos to leave via the front door. Mike seemed to know most of them, which meant they were also from the plant. The last two of the group were a sandy-haired youth and a dark-haired girl, following a few paces behind the rest and talking together about something. Murdoch swept a casual eye over them as they passed, and suddenly something convulsed inside his chest. It was *her*.

For a moment his mind froze up. She was only a few feet away from him, and for some reason his idiotic brain couldn't put together anything to say. And then he realized that she had stopped and was looking at him curiously with a faint flicker of recognition on her face.

Suddenly she smiled. "Hello there," she said. "How's the kitten?"

Murdoch gasped in surprise. "I don't believe it!" he exclaimed. "You can't remember that."

"Why not? I don't see kittens under cars very often."

"That's incredible."

"I detect an American," she remarked. "Is your friend one too?"

"That's right . . . from California . . . both of us. We're over here for a while."

"With EFC?"

"No. As a matter of fact we're—"

"Hey, Anne," a voice called from the doorway out to the street. "Come on. We're all waiting. Some of us are getting hungry." Murdoch looked around and saw that it belonged to a tall, broad-shouldered, athletic-looking character with a reddish face who was wearing a dark blazer.

"Stay on and have one with us," Murdoch suggested. "You can talk to that bunch any day of the week."

"It's nice of you to offer, but we're all together," she replied with a laugh. "I've got to go, I'm afraid." She turned her head and called to the door, "All right. Patience, Trevor. I'm on my way now." To Murdoch she said, "Take care of the kitten," and then she was gone.

Murdoch turned back toward the bar to find Lee and Mike sporting derisive smirks.

"She remembered me," Murdoch said defensively. "Didn't you see? She's in love already."

"Like hell," Lee told him. "She remembered Maxwell."

"At least I've got her name now," Murdoch said defiantly.

"Fast operator," Lee murmured. "I'd better go buy some flowers for the wedding."

They ate out with Mike and arrived back at Storbannon well after midnight to find Charles and Cartland back from London, and still up talking in the library.

"You two scoundrels look a little the worse for wear, if I'm not mistaken," Charles observed as they came in. "You've tracked down the local lassies already, I'll be bound."

"Wrong, Grandpa," Murdoch said. "We had a night out with one of Elizabeth's physicists. Nice guy."

"Did you get the tour round the plant?" Cartland asked.

"Yes, we did," Lee told him. "Quite a place."

"How'd it go down south?" Murdoch asked, looking at Charles.

"Oh . . . we had a busy day, right enough." Charles replied. "What about the tests here? Have we got a complete set of preliminary data ready for analysis yet?"

"Well, the final group has been running all day," Murdoch said. "We should have the output by morning. Why?"

"I want to aim at getting some kind of a tentative interpretation by this time next week, if we can," Charles told him. "A week from tomorrow, the Minister himself is coming up here with a couple of his scientific chappies. They want to see it for themselves." He sighed and rubbed his beard resignedly. "It looks as if we've really started something now, I'm afraid."

CHAPTER TWENTY-EIGHT

The Honorable Graham Cuthrie, His Majesty's Minister for Advanced Technology and Science, stared over Murdoch's shoulder at the screen and went over in his mind the things that Charles had said. Then he took a sheet of blank paper off the top of the desk beside him and drew a large cross from corner to corner with a red broad-tipped pen. Slowly and deliberately he folded the paper in two and tore it across, then placed the pieces on top of each other and tore them again.

"There is an event," he declared. "The paper with the red X on it has been torn up." He looked dubiously across the lab at where Charles was standing by the workbench. On the other side of the room with Lee and Cartland, Professor Norman Payne, Chairman of the Minister's Advisory Committee on Advanced Research, and Dr. Catherine Hazeltine from the National Physical Laboratory at Teddington stood silently watching with interest. Cuthrie continued, "The event of my tearing this sheet of paper is now established as part of the past. It's fact. Are you suggesting that it can now be changed?"

Charles made no reply, but simply nodded at Murdoch. Murdoch composed a simple line of text on the screen: "Do not tear the sheet that has the red X drawn on it."

"You tore it at exactly ten seconds after eleven-seven," Murdoch said, glancing back at Cuthrie. "I'm setting this message to arrive at a point in time five seconds before that. Whether or not anything changes will depend on whether or not the 'you' that exists at that moment decides to take any notice of it." Cuthrie sniffed suspiciously. Without further ado, Murdoch turned back to the console and pressed the *Transmit* key.

Cuthrie took a sheet of blank paper off the top of the desk beside him and drew a large cross from corner to corner with a red broad-tipped pen. As he raised the sheet for everybody in the room to see, a line of text appeared suddenly on the screen in front of Murdoch and caught Cuthrie's eye. Cuthrie jerked his head up sharply in surprise and found Charles watching him with a faint expression of amusement.

"Where the devil did that come from?" Cuthrie asked uncertainly.

Murdoch leaned forward to read the numerical data that had appeared along with the text. "From a point in time that was in the future when this appeared on the screen," he said. "In fact, from just about now."

"But . . . how could anybody know that I was intending to tear it up?" Cuthrie asked in a bewildered voice. "I never mentioned it in any way at all."

"I think that perhaps you're missing the point, Graham," Catherine Hazeltine suggested. "From what Sir Charles said earlier, you *did* tear it up . . . on a timeline that has been reconfigured to the one we're all on now as a result of what is now on the screen. Am I right, Sir Charles?" Charles nodded but said nothing. Lee and Cartland looked as if they were enjoying themselves as they watched.

"My God!" Cuthrie breathed, staring at the screen again with a new light of sudden respect in his eyes. Professor Payne thought for a moment, and then stepped a pace forward. "May I have that for a moment?" he asked. Cuthrie passed him the sheet. Payne produced a pen from his pocket and scrawled a large black circle on top of the red cross.

"That circle is now there," he told them. "I've drawn it. Fact. If I understand you correctly, you're telling us that the event of my having done that could be changed, even though it's happened. Very well. Show me."

"May I have that for a moment?" Payne said, moving a step forward. Cuthrie passed him the sheet. Payne produced a pen from his pocket and poised his hand over the red cross.

"Hold it!" Murdoch called out. Payne looked up, puzzled. "If you were thinking of drawing a black circle, don't." Murdoch pointed to another line of text that had just appeared. "It's telling you here not to." Payne gasped incredulously and stood staring first at the screen, then at the paper, and then back at the screen again, temporarily at a loss of words.

"You *did* draw one!" Catherine Hazeltine whispered. "It's happened again. This is impossible!"

"Let me try something else," Cuthrie said, taking the pen and paper from Payne's unresisting fingers.

"Before you do, let me just clarify what's happening," Charles said. "It's futile to try and catch the system out by trying to set up paradoxes. All that will happen will be that the timeline will reconfigure to a new one on which all our memories and records—such as what's drawn on that piece of paper—will be fully consistent with the new events resulting from the information impressed upon it. In other words you won't see a paradox however hard you try.

"When you think about the problem, it makes sense. By definition a paradox can't exist. It's to be expected, therefore, that the logic that governs the process will not permit one to exist. It's a strange form of logic when judged by ordinary standards, to be sure, but then ordinary standards never took account of anything like this."

"What it boils down to is that it's a waste of time trying to fool it," Cartland summarized. "You won't.

What we should be doing is thinking about how to use it."

"Are you sure you're all right in here on your own?" Morna asked anxiously. "It must be awfully boring for you sitting around all day. Mrs. Paisley is preparing you some lunch—turkey-and-ham salad. It'll be ready in about five minutes." The RAF pilot, who had flown the three visitors directly to Storbannon from London, grinned up from the armchair in the library, from where he was watching a movie on the vi-set. He was young, probably not much over twenty, and with boyishly styled hair and a freckled face that had immediately aroused Morna's motherly instincts.

"Don't worry about me, miss," he replied cheerfully. "There's plenty to read if I get tired of this, and I'm nice and comfy. To tell you the truth, I could do with a few more days like this."

"Are you sure there's nothing more I can get you?" Morna asked.

"A cuppa char'd go down nicely . . . if it isn't too much trouble."

At that moment Cartland breezed in from the hall-way and caught the tail-end of the conversation.

"How about a noggin instead, old boy?" he suggested. "If you've got a few hours to kill, you might as well do it in style."

The pilot hesitated. "Well, I am on duty, sir . . . But thanks very much; a small beer'd go down a real treat."

"Newcastle okay?" Cartland asked as he walked across to the cabinet by one of the walls. "It's export."

"Just the job."

"Och, ye must be all coming out for lunch," Morna said to Cartland. "I'd better go and give Mrs. Paisley a hand." She hurried out of the door and turned in the direction of the kitchen. Cartland poured two beers and brought one across to where the pilot was sitting.

"Thank you very much, sir," the pilot acknowledged. "Good health."

"Cheers, old boy." Cartland took a sip from his own glass and studied the insignia on the shoulder of the pilot's jacket. "Which Command—Air Support?"

"Eighty-third Squadron."

"Ah, let me see now . . ." Cartland thought for a second. "Number Three Transport Group, isn't it? Based at Northolt."

"That's right," the pilot said, slightly surprised. "You must be ex-RAF."

"I was in Orbital Command for nearly ten years. Transferred from there to liaison and advisory."

"Shuttles and sats?"

"Yes," Cartland said. "You ought to think of pushing for it. That's where all the fun is. It'll get better too when Europe sets up the Integrated Space Wing. You could get a lunar trip, or maybe even a joint Mars effort with the States. Who knows?"

"I've been thinking about just that," the pilot told him. "I'll need my advanced nav and some more hours logged first though." He took a drink from his glass and nodded approvingly. "This is good stuff. Beats the southern brew, never mind what I say when I'm back 'ome."

"Where's that, London?"

"Near enough. Gravesend—just down the river a bit." The pilot sank back in the chair and went on absently after a few seconds, "I had a pal in Orbital Command . . . from Southampton 'e was. He copped it on *Centurion*." The pilot shook his head sadly. "A bad business that was. . . ."

Cartland frowned at him uncertainly. "Sorry . . . I'm not quite with you. What's *Centurion*?"

The pilot took a long gulp from his glass, obviously in an attempt to disguise his sudden embarrassment. "Oh, Gawd! I shouldn't have mentioned that, sir. It was a slip of the—"

"That's all right. I understand," Cartland said. He waited curiously for a moment all the same, but the pilot was clearly not about to volunteer anything further. Cartland glanced at the name-tag stitched above the pilot's breast pocket.

"William G. O'Malley, eh?" he said to change the topic. "That doesn't sound like a long line of Gravesenders to me. There must be some Irish in there somewhere."

223

"My old man was from Galway," the pilot told him, sounding relieved. "I used to go there a lot on 'olidays when I was a kid. Nice place."

At that moment Morna came back in to inform Cartland that lunch was about to be served in the dining room.

"I hope you're taking care of him too," Cartland said, indicating the pilot with a nod of his head.

"Mrs. Paisley's preparing something for him now," Morna replied.

"Good," Cartland said. "Must look after the troops." He walked back to the door, then stopped and looked back at the pilot. "Help yourself to another beer if you feel like it," he called back.

"Thank you very much, sir. I don't mind if I do."

"Take it easy though, old boy," Cartland cautioned. "It wouldn't do to go flying that lot into Big Ben on the way home. They'd never put you in Orbital Command then. . . . More likely, the Bloody Tower."

"From what we can tell at the moment, I don't think that a coherent dialogue between past and future universes would really be feasible," Charles said across the luncheon table. "Or at least, I can't see that it would make much sense."

"Why is that?" Cuthrie asked over a piece of caviared toast.

"Well," Charles replied. "Imagine ourselves attempting to conduct a dialogue with the 'us' who exist, say, an hour ahead of now. We could ask questions, and they could reply, but every time they did so, the very act of their replying would restructure the timeline that they themselves exist as part of. Thus they would become new versions of themselves who never sent any reply, and without any recollection of having sent one."

"Unless they made it their business to send back exactly what they had already received themselves, when it was time to send it," Payne pointed out.

"If they had already received the information, there would be no point in their doing anything like that," Charles replied. "They could send it, I agree, but it wouldn't achieve anything or tell them anything they

224

didn't already know. Therefore I assume they wouldn't bother. That was why I said that an attempt at a meaningful dialogue wouldn't make much sense."

"But there's nothing to stop messages being sent both ways," Cuthrie said, just to be sure.

"No, there isn't," Charles confirmed. "But every successive response from the future would come from different individuals on changed timelines. Hence such an exchange couldn't be what you could call coherent."

"But that kind of thing would be just entertainment," Murdoch said, joining in. "The real power of the whole thing is that information can be sent back to alter past events. You've seen that done already."

"And I think it's going to take me a few days to grasp fully what it all means," Catherine Hazeltine said.

"It's a servoloop through time," Cartland told them.

Payne thought about the statement and nodded slowly. "That's a good way to put it," he agreed, smiling faintly.

"Ye-es . . ." Cuthrie murmured. "I see what you mean . . . a feedback-loop through time. A feedback system works by measuring the difference between the desired output of a process and the actual output, and generating an input to correct for any error. That's exactly what you can do with this machine, isn't it. . . ." His voice took on a note of awe as the full implications at last dawned on him. "There's no need to rely on trying to predict and forecast as best we can any more. We can *monitor the actual consequences* of our decisions and actions, and change them until they produce the required results! My God . . . it's staggering!"

The room became very quiet for a while as the enormity of the whole thing became clear. The whole future course of civilization could be completely transformed. The wasted efforts, the futile ventures, the uncertainties, and the risks—all of them could be done away with forever.

At last Charles spoke. "Up at Burghead, they're trying to solve a difficult problem right now. Perhaps they could know immediately whether or not they're using the right approach and, if they are, what it's outcome will be. Billions are being spent on studies and experiments on star-probe designs; perhaps we could obtain the answers now. Will the space colonies succeed? Perhaps we could know in advance before we commit anything. And who knows what else might be possible?"

"It sounds insane," Catherine protested. "How can we obtain information from the future when the future contains it only by virtue of having been the present? It's a closed circle." She looked appealingly from side to side. "We ask somebody in a future universe a question, and get an answer. But the only reason that person knows the answer is that he remembers being told it when he was us and asked it. But who *discovered* the answer? Where did it originate from? It's ridiculous."

"I can't answer that for sure yet," Charles confessed. "That's why I don't want us trying to use the machine for anything like that at this stage. The only thing I can suggest as a possibility is that the effort that went into finding the answer was expended on a timeline that did exist, but which was subsequently restructured."

"But the answer can still be sent back and preserved on the new timeline?" Catherine still could not help sounding distinctly skeptical.

"Quite," Charles said simply. "That must be clear from what you've already seen."

"When you think about it, it might not be as ridiculous as it seems at first sight," Payne said. "Compare it to the invention of language. To somebody who had no concept of it, the idea of later generations being able to profit from the knowledge gained by previous generations might seem equally ridiculous. To somebody like that, the idea of lots of people all being able to know something that had only had to be learned once might seem to be every bit as much 'cheating' as this business does to us. Maybe that's a good way to think about it—simply as extending the same process further."

"I suppose that makes about as much sense as any other way of looking at it," Catherine conceded, although still sounding dubious.

226

Cuthrie had been looking thoughtful while he followed the conversation. When the silence had lasted for a few seconds he said, "I must admit, I hadn't really appreciated how big all this is until today. It could have repercussions that will affect every nation on Earth, radically . . . the whole race. I'm not at all sure that something like this can stop with the British Government. There may be a lot more people who should be brought in on it."

"I was wondering about that too," Charles said, nodding. "Let's see what they say when you report back to London. I'm not at all sure how we should handle it."

"But how can anybody even begin playing around with something like this?" Payne asked. "How can anybody presume to make decisions that could change the lives of everybody on the planet? Whose priorities come first when there's a conflict of interests? Who decides? The whole thing sounds monstrous."

"Haven't people been presuming just that all through history anyway?" Charles suggested soberly. "Passing laws, industrializing countries, declaring wars . . . what's the difference?"

"And maybe you're forgetting that it's already happened," Lee said, nodding his head to indicate Murdoch while he addressed the others. "The Burghead black holes. We're already part of a universe that has been restructured. I don't see any bad effects of it."

"That's true," Payne admitted.

"But we don't really know anything about what happened or why," Murdoch pointed out. "The message that came back was too short. We don't know what the situation was for sure in the universe that it came from, or exactly what it was that we avoided, or . . . anything about it."

"That's the problem," Cuthrie declared. "There's nothing to *measure* exactly how beneficial, or otherwise, this messing around with timelines is. Take the example that Murdoch just mentioned. As he said, we don't know anything for sure about the timeline that was changed. For all we know, it could just as well have been changed for the worse as for the better. We know a little bit about one hazard that appears to have been avoided, and nothing at all about anything else that may have been affected. The people who existed on that timeline no doubt knew a lot more than we do, but *we* don't know any of that . . . and they don't exist any more. How can we even begin to think about a policy on how to use this capability when there doesn't seem to be a way of telling whether or not it's going to do any good?"

"We need an experiment," Charles said after another silence. "A carefully designed, comprehensive experiment conducted under controlled conditions. Not a few scraps of data such as we had about the Burghead problem, but a fully detailed package of information that describes exactly what in the past is to be changed, why, how, and everything about the situation that such an action is intended to affect. Then the people in the past who receive that information will be in a position to compare exactly the situation that they come to experience with the one that they would otherwise have experienced. Then they'll be able to measure just how effective the exercise has been." He looked at Cuthrie. "Given that, your Government would have all it needed to decide its policy."

"I agree," Cuthrie said simply.

"Fine, but there's a small problem," Cartland said. "Whatever you pick for an experiment will have to be a bit more significant than drawing crosses on pieces of paper, won't it? If you want to measure the *goods* and *bads,* it'll have to have effects that can be interpreted as good or bad . . . and to be sure about it, significant effects that can't be mistaken, which means it will affect the lives of lots of people." He looked challengingly around the table. "So now, who's willing to play God? Who would care to suggest an experiment and be responsible for its consequences?"

A long silence ensued while the others exchanged helpless looks.

There were no takers.

CHAPTER TWENTY-NINE

The Right Honorable Kenneth Lansing, Prime Minister to the Crown, stood erect with his hands clasped behind his back, staring out over the stone balustrade of the Members' Terrace at the gray-green water of the Thames sliding slowly by beneath Westminster Bridge. He stood motionless for a long time, and then pivoted himself abruptly to face Cuthrie, who was watching and waiting in silence.

"I don't like it, Graham," he declared. "The whole security aspect of it worries me. Too many people know about it already. First there's Ross and his crowd in Glenmoroch, then a whole bunch of Courtney's people at Burghead, and on top of that God only knows how many people in EFC. It's probably halfway around Europe by now, if the truth were known. I can't see any way now that the story can be contained."

"I think you're right," Cuthrie replied in a worried voice. "It's more the EFC end that bothers me though. Courtney's people are only concerned with solving the reactor problem. And in Glenmoroch, Sir Charles is no fool. That other fellow there—Cartland—has a first-rate career record in the RAF; I don't think there's much to worry about as far as he's concerned either."

"What about those two Americans?" Lansing inquired.

"One of them is Ross's grandson," Cuthrie replied. "I've had a check done through a nameless friend at the Yard—brilliant academic record; nothing medically or psychologically abnormal; no police record, apart from something to do with a student prank about ten years ago; no strong political inclinations or affiliations; no debts or financial problems; very level-headed by all accounts; good relationships with his family, and especially strong ties with his grandfather. In short, a negligible risk."

"And the other one?"

"Generally the same kind of character. He was born in Japan, but that's of no significance; his father's a VP of a U.S. fusion corporation. The two of them were in business together until around the middle of last year . . . offering a kind of consulting service in plasma dynamics. Fulfilled all their contracts, paid their bills and taxes. They're both extremely individualistic, with an aversion to the more usual types of structured career environments—the last of the gifted, amateur entrepreneurs, perhaps . . . or maybe the first of the next breed."

"Mmm . . ." Lansing frowned and rocked to and fro on his heels, keeping his hands clasped behind him. "You don't think that could be significant?"

"I don't think so," Cuthrie said, shaking his head. "As I said a moment ago, I'm more worried about something leaking out through EFC, either at Burghead or, more likely, at the Brussels end."

"Damn EFC!" Lansing muttered. "Why in God's name did Ross have to go telling them about it at all? Why couldn't he have brought it to us in the first place?"

"He err . . ." Cuthrie faltered for a second, not quite knowing how to phrase an answer. "He had the end of the world to worry about. . . . Didn't think it could wait."

"End of the world . . . stuff and nonsense," Lansing growled. "Another damned individualist, if the truth were known. Always has been. He only came back to this country and shut himself up in that castle of his because the Americans wouldn't change the Defense Department to suit him. It must run in the family." He turned away to stare out across the river at the Albert Embankment on the far side, and then wheeled back again. "What does Courtney have to say about it?"

"I talked to him this morning," Cuthrie said. "He insists that his only interest is to get Burghead operational as quickly as possible. If Ross has the know-how to help him do that, then he'll use it until somebody tells him he can't."

"Did he give any reason for taking it straight to

230

Brussels before he'd even consulted with us?" Lansing asked.

Cuthrie raised his eyebrows and drew a long breath. "He said that he could hardly go inviting outside people into EFC's property and at EFC's expense without telling EFC why they're there and what they're doing. I ah . . . I think it was his polite way of reminding us that EFC runs Burghead, and we don't—in other words, to go to hell."

Lansing turned a brighter shade of pink behind his white moustache and emitted an indignant *"Hrmph!"*

"Well, we can't really push the big corporations around any more these days, Ken," Cuthrie pointed out. "I'm fairly certain that Courtney is acting as a policy mouthpiece for Brussels. As soon as they found out about what Ross had stumbled on and when they realized how potent it was, they practically insisted that Ross bring the British Government in on it. Why did they do that? As I see it, they were taking out insurance to make sure that they would come through in a good light later: Nobody would be able to accuse them of attempting to keep the whole thing under wraps and impede the communication of fundamental scientific knowledge for commercial gain. They're making sure that their respectable image will still be shining and bright at the end of it. What they're telling us through Courtney is that they're only minding their own business; the further issues that the whole thing raises is our problem."

Lansing narrowed his eyes thoughtfully for a moment. "No . . ." he said slowly. "I think there's more to it than that. This is too big for them not to want to be in on it. They're worried in case we clamp down on Ross with the Official Secrets Act or something and block their private information-channel through Burghead. That's why they want a clean record of having played it straight. If we do anything like that now, EFC will go running straight to the Consortium governments and use them as a lever to get the information instead. Then they would be able to point fingers at us for trying to block the spread of scientific information, sabotaging a European-funded project for reasons of national self-interest, and all kinds of

231

things like that. They've set it up rather nicely. If we leave Burghead and Ross alone, EFC will benefit, but it will be us, not them, who'll look bad when the lid eventually comes off. If we put out feelers through the diplomatic grapevine to get the other Consortium governments involved, then EFC will still be in the club. The Consortium governments could hardly cut EFC out of it when it was EFC who had done the correct thing and brought the governments in on it in the first place, could they? Either way they've guaranteed themselves a leading place in developing whatever kind of technology comes out of it." Lansing fell silent and began pacing slowly along the terrace.

Cuthrie fell into step beside him. "I agree that we can't clamp down on Ross or pull the rug out from under Burghead now," he said. "Things have gone too far. In the long run it would be bound to backfire on us. There'd be an almighty row. I'd even go as far as to say it could lose us a seat on the Federation, if the Federation ever gets set up. If it came to the crunch, Europe could get along without Burghead for a while if it had to, but *we* couldn't."

They reached the end of the terrace and turned to retrace their steps. Other members of the House were beginning to appear through the doors leading into the Parliament buildings, catching a breath of air before the commencement of the next session.

At last Lansing said, "Supposing for the sake of argument that we did try to hush things up and keep it to ourselves for the time being. What would EFC do?"

"I thought we'd already agreed on that," Cuthrie said, shrugging and sounding slightly surprised. "They'd protest to the Consortium governments."

"And what would the Consortium governments do?"

"Well . . . I suppose we'd hear about it through the diplomatic channels to begin with. If we chose not to play ball, I suppose they'd take it further and begin recruiting allies . . . probably the Americans. They'd put the squeeze on us from Washington."

"And suppose that it went the other way," Lansing said. "We get together with the Consortium governments and try to cut EFC out. What would happen then?"

"In that case EFC would go to the Americans," Cuthrie replied. "Not openly, mind you, but I'd stake a million to one that it wouldn't be long before the Americans knew what was going on . . . probably as a result of a contrived leak through the U.S. fusion community."

"So either way it's out of the bag, isn't it," Lansing mused. "The EFC knows about it already, the Consortium governments are bound to find out about it whatever happens if they don't know already, and unless we allow ourselves to be pulled up and down on strings held by EFC, the Americans will be in on it too . . . and probably a few more before very long."

"It looks like it, Ken," Cuthrie agreed glumly. "EFC would prefer to be part of a small club, I'm sure, but they won't hesitate to make the club bigger if there's no other way for them to stay in."

"And then what?" Lansing asked.

Cuthrie thought for a second. "Then they'd all start building their own machines," he said. "Oh, God! Can you imagine the chaos with a half-dozen of the damn things all working against each other?"

"Only because each one would know that the others were building them," Lansing said. His voice became thoughtful, as if thoughts that had been forming in his mind for a while were at last coming to the surface. "They'd all be paranoid with suspicion of each others' motives because none of them would ever know for sure what the rest were up to. And that would all be because they had been kept in the dark to begin with. But . . . on the other hand, if they were *all* in on it from the very start . . ." He stopped abruptly and stood with a strange expression on his face.

Cuthrie stared for a moment and then gasped as he realized what Lansing was driving at. "Good God!" he exclaimed. "Surely you're not suggesting—"

"Why not?" Lansing demanded. "Why wait for them to grab a share in it? If they're going to get a slice anyway, let's give it to them and capitalize on being magnanimous. Let's preempt the whole bloody lot of them—EFC, the Consortium gang, the Americans, and whoever's in line after that. We *will* contact the Consortium governments through the usual channels just as EFC are moralizing that we should, but while we're at it we'll include the U.S., the Commonwealth, the Japanese . . . the Soviets too. Why not?"

"What? All of them? You can't be serious!" Cuthrie gasped as if Lansing had suddenly taken leave of his senses.

"Why not?" Lansing repeated. "Then we'd beat all of them at their own game."

"But don't you realize the defense implications that something like this could have?" Cuthrie protested. "We can't make a present of it to the Soviets and God alone knows who else."

"And do *you* realize the consequences if something like this were *allowed to become* a defense issue?" Lansing countered. "That's the real risk. The only safe alternatives are total security or no security. Anything in between would be disastrous. It's already too late to hope for the first, so we must go all-out to insure the second before anybody has time to cultivate any vested interests. You said yourself earlier that this could affect the whole world. So let's make it the world's . . . and let the world decide how it wants to use this knowledge." He walked over to the balustrade and braced his arms along the top to stare out across the river. Cuthrie joined him, still looking somewhat shaken at the Prime Minister's suggestion.

"Don't look so worried, Graham," Lansing said in a more jovial voice. "Think of it—possibly the most potent scientific breakthrough in history. And we, this country, will have given it to the world, freely, of our own choosing, and without duress. What a precedent to launch whatever follows from it! Think of the prestige. I'm sure we'll be able to get far more of a return one way or another than we ever did from peddling a few barrels of oil to the Consortium mob." He turned and clapped Cuthrie heartily on the shoulder as a new thought struck him. "And if something goes wrong somewhere, then from what you say, we can always send a message back to somewhere and change it, hah-hah, hah-hah, hah-hah!"

"It looks worse than it is. The edges are a bit torn, but it's clean and that's the main thing." She swabbed a few final traces of clotted blood from around the gash in Murdoch's right arm, and straightened up to replace the bowl of surgical alcohol on the cart by the chair on which he was sitting. "The binding compound will hold it without stitches, and the diffusive shot should stop any infection. How did you do it?"

"In the Reactor Building," Murdoch replied. "Some idiot kicked a cover-plate off a catwalk thirty feet up. A foot closer and it would have been my head."

"Weren't you wearing a hard-hat?"

"Err . . . no."

"Tut tut." She shook her head reproachfully and moved the cart away.

Murdoch watched as she unloaded the tray she had been using into the sterilizer, then glanced at the nurse who was sitting at a desk nearby with her back to them. He wished the nurse would go away and find something to do elsewhere, but she seemed to have sprouted roots. "Your name's Anne, isn't it?" he said, looking back.

"That's right. You must remember it from the Bull."

"You've got a good memory," Murdoch complimented. "You remembered Maxwell too."

"Maxwell?"

"The kitten. That's his name—James Clerk Maxwell. My grandfather called him that."

Anne closed the sterilizer and moved over to a sink to rinse her hands. Then she placed a lint dressing and a bandage roll on another tray. "I take it you're staying here with your grandfather for a while," she said. "Is he something to do with EFC?"

"No." Murdoch shook his head. "He's a theoretical physicist who's doing some work for Dr. Muir's people. We—that is, myself and the pal of mine you've seen—are helping out. We're in the same line."

"I see," she said. "Arm out." Murdoch held out his arm. Anne bent close to him, placed the dressing

235

over the wound, and began winding the bandage round with quick, nimble fingers. Her nearness and fragrance were making him sweat.

"Do you live around here?" he asked, keeping his voice low in an attempt to exclude the nurse from the conversation.

"Nairn . . . about fifteen miles away."

She wasn't wearing a ring, he noticed. Maybe doctors didn't when they were working. Oh, to hell with it.

"What do people do after work in Nairn?" he asked. "Or maybe on Saturdays?"

"Oh . . . you'd be surprised." She caught his eye for a second and held it in mock reproach. Her mouth was twitching in a hint of a smile that seemed calculated to keep him guessing. Murdoch sensed that all he had to do was play the next ten seconds exactly right. A sudden excitement surged through him as he realized that he was on the easy home straight.

"ANNE . . ." The voice called out suddenly from the other side of a half-open office door at the far end of the room. It sounded reedy for a man's, almost shrill. A moment later, the man himself appeared in the doorway. He had overgrown, frizzy hair, and was wearing a pair of gold-rimmed spectacles halfway down his thin, pointed nose; his white coat ranked him as another doctor, probably the one Anne worked for, Murdoch guessed. He appeared irritated. "Anne," he said again. "I've got the Health Authority woman on my line about that RCM req. that you put through. She's querying some figures in the specification. Come and have a word with her, will you. I can't talk to her about this electronics gibberish."

"I'll be right there," Anne said. "Just tidying up Mr. Ross's arm."

"Oh, Nurse Reynolds can finish that off. Come and get this wretched woman off my phone."

Anne secured the bandage with an adhesive pad and smoothed it down. "The wound's quite deep," she said quickly to Murdoch. "You should try and rest it for a while. We'll put the arm in a sling for a few days to keep it out of action." She turned to the nurse, who had risen from the desk and moved over toward

236

them. "Could you fix Mr. Ross up with a light sling, please. Also arrange for him to come back for us to have another look at it in a week's time." With that she disappeared through into the office, and the door closed. The sign on it read DR. M.J. WARING. Murdoch glowered at it, hoping that his stare could focus malevolence on the man that the name symbolized—a somewhat impractical attempt at voodoo.

"It's really none of my business, but I couldn't help overhearing," the nurse whispered as she positioned a narrow band of black material around his neck. "I think you'll be lucky if you're not wasting your time."

Murdoch scowled at her. "How come?"

"I believe she's already going out with someone. She's the kind that tends to keep to one at a time, if you know what I mean."

"Big guy, red face . . . looks like a prize-fighter?"

"Yes. You know him then?"

"I've seen him around." Murdoch sighed resignedly. He looked at the nurse again. She was slightly on the plump side, but quite pretty with bright, blue eyes and blonde curls beneath her cap. "What are you doing on Saturday?" he asked on impulse.

"Tied up, I'm afraid. I've got to go to a wedding."

"Oh, really? Whose?"

"Mine, actually."

Murdoch decided it just wasn't one of his days.

Lee was sprawled on a seat in the waiting room outside, browsing through a magazine, when Murdoch left the clinic. He looked up, tossed the magazine aside, and hauled himself to his feet.

"How's the arm? Didn't they amputate?"

"It's okay. It wasn't as bad as it looked; a lot of it was just blood and skin. It looks as if you'll be doing all the driving for a day or two though."

"Still feel sick?" Lee asked as they walked out into the corridor and turned in the direction of the elevators.

"No. That's worn off now. They gave me something to get rid of the nausea."

They stopped in front of one of the elevators, and Lee pressed the call button.

"So . . ." Lee said after a few seconds. "Was she there?"

Pause.

"Yes." Murdoch continued to stare blankly at the doors in front of him.

"So?"

"So what?"

"So, did you get a date?"

"I don't know."

"What the hell do you mean, you don't know?" Lee demanded. "Either you're seeing her or you're not. What happened?"

"You wouldn't believe it." The doors slid open, and they stepped inside.

"You screwed it up," Lee declared flatly.

"I did *not* screw it up. Her boss screwed it up. He came muscling in at exactly the wrong moment. Another minute and I'd have been all fixed up."

"That's the lousiest excuse I ever heard. Come on, be honest—you blew it."

"I did *not*. Look, I've gotta come back in a week for a check. We'll see then what happens. I'll lay you money on it."

"Five pounds," Lee said at once.

"You're on."

"You'll screw it up."

"We'll see."

A week later Murdoch returned and was told that Anne was off for the day, visiting her family in Dundee. His arm was healing satisfactorily, and there was no need for him to come back again. The visit cost him five pounds.

CHAPTER THIRTY

Through April and into May, groups of scientists, political advisers, and delegates from various governments visited Storbannon to meet Charles and his team, to learn more of the breakthrough and what it meant, and to see the machine for themselves. Most of the visitors spent a few days there, and the Guest Wing was reopened to accommodate them. The place began to acquire the atmosphere of a cosmopolitan, residential club for the world's scientific and political élite. As further research into the machine and its workings continued, a model gradually emerged of a dynamic timeline continuum in which spontaneous fluctuations at the quantum level could occasionally manifest themselves as major changes in events at higher levels. This meant that a future situation as described in a message that was sent back could be found to have changed when the recipients of the message eventually arrived there, even if no action was taken because of the message. The discovery of this fact, achieved through a long series of experiments that involved sending back random numbers, in no way detracted from the value of the new technology; on the contrary, it implied that the outcomes of major undertakings frequently hinged on apparently trivial details, and the ability to know in advance just how significant such details would be promised undreamed-of possibilities. In fact the whole thing seemed too awesome. Everybody who became involved agreed on the need for a full-scale experiment along the lines that Charles had originally suggested, but nobody was willing to take the initiative in proposing the actual form that such an experiment should take. The enormity of what it implied had mentally paralyzed all of them.

At Burghead, the physicists working on the reactor problem progressed with the task of integrating Charles's theory into their design calculations. By the end of May they had reached a point where a series of moderate-power tests of the reactors and the accelerator system were needed to check their preliminary results for a revised arrangement of target geometry. A schedule of tests was drawn up accordingly, and arrays of instruments were set up around the target chambers to capture details of the complex interactions that were expected as conditions approached the onset of the extreme nonlinearities featured in Charles's equations. Murdoch had not yet seen the Burghead system running. Accordingly he drove up to the plant

239

on the day the tests were due to begin, and by mid-morning was in the main control room in the Reactor Building, watching the checkout procedures as the accelerators were brought up to the power levels required.

Mike Stavely scanned a column of mnemonics that had just appeared on one of the displays in the mosaic of screens and indicator panels before him while Murdoch watched over his shoulder. All the stations in the control room were manned, and on every side displays changed and lights flickered as the computers analyzed, summarized, and reported the status of every section and subsystem of the nine-square-mile complex. Elizabeth, Courtney, and a few of the other senior executives were standing around in small groups to observe the tests getting under way.

Mike turned his head slightly to speak into a microphone projecting toward him from one side of the console. "FIC's third phase are all plus. Sequencer has unlocked. How are the quad-field stabilizers?"

"We've still got orange," a voice replied from a grill above one of the screens. "Status checkout still running."

"Advise as soon as complete, will you," Mike said.

"Will do."

Mike flipped a couple of switches, entered a code into a touchboard, and spoke into the microphone again. "Are you there, Linac One?"

"Reading," a different voice replied.

"We need vacuums, RTX affirmations, and pilot lineup vectors."

"Coming up now," the voice advised. "Vacuums are *Go*. RTX slaving to your Channel Five."

Murdoch watched for a moment longer as another screen filled with hieroglyphics, and then he sauntered across to where Elizabeth was standing with Simon Vickers and one of the engineers. "From what I can tell, it seems to be going fine," he said.

Elizabeth nodded. "Yes, all on schedule. With a bit of luck we'll see some one-shot firings before the end of today. I hope it goes smoothly from here on. If things ease off a bit, I'll be able to get down to Stor-bannon again. How are things going down there?"

"We're getting some pretty interesting people com-ing through," Murdoch replied. "It's a pity you couldn't get down in the last couple of days. We had a bunch of people from all over talking about possible cosmo-logical implications. You'd have liked it."

"Cosmology?" Elizabeth looked puzzled. "What's the machine got to do with cosmology? I'm not sure I follow."

"It's amazing," Murdoch began. "They—" He stopped as Vickers returned his eyes from something that he had been watching on the far side of the room and nodded to acknowledge Murdoch's presence. "Hi, Simon."

"Good to see you again, Murdoch," Vickers said. "You've come up to see us begin the tests, eh?" He glanced quickly around. "Where's Lee? I'd have thought he'd be around to see the system working as well."

"He's not feeling too well," Murdoch said. "He was in bed most of yesterday, and couldn't get up today. Said he felt washed out."

"Oh dear, I do hope it isn't anything serious," Elizabeth said. "Have you had a doctor there?"

"He said it was just a bug," Murdoch told her. "Thinks he'll be okay tomorrow."

"I hope he's right," Vickers said dubiously. "It couldn't be that funny thing that people around here have been coming down with, could it?"

Murdoch shrugged and sighed. "You know Lee. I wouldn't have thought so though. It seems to be affecting just Burghead people."

Since the beginning of May, eight of the Burghead technical staff, all of whom worked in the Reactor Building, had succumbed to a mysterious sickness that had not yet been fully diagnosed. There had been a minor flurry of speculation in the press and news media that the sickness could have some connection with the fusion-related activities going on at Burghead, but this had died away after official statements that the effects had nothing in common with any that would have resulted from radiation.

One of the technicians at a nearby panel called the engineer over to point out something on a display, and Vickers moved away to join them. Murdoch and Elizabeth began walking slowly toward one side of the room and stopped in front of the large window that looked down over the reactor bay. The bay was brightly lit, and a number of technicians were moving around among the mass of tubes and steelwork surrounding the reactor housing.

"What were you saying a minute ago about cosmology?" Elizabeth asked.

"In the last couple of days we've had a German cosmologist and a Russian astronomer getting interested in the fact that matter-annihilation produces tau waves," Murdoch told her. "They pointed out that celestial black holes annihilate matter on a huge scale; therefore they ought to produce tau waves on a huge scale."

"I see . . ." Elizabeth said, starting to sound interested. "That's an intriguing thought. What happened then?"

"They used some of Grandpa's equations to try to estimate how far back in time the tau radiation from a supernova collapse should rematerialize in normal space, and what the characteristics of the transfer would be. The results were interesting, to say the least: They gave a concentration of energy equal to about a hundred times the amount radiated by an average galaxy, rematerializing inside a volume of about one millionth of a galactic diameter. And it would rematerialize approximately four billion years ago!"

Elizabeth's jaw dropped open in amazement as she saw the implication. She stared incredulously at Murdoch for a second, and then gasped, "Not quasars!"

"Yes, quasars!" Murdoch exclaimed. "They must be. The quasars that we see today from four billion years in the past must be nothing less than the white holes that today's black holes are feeding through tau space!"

"A closed system," Elizabeth breathed. "The quasars evolved into today's galaxies, which produced the supernovas, which produced the black holes. The whole thing is a closed system."

"And you haven't heard all of it," Murdoch said, nodding vigorously. "How do you think the number works out when you figure the same thing for when the whole universe caves in at the end of it all—the 'Ultimate Collapse'? That'll be the biggest black hole ever. Every particle of matter and photon of radiation will be squeezed into tau space and shot back through time. Guess where to."

Elizabeth's eyes widened even further; she had already guessed the answer.

"Forty billion years!" Murdoch said, still nodding. "It will reappear forty billion years in the past. That's what caused the Big Bang! The Big Bang was the end of the universe projected back through tau space. They're both the same thing! How's that for a total recycling system? It has to be the biggest reset loop ever!"

Before Elizabeth could form any reply, a technician came out of an office that opened out onto the control room floor, looked around, and came over to where they were standing. "Excuse me," he said. "There's a call for Mr. Ross in the Supervisor's Office."

"Who is it?" Murdoch asked.

"A Dr. Patterson."

"Who's Dr. Patterson?"

"You'd better go and find out," Elizabeth suggested.

Murdoch followed the technician into the office and was ushered across to a swivel-mounted vi-set on one of the consoles. His eyebrows lifted in surprise as he moved around in front of the screen. It was Anne, from the Medical Department.

"Hello," he greeted brightly. "What can I do for you?" Then he saw the serious expression on her face, and his smile faded. "What's up?"

"I've some bad news for you, I'm afraid," she replied. "Your friend, Mr. Walker, was taken very ill at Storbannon late this morning."

"Lee? What's wrong with him? Where is he now?"

"We're not exactly sure," Anne said. "He collapsed about halfway through the morning and was taken to the hospital at Kingussie. The Emergency Unit at

Kingussie contacted us and asked us to get in touch with you. I understand that he doesn't have any direct relatives over here."

Murdoch was unable to think clearly with the suddenness of the news. "No . . . that's right, he hasn't," he mumbled. "How much do you know yet. Is—is it serious?" He frowned suddenly as the meaning of something that Anne had said at last percolated through. "Why did Kingussie contact you about it? Is it the same thing as you've had breaking out around here in the last couple of weeks?"

Anne bit her lip, hesitated for a moment, then nodded almost imperceptibly. "It's impossible to say for sure at this stage, but . . . it sounds as if it could be."

"If it is, how serious is it?" Murdoch asked, sounding worried.

Anne avoided a direct answer. "Can you come over to the Medical Department?" she suggested. "There are some things we'd like to ask you. We'll tell you as much then as it's possible to tell."

"Of course," Murdoch replied. "I just want to call Storbannon first to find out what happened. Then I'll be right over."

He called Storbannon immediately after Anne cleared down. Robert answered and transferred the call to Cartland.

"It's a bloody bad show, I'm afraid," Cartland told him. "Robert took him in a tray of something to eat because he hadn't had anything for two days. Then we heard an almighty crash in there a few minutes later. He seemed to be having some kind of seizure, mainly in his arm. He didn't seem to be able to see anything, and we couldn't get any response when we talked to him. I did what I could, and Robert called an ambulance from Kingussie. That's about all I can tell you. What else have you heard?"

"Only that it could be the same as that thing people here have been coming down with, and nobody knows what it is," Murdoch replied. "I'm going over to talk to them now. I'll call you again as soon as I get out."

"I'd appreciate it," Cartland said. "I found his U.S. social security card and all that stuff, and sent it off

with the ambulance in case they needed it for anything. Do you want me to call his folks in the States?"

"Better wait until I've had a chance to talk here,"
Murdoch suggested. "I may have more news later."

"Jolly good. Okay then, Murdoch, I'll wait until I
hear from you."

Murdoch cut the call, left the control room, and
headed for the elevator bank. Minutes later he was
up at ground level, hurrying out of the main entrance
of the Reactor Building.

CHAPTER THIRTY-ONE

Murdoch arrived in the Medical Department and was
greeted by the blue-eyed nurse; there was no sign of
Anne. The nurse showed him to a door marked DR.
M.J. WARING, which opened off the waiting room.
From its position, Murdoch guessed that it was another door into the same office that he had seen from
the room in which his arm had been treated. The
nurse knocked once, then opened the door and showed
him in without waiting for a reply; evidently his arrival
was being awaited.

The frizzy-haired doctor, who Murdoch had already
guessed had to be Waring, was sitting behind the desk
inside, clad in a white coat and peering up over his
gold-rimmed spectacles. Sitting next to Waring was
another man, whose face was unfamiliar. He gave the
impression of being tall, even though he was seated,
and was lean, gray-haired, gaunt-faced, and of dis-
tinguished appearance. He was dressed in a three-
piece suit of dark charcoal pinstripe, and was resting
his hands on the desk in front of him, fingers interlaced loosely, to reveal brilliant white shirt cuffs fas-
tened by heavy, gold links. Frizzy-hair motioned Murdoch into a chair on the opposite side of the desk,
and waited until the nurse had left and closed the door
before he began speaking.

"Mr. Ross, I take it. You are Mr. Walker's colleague from the United States?"

"Yes."

"I'm sorry about what's happened, naturally. I don't think we've met before. My name is Waring, and I'm in charge of this department. This is Sir Giles Fennimore. Sir Giles is a specialist from London who is up here to investigate the cases of sickness that have been occurring at Burghead. No doubt you've heard about them."

"How do you do," Murdoch said awkwardly, not quite knowing what form of address was appropriate. Fennimore inclined his head slightly without smiling. Murdoch looked back at Waring. "A specialist in what? Have you found out what this thing is?"

"It appears to be a disturbance of the central nervous system," Waring replied. "The cause has not yet been positively identified." He paused for a moment. "It is of an extremely virulent nature, and all the cases that we have seen to date have exhibited rapid deterioration." His voice fell to an apologetic note. "I'm afraid that, so far, there have been no indications of any subsequent . . . improvement."

Murdoch could only nod his head numbly. "I see," he managed, in a voice that caught somewhere in his throat. A few seconds of heavy silence passed.

Then Fennimore leaned forward and brought his hands up to his chin. "You should be aware, Mr. Ross, that we cannot be absolutely sure at this stage that your colleague is suffering from the same complaint as the others from Burghead," he said. "However, from the information that we have received from Kingussie, it does sound highly likely." His voice was quiet, but at the same time firm in the kind of way that could command instant authority and respect without needing to sound overbearing.

"We should know the answer to that very shortly," Waring said. "Mr. Walker is being moved here from Kingussie at this moment. We expect him to arrive within the next fifteen minutes or so."

Murdoch studied the two expressionless faces across the desk. There was something very strange about this whole business, he told himself. Why had Fennimore, a "sir" who was clearly far removed from being a prescriber of pills and bottles for family medicine closets, come all the way from London to investigate

246

a few cases of an obscure sickness in a place as remote as this? Why was he here?

And surely it wasn't normal for a patient admitted to a regular hospital to be transferred to the medical facility of a privately owned industrial plant . . . or, come to that, any industrial plant. Why were they sending Lee here? The only possible reason was that Fennimore was here. But how had the people at Kingussie known that Fennimore was here? More likely they hadn't known, Murdoch thought. They had probably been alerted, presumably along with lots of other places as well, to watch out for any further cases of the Burghead type, and report them to some kind of agency that knew of Fennimore's movements. Why?

And given that Fennimore had been informed through some channel such as that, surely it would have been far simpler to send him to Kingussie rather than have Lee brought to him . . . unless, of course, the medical people at Burghead knew something that the doctors at Kingussie didn't know. And the doctors at Burghead had seen this sickness before.

All very strange. But Murdoch was neither in a position, nor in a frame of mind, to cross-examine anybody.

"We would like you to answer a few questions about Mr. Walker if you can," Waring resumed. "It could be of considerable help to us."

"Sure. . . ." Murdoch shrugged and spread his hands. "Anything you want to know." Waring reached out and tapped a pad on the touchboard of the terminal standing on a small table by the desk. Evidently the conversation was going to be recorded.

"How long have you known Mr. Walker?" Waring asked.

"About six years. When I met him, we were both working for the Fusion Electric Corporation in California. That was in . . . 2004, I think. Yes . . . about six years."

"And you've known him fairly closely ever since?"

"Pretty much. We went into business together in 2006."

"What kind of business?"

"Technical consulting."

"Did it involve any hazardous environments? Any time overseas?"

"No, none that I can think of. We did all our work in the States."

"He didn't go abroad at all during that time?"

"To Mexico once, and Canada a couple of times . . . oh, and a vacation in Hawaii."

"When was that?"

"About three years ago."

"I see. Do you know if Mr. Walker ever suffered from any major ailments or diseases during his early life?"

"None that he ever mentioned, but he didn't talk much about that kind of thing. Certainly there was nothing disabling; he's always been pretty active."

"In the time that you have known him, has he ever complained of minor visual disturbances—haziness, blurring, dimness of vision, temporary blind spots, anything like that?"

"Never."

"Has he ever shown any signs of susceptibility to fatigue, or complained of dizziness, unsteadiness of the legs, or problems with balance?"

"Never . . . unless you count the last couple of days."

"How about emotional abnormalities—things like inexplicable euphoria, apathy, inability to concentrate, sudden depression, or laughter for no reason? Ever anything like that?"

Murdoch could only shake his head. "No, nothing like that at all, ever." He sighed. "He's always been the exact opposite: totally in control of himself physically and mentally for as long as I've known him. I've never known him to be sick before. It's a complete shock."

"I see, Mr. Ross," Waring said. "Well, thank you very much for your help."

"I don't really feel I've been much help at all," Murdoch said.

"On the contrary, you've given us some valuable information," Waring told him. He turned to look at Fennimore. "Do you have anything to add, Sir Giles?"

"Just one thing." Fennimore raised a pair of mild,

gray eyes; Murdoch suddenly had the eerie feeling that they were looking in through his own, and reading the currents in his brain directly. "Was Mr. Walker in the California area around the time of August–September last year?"

"Why, yes," Murdoch answered, slightly surprised by the question. "We lived there. We ran our office in Palo Alto."

A flicker of concern passed momentarily across Fennimore's face. "Were you there at that time as well?" he asked, in a voice that had suddenly taken on a sharper tone.

"No, I wasn't," Murdoch told him. "I moved to New York in late July. Lee was due to follow on after he'd cleared up a few outstanding things. Why?"

"It's just something that we're curious about," Fennimore replied. His voice sounded more relaxed. He sat back in his chair in a manner that said that the matter was closed. Murdoch's suspicions of something strange going on behind it all increased. Before he could frame a question, the call-tone sounded from Waring's vi-set. Waring excused himself and tapped a pad to accept the call. It was the blue-eyed nurse.

"The ambulance from Kingussie has just landed," she announced. "They're bringing Mr. Walker up now."

"Thank you, nurse," Waring acknowledged. "We'll be through there straight away. Tell Anne we need to talk to her, and come and collect Mr. Ross, would you." He cut the screen and turned to face Murdoch. Fennimore was already getting up from his chair. "I'm afraid you'll have to excuse us, Mr. Ross," Waring said. "We have to begin a detailed examination at once. I really don't see that it would serve any purpose for you to wait here since we may be some time. I suggest that you go back to Glenmoroch. We will call you there as soon as there is anything definite to report. We will arrange for Mr. Walker's next of kin to be notified as a matter of routine. Thank you once again for your assistance."

Waring rose to his feet and turned to follow Fennimore, who had already disappeared through a door at the rear of the office. At the same time the door leading out to the waiting room opened, and the nurse appeared, holding the door aside for Murdoch to leave. Still in a daze, Murdoch stumbled out of Waring's office and into the waiting room. The nurse hurried away through another door while he stopped for a moment to collect his wits. The sight of the room triggered off the recollection of Lee sprawling across one of the seats, thumbing casually through a magazine, on the day that Murdoch had hurt his arm. It seemed like only yesterday.

Voices sounded from the corridor outside. Murdoch moved over to the door and looked out just in time to see a figure wrapped in bright red blankets being rushed by on a gurney from the direction of the elevators by two white-clad orderlies. Its features were glazed, waxlike, and bloodless; Murdoch almost failed to recognize them. He was still staring, paralyzed with shock, when the gurney was whisked out of sight through another door farther along the corridor.

"Hello, Mr. Ross," a voice said quietly behind him. "I'm so sorry this has happened." Murdoch turned his head dazedly. It was Anne. She had been following a few paces behind the gurney, evidently after having met the ambulance on the landing pads outside. "Are you feeling all right?" she asked.

Murdoch pulled himself together and shook his head to clear it. "I'm okay," he murmured. "It's all a bit . . . sudden, that's all."

"Of course," she said. "Would you like to sit down for a minute? Maybe I could ask the nurse to get you a cup of tea or something." Murdoch shook his head.

"There's no need. I'll have something when I get back." He paused, wondering how to phrase any of the questions that were tumbling through his mind. Before he could say anything, one of the waiting-room doors opened, and the nurse poked her head through.

"Dr. Waring says he'd like to talk to you straight away," she said, looking at Anne.

"Tell him I'm on my way," Anne replied. The nurse vanished. Anne looked back at Murdoch. "I'm sorry but I'll have to go. Try not to worry too much. There is a chance that it's not as serious as we think."

She began moving away in the direction of the door through which the gurney had been taken.

"I need to talk to you," Murdoch called after her on a sudden, uncontrollable impulse. Anne stopped, turned, and raised her eyebrows, giving the uncanny impression that she already knew what he was going to say although Murdoch wasn't quite sure himself. He gestured helplessly with his arms. "Look . . . all I've been doing in there is answering questions. I still don't know anything about this thing, or what it is, or . . . *anything*. You've seen this before. What the hell's going on around this place?"

"I understand your situation," she said dubiously. "But I'm not sure I could really tell you any more than Dr. Waring already has."

"He hasn't told me anything," Murdoch protested. "Look, that's my partner they just took through there. He's six thousand miles from home, and I'm the only person on this side of the Atlantic who's got anything to do with him. Surely I've got a right to know something."

Anne hesitated for a moment; her expression softened. "I can't talk to you now," she said. "They're waiting for me. You heard the nurse."

"I know," Murdoch said. "But later maybe, after work. We could have a coffee someplace. Thirty minutes."

"We might be a while," Anne warned him.

"I'll go back to the Reactor Building and stay on the same number you called me on earlier. I'll stay there until you're through here, okay?"

Anne took a long breath, then nodded quickly. "Very well. I'll call you there as soon as I'm ready to leave. Don't expect too much though." With that she turned, walked away, and disappeared out of the corridor.

CHAPTER THIRTY-TWO

He met her in the Burghead cafeteria at six-thirty. The place was fairly busy with technicians and engineers snatching a break and a meal before continuing the day's tests on into the evening. Murdoch and Anne found a quiet table in a corner by a window looking out over the VTOL pads, away from the chattering groups of people.

Waring and Fennimore, she told him, had confirmed that Lee was suffering from whatever had afflicted the other eight. She went on to summarize as much as she knew about the disease: It took the form of a rapid deterioration of the myelin insulating sheaths that encased the nerve fibers of the brain and spinal cord; it was caused by a virus that had been isolated, but that did not belong to any of the strains familiar to medical science; the origin of the virus had not been established; no method of halting the disease had been discovered so far. She also told Murdoch that Lee was being moved that night to a special section of the Intensive Care Unit at the Royal Infirmary in Glasgow, which had been set up to take care of the Burghead victims.

"You asked me to be frank," she concluded, speaking in a low voice. "At present it doesn't look as if any of them has much of a chance of recovering. The symptoms are almost certainly terminal."

"How long?" Murdoch asked stonily.

"It's difficult to say. . . . A few months at the most, perhaps."

Murdoch stared at the top of the table for a long time without saying anything. He had often tried to imagine what it would be like to be alone with her and talk to her, but never had he dreamed it would be like this. "Why Burghead?" he asked at last. "What's the connection with this place? Has anybody found out?"

Anne pursed her lips and toyed with the handle of

252

her coffee cup for a while as if she were trying to decide something in her mind. Murdoch watched her in silence. At last she looked up.

"I don't know why I should tell you this, but you seem to be a fairly level-headed kind of person. And besides, you'll know about it before very much longer anyway. . . ." She paused to draw a long breath. "It doesn't have any connection with Burghead. The first few cases happen to have broken out here. As far as we can tell, that has nothing at all to do with the cause of the disease."

"What?" Murdoch stared at her uncertainly. "What do you mean, 'first few cases'?"

Anne nodded. "We're starting to get reports of other occurrences—from all over—people who have nothing to do with Burghead or any other kind of fusion establishment. The only thing that the victims seem to have in common is that they were all in the West Coast area of the U.S.A. at around August–September last year. The eight from the plant were there on an exchange program. We don't know why the symptoms appeared in them sooner than in people in other places. Presumably all the victims contracted the virus in August–September last year, and since then it's been gestating. Some local factor may have triggered it into an active state slightly earlier here—a dietary difference, maybe. It could have been anything."

"That explains something, anyhow," Murdoch said slowly.

"Oh, what?"

"That guy Fennimore wanted to know if Lee had been in California at around that time. Now I know why. Lee was there right through to the end of December."

"Were you there with him?" Anne asked, sounding suddenly alarmed.

Murdoch shook his head. "No. I moved to New York in July. Fennimore asked that too."

"Well, that's something anyway," Anne said, sounding relieved.

"Who is Fennimore?" Murdoch asked. "What's he doing here? Okay, so some new kind of disease is breaking out in places. Why is it being hushed up?"

253

"I can't tell you very much about him," Anne replied. "He's an adviser on some aspects of medical legislation to the Government. He visits Dr. Waring occasionally. I never really get to speak to him."

"What kind of legislation?" Murdoch asked.

"I really can't tell you any more than that."

Murdoch eyed her suspiciously for a second or two. He had the distinct feeling that she was holding something back, but he realized that she had already said more than was necessary; he was hardly in a position to demand answers. He rubbed his chin thoughtfully for a while and reflected upon the things she had told him.

"So what does it point to?" he asked at last. "This virus, wherever it came from, first showed up on the West Coast about nine months ago."

"Yes."

"And for most of that time it's been gestating. But in the last few weeks the first symptoms of it going into an active state have started to appear . . . all in people who were there at that time." Murdoch's eyes widened slowly as the full implication dawned on him. He looked up sharply, but Anne kept her eyes averted as if she knew already what he was going to say. "So what will happen when it starts there?" he said. "There are millions of people who live there. It's one of the most densely pop—"

"It's already started," Anne said, looking straight at her cup and barely moving her mouth. "We've had data coming through via London all day. It's not being released for publication, but the media are bound to put it together for themselves before long."

Murdoch gaped at her, horrified. "Where?" he gasped. "How many? How bad is it?"

"Mainly in Northern California," she told him. "A lot in San Francisco; some in the Los Angeles area; a few in other parts of the world, but mainly other places in North America, primarily cities. In total about three thousand cases have been confirmed, but the rate of incidence is getting faster."

"Three *thousand!*" Murdoch was stunned. *"Jesus!* And there's no way of stopping it yet? How fast will it spread?"

"Once the virus activates, it becomes infectious," Anne said. "Now that it's started to appear in its active form, there's nothing except whatever natural immunity exists to stop it spreading through a whole population. We don't have any information on that yet." She looked up at last and met his eyes. Her face was grave. "All the signs point toward a major epidemic breaking loose, and not just in North America. How many places do you think it will have been carried to in the last nine months? It's probably in its gestating form already among the population of just about every city in the world."

By early the next morning, news bulletins were carrying some mention of outbreaks of an unidentified disease that had occurred in various places, notably in the western United States; the details were evidently too sparse and too scattered for the media companies to have formed any global picture yet. A statement issued by the U.S. Health Department was couched in vague and reassuring terms, and little was reported in the way of public reaction.

Murdoch called his father in Chicago to find out if there were any differences in the story being told nearer the scene. It turned out that Malcom wasn't even aware that any such story was being told at all and didn't seem overly interested in the subject. Murdoch had no overt reason to press the matter further, so he switched the conversation to family matters and let it go at that.

After that, Murdoch called Lee's family in California, his second call to them since returning from Burghead the previous evening, to ask if they had received any further news on Lee. They had not. The general situation, however, was receiving more attention there than seemed to be the case in Chicago.

The latest development that night—it was approaching midnight local time—had been an admission by the State Governor that there was a risk that the outbreak reported earlier in the day could grow to major proportions. The Governor had revealed in part of his statement that isolated cases of the disease had been appearing for some time, and that a crash program to develop a vaccine against it had been in operation for a while as a precaution against the situation that now appeared to be developing. The program had proved successful, and a plan had already been worked out with the Federal authorities for distribution of the vaccine to affected areas for mass inoculation. The plan had been set in motion, and hospitals and clinics throughout the state were being alerted to make suitable preparations. There was no cause for alarm. By 8:30 British time, the British news bulletins were already carrying extracts from the California State Governor's statement, and had taken on a more serious tone.

Murdoch was somewhat puzzled by these announcements. According to Anne only the evening before, no hope for a cure was even remotely in sight. But the Governor of California had stated only hours later that a vaccine had been sufficiently developed for mass distribution to commence. Murdoch was convinced that if Anne had known of the vaccine, she would have mentioned it, even if only in general terms. The implication was, therefore, that she hadn't known about it. But if she was a doctor who worked at one of the places where interest in the disease seemed to be focused, why would she be kept in the dark about something like that? It didn't make sense.

The other thing that puzzled Murdoch was the Governor's alleged statement that work on the vaccine had been going on "for some time." How long was some time? Anne had said that the Burghead victims were among the earliest reported; but the cases at Burghead had appeared only in the previous couple of weeks. Murdoch was not an immunologist, but he found it difficult to believe that a drug to combat a hitherto unknown strain of virus could be developed, tested, and put into volume manufacture in so short a time. Therefore "for some time" meant a lot more than merely a couple of weeks, which suggested that somebody, somewhere, had been expecting something like this to happen. Who? Where? What the hell was going on?

But although Murdoch was concerned, his main fears were not for lots of potential victims, most of whom he didn't know, but for one particular already confirmed victim in an isolation unit in Glasgow. The more he brooded about it, the more the vague thought that had begun to form the evening before when he was driving back from Burghead took shape. Whatever had caused the disease was already fact; there was one possible way, however, by which that fact might be changed. Murdoch voiced it at last to Cartland after they had finished making calls and monitoring the news, and had sat down for breakfast. Charles had gone to Burghead early that morning and was not available to be consulted.

"The *machine?*" Cartland repeated incredulously. "You want to use the machine to change it?"

"Why not?" Murdoch demanded. "Even if they have come up with a vaccine, it can't fix the damage that's already been done. It can't help people like Lee. The only way to help them now is to go back and catch what started it. Only the machine can do that."

"But . . . we can't!" Cartland protested. "We agreed that we weren't going to fool around with it for things like that—not for a while anyway."

"Screw what we agreed!" Murdoch shouted suddenly. "For Christ's sake, the guy is dying! Are you saying we just sit on our asses here and do nothing when the way to stop it might be right down there under our feet in the goddam basement?"

Cartland blinked uncertainly, momentarily taken aback by Murdoch's outburst. "How?" he asked. "It's all very well to say catch what started it, but as far as I can see, nobody seems to know what *did* start it. So exactly what are you proposing that we change?"

"I don't know," Murdoch admitted, at the same time calming down somewhat. "But I'm pretty sure there are people around who know a hell of a lot more than they're letting on about. This guy Fennimore, for instance—we've got to get at him and find out more of what he's up to. Then maybe we'll be able to figure out where we go next."

Cartland sat back in his chair and thought about it. At length he nodded decisively to indicate that he was prepared to go along with what Murdoch had said.

"So how are we going to do that?" he asked, looking back up at Murdoch. "We don't even know where Fennimore might be this morning."

"We don't," Murdoch agreed. "But I know somebody who might. I'll call her first thing after breakfast."

Murdoch called Burghead fifteen minutes later and asked for the Medical Department. Anne was not there. The blue-eyed nurse was unable to tell him where Anne was, and put him through to Waring instead.

"I'm afraid that Sir Giles is traveling to the United States this morning," Waring told him in answer to his question. "Dr. Patterson has gone with him to assist. Their plane should have left two hours ago from Edinburgh."

Murdoch was stunned. "Nobody said anything about that yesterday," he said.

"I see no reason why they should have," Waring replied in a not-too-friendly voice. "But as a matter of fact they didn't know yesterday. It was only decided at the last moment very early this morning." Murdoch had a good idea what the sudden visit to the States was in connection with, but he was hardly in a position to talk about it. Waring's tone had already as good as told him that it was none of his business.

"Have you any idea how long they're likely to be gone?" Murdoch asked instead.

"No, I haven't," Waring replied. "But there's no reason why you should want to speak with Sir Giles anyway. He is a consulting specialist and does not carry prime responsibility for the patient . . . I assume you're calling to inquire about Mr. Walker. That now rests with the Royal Infirmary at Glasgow. The physician in charge there is a Dr. Fisher, who, I understand, has already spoken to your Mr. Cartland. Also, Mr. Walker's next of kin in the United States have been notified and will be informed should any change occur. For further information I must refer you to Dr. Fisher. I really can't be of more help than that, I'm afraid. Now, if you'll excuse me, I am extremely busy."

"I see. Thanks anyway," Murdoch said, and cut the call.

"Finnicky bugger," Cartland commented from where he had been watching on the far side of the room. "Why didn't you try pumping him a bit harder?"

Murdoch shook his head. "It wouldn't have done any good. You won't get any more out of him." He turned away from the vi-set and frowned as he tried to think. "Who else do we know who might give us a lead on it?" He turned back to face Cartland. "What about Grandpa's pals in London? There must be somebody among them who's got connections with whatever part of the Government Fennimore's mixed up with."

"Probably, but I'm not sure that's the best way to go about it," Cartland said dubiously. "You'd need months to fight your way through that lot, especially since you don't have anything in the way of real facts to wave around." He thrust his hands into his pockets and paced slowly over to the window, where he stood staring out for a few seconds. "A better way would be to start nearer home."

"Where?" Murdoch asked.

Cartland turned to face into the room again. "Burghead surely, I'd have thought. If there is something peculiar going on behind the scenes, this fellow Fennimore and that bloke you were talking to a minute ago can't be the only ones there who know about it, can they? I mean, they can't be running some kind of private venture inside a place like that, with nobody else having an inkling of it. Surely Courtney must know something about what Fennimore's doing there. Good God, he *is* supposed to be running the show, after all."

"That's a thought," Murdoch agreed. "But do we know him well enough to just go walking in and demanding answers to something like this? If the whole thing's being hushed up for some reason, Courtney might know about it, but why should he talk to us?"

"Well, you were about to try to get Fennimore to talk a few minutes ago, and you don't know him at all," Cartland pointed out. "But if it bothers you, why not try approaching Courtney through Elizabeth?"

"Of course!" Murdoch snapped his fingers. "What's wrong with me, Ted? I'll call her now and see if she can get me in there today. Do you think I should contact Grandpa there and get him in on it too.

"I wouldn't at this stage," Cartland said. "Wait until you've got some answers. Save your big guns until you've got something worthwhile to fire at. If you do need to get involved with London later, that would be the time to wheel in Charles. But if Liz can arrange something and you feel you need some moral support, I'll come along to Burghead too. How about that?"

"Fine," Murdoch said. "Thanks. I think maybe I'll be needing some."

CHAPTER THIRTY-THREE

"I'm sorry, but what you are asking would be grossly irregular and a flagrant breach of professional confidence," Courtney declared from behind his desk later that same day. In front of him Murdoch, Cartland, and Elizabeth listened solemnly. Elizabeth's warning of Courtney's initial response was proving to be accurate. Courtney went on, "Some weeks ago, I was approached by the Ministry and asked to agree to Sir Giles Fennimore's participation in certain investigations that our own medical people were conducting. It was, and still is, my understanding that Dr. Waring contacted London in the first instance, and on his own initiative to seek professional advice, which of course is his prerogative. Naturally I agreed to that request. I do not concern myself with day-to-day details of an issue that has no direct bearing on the operations of the facility. And even if I did, I would hardly feel obliged to divulge such information to persons whose responsibilities lie outside that area entirely." He punctuated his words with a cool glance in Elizabeth's direction, conveying in no uncertain terms that the matter had nothing to do with her or with anybody from Storbannon, and she should have known better than to have imagined otherwise.

"I understand your position," Cartland replied from his chair on one side of Elizabeth. He kept his voice calm, but at the same time managed to preserve a note of underlying urgency. "But, believe me, we do have valid reasons for asking you this, and they are important. It's impossible to believe that Fennimore just happened to appear here by chance just after the first cases were reported. He knew what he was looking for, which means that somebody had reason to believe that something like this was going to happen sooner or later somewhere. In other words, whatever caused this epidemic that's just starting has been known about for some time. It's vital that we find out who it was that knew about it, and where to contact them. They must have been involved in Fennimore's coming here, and it seems only reasonable to assume that they would have given you at least a hint of why. And that's why we've come to you."

Impatience flickered across Courtney's face for the first time. "Mr. Cartland," he said. "You must understand that matters discussed between myself, acting in my capacity as managing director of this facility, and a department of the Government have to be treated with considerable discretion. I'm sorry, but I have nothing further to add."

Elizabeth stood up and stepped forward to plant her hands on the edge of the desk. Courtney's face registered surprise.

"Lee is *dying*," she said, struggling to keep her voice calm. "So are eight people employed by this facility. So are several thousand people in America and other places, and who knows how many a week from now. If you know *anything* more than you've indicated, which you *must,* Ralph, *please* . . . we have to know what it is."

"Naturally you have my sympathy about Lee," Courtney said in a milder voice. He glanced at Murdoch and then looked back up at Elizabeth. "And I'm sorry about the others too. But aside from that, *if* I knew any more than I've already told you, I fail to see what connection it would have with anybody here apart from reasons of, if you'll pardon the expression, morbid curiosity. And *if* I knew anything more, that

261

would certainly not constitute a sufficiently good reason for me to break the confidence that my title imposes. As I have already stated, I have nothing further to add."

Elizabeth backed off, sat down again, and closed her eyes wearily. Beside her, Cartland frowned at his feet, unable to find a continuation. Murdoch gripped the sides of his chair tightly in his effort to contain his rising irritation at all the verbal niceties. None of it was getting them anywhere.

"Look, why don't we stop all this fencing around," he growled, looking directly at Courtney. "We're seeing the first stages of an epidemic that shows every sign of taking hold worldwide. We don't know what caused it, but we think there are people around who might. If we knew more about it, there's a chance we could stop it from ever having started in the first place. We could use the machine at Storbannon." With that he sat back and scowled as he waited for his words to take effect. Next to him, Elizabeth stiffened visibly. On her far side, Cartland pursed his lips in a silent whistle.

Courtney's face remained a mask of composure, devoid of any trace of reaction or emotion. For a moment, Murdoch thought that he hadn't heard; then he saw that Courtney's eyes had taken on a strange and distant fixation. Elizabeth raised her head and watched, suddenly with hope showing in her eyes. She had seen that look on Courtney's face before, and knew that behind those eyes, his mind was already racing through all the permutations and variations with the speed and precision of one of her department's computers; within seconds every alternative and implication would have been sorted, categorized, and neatly slotted into place. Murdoch and Cartland waited in silence, unsure of what exactly was happening, but sensing that a new, subtly different atmosphere had crept into the room.

At last Courtney brought his fingers together and raised them to his brow, held the pose for a few seconds, then slowly lifted his head until his fingertips were brushing the underside of his chin. He exhaled a long breath, and began speaking slowly and deliberately, his eyes focused on some distant point behind them.

"For reasons that I've never made it my business to pry into, the World Health Organization has been expecting something like this for some considerable time," he began. For a moment Murdoch was confused; then he realized to his astonishment that Courtney had dismissed any need for further explanation and had already reversed his decision without wasting further time by saying so. "The first I knew about it was when the Ministry got in touch somewhere around the beginning of this month," Courtney continued, dropping his earlier formal tone. "They told me that Waring had reported what they thought might be the first signs, and they wanted to send Fennimore up here to look into it. There may have been a few odd outbreaks appearing in other places as well around that time; I don't know. Anyway I agreed, naturally. Fennimore has been involved for some time—ever since last year, I gather—with some kind of joint U.S.-U.K. research effort aimed at developing a vaccine to combat the epidemic when it came. The organization that Fennimore represents appears to have known for a while that it would begin in the western U.S.A., but I don't think they were sure exactly what form the disease would take. That was why they were interested in getting information on the first cases as early as possible. I've never considered it my business to press for details beyond those that Fennimore and Waring chose to volunteer, which were very few. However, if it helps you in any way, I do know that Eurospace, NASA, and the Soviet Aerospace people have all been actively involved. Don't ask me why." Courtney shrugged and showed his palms to indicate that he was through.

Cartland had looked up and was sitting forward in his chair with suddenly increased interest. "What have the space agencies got to do with it?" he asked. "Can you give us any more details about that? That adds a whole new perspective to the thing."

Courtney sighed and shook his head apologetically. "I don't pretend to be an expert on such things," he said. "I think there might be a connection with satellites though . . . or, at least, one particular kind of satellite."

"Can you be specific?" Cartland asked.

"Well, I might be misleading you," Courtney warned. "But I've seen the word *Centurion* used several times. From the contexts, it seemed to be a satellite of some description, although I could be mistaken."

"*Centurion*?" Cartland screwed his face into a frown and slumped back into his chair, where he thought hard for a few seconds, at the same time tugging at one side of his moustache.

"Doesn't that mean anything to you, Ted?" Murdoch asked.

Cartland thought for a moment longer, then shook his head in an admission of defeat. "No . . . no, I can't say it does. Extraordinary."

Courtney looked from Cartland to Murdoch and then to Elizabeth. "I'm sorry, but that really is the best I can do." He pushed himself away from the desk and straightened up in his chair to indicate that the meeting was over. "It goes without saying that if I didn't trust your motives and your integrity, I would never have said the things you've just heard," he said to all three. "I don't feel there is any need to spell out the rest. I'm sorry it couldn't have been more. If I can help you further in any other way, let me know."

"Thank you, Ralph," Elizabeth said as they got up to leave. "Obviously we'll treat everything you've said with discretion." She turned toward the door, and Murdoch moved to follow.

Cartland was still sitting fingering his moustache and shaking his head thoughtfully. "*Centurion* . . ." he muttered, half to himself. "You know, it's a funny thing. I'm sure I've heard that word somewhere before, and not very long ago either. Where on Earth was it? . . "

Fifteen minutes later they were back in Elizabeth's office in the Mathematics and Physics Department. Elizabeth ordered coffees and sat down at her desk, while Murdoch settled himself in a chair below a large blackboard covered with symbols and equations. Cartland remained standing by the window, staring out over the central area of the complex. He had been noticeably quiet all the way back from Courtney's office.

"Well, Murdoch," Elizabeth said. "It looks as if you saved the day for us. I'll have to take a course in direct American speech sometime. It certainly seems to produce results. I wonder where we go from here."

"The only way I can see is to try and track Fennimore down in the States," Murdoch answered. "Maybe we could try approaching Waring now; he must know where Fennimore is. After all, we have more or less got Courtney's backing now. It's not the same as when I tried calling Waring first thing this morning."

"Mmm. . . ." Elizabeth sounded dubious. "I'm not convinced it'll be that easy. If I know Waring, he's just as likely to go protesting back to Courtney for having spoken out of turn. It might be better to try contacting Fennimore directly through the State authorities in California; Fennimore must have gone to California. Who would the people be to try first there? Do you know?"

"Not really," Murdoch confessed. "And if the news reports are anything to go by, I wouldn't mind betting that it'll be pretty near impossible to get through to anybody there right now. They're probably being swamped with calls from all over."

"Maybe we ought to talk to Charles," Elizabeth suggested.

"Maybe," Murdoch agreed. He didn't sound very happy at the idea; there was still not much in the way of hard facts to talk to Charles about. Elizabeth sensed his reluctance and lapsed into silence.

A muted whine of aircraft engines floated in from outside the building, and after a few seconds an EFC VTOL rose slowly from behind the Domestic Block and began climbing away to the south. Cartland watched it absently through the window. Then his body stiffened suddenly. He spun round and snapped his fingers.

"The pilot!" he exclaimed. Murdoch and Elizabeth frowned at him quizzically. "*That* was it—the RAF pilot! He said something about *Centurion*." Cartland began pacing excitedly back and forth in front of the window, still making snapping motions with his thumb and forefinger. "Air Support Command, Northolt . . . Eighty-third Squadron, that was it. . . . What the hell was his name? *Irish!* Irish name, Irish name . . . oh damn!"

"What is it, Ted?" Elizabeth asked in a mystified voice.

Cartland didn't seem to hear. "May I use your phone, Liz?" he asked, stopping abruptly in his tracks. "I think I may have a lead."

"Of course." Elizabeth gestured toward the vi-set by her desk. Cartland swiveled it around to face him, activated it, and called up a screen of directory data. Murdoch got up from his chair and moved round to stand beside Cartland and watch. Cartland found the call-code for the Royal Air Force base at Northolt, on the western outskirts of London, tapped it into the touchboard, and was through in a matter of seconds. After a short ritual exchange with the operator, he was looking at the features of the Station Adjutant of Number 83 Squadron.

"Good afternoon," he said briskly. "My name is Edward Cartland, formerly Group Captain. I wonder if you can help me. I need to contact one of your personnel as a matter of extreme urgency. I don't remember the name, I'm afraid, but he is a flying officer, and his name is distinctly Irish. He comes from somewhere in Gravesend."

The adjutant eyed him suspiciously for a moment, then shifted his gaze off-screen to consult some invisible oracle. "Irish, eh? Nah then, let's see what it says 'ere." His lips moved soundlessly as he read from something. "We've got a Ryan and an O'Keefe," he said, without moving his head to look back at Cartland.

"No . . . neither of those," Cartland told him. Then his face lit up suddenly. "It was an O' something though. O'Rourke, O'Brien . . . something like that."

"O'Malley?"

"*O'Malley!* That was it! How can I get in touch with him?"

"Aircrew," the adjutant pronounced solemnly. "I'll put yer through to the Ops Room." The screen blanked out for a moment, and then came alive again to present

266

the face of a good-looking, red-haired WAAF, smartly attired in an air-force-blue shirt and dark tie.

Cartland repeated his request, this time in a far more agreeable and less formal tone of voice. From behind Cartland and just outside the viewing angle of the camera, Murdoch watched intrigued, with no real idea of what was going on. Elizabeth was leaning forward with an elbow propped on the desk, and looking equally mystified. The WAAF turned sideways to interrogate a terminal just visible at the edge of the screen, and then swung back to present a full-face view.

"Flying Officer O'Malley is away on a forty-eight-hour leave," she crooned in a sultry, slightly husky, voice. "You should be able to reach him at his home. I'll give you the number." As she spoke, a Gravesend code appeared in a box at the bottom of the screen. Cartland touched a pad to lock the number into the vi-set's local memory.

"Thanks a lot, lovely," he acknowledged. "You've been a big help."

"Tell him that Monica sends her regards. He'll know who you mean." The WAAF winked saucily and vanished.

Cartland blinked in surprise at the blank screen, then turned his head to look at Murdoch. "Good Lord!" he exclaimed. "Did you see that? How extraordinary! It's enough to make a chap want to join up again."

He was already hammering in a rapid-fire command sequence to place a call to the number that he had stored. The screen lit up again and revealed a stout, middle-aged woman wearing a stained pinafore over a flower-patterned dress. Her expression changed to what could have been belligerence as she recognized Cartland's distinctly military appearance and bearing.

"Yes?" she demanded.

"Ah, good afternoon, madam. Do you have somebody called O'Malley there—a Flying Officer O'Malley of the RAF?"

"And who would be wanting him?" the woman asked, in a broad Irish brogue.

"My name is Cartland."

The woman sniffed suspiciously and turned her head to call back to somewhere over her shoulder. "*Bill. . . .*" A short pause followed, then, "You've a gentleman to talk to you on the line here." Another voice, indistinct and unintelligible, called something in reply from the background. "A Mr. Cartwheel or something, I think he said," the woman answered.

"I don't know any Cartwheels," the other voice said, becoming louder and clearer.

"Well, it's yourself he's asking for. You'd better come in here and talk to him."

" 'Arf a minute."

"He's coming to talk to you now, Mr. Cartwheel," the woman said out of the screen.

"Thank you," Cartland acknowledged. A few seconds later the woman moved out of view and was replaced by the face that Cartland had last seen two months previously in the library at Storbannon. O'Malley's shoulders were bare, and he was wiping shaving lather from his face with a towel. It took him a moment to recognize who was calling.

"Strewth! I remember you . . . from that big 'ouse up in Scotland. Fancy seein' you again! What can I do for you, sir?"

"Good to see you," Cartland replied. "I'm sorry to come busting in on your forty-eight and all that, but I think you may be able to help me with a little problem I'm having."

"If I can, sir. What's up?"

Cartland's tone became more serious. "Look, I hate to drag this up again, but it could be important. Do you remember when we were talking a couple of months ago? You mentioned a pal of yours who got killed . . . came from Southampton."

"Yes, I remember." O'Malley looked suddenly apprehensive. "What about him?"

"When you mentioned him, you said that it happened on something called *Centurion.* I'm trying to find out what *Centurion* was. It's an extremely urgent matter."

O'Malley's face dropped. "I should never have said that, sir," he protested. "I can't talk about that. They'll 'ave me shot." He squared his shoulders visibly and

268

recited, "I'm sorry, but that is security-restricted information. I am not permitted to say anything." Then he relaxed and peered suspiciously out at Cartland. "Besides, 'ow do I know you're not from friggin' Air Force Security, tryin' to catch me out?"

"I can assure you that I'm nothing of the sort," Cartland began, then realized the futility of it and sighed resignedly. "Oh damn!" He had half-expected as much. He drummed his fingers on the edge of the vi-set while O'Malley watched woodenly. Then Cartland looked up at him again. "Look, I appreciate your situation, and I don't want to put you on the spot, old boy. But can you tell me who this chap was and which unit he was with? That much can't be classified information. After all, I could be simply an old friend trying to trace him, couldn't I? You don't even have to know that anything's happened to him at all."

O'Malley considered the proposition, then nodded. His voice dropped instinctively to a lower note. "His name was Pilot Officer Barry Lewis from Communications. He was with Six twenty-sixth Squadron, Orbital Command. Copped it about eight or nine months ago. I can't say more than that."

While O'Malley was speaking, Cartland had entered a code into the vi-set to record the audio channel. He nodded his head in satisfaction. "Thanks a lot, old boy," he said. "Enjoy your leave. Oh . . . there was one other thing: Monica sends her love from Northolt. Just thought you'd like to know."

O'Malley's face fell in sudden alarm and dismay. "Quieten it down, for Christ's sake, sir," he hissed. "I've got me bird in the next room 'ere."

"Oh, good heavens! Err . . . sorry about that," Cartland mumbled. Then he raised his voice to a louder level. "Well . . . thanks again. Keep working on those nav exams. We'll see you in orbit by next year, eh?"

"I hope so, sir." O'Malley grinned. "Good luck with your problem."

Cartland cleared down and replayed the audio that he had recorded, at the same time keying the important details onto a scratchpad area of the screen. Then he recalled the directory and located the section for Buckinghamshire.

"Ted, would you mind telling us what on Earth you're doing?" Elizabeth asked.

"I've seen that guy before," Murdoch said. "He was the pilot who flew the plane when Cuthrie and the others came up to see Grandpa's machine for the first time. How did you know that he knew about *Centurion*?"

"It'd take too long to explain now," Cartland muttered, scanning down a screen of entries and then switching it for the next. "I'll tell you all about it when I've made this call."

"Who to this time?" Murdoch asked.

"It's time to wheel in the old pals," Cartland told him. Murdoch glanced at Elizabeth. She shrugged. "Ah! Here we are," Cartland said suddenly. "RAF Orbital Command Headquarters, High Wycombe." He selected the number with a movable cursor and flagged it for automatic calling. A short silence descended while he waited.

When the call was accepted, Cartland asked for a Wing Commander Wallace of Communications. After a couple of transfers of the call, the screen stabilized to show a bull-necked, broad-shouldered, but jovial-looking officer in his fifties, sporting the nearest real-life approximation to the much-caricatured RAF handlebar moustache that Murdoch had ever seen. The officer squinted for a moment, then his face broke into a smile of incredulity and evident delight.

"Teddy Cartland!" he roared. "Ted, old boy, how are things these days? Talk about a face from the past!"

"Hello, Wally. Oh, not so bad, you know. How's the old firm?"

"Same as ever. What is it then, social or business?"

"Social, actually. I'm thinking of throwing a party. Thought you might like to come along," Cartland told him.

Wallace leaned away and appeared to reach an arm out to somewhere below and to one side of the view being shown on the screen. Then he moved back into full view. "That's strange," he said matter-of-factly. "Our recorders here seem to have packed up all of a sudden. I don't know—can't trust anything these days." His expression at once became more serious. "Okay, Ted. What business?"

"Well," Cartland replied. "The truth is I'm in a bit of a pickle over something, and you're the only person I can think of who might be able to help sort it out. Do you want to hear more?"

"Of course. Shoot."

"I'm trying to track down an OC type from your mob. Name's Pilot Officer Barry Lewis, Six twenty-sixth Squadron."

"Mmm, Six twenty-sixth Squadron . . . based at Greenham Common." Wallace frowned and looked at Cartland quizzically. "That sounds fairly routine, Ted. Why didn't you go through Adastral House?"

"I think it might be a bit delicate," Cartland said. "He bought it about eight or nine months ago. I need to know where and how. I don't want you to go into it now. Could you call me back later tonight if I give you a number?"

"Oh, I see. It's like that, is it." Wallace looked slightly dubious. "It might be a better idea if I met you somewhere instead for a drink," he suggested. "That would be better if there's a lot to talk about."

"Oh, come on, Wally, I'm right up the other end of bloody Scotland!" Cartland protested, his voice rising. "What do you want me to do, hop on a bike? We've known each other too long to start playing silly buggers. The number's a private one and there's no chance of any wires."

Wallace thought for a moment, then nodded. "Very well," he said. "I'll see what I can do. Give me the number. I probably won't be able to get back to you until late though."

Cartland became very quiet for a while in the car when he and Murdoch were about halfway back to Storbannon later that evening. Murdoch drove for a few miles in silence, and then began giving Cartland increasingly frequent curious looks.

"What's on your mind?" he asked at last.

"Err . . . what, old boy?" Cartland asked, coming back suddenly from his reverie.

"What are you so deep in thought about?" Murdoch asked.

"Oh . . . it's nothing really."

"Come on. Give."

Cartland pondered for some time. At last he said, "I think I know now what *Centurion* was."

Murdoch waited for a moment expectantly, then shot across a look of surprise and bemusement. "Well, don't just sit there, Ted. Tell me. What was it? How did you figure it out?"

"It was when O'Malley said it happened eight or nine months ago," Cartland said. "I've been thinking about it, and there's only one thing it could have been. It all fits."

Silence.

"Well, what, for Christ's sake?"

Cartland shuffled uncomfortably in his seat. "It's a rather delicate issue," he said, sounding somewhat awkward. "If you don't mind, I'd rather not go into it now in case I'm wrong. I'd rather wait and see what Wally has to say when he calls tonight. Sorry to sound a bit melodramatic and all that, but there are good reasons."

Murdoch gave him another long, puzzled look, shook his head in resignation, and flipped the car into manual mode to exit from the Kingussie bypass onto the Glenmoroch road.

CHAPTER THIRTY-FOUR

It was almost ten o'clock that night when Wallace called. Murdoch and Cartland were together in the sitting room when Charles put the call through from the study. Cartland took it.

"Are you alone?" Wallace asked.

"There's one other person with me, but you needn't worry about him," Cartland replied. "What have you got for us?"

"Pilot Officer Barry Lewis, Six twenty-sixth Squadron, Greenham Common," Wallace recited. "Killed on active duty, August 12 last year. He was—"

"Ah hah!" Cartland breathed, nodding slowly. "Was he killed while actually engaged in orbital duties?"

"Err . . . yes, as a matter of fact." Wallace looked surprised.

"Then I'm not sure that you need say any more, Wally," Cartland said. "He was on QX-37, wasn't he?" Behind Cartland and to one side, Murdoch's eyes widened in sudden surprise. QX-37 had been in the news the previous August. It was the designation of an orbiting observatory that had been destroyed by the billions-to-one-against chance event of being hit by a sizable meteor during the annual Perseids shower. On the screen, Wallace's expression changed from surprise to mild indignation.

"Do you mean to say that after all this, you knew all the time? Are you playing games with me, Ted?"

"Not for certain," Cartland said. "I had an inspired guess after we spoke this afternoon, but I still needed the confirmation. There's just one other thing I need to know now: After QX-37 was hit, did they blanket the whole thing with a new codename—classified?"

"How on Earth did you know that?" Wallace asked, now looking completely taken aback. "That's a top-security classification."

"Never mind," Cartland replied. "They did, didn't they. Was that codename *Centurion*?" Wallace hesitated visibly for a moment, then nodded once. Cartland relaxed and emitted a long, satisfied sigh. "Thanks, Wally," he said. "I can fill in everything else I need myself now. Believe me, you may have done a lot of people a lot of good."

"I'm glad to hear it. Well, you know me—no questions, eh? Is that all you want?"

"That's fine."

"Good. Well, drop in for a drink when you're back this side of the wall, won't you."

"I will, Wally. And thanks again."

Murdoch was looking strangely at Cartland as Ted cut the call and turned away from the screen. Cartland looked up at him and stood waiting for him to say something.

Murdoch shrugged and threw out his hands. "Okay," he said. "I know what QX-37 was, but I still don't get it. Why couldn't you have told me that earlier? And why should an astronomical satellite have anything to do with it?"

"You heard the public version of it," Cartland said. "But there was more to QX-37 than ever got into the news or the documentaries. Sit down and I'll tell you the full story." Looking puzzled, Murdoch moved over to one of the armchairs and sat down on the edge of the seat. Cartland noticed that the door had been left ajar, ambled across the room to close it, then turned and began pacing slowly toward the window.

"QX-37 was a joint Anglo–U.S. project," he said. "I worked on parts of the design study when I was at Cornell, which is why I know something about it. There were a few astronomers up on it with a few telescopes and things, but that was really a cover. Primarily it was built as a biological research lab for conducting experiments that were considered by some people to be too dangerous to be performed anywhere down here. That was what QX-37 was really all about."

Murdoch's mouth fell open in surprise as he listened. Cartland reached the window, stared out for a moment, and then pivoted abruptly and stood looking at where Murdoch was sitting, and waited for a response.

"Too dangerous?" Murdoch's face knotted into a bemused frown. "What kind of experiments?" Then his expression changed to one of disbelief as the implication dawned on him. "Not . . . not virus research, or something like that?"

"Exactly," Cartland confirmed. His tone was ominous. "In particular, a lot of the work was connected with finding out more about certain extremely virulent and difficult-to-handle strains . . . such as those responsible for multiple sclerosis and poliomyelitis." He paused to allow Murdoch time to complete making the connection, and then continued, "I don't know if you remember, but a few years ago there was a lot of fuss about proposals to conduct research into possible ways of curing things like that by engineering enzymes that would neutralize such viruses by mutating their DNA.

274

The experiments involved would hinge on mutating viral strains in all kinds of ways, and a lot of people weren't happy about the idea. They weren't convinced that fail-proof containment measures could be guaranteed, and stirred up a huge, neurotic lobby over it. In the end they got their way, and the project was dropped—at least publicly, anyway."

"But not behind the scenes, huh?" Murdoch completed.

"Quite." Cartland clasped his hands behind his back and began pacing again. "The work had to be done. The potential benefits were enormous, not just because of the hope of being able to control a few diseases but for all kinds of other things to do with DNA manipulation . . . such as eliminating permanently a whole range of congenital defects. Anyhow, to cut a long story short, a decision was taken to move the whole show up into a specially constructed space lab, away from the Earth's surface completely. It seemed to be the ultimate in isolation. The project was approved secretly, and a small astronomical observatory and lab were included to make it look legitimate. That was the only part of it that the public heard about, and they knew it as QX-37." Cartland shrugged and stopped pacing to stare moodily into the hearth. "You know the rest."

"The Perseids or something, wasn't it?" Murdoch said.

"Yes. It's a meteor stream that intersects the Earth's orbit every year just before the middle of August . . . probably the remains of a broken-up comet. The chances of anything as small as QX-37 being hit by anything at all were too small to imagine, let alone being hit by anything big. But . . . they were finite nevertheless." Cartland shook his head and sighed. "You know, Murdoch, it's bloody ironic. There was absolutely nothing wrong with the containment measures that had been proposed in the first place. Why do these damned government people always give in to a handful of crackpots who know nothing except how to make a lot of noise? It was the same with nuclear power thirty years ago. I don't know. . . ."

"If you knew that much all along, you must have

been pretty worried when QX-37 broke up and re-entered," Murdoch said. "So must the other people who knew about it. I guess that explains why Fennimore and his bunch have been on the lookout for something."

"I was, naturally," Cartland agreed. "But I didn't really think that anything viral would have survived the burnup. I talked to a few people I knew on the inside, and they didn't think so either. Evidently we were wrong."

"What do you figure happened?" Murdoch asked.

"It's impossible to say for sure. No doubt some of the cultures were kept frozen in storage. The container they were in could have been protected from the burnup heat by the shell of the structure, and disintegrated later when the whole thing had slowed down at lower altitudes. The viruses must have been released into the atmosphere below ten miles, I'd say; anything that small released higher up in the stratosphere would stay up there for years. If you remember, the debris of QX-37 reentered over the Pacific just east of Japan. From there it would take wind-borne viruses something like . . . oh, two or three weeks maybe, to reach the West Coast of the U.S.A."

"And Wallace said it happened on August 12," Murdoch mused. "That gives us late August or early September for the viruses showing up in California. Those are the dates that Fennimore and Waring asked me about."

"Exactly. It all fits."

"And I can see why somebody would want to smokescreen the whole subject by giving it a new codename," Murdoch said. "There was too much risk of loose talk getting out that linked QX-37 with viruses. Once that happened, people would have figured out the rest in no time at all."

Cartland moved away from the fireplace and perched himself on the arm of the chair opposite Murdoch. "Well, at least it looks as if we've got an idea of what's behind it all now," he said. "But I can't see that it's going to help much. The machine downstairs can't change anything. It can't change QX-37 going up in the first place, because that happened over two years ago, and there wasn't any machine at Storbannon at all then. What else can we do—send a message to God instead, to change the orbit of the Perseids?"

"No . . ." Murdoch said, sounding thoughtful. "But maybe it could do something else. . . ." He sank back in the chair and lapsed into silence for a few seconds while Cartland watched curiously. "Fennimore has to be part of a research group that's been working on the quiet for the best part of nine months," Murdoch said. "That vaccine that they're about to administer in California can't have been developed in the last week or two. They must have known what kinds of viruses were being bred up on that satellite. In fact they probably knew early on which strains had been released because they probably picked them up from atmospheric samples even before anything had reached the West Coast at all. So they've probably had something like eight months to work on it. But suppose they'd known in *January*—after the machine here was working—what they know now! Suppose that the data on how to make the vaccine were to be sent back to then! Don't you think that might change things?"

"Good Lord!" Cartland's voice trailed away in astonishment. Then as he thought about it, his look of amazement changed to a frown. "I'm not so sure it would," he said. "I mean, yes—it might protect anybody who hadn't caught the virus by January, but from what Anne told you, nobody was catching it in January. The people who are going down like flies now all caught it last September . . . people like Lee, for instance. How could it help them? The only people it could help are the ones who are picking it up right now because the virus has come out of gestation and become communicable. If the vaccine was available a month ago, a mass-inoculation might have prevented a second wave from spreading, but how could it stop the first wave? The victims of that have been carrying it since September. What can the machine do for people like Lee?"

"It might not be as hopeless as that, Ted," Murdoch insisted. "How much do you know about viruses? Can an antidote neutralize a virus that's already in the system, but which hasn't become active yet? If it

277

can, and if Fennimore and company's vaccine works that way, then maybe there's a chance."

Cartland nodded slowly as he listened. "It's possible, I suppose," he mused in a faraway voice. Then he looked up and threw out his hands. "I don't know, old boy. Not my department. Maybe we've reached the point where we have to talk to Charles about it. He shouldn't have any problem getting his friends in London to sit up and take notice when we tell him what we know now."

They told Charles the whole story first thing the next morning. Charles immediately called Cuthrie, who promptly got in touch with Lansing. In the middle of the afternoon, Cuthrie called back to say that certain departments were already in touch with their American counterparts, but that nothing concrete had filtered back to him yet. Meanwhile the latest reports were that the inoculation program in California had been begun in haste. The number of confirmed cases had topped fifteen thousand in that state alone, and there could be no further disguising of the fact that something serious was happening.

The inoculations were stopped less than twenty-four hours later; by that time, 811 of the people treated had died from severe neural disorders.

The disease became known as *omnisclerosis californians*. In a stormy session of Congress, the U.S. Secretary for Health faced accusations that ranged from incompetence to criminal irresponsibility. The President declared Northern California a disaster area, and tens of thousands fled the state as alarm spread and rumors multiplied.

During the nine months that had passed since September, the gestating virus had been taken by carriers to thousands of other points around the world. Since the beginning of May, when the symptoms became visible, a medical task-force at the World Health Organization's headquarters in Geneva had been carefully following the pattern of these scattered outbreaks, and making detailed plans to check further spreading by means of the U.S.-produced vaccine when it became available. With the sudden withdrawal of the vaccine, the plans collapsed in ruins. The world was left without any defense to offer. When this became public knowledge, which would surely be only a matter of time after the disaster in California, the real trouble would begin.

CHAPTER THIRTY-FIVE

Graham Cuthrie, bareheaded and wearing a light tan trenchcoat over a dark-blue suit, stood near one end of the Customs barrier in the Arrivals section of Number Three Terminal at Heathrow Airport, London, watching the lines beginning to form as the passengers began trickling through from the Boeing just in from San Francisco. Next to him was Desmond Sawyer, a young official from the U.K. Ministry of Health, and standing behind them were two uniformed policemen and a girl dressed in the blue-and-white of British Airways. A British Immigration officer was standing slightly apart from the group.

A minute or so went by. Then a tall, gray-haired, gaunt-faced man, carrying a black briefcase and accompanied by an attractive, dark-haired girl, detached from the throng coming through from the arrivals gate.

Sawyer touched Cuthrie's arm and indicated with a nod of his head. "That's him. He's seen us."

"Who's the girl with him?" Cuthrie inquired.

"Her name's Patterson. She's a doctor . . . works with Waring up at Burghead. She went along to help out," Sawyer replied. Cuthrie nodded.

The two arrivals drew up facing the reception committee, and Sawyer stepped forward a pace to greet them. "This is Sir Giles Fennimore, and this, I presume, is Dr. Patterson," he said. He glanced at Fennimore. "I take it you know the Minister, Sir Giles, even if you haven't met—Graham Cuthrie." A few seconds of brief handshaking and cursory formalities followed. The Immigration officer unlocked a gate in the barrier and beckoned them through. The two policemen and the British Airways girl stood aside to let them pass and then followed, watched by a mixture of curious stares and a few dirty looks from the regular passengers standing in line at the other gates farther along.

Fennimore looked up at the large clock high on the wall above the center of the Customs Hall. "You'll be lucky to make it," he said to Anne as the group began walking briskly toward one of the exits. "The Geneva flight leaves in eight minutes." Anne looked inquiringly at the British Airways girl.

"It's under control," the girl told her. "We've got a car waiting at a side door to take you across to the terminal, and you'll be escorted through to the plane. The pilot has orders to hold takeoff until you're on board." Anne nodded. One of the policemen took the bag that she was carrying as she struggled to keep up with the airline girl.

Behind them, Fennimore, Cuthrie, and Sawyer fell back a few paces. "What happened?" Sawyer asked. "The prototype batch that was tested on the volunteers gave no adverse side effects. What went wrong?"

"It's all been a gross exaggeration," Fennimore said, keeping his voice low. "*One* production batch from *one* plant in New Jersey was incorrectly processed. Every shipment of that batch has been traced. There's nothing wrong with the rest. It's inexcusable that it happened, but the time-pressure of the whole thing has been impossible. Nobody knew for certain what the gestation period would be. For all that anyone at WHO knew in September, it could have been starting by Christmas."

"What?" Cuthrie muttered in amazement as he listened. "There's nothing wrong with it? Are you saying that the vaccine *could* be used safely?"

"I'm certain of it," Fennimore told him. "But it won't make any difference now. Everybody's panicking. They'd never allow it to be used again now, no matter what anybody tells them. Even if they did, the public wouldn't accept it again. It's too late."

The group stopped at the mouth of a corridor that led off from the main concourse.

"This is where we leave you," the airline girl announced. "The car for Dr. Patterson is outside the

280

next exit. Your plane is that way." She pointed along the corridor. "The policemen will go with you to the pad."

Fennimore glanced at Cuthrie as the policeman who had been carrying Anne's bag passed it to the Immigration officer. "There's an RAF jet waiting for us," Cuthrie explained. "We're going straight on up to Scotland. We thought you'd be in a better position to report back to London after you've had a chance to talk to Ross yourself."

Fennimore nodded but looked dubious. He looked at Anne and managed a tired shadow of a smile. "Well, Anne, it seems that neither of us are being given time for our feet to touch the ground. Thank you for your help; it has been invaluable. Good luck with the WHO people. Make sure they get the true facts before any of this hysterical nonsense catches up with you."

"I'll do my best," she said. "Do you know where you'll be if I need to get in touch?"

"Desmond's office will know," Fennimore said. "But don't worry about it. I'll be calling you anyway."

Anne turned and walked away, accompanied by the Immigration officer and the girl. Fennimore, Cuthrie, and Sawyer began following the two policemen along the corridor toward a door marked NO EXIT.

"So what exactly is it that's causing the problem?" Cuthrie asked Fennimore. "Desmond here said earlier that it seems to be a single strain that was rugged enough to survive the burnup—a mutant of the multiple-sclerosis virus. Is that correct?"

Fennimore nodded. "It was a mutant strain to begin with. We had a vaccine fully developed by February. But when the first actual cases appeared, some yielded strains that had been further mutated beyond anything that was ever engineered on *Centurion*—probably by high-altitude cosmic rays. We had to modify the vaccine in a hurry and revise the manufacturing directions. That must have been how the mistake was made in the New Jersey plant. There simply wasn't enough time."

One of the policemen opened the door and ushered them through to the outside. They were in a small, walled-off area of the airport that contained an assortment of ground vehicles and aircraft. To one side of the space, in the center of a clear area, a VTOL jet bearing RAF roundels was standing with engines already running and heat-shimmers dancing around its exhausts. The passenger door was open, and an airman in flying tunic was waiting at the bottom of the extended access steps.

"So what happened in New Jersey?" Sawyer asked as they hurried across the expanse of concrete toward the plane.

"Two steps were inverted in the purification cycle," Fennimore told him. "A molecular structure formed in an intermediate reaction was not broken down as it should have been. When the vaccine was injected, the molecules selectively blocked the sodium ion-channels through the walls of the nerve fibers. Instead of administering an antidote, we were administering a lethal neural toxin."

"My God!" Cuthrie breathed, horrified.

Nothing more was said while they boarded the aircraft and sat down in the comfortably upholstered passenger cabin. The airman who had been waiting for them closed the door and then went forward to join the pilot, leaving the cockpit door open behind him. The voices of the pilot and Heathrow Control came floating through.

"Hello, Control. This is Air Force Oscar Baker 270. Our passengers are aboard, and we're ready for takeoff. Request immediate clearance, please."

"One moment Oscar Baker. Control calling TWA 635. Come in, please."

"Trans World 635 answering. What's up? We're ready to go."

"Hold takeoff until further instructions, 635. We have an RAF priority."

"Roger. 635 holding."

"You are cleared for immediate takeoff, Oscar Baker. Turn onto bearing two-eight-five at ten thousand feet. Switch to channel four and lock AFCS to Luton beacon."

"Wilco. Oscar Baker taking off now."

The engine note rose and became more insistent,

and seconds later the airport buildings were falling away outside the cabin windows. Fennimore sank back into the soft leather folds of his seat and closed his eyes with a grateful sigh. "Heavens, I don't know, Cuthrie," he murmured. "If this goes on much longer, I'll be permanently deformed into the shape of an airplane seat. I don't think I've slept in two days." Cuthrie smiled faintly but said nothing.

Fennimore relaxed with his eyes closed for half a minute or so, and then hauled himself into an upright posture with a shake of his head and a few blinks. "Now," he said, looking across at both Cuthrie and Sawyer. "What's all this nonsense about some kind of time machine somewhere in Scotland? Who is this crank Ross? I hope you realize how unfortunate this could be if it turns out to be a waste of time."

"He's no crank, I assure you," Cuthrie said. "He's probably as accomplished in his field as you are in yours . . . Nobel Prize winner for physics, no less. He's been working privately in his own lab for a couple of years, but before that he did most of his stuff in the States. In fact he lives near a place called Glenmoroch, not far from Burghead. I believe he's been to Burghead several times, doing some consulting work for EFC to help solve the reactor trouble they've been having there. He works with an ex-RAF technical wizard called Cartland and a couple of young Americans, one of them his grandson. They're both from California; in fact the other one was one of your early Burghead cases."

"Ross? . . . Americans? . . ." Fennimore repeated slowly. He jerked his head around sharply. "Is the other one called Walker?"

"Yes, he is as a matter of fact," Cuthrie replied. "You've met him then, obviously."

"I happened to be at Burghead on the day Walker was admitted," Fennimore said. "And I've met Ross too . . . the younger one, that is."

"Well?" Cuthrie challenged. "Did he strike you as the kind of person who'd waste his time messing around with a bunch of cranks?"

"I'm afraid I really can't recall all that much about him," Fennimore confessed. "Too much has happened since then, or maybe I'm just tired." He paused to think for a few seconds, then shook his head. "But . . . changing the past. . . . Really, it's too absurd for words. To be honest with you, Cuthrie, the only reason I'm here at all is that the Prime Minister literally insisted through the Ministry. If you want my personal opinion, I've never heard such hogwash."

"Maybe you'll change your mind when you've talked to Ross yourself," Cuthrie replied.

"You sound very sure of yourself," Fennimore commented. "Do you really believe they can do anything like that? How can you, in your position?"

"I have to," Cuthrie said simply. "I've seen them do it."

"Pah! And I've seen some clever conjurors too," Fennimore declared. "And it wouldn't be the first time that one has fooled a panel of reputable scientists. Scientists are good in their own specialties, but they're simply not experienced in detecting deliberate fraud; Nature is often complex, but never dishonest. Did you ever hear of somebody called Uri Geller in the seventies?"

"Yes, and the rest," Cuthrie replied. "And Ross isn't another of them. Let's wait and see how you feel about it a couple of hours from now."

CHAPTER THIRTY-SIX

Sir Giles Fennimore sat in an armchair in the library at Storbannon, staring with dazed eyes at the things written on the pieces of paper that he had brought with him from the lab. Sawyer, looking equally bemused, was sitting to one side of him while Cuthrie watched impassively from where he was standing with his back to the hearth. Charles, Cartland, and Murdoch looked on from various other points around the room. At last Fennimore looked up and found his voice.

"I still can't believe this," he said, looking at Charles. "You can assure me that this is genuine? It really isn't some kind of trick?"

"You don't have to take my word for it," Charles replied. "Enough of Graham's people have been here and gone through it all." He held up a hand as if to stifle a protest. "I know what you're thinking—good scientists have been taken in before. But aside from that, do you think I'd play cheap tricks at a time like this? If the circumstances were different, then aye, I might have been tempted. But with things as they are, I'd hardly stoop to raising any hopes just for the fun of it. In short: Yes, the machine is genuine."

Fennimore looked from Charles to Cartland and then to Murdoch, as if seeking confirmation in their faces. He was even more drawn than when Murdoch had seen him at Burghead, and his eyes seemed to harbor a permanent haunted look. Since the day before his departure to the United States, he had aged ten years.

"That device downstairs really can alter the past?" Fennimore whispered.

"Haven't the trivial things we've shown you proved that?" Charles asked. "We've been doing exactly that for the last two hours."

Fennimore looked down again at the papers in his hand, and cast his mind back over the things he had seen in the lab. By this time he was too weary for further rounds of questions, answers, and reasons. "What is your proposal?" he asked simply.

"Earlier on, we asked you if the vaccine would neutralize a virus that was already resident in the body in its gestating state," Charles answered. "You said that it would."

"That is correct," Fennimore confirmed.

Charles nodded and continued, "Murdoch has proposed a solution to the complete problem—change the whole timeline all the way back to January. He wants complete details of how to prepare the vaccine sent back to then. Then, hopefully, the inhabitants of that universe will be able to take timely action to protect not only the people who are at risk now, in June, but also those who, in this universe, are already victims of the active virus, and therefore incurable."

Fennimore gasped. "*January!* But I thought you said that the machine only had a range of one day.

285

How could you possibly do anything that would affect what happened in January?"

"It's a long story," Cartland came in. "We might as well let you in on a secret: The machine has, we believe, already been used for something similar. We'll tell you all about that later. But to answer your question for now, we already possess a computer program that employs an ingenious method to jump a message as far back as January in one-day hops. In a nutshell, it uses itself as a relay. The program worked before; therefore it can work again."

"It's *already been used* for something like this?" Fennimore stared incredulously. "You mean in connection with this situation?"

"No," Charles replied. "For something entirely different. We can talk about that later, as Ted says. But to do something about the present situation, obviously we will need your help and cooperation."

Fennimore shook his head rapidly. "But . . . it's outlandish. From the things you said earlier, an action like that could affect all kinds of people's lives radically. Surely you're not suggesting that we—just a handful of individuals making a decision in isolation, without reference to anybody—can take it upon ourselves to change what might turn out to be a large section of the world all the way back to January? How can anybody presume such a right?"

"I'm not proposing that we do," Charles replied. "I agree with what you say. It's for the governments of this world to decide. They need a full-scale, controlled experiment to convince them of the potential of this technology. This could be the perfect opportunity to give them one. But before they'll even go as far as approving such an experiment, they'll need something that will make their minds up for them that it can be of real benefit. It's a vicious circle. The only way to break out of it is to present them with a *fait accompli* and let them draw their conclusions from that. That's what I'm proposing we do here."

"Are you sure that the governments are that deeply involved?" Fennimore asked with a trace of suspicion in his voice.

"Oh, come on!" Cuthrie exclaimed. "What do you

think I'm doing here? And didn't you say yourself that it was Lansing who insisted on your coming here?"

Fennimore closed his eyes for a moment, drew a long breath, and then nodded. "Very well. Exactly what kind of *fait accompli* have you in mind? What would it be designed to achieve?"

"A pilot test," Charles answered at once. "I don't want to do anything that would affect January; that exercise should be reserved for the main experiment, and be conducted in such a way that all of the appropriate government leaders and their advisers know about it." He paused. "I just want to go back five days. I've been thinking about the tragic error in California that you told us about, and it seems an ideal candidate for what I have in mind. I want to go back five days and have the bad batch of vaccine intercepted. That in itself, I'm sure you will agree, constitutes a worthwhile objective. But as well as that, I want the value of this pilot test to be endorsed by somebody whose reputation and integrity are beyond question, and whose authority is indisputable. I want *you,* Sir Giles, to be the witness."

Fennimore gaped in undisguised astonishment as what Charles was saying slowly dawned on him: Charles was offering to wipe away the nightmare that Fennimore had been living for days. One simple message sent from the machine downstairs would be all it would take. For the moment, Fennimore was unable to find any words to reply.

"I assume that you now possess complete details of what went wrong with the New Jersey batch—how, what the effects were, when it happened, and all that kind of thing," Charles went on. "Is that correct?" Fennimore nodded. "I'd like you to send all of that data," Charles said. "Data that nobody could possibly have possessed five days ago. And I'd like you to compose it in a way that only you would recognize, perhaps by including phrases of your own private shorthand if you use one, or any special symbols or abbreviations. You see, it will be *you* who eventually reads it; I want to make sure that you'll have no doubts as to who sent it. When that happens, there must be no doubt whatsoever as to its authenticity."

"There's another thing too," Cartland said. "Don't forget that Murdoch and I only figured out the *Centurion* story in the last couple of days. If you're going back five days, you'd better put in something about that as well. Otherwise we might not be so lucky on the new timeline."

"That's a good point," Charles agreed. "Aye, we'll put all that in as well." He turned and looked inquiringly at Fennimore. "Well, that's my proposal. What do you say to it, Sir Giles?"

The call-tone from the bedside vi-set brought Fennimore out of a deep sleep. He switched on the lamp to light up his room in the Glasgow Hilton, and glanced instinctively at his watch; it was almost two A.M. Stifling a yawn, he reached out for the screen, pivoted it toward him, and accepted the call. The caller was Desmond Sawyer from the Ministry in London.

"It's looking as if the balloon's going up," Sawyer said without preamble. "Your San Francisco tickets are fixed for flight twenty-eight out of Edinburgh at seven-thirty in the morning. A car will pick you up from the hotel at six-forty-five."

"It's started, ¬has it?" Fennimore said.

"I'm afraid so."

"What about Dr. Patterson?"

"I've just called her. She'll meet you on the plane; you've got adjacent seats. Everything else is fixed at the other end."

"Very good," Fennimore said. "Call Fisher at the Glasgow Royal in the morning, would you, and tell him what's happened. I'll call him when I get to San Francisco."

"I'd already planned to," Sawyer said. "Well, I'll let you get some sleep for what's left of the night. Good night. Have a good trip."

"Night, Desmond. Thanks."

Fennimore cut off the screen, turned out the light, and settled down to go to sleep. Two minutes later the call-tone sounded again. "Damn and blast it!" he muttered as he fumbled for the lightswitch again. This time the face was not familiar. It was an elderly man, possibly in his late sixties or early seventies, with white hair and a proud, jutting, gray beard. His face was rugged and ruddy in hue, and somehow gave the impression of belonging to a body large in stature.

"Yes?" Fennimore inquired irritably.

"I'm sorry to have to disturb you at this time of night," the caller said in a distinctly Scottish voice. "You are Sir Giles Fennimore?"

"Yes."

"My name is Sir Charles Ross. Among other things I'm engaged as a consultant physicist to the EFC at Burghead."

"Kindly get to the point," Fennimore said. "What do you want? It's two o'clock in the morning."

"I'm sorry, but it was vital for me to contact you before you leave for San Francisco in the morning."

Fennimore's eyes widened suddenly, and he hauled himself into a more attentive position. "Who are you?" he demanded. "How do you know about my going to San Francisco? I only found out about it myself for certain a few minutes ago."

"I told you, my name is Ross. I have some important information for you."

"What kind of information?"

"It concerns *Centurion*."

Fennimore's face at once became serious. "What do you know about *Centurion*?" he asked in a guarded tone.

"The specification being used for production of the vaccine at the New Jersey plant contains an error in the purification cycle," Ross said. "The batch being manufactured there will not reproduce the prototype results; it will induce lethal side effects. It's imperative that distribution of that batch is stopped."

"My God!" Fennimore gasped, staring at the screen in disbelief. "How do you know about all this? Why haven't we met before? Which department are you with?"

"I'm not with any department," Ross replied. "I'm engaged in private research."

"Then who told you about it?" Fennimore demanded.

"You did."

"Me? When?"

"About four hours ago," Ross said.

Fennimore's bewilderment increased visibly. "Don't be absurd," he said curtly. "I've been here all evening. I've never seen you before."

Ross hesitated for an instant. "Err . . . you were five days in the future at the time," he explained. There was a hint of apology in his tone.

Pause.

"Are you some kind of lunatic?"

"Would a lunatic have been able to tell you about *Centurion* and New Jersey?" Ross asked.

"No," Fennimore admitted after a few seconds' thought. "Perhaps you'd better explain yourself . . . from the beginning, please."

"It might take a while," Ross replied. "It would be better if I came to talk to you there."

"What, at this time of night?" Fennimore objected. "I've got an early plane to catch, as you seem to know perfectly well already."

"Allow me to show you something that might persuade you," Ross said. "Would you activate your hardcopy unit, please." Fennimore looked puzzled, then stretched out his arm to tap a pad below the screen of the vi-set. Moments later, the slot in the base of the set began disgorging sheets of paper. Fennimore took the first from the tray beneath the slot and scanned it hurriedly. After a second or two, he gasped aloud and looked up at the screen.

"Where did you get this?" he demanded. "Who wrote it?"

"Who do you think wrote it?" Ross asked. "Who's the only person who could have written it?"

"But I never . . ." Fennimore's voice trailed away. He shook his head in total confusion.

"Now can we come and talk to you?" Ross asked.

"We?"

"I have two colleagues I'd like to bring, if you've no objection."

Fennimore looked down at the sheet again, then reached out and retrieved another. He read the first few lines of symbols on it, shaking his head slowly while Ross watched in silence. When he looked up, his face had lost color noticeably. "Yes . . . perhaps we had better talk," he faltered. "Bring your colleagues if you wish. How long will it be before I should expect you?"

"Give us about an hour," Ross replied. "We're a bit of a drive away. We'll call your room when we get there. Apologies for disturbing you, once again. I'm sure that when we've finished, you'll agree that it was necessary, however."

"I certainly hope so," Fennimore said in a still shaky voice. "Very well then, I'll expect you in about an hour."

After he had cleared the call, he got out of bed, rinsed his face, and dressed. Then he sat down at the table by the foot of the bed and began studying carefully the sheets of data that Ross had copied through. As he read, the expression of complete and utter mystification on his face only deepened further.

CHAPTER THIRTY-SEVEN

"The biggest single obstacle that the human race must learn to overcome is its persistent and morbid tendency to believe that certain things are impossible," Cuthrie said. The rows of faces arrayed in front of him around the conference theater listened in attentive silence. "I submit that there is no such thing. It was not very long ago that self-propelled carriages were proved to be 'impossible' on principle; survival at velocities above fifty miles per hour was once considered 'impossible'; heavier-than-air flight was 'impossible'; and so were rocket propulsion, space travel, nuclear fusion, feeding the Third World, and stabilizing global population. Throughout history, today's children have yawned at yesterday's miracles."

The conference was being held in the Health Ministry's new skyscraper in the center of London. The attendees were scientific and policy advisers from the various governments that had so far been brought into the Storbannon secret. They had come to London in response to an invitation extended by the British

Government following certain approaches that had been made to Lansing by the World Health Organization in Geneva. Three weeks had gone by since Charles's call to Fennimore in his hotel room in Glasgow.

Cuthrie continued, "Yet even the most optimistic among us have always been obliged to constrain their philosophies to the observation that 'We can't change the past, but we can do something about the future.' That has remained the ultimate impossibility which has never been seriously questioned." He paused for effect, and swung his gaze slowly from one side of the room to the other. "But today, lo and behold, even that ultimate of impossibilities lies demolished at the end of the trail marked by the ruins of all the rest. The question confronting us is not 'Which direction do we take from here?'—for surely there can be no doubt about that, but, 'How do we take the next step?' "

Cuthrie paused again to invite comments, but the silence that greeted him was total. Charles had already spoken at some length, firing the imaginations of everybody present with visions of the future heralded by the new physics. But the visions had been of distant futures that lay at the ends of long, winding roads ahead, with nothing specific to guide the first moves needed to get to them. Charles had provided the tools for shaping a world, but where were the directions for using them? The paralysis that had gripped the minds of everybody who had grappled with the problem was still as much in evidence as it had been months previously. The moving finger, having writ, could now be erased; but nobody was willing to take a contract to do the rewrite.

"We have all been agreed for some time that the next step must be a fully controlled test," Cuthrie went on. "So far, however, nobody has been willing to decide what form such a test should take. We think that an ideal opportunity for such a test now exists, and we have called you all here in the hope that, as a result of what will be said today, your respective governments will see fit to add their endorsements to a decision for us to proceed." A sudden stir of interest ran around the rows of listeners at these words. Cuthrie waited for a moment, then concluded, "Murdoch Ross is going to describe to you what we have in mind. I think most of you have been to Storbannon at some time or other, and have already met Murdoch. For anybody who hasn't, he is from the United States and is the grandson of Sir Charles Ross, who spoke earlier. He is also a mathematician, and has been participating in the work that Sir Charles has described. Murdoch?" Cuthrie glanced across at where Murdoch was sitting, nodded, and sat down amid an undercurrent of murmuring from all sides.

Murdoch climbed to his feet and straightened up to face the august gathering. Charles had been the one to suggest that since the whole topic of the conference had been essentially Murdoch's brainchild, Murdoch should present it. Murdoch had accepted, although with some misgivings at the prospect of having to address an audience of delegates from the world's governments. Now, as he stood facing them with an expectant silence beginning to descend, everything that he had carefully prepared in his mind was already scrambled into a hopeless mess. He looked down at the notes that he had brought with him, but they no longer meant anything. Words poured into his head, but his mouth was unable to string them together into anything coherent.

And then he thought of the breathing vegetable that he had gone to see a few days previously in Glasgow— through which fluids circulated, and inside which proteins continued to assemble themselves only because of the never-faltering vigilance of machines . . . which lay still only because of drugs and surgically implanted neural bypasses . . . which contained something that had once been a brain, but would never again think. He pushed the notes away, and looked up.

"In early May, almost two months ago, the first cases of *omnisclerosis* appeared," he said. "Today the number of confirmed cases worldwide is not far short of a hundred thousand, despite the intensive inoculation program that has been in operation for almost a month. In the past seven days there have been fifty-seven deaths among the earliest-reported victims. Also, we are told, no cure is currently in sight that will arrest the disease once the virus comes out of its gestating state and begins replicating its DNA. Therefore, in the months ahead, we can expect the death-toll to rise to at least a hundred thousand. That much seems certain.

"But that is not all. The gestation period is eight to nine months. Without doubt there are many people all over the world who are already unwitting carriers, and who, for one reason or another, will not be traced and treated before the viruses that they are carrying become active. And we know also that when that stage is reached, not only will those people be incurable, but the disease they are carrying will become communicable.

"Thus, one hundred thousand carriers have already been spreading it to who-knows-how-many more potential victims in who-knows-how-many parts of the world. So how many times one hundred thousand people will be under a death-sentence eight to nine months from now?"

He paused for a moment to let his listeners reflect on the question. A solemn hush had descended on the auditorium. Murdoch did not mention anything of the connection of the QX-37 orbiting laboratory with the whole business. The origin of the virus was still officially a mystery, and the question of how to handle the QX-37 issue was not Murdoch's problem; he was quite happy to let things remain that way.

He resumed, "Even if the inoculation program were one hundred percent successful, and *every single* carrier were traced and treated to contain any further spreading, we would still be left with one hundred thousand certain deaths. But that, of course, would be an unrealizable ideal situation. In reality we have to accept that the final count will be far higher than that before it's all over." He leaned forward to rest his hands on the edge of the table in front of him and swept his eyes around the conference theater.

"*But* . . . just *suppose* that the vaccine had been available as little as three months ago, or maybe less, before even the first few cases turned malignant. *Suppose* that, three months ago, we had known in advance the name of every malignant case that subsequently developed. *Suppose* that the inoculation program had been commenced then, instead of three months and one hundred thousand people too late. . . ." Excited mutterings began breaking out around the room as the gist of what Murdoch was driving at became clear. He spread his hands in appeal and raised his voice to carry above the rising hubbub.

"*Not one case* of malignancy would have appeared today. Fifty-seven people who are dead wouldn't be. One hundred thousand people who are condemned to death would be living normal lives. And hundreds of thousands, *maybe millions,* who are already sentenced to join them would be reprieved. *And* you would have had your experiment." He cast a final look around the room. "That is what I'm proposing." Then he sat down. Cuthrie raised his eyebrows; beside him, Charles caught Murdoch's eye and nodded approval.

The first response came from Leonard B. Kenning, the U.S. Presidential Science Adviser. "Are you saying we change the whole timeline for three months back?"

"Three months wouldn't give enough time," Murdoch replied. "The vaccine would still have to be manufactured and distributed, probably after thorough testing. I'm saying make it *six* months—for as long as the Storbannon machine has been available."

"*Six months?*" a representative from Germany protested. "Who knows what else might be affected? Everything interacts with everything in our society. We could drastically affect other things that have no obvious connection with the epidemic. The whole idea is simply too . . . too outrageous."

"We do it all the time anyway," Murdoch pointed out. "Every day of the week, governments make decisions that will affect every individual on the planet, but that doesn't stop them. And if you do nothing, won't that affect every aspect of society just as drastically? And could any alternative that you create be any worse? I don't think so. That's why this situation is ideal for the experiment you've all been asking for."

"Surely we need more time before something like this," an Italian insisted. "Something smaller to begin with . . . something we can progress slowly from. Oh, I don't know, something like—"

"There isn't time," Murdoch said simply.

"Let's get straight what you're suggesting," an Australian scientist piped in. "You're saying that we package the whole thing up—how to manufacture the vaccine and all that business—and send it back to the world of six months ago. Am I right?"

"More than just that," Murdoch replied. "Every scrap of data on the situation that led to our making the decision . . . even significant events that may appear totally unconnected with it. Then the world of six months ago can make *informed* decisions on the action it wants to take. It will be able to judge reliably exactly what it has gained and what, if anything, it has lost, and why. When that world gets to *its* July, it will know where to go next, unlike us." Murdoch's expression lightened somewhat. "And the beauty of it from our point of view is that whatever that world does, we will all still be part of what grows out of it."

"That's the part that bothers me," the Australian said. "Never mind all this high-sounding talk. I'll be honest; I'm bothered about *me*. I don't like this idea of somebody somewhere pressing a button, and me being—what do you call it?—reset into somebody else. It gives me the creeps. Why should I agree to it?"

"Fifty years from now you'll probably grow up taking the process for granted," Charles threw in.

"Maybe so," the Australian conceded. "But I don't happen to have grown up fifty years from now." A few heads here and there were nodding in agreement.

"It happens naturally all the time anyway," Charles said. "The timeline reconfigures spontaneously. Within the last few seconds you could have been reset from somebody who existed on another timeline to the one we're on at this moment, without even knowing it."

"That's all very well to say in theory," the German who had spoken earlier objected. "But how can *you* know for certain that it happens all the time? From what I have gathered, that supposition follows merely from abstract mathematics and indirect inferences from a few trivial tests with random numbers. And as for the claim that we can never be cognizant of the process, that sounds far too contrived to me for comfort. It certainly doesn't constitute a sound basis for

296

anything as drastic in its effects as what's being proposed."

"It's still an act of faith," another voice declared. "We can't sanction something like this purely on the say-so of a handful of people."

"Evidence," another muttered loudly. "Give us some evidence." Other voices began joining in. Fennimore and Charles exchanged looks and then turned their heads toward Cuthrie. Cuthrie gave a slight nod, raised his hand for silence, and then gestured toward Charles.

"Nobody in this room should have any qualms about being reset along with altered timelines," Charles said, speaking in a firm, authoritative voice that compelled silence. He threw a defiant stare around the room. "You see, it's already happened . . . to all of you!" He paused, but everybody was momentarily too confused to offer any response. He went on, "We are here now, saying these things, as a result of a reset that the machine has already caused! Another timeline did exist on which this conference was never called, and on which everybody in this room was at this moment somewhere else, doing something different. That timeline no longer exists."

For the next five seconds a falling pin would have sounded like a landmine.

"What the hell are you talking about?" the Australian demanded at last.

A dozen other mouths started to open, but the words froze as Fennimore, who had been introduced at the beginning of the proceedings, rose slowly to his feet. He stood erect and dignified, and stared calmly out at the rows of faces until satisfied that the attention of everybody in the room was focused upon him. Then he began speaking in a slow, clear voice.

"A few minutes ago, Murdoch Ross accurately summarized the seriousness of the present situation. The situation is serious despite the strenuous efforts being expended on the inoculation program, which, I can assure you, is contributing substantially to containing further spread of the disease. In other words although the program cannot be totally successful, the

297

situation today would be indescribably worse without it.

"Imagine, if you will, the world as it would be at this moment if the program had not been implemented when it was. Almost certainly the western U.S.A. would be in a state of virtual quarantine, the outbreaks in other places would have consolidated, and Murdoch's figure of hundreds of thousands would probably already be fact. And without any effective defenses to offer, the world would be facing merely the beginnings of what was to come." He stopped for a second to allow the audience time to dwell on the picture.

"The situation that I have just described came very close to becoming a reality," he resumed. "Just how closely has been something which, up until now, has been known only to myself and a handful of people in the world. It was avoided only as a consequence of certain remarkable events which took place in the early hours of the morning of June 1. Those events I will now describe to you."

Murdoch studied the faces of the delegates as they listened. They were expectant and tense, waiting for the testimony of what they now recognized was the star witness, for whom everything else had been the buildup. It was out of his hands now, Murdoch told himself.

Fennimore went on, "The virus was first identified as an unknown strain in routine analyses of air samples collected late last year. I was a member of a joint Anglo-American study that was initiated to assess the possible effects of the virus on humans, and to explore methods of combating those effects in the event of their proving dangerous. To avoid the risk of needless public alarm, a decision was taken not to publicize these investigations, which at that time were viewed as being purely of a precautionary nature.

"By the early weeks of this year, the virulence of the strain had been established, and a probable pattern of geographical spread had been determined, centered upon Northern California. At this stage the gestation period was not known with confidence; accordingly the search for an antidote was intensified, and medical

298

centers throughout the world were alerted to watch for unusual symptoms associated with disorders of the nervous system. A communications system was set up to channel reports of such occurrences through the World Health Organization in Geneva to special offices in Washington, D.C., and London, from which centers the research was being directed.

"Evidence of the gestating virus was obtained from tissue samples collected in the course of routine clinical tests on hospital patients residing in the San Francisco area. These patients were approached, and a group selected for reliability agreed to undergo voluntary tests of the vaccines being developed. By the end of April, a satisfactory antidote formula had been derived. At the same time, plans for a mass inoculation were worked out with the Federal health authorities, and arrangements for volume-manufacture of the vaccine were made with a number of pharmaceutical companies in the United States.

"The first outbreaks appeared in early May, some of the earliest occurring in Scotland. I spent a considerable amount of time in May working with the staff of a medical facility in Glasgow who were treating these cases, in order to acquire as much information as possible on the disease in the most advanced stages available for study. I flew to San Francisco on June 1 to report my findings and to observe the effectiveness of the measures being proposed to counter the epidemic that was by then clearly imminent. The program of inoculation had been scheduled to begin there on June 2."

Fennimore paused to fill a glass from the water pitcher on the table. As he drank, he scanned rapidly across the faces before him. They were still waiting. Everything that Fennimore had said so far had been simply a frank account of things that had been going on behind the scenes for some time; he had made no reference at all to Storbannon or the machine. But the audience could sense that he was about to come to the point of his statement. He set the glass down and resumed his former posture.

"Some hours before I was due to leave Scotland, in the early hours of June 1, I was contacted by Sir

Charles Ross, whom I had neither met nor heard of previously." Fennimore's voice rose to a louder note. "Sir Charles, who had not been involved with this matter in any way whatsoever, who was not included among the few people with access to information pertaining to it, and whose work had no connection with medical research in any form, was able to produce complete details of a production batch of the vaccine which, for reasons that are still being investigated by United States Food and Drug Administration officials, had been made defectively!" A chorus of surprised mutterings broke out at once. Fennimore spoke on above the sound.

"Furthermore, Sir Charles was able not only to specify the chemical nature of the defect, the precise point in the manufacturing process at which it had occurred, the reference number of the batch concerned, and the name of the manufacturing plant that had produced it, but also to describe in detail the effects that such a defect would have on the human organism, namely selective blocking of certain neural ion channels with a high probability of death within hours.

"*Every one* of those statements was subsequently shown to be accurate in every respect! Had Sir Charles not intervened in this way, there is no doubt that that batch would have been shipped and administered as intended. What the consequences of that would have been, I dread to think. Almost certainly, they would have included withdrawal of *all* batches of the vaccine, and therefore necessarily the postponement of the whole inoculation program for an indefinite period."

The reactions of the listeners ranged through the whole spectrum of various degrees of bewilderment. A few had already seen the full implications and were just staring wide-eyed and open-mouthed. Some were frowning as they wrestled to make sense out of what Fennimore was saying. Others just shook their heads and gave up.

"Are you saying that he got that information from the future through the machine?" the Australian asked in a choking voice.

"How else?" Fennimore answered simply.

"But how can you be certain of that?" the German challenged. "How can you *prove* word didn't leak out in some other way? Such things do happen, after all. You do not *have to* introduce the hypothesis of a time machine to explain it, since we already have other, perfectly adequate, alternative explanations that are familiar." He shot an apologetic look at Charles. "No disrespect to anybody, but that information could have leaked out and come from other sources, and merely have been purported to have been received through the machine. How do we know? What *proof* is there that *positively excludes* such alternatives?"

"A very proper and correct question," Charles approved, nodding. He turned his head and looked up at Fennimore to invite a reply.

"For one thing, I can state categorically that nobody concerned with producing the vaccine had any inkling of the existence of the defect until I brought it to their attention and insisted that they check," Fennimore said. "But beyond that, the document that Sir Charles presented to me on June 1, and that contained all the data I have referred to, was of a unique nature. It was written in specialized biochemical terminology, and contained numerous contractions, conventions, phrasings, and other characteristics that identified its author beyond any shadow of a doubt—at least it did to my satisfaction, but that was really all it needed to do." Fennimore paused for an instant. "There was only one person who could have written that information in that particular fashion: *I myself!* And yet I had never seen it before; neither was I previously aware of the content."

Gasps of amazement were starting to come from all around. The Australian had turned a light purple and seemed to have gone into some kind of trance. Fennimore had the feeling that bedlam could erupt at any moment. He pressed on.

"The document was dated as having originated on June 5," he told them. "Five days *after* the occasion in question! I had not written it. Therefore I was obliged to accept Sir Charles's explanation, ludicrous in the extreme though it sounded, that another 'I' must have—an 'I' who existed five days in the future. And an 'I,' furthermore, who existed in a universe that I did not subsequently come to experience, for I have never composed or contributed in any way to the creation of any such document.

"On June 1, the information supplied by Sir Charles was completely new to me. After my arrival in the United States on June 2 and discussions with the other people involved with the project, I was satisfied that nobody else could have provided the information that Sir Charles had supplied. It could not have been leaked prior to June 1 because nobody knew about it; furthermore, I know that the document could not have been forged, since I would have to have been a party to it. Therefore there was no option but to accept Sir Charles's claim: that a different future had existed on a different timeline, and on that timeline, the defective batch was in fact distributed and administered."

A few seconds passed by before the audience realized what Fennimore had said.

"What!" The German was half out of his seat. "What do you mean, 'was distributed and administered'?"

"Exactly that," Fennimore replied calmly.

"How can you be sure?" somebody else demanded.

"Because the document said so, and for the reasons that I have already given, I am quite satisfied as to its authenticity. *I* wrote it."

"Said so?" the Australian repeated in a bewildered voice.

"Yes. In the universe from which the document originated, the inoculation program was stopped on June 3 after eight hundred and eleven people had died from receiving the defective vaccine. The whole state was in panic, and Congress was in uproar. I think I can see very clearly why the inhabitants of that universe would have seen fit to send a message back five days with the hope of changing things. In that universe, after over eight hundred deaths, which incidentally have been avoided on our present timeline, there could have been no choice but to abandon the program. Reassurances would have been of no avail against public opinion after such an error. The only future they would have had would be the one that I described when I began speaking." Fennimore nodded his head solemnly and looked from side to side. "Yes, ladies and gentlemen, I can see very clearly why they changed it."

He waited a moment for any questions at that point, but there were none. "In conclusion, my position is that I have no doubts as to the benefits that this technology can bestow if used wisely, and I am convinced that we should use the opportunity that we have to learn more than we know now. We should not shirk from it. I endorse fully the action that Murdoch Ross and his colleagues are advocating. Thank you. That is all I have to say." With that, he sat down.

A state of mass stupor seemed to have taken possession of the audience. From one side of the auditorium to the other, faces stared back with wide, glazed eyes. After a few seconds of total silence had dragged by, Murdoch turned and leaned across toward Charles. "What do you think they think?" he muttered from the corner of his mouth.

"Och, ye'll get no sense out of any o' them now until after lunch," Charles replied. "But I think they'll go along with it. The real test will come when they go running back to the people that sent them. That's when the shilly-shallying will start."

Fifteen minutes later, when the conference was breaking up for lunch, the Australian stopped on his way to the door and looked down at where Charles was sitting.

"You're a slippery old so-and-so, you know," he said in a voice that was a mixture of reproach and grudging admiration.

Charles turned his face upward in surprise. "Why? What am I supposed to have done now?"

"After all this insisting that the machine wouldn't be used for messing around with timelines until everybody had been consulted, you go and spring this on us. You go sending messages back that change the whole U.S. inoculation program . . . without a word to anybody about it. It contradicts everything you've

303

been saying. Come on, admit it—you've conned the lot of us."

Charles glared up and dismissed the accusation with a wave of his hand. "Hell, that was nothing to do with me at all," he said. "It was some other Charlie Ross in some other universe who did that. Go talk to him about it."

CHAPTER THIRTY-EIGHT

"Well," Charles said as he paced slowly to and fro in front of the snow-crusted library window. "I still think the only workable approach is the one on which we've already more or less agreed: Keep it simple to begin with by using the results of complex algorithms that nobody can know in advance, and adhere strictly to a rigid, predefined schedule. Then later on maybe, we could try repeating the whole thing using random numbers or something like that." He stopped and turned to look questioningly at where Elizabeth was listening in one of the armchairs.

"Yes, but that still wouldn't completely eliminate the element of human choice," she pointed out. "For example, somebody would still have to make a decision at some point of which algorithms to use. Until somebody makes that decision, obviously the actual results that will be obtained must remain undetermined. Whatever you do, you can't get away from human choice still being part of it. There's nothing that predetermines what we may or may not decide to do."

"I agree with you," Charles said, raising a hand. "But what else can we do? We're really going round and round the same circle all the time. And besides that, all this speculation will be just guessing in the dark until we've accumulated some tangible data. I say let's not try and prejudge how it might or might not work; let's just go ahead and set up a schedule of tests along the lines I've suggested, work through it systematically and with no deviations, and then see where we go from there."

Elizabeth considered the suggestion for a few seconds, then nodded. "Very well. You're right, I suppose, Charles. And after all, it is your machine. Let's do it that way then."

"Good." Charles came away from the window and sat down in the chair facing her. "We'll put it to Ted when he comes back upstairs. If he agrees, then we could start thinking about a broad outline form for the schedule right now, this afternoon. The general form that I had in mind was to break it into a series of phases, each designed to isolate one of the variables. The first thing I'd like to——" He stopped speaking abruptly as a loud crash sounded from somewhere outside the library. It sounded like a door being thrown open. Running footsteps clattered for a second, then the library door burst open, and Cartland exploded into the room.

"Extraordinary!" he shouted. "It's unbelievable! The machine!" He gesticulated wildly in the direction from which he had come. Charles and Elizabeth were already on their feet, staring at him in astonishment.

"What in God's name's wrong wi' ye?" Charles demanded. "Is it a ghost you've found down there or something?"

Cartland continued to wave his arms, at the same time hopping excitedly from one foot to the other. "It's gone berserk! There's all kinds of stuff coming out of it . . . reams of stuff!"

"What kind of stuff?" Elizabeth asked.

"I don't know. Something about black holes."

"Black holes?" Charles stared at him incredulously. "What about black holes?"

"I don't know," Cartland told him. "But that's not the point. It's coming from *May!* The message says it's come all the way back from the end of May!"

"That's preposterous," Charles declared.

"Come and see for yourself," Cartland said, at last calming down a little.

Charles strode out of the library and made for the door that led down to the lab. The other two followed close behind. Inside the lab, the hardcopier had stopped running, but a small wad of output sheets was lying in its catcher tray. Charles snatched them up and began scanning them rapidly. As he did so, his face creased into a frown of noncomprehension. After a few seconds he passed the first sheet to Elizabeth and began thumbing through the rest.

"How do you know this is genuine?" Charles asked. "How can it be?"

"Unless somebody in May found a way of extending the machine's range," Cartland suggested, but even as he said it, he shook his head. "No. That's not possible surely. The power it would need would be unimaginable. It would have to be a whole new machine. If anything like that was going to be working by May, we'd have had to have begun designing it a long time ago, and we didn't."

"Is it conceivable that somebody else has built *another machine* that we don't know about?" Charles mused, half to himself. He thought for a moment and shook his head decisively. "No, of course not. Obviously this message was sent in the code that our circuits are designed to handle. It's impossible to believe that another machine would use exactly the same protocols. The message must have been transmitted from this same machine."

Elizabeth was studying intently the sheet that Charles had handed to her. When she at last looked up, there was a strange expression on her face. Charles and Cartland looked at her curiously.

"Charles," she said quietly. "Does anybody else from Burghead, apart from me, know about your machine?"

"Of course not," Charles replied, sounding surprised. "Why?"

"Is anybody else from Burghead likely to learn about it within the next twenty-four hours?" she asked.

"Not for any reason I can think of. Why? What are you getting at?"

"Then this message is genuine," Elizabeth said simply. "It was originated in May." Charles's and Cartland's faces asked the question for them. Elizabeth explained, "There is information here of an extremely technical nature concerning the design of the Burghead reactors. Only somebody who was from Burghead and intimately involved with the physics of it could have supplied that information. If this message was sent from somewhere inside the machine's range, in other words within the next twenty-four hours, then I must have been involved with sending it. But if it did come from within that time, it would be a hoax because it claims to have come from May. I can think of no reason why I would wish to be a party to any hoax of that nature. Why should I? If it's not a hoax, it must have come from where it says it came from. Don't ask me how, but that's the only logical interpretation."

Charles stared hard at her for a long time, then nodded his head slowly. "Aye, Elizabeth, I think you're right," he said. He shifted his gaze back to the machine and shook his head wonderingly. "But how on Earth—"

"They downline loaded it!" Cartland exclaimed suddenly, snapping his fingers. Charles looked at him, momentarily puzzled. "A kind of bootstrap," Cartland said. "Somebody in May must have found a way of programming it to transmit to itself, to itself, to itself, all the way back in one-day stages. It *has* to be something like that. When you think about it, it's feasible."

An intrigued gleam came into Charles's eyes. "Aye . . ." he said, nodding his head slowly and thoughtfully. "There could be something to that, Ted. If that was how they did it, the program they used must have appeared in the computer first to read the message in after it. We'll see if we can get Lee to have a look at it when he and Murdoch get back from Kingussie. Did they give any idea of how long they thought they'd be?"

"I don't think they'll be back until after tea," Elizabeth said. "Maybe not until later this evening. Lee came back into the house just before they left and asked Mrs. Paisley to leave them out some sandwiches."

"Ah well, we'll just have to wait," Charles said. "In the meantime let's have a look at the message and see what all this business is about black holes."

At that moment the door opened, and Morna walked

307

in. She stopped abruptly when she saw them, and brought her hand up to her mouth.

"Och! I did not think there was anyone down here. I thought ye were all still upstairs in the library."

"What do you want?" Charles asked a trifle impatiently.

"I was lookin' to find Maxwell. His dinner was ready over an hour ago, and it has not been touched. He's always appeared in the kitchen on time to the minute."

"Well, he's not here I'm afraid, Morna," Charles said. "He's probably got himself shut in a cupboard somewhere. We are rather busy."

"I'm sorry to have bothered ye," Morna said, backing toward the door. "I thought ye were all in the library."

Just as she closed the door, a flashing symbol appeared on the main screen of the machine's console, indicating that an incoming message was being received. Then the symbol became steady.

"Another one!" Charles gasped in amazement. "My God! What have we started with all this?" Cartland was already at the console, hammering in a command for whatever had come in to be displayed. A second later the screen came to life. The message on it read:

To Sir Charles Ross and colleagues at Storbannon, Saturday, January 16, 2010.
Greetings from Wednesday, July 28, 2010, on behalf of His Majesty's Government.
IMPORTANT
This is a preliminary message only. The storage capacity of your machine as it exists is inadequate for the main message to follow. Connect the system computer into your datagrid terminal, and reserve 50 Megabytes of network storage.
Main body of message will follow in one hour.

EPILOGUE

"It looks pretty busy," Lee observed as he looked out of the car at the crowds of shoppers threading their way along the snow-cleared sidewalk of the town's main street. He looked along the line of parked vehicles beside them. "You're gonna have problems finding a space here."

"It just needs patience," Murdoch said, slowing the car to a crawl. "Ah, what did I tell you—there's one." He brought the vehicle to a halt just ahead of an empty space, checked behind them, and reversed into it.

"They don't exactly have a surplus of parking lots in this town," Lee observed, looking around.

"What would you pull down to make some more?" Murdoch asked him.

"Mmm, okay, point taken. Where to first?"

"Well, if you still want a beer, why don't we do that now. Then we won't have to carry lots of junk all over town. There's a place you'd like just around the corner, all oak beams and stuff. Must be three hundred years old."

"Sounds fine."

Murdoch climbed out into the road and closed the car door. Lee opened the door on the other side, then paused for a moment to check his pockets for the list of things he needed to buy. Then he got out and turned to close the car door behind him.

Murdoch was halfway around the car when a startled shriek, coinciding with an ear-rending S-Q-U-A-W-K, stopped him dead in his tracks. At the same instant, Lee, who was just straightening up on the other side, spun around. They were just in time to see a girl who was coming out of one of the stores stumble over something and drop most of the packages she had been carrying.

"Oh, shit!" Murdoch groaned as he recognized the ball of black-and-white fur streaking away from beneath her feet and into the crowd. Lee yelled something and leaped away in pursuit. For a second Murdoch stood staring helplessly.

And then he noticed for the first time how stunningly attractive the girl was, with long, dark hair, and elegantly dressed in a brown sheepskin coat with matching knee-length boots. He hurried across the sidewalk to see what he could do to help.

Naturally . . .

ABOUT THE AUTHOR

JAMES HOGAN was born in London in 1941 and educated at the Cardinal Vaughan Grammar School, Kensington. He studied general engineering at the Royal Aircraft Establishment, Farnborough, subsequently specializing in electronics and digital systems.

After spending a few years as a systems design engineer, he transferred into selling and later joined the computer industry as a salesman, working with ITT, Honeywell, and Digital Equipment Corporation. He also worked as a life insurance salesman for two years ". . . to have a 'break' from the world of machines and to learn something more about people."

In mid-1977 he moved from England to the United States to become a Senior Sales Training Consultant, concentrating on the applications of minicomputers in science and research for DEC.

At the end of 1979, Hogan opted to write full-time and he is now living in Florida.